HOW TO LOSE A LAIRD

Books by Anna Bradley

The Sutherlands
LADY ELEANOR'S SEVENTH SUITOR
LADY CHARLOTTE'S FIRST LOVE
TWELFTH NIGHT WITH THE EARL

The Somerset Sisters
MORE OR LESS A MARCHIONESS
MORE OR LESS A COUNTESS
MORE OR LESS A TEMPTRESS

Besotted Scots
THE WAYWARD BRIDE
TO WED A WILD SCOT
FOR THE SAKE OF A SCOTTISH RAKE

The Swooning Virgins Society
THE VIRGIN WHO RUINED LORD GRAY
THE VIRGIN WHO VINDICATED LORD DARLINGTON
THE VIRGIN WHO HUMBLED LORD HASLEMERE
THE VIRGIN WHO BEWITCHED LORD LYMINGTON
THE VIRGIN WHO CAPTURED A VISCOUNT

Drop Dead Dukes
GIVE THE DEVIL HIS DUKE
DAMNED IF DUKE
THE DUKE'S CHRISTMAS BRIDE

Cairncross Castle
WHAT HAPPENS IN THE HIGHLANDS
HOW TO LOSE A LAIRD

Published by Kensington Publishing Corp.

HOW TO LOSE A LAIRD

ANNA BRADLEY

kensingtonbooks.com

KENSINGTON BOOKS are published by

Kensington Publishing Corp.
900 Third Avenue
New York, NY 10022

ISBN: 978-1-4967-5521-6
ISBN: 978-1-4967-5524-7 (ebook)

First Kensington Trade Edition: June 2026

10 9 8 7 6 5 4 3 2 1

Printed in the United States of America

The authorized representative in the EU for product safety and compliance
is eucomply OU, Parnu mnt 139b-14, Apt 123
Tallinn, Berlin 11317, hello@eucompliancepartner.com

For Michelle, forever in our hearts

Chapter 1

Dunvegan, Isle of Skye, Scotland
October 1775

"You needn't behave as if you're innocent, sir. I recall with perfect clarity the circumstances of our first meeting, and the catastrophe that followed it."

There was no reply. A lucky thing, as it would have been jarring indeed if there had been. A shadow fell over her notebook, but Freya didn't look up, focusing instead on her pencil and the lines and curves flowing from the blunt tip.

"You insult my intelligence if you believe I will trust you, after what happened the last time. I'm no fool, to be seduced again by your pretty wiles. You, sir, are no gentleman."

As if in answer, the shadow shifted, drifting eastward on the light breeze coming off Loch Dunvegan far below her perch on the castle roof. Light spilled over her, illuminating the page and bathing her bare head in warmth.

She did look up then, blinking against the sunlight emerging from behind the passing cloud. "Ah, it's just as I suspected. You think to beguile me again. You may do your worst. You may glow and billow and float all you like, but I won't be taken in by your beauty. You're a rogue and a cheat, and I'm too clever a lady to be duped a second time."

She'd only seen these sorts of clouds once before, but she'd sketched them then, too. It would be helpful if she could find that earlier sketch so she could compare them and be certain she was looking at the same formation.

She plucked up her sketchbook, balanced it on her knees, and began turning over the leaves, one by one. Hundreds of sketches filled the pages, some of them messy, sprawling things that took up every available inch of a page, while others no larger than the tip of her thumb were crowded into the margins.

There were sunrises and sunsets, and sketches of Loch Dunvegan when it was as smooth as a pane of glass and as angry as a nest of hornets, with the crushing waves threatening to reduce the rocks below the castle to powder. There were drawings of the midday sun perched high amidst a canvas of clear blue sky, and drawings of the moon presiding over a sea of velvety darkness. She had an entire notebook filled only with drawings of the stars, twinkling like pinpricks of silvery light in the midnight sky.

Those sketches were from the summer when she'd turned eight years old. Her father had spent hours on the roof with her that summer, teaching her all about the constellations.

Orion, Cepheus, Draco, and Cassiopeia . . .

They'd sat together on this very roof, gazing into the darkness above, with the warm breeze stirring her hair, and her father's voice, deep and quiet and filled with wonder.

It seemed like a lifetime ago now.

There were dozens of notations scribbled across the bottom of each page of this notebook. The scrawled numbers and calculations would look like nonsense to an untrained eye, but to her the recordings of shifts in temperatures, rainfall estimates, wind speeds and directions, and notations of the height of the waves that came crashing against the castle walls on stormy days were a subject of endless fascination.

She turned over the next leaf, and a laugh caught in her throat at the awkward row of trees marching across the page. "Oh, dear. Those aren't very good, are they?" She'd been attempting to catch the motion of the wind through the woods surrounding the castle, but the branches looked more like the ruffled feathers of an outraged bird.

And there were clouds. Dozens of clouds. Light, airy ones, like puffs of smoke from a pipe, and long, diaphanous ones that looked as if they'd been stretched by a giant hand until they were no more than wispy white shadows.

One would never suspect the clouds above her now of being harbingers of chaos. The sun was still shining, and the sky behind the charming billows was an ocean of bright blue. They looked harmless enough, like the seed heads of cotton grass, soft, bright white bits of fluff that made one's finger itch to stroke them.

But their beauty was a deception.

It was foolishness, to imagine a beautiful thing must also be a benign one. Pure folly, to believe destruction couldn't come out of a clear blue sky.

It could. It *did*. If she'd learned nothing else these past few months, she'd learned that.

She turned to the next page, then the next, and . . . ah, yes, here it was. This was the sketch she'd been looking for. It was a drawing of a thick bank of clouds, except there was no sun to be seen in this sketch. These clouds were the same strange, bright white as those above her now, but these were edged with an ominous band of dark gray that would prove to be prophetic.

They were dense, towering things, and the storm that had followed that unusual mass of clouds had wreaked havoc on Dunvegan and the surrounding areas. Crops had been destroyed, and half a dozen villagers were injured by the debris the wind had tossed about. It had come in such violent gusts that entire trees had been torn from the ground, exposing their raw, tangled roots to the world. There'd been something almost obscene about it, like getting a peek beneath a lady's skirts.

She'd written the date in the bottom left corner of the page.

October 21, 1774.

No, that couldn't be right, could it? Had it only been a year since she'd sketched these clouds? It seemed impossible, given how much had happened since then, but there it was, in her own messy scribble, as plain as day.

Now a second storm was coming, and Dunvegan was directly in its path.

Not so long ago, the threat of such a storm would have had her scrambling to warn her sisters, but what good did a warning do? The storm would come either way, and there was little they could do about it aside from tucking themselves into the safest corner of the castle until it passed.

In the end, all her sketches and notes and calculations served little purpose. Catriona might persist in calling her abilities a "gift," but unlike Cat's cures and Sorcha's falconry, it was little more than a hobby, and a rather silly one, at that.

Now, if she were able to *control* the weather, as some of the more suspicious villagers believed, that would be another thing entirely. What would it be like to have the wind at her fingertips? To have the power to summon the thunder with a wave of her hand?

She settled herself more comfortably against the stones at her back, smoothed her skirt over her bent knees and took up her pencil, suppressing a sigh. It was a forlorn little stub of a thing, no longer than her thumb.

She needed a new one. A new notebook, as well, as this one was in a shocking state. The once pristine white pages were now smudged and grubby with overuse. There was hardly a sliver of blank space left, aside from one small corner at the top of the page.

She pressed the dull tip to the paper, and her hand moved idly over the space until a face began to emerge. *Her* face, except it wasn't the same face she saw reflected in her looking glass every morning. This face was sharper, the chin ending in an obstinate point, and her eyes looked wild, her eyebrows two dark, arched wings above them, and her mouth—my goodness, that was a wicked curve of a smile on her lips.

Why, she looked marvelous! Like herself, but fiercer. She added a mane of untamed curls and a pair of upraised hands with lightning bolts shooting from the fingertips, then traced her finger over the pencil lines, a laugh bubbling in her throat.

How wonderful! No one would dare trifle with such a ferocious creature.

But alas, she was no witch, no matter what the gossips said. The sketch was a lie, just as so many of her other sketches were. Anyone looking through her notebook might be fooled into believing she lived in the world she spent so much time depicting, when the truth was, she only recorded it.

She had lived, once. Her life in Dunvegan had been quiet enough even then, but there'd been a time when she'd walked into the village every day. Back then, the villagers had greeted her with nods and smiles. She'd had friends there, people who were pleased to see her.

But no longer. It had been months since she'd left the castle, months since she'd spoken to a single soul aside from her sisters, and Lord Ballantyne.

If only she . . .

No. There was no sense in wishing for the impossible. It would only make her melancholy, and anyway, it was better this way.

Safer.

Still, it was an amusing sketch. Carefully, she tore it out of her notebook and slipped it into the pocket of her cloak, then set her pencil and notebook aside in favor of watching the clouds skimming across the sky. Cool fingers of light played over her face. She closed her eyes, and bursts of pale yellow and muted orange danced behind her eyelids.

The impending storm would come, whether she told anyone or not. There was no one around to warn, in any case. Catriona had gone off to the village with Lord Ballantyne, and Sorcha was . . . well, she hadn't any idea where Sorcha was. In the woods somewhere, no doubt, getting up to goodness only knew what sort of mischief.

But the storm was still hours away. Even as much as a day might pass before it hit, and in the meantime, there was sunshine to be had. Weak sunshine, with hardly a breath of warmth to it, but still rare enough a Highland lass knew to appreciate it as the gift it was.

Perhaps a wee nap was in order? Goodness knew a sound sleep was rare enough these days. A wise lady seized it when it presented itself, rather like sunshine in October.

But her eyelashes hardly had a chance to brush her cheeks before she was startled awake by a noise so strange, so utterly out of place she was on her feet and peering over the edge of the wall surrounding the turret's roof before her eyes had fully opened.

From here, she could see for miles around the castle. The turret had been added to the original castle structure in the twelfth century. Most people considered it an ill-advised addition, jutting as it did like a scolding finger into the sky.

It was an ugly old thing, to be sure, but she loved it despite its oddities. Or perhaps because of them. She could never quite make up her mind. Whatever the case, there was no denying it was the turret that distinguished her castle from every other castle on the Isle of Skye.

Awkward or not, Castle Cairncross was famous for its turret.

Or perhaps infamous was a better word. Yes, infamous was a more apt description these days, but it did her no good at all to dwell on it.

It was much better not to think of it at all.

As for the strange noise, it had disappeared as suddenly as it arrived. She scanned the wood, then the narrow pathway to the village that wound behind the old stables, but all was silent, and the front drive, the wood, and the pathway were deserted.

Had she imagined the voices, or drifted off to sleep, and dreamed—

No! There it was again, a man's voice. A single male voice on its own wasn't cause for alarm, not since Lord Ballantyne had come to Dunvegan. If there'd been only one deep voice, she would have assumed he and Catriona had returned from their errand in the village.

But there were *two* male voices—a deep, cold one and a second one, warmer and with a hint of amusement.

Whoever they were, they were close. *Too* close.

She braced her arms on the ledge and leaned as far over the edge of the wall as she dared, and . . . oh, dear God, there they were, right below her!

Two men, both strangers.

She was no connoisseur of the male form, but they were much larger than the usual sort of man—big, strapping fellows with broad shoulders and massive hands. The man on the left with the dark hair was a veritable giant, and he looked . . . well, it was difficult to tell from here, but his mouth seemed to be turned down in a scowl as dark as midnight itself.

There could only be one reason they were strolling boldly up her drive as if they had every right to be there, coming closer to the front door with every step.

Oh, no. No, no, no. Not now. Not *again*.

She stumbled backward, away from the wall, her heart pounding in her chest. No good ever came of strange men approaching Castle Cairncross, especially men who could snap a lady's neck with a mere twitch of their fingers.

What was she meant to *do*? There was no one nearby, not a single person to warn.

Two men she'd never seen before were a heartbeat away from her front door.

And she was here alone.

* * *

"So, this is Castle Cairncross." Callum paused several paces from the top of the drive and took in the massive, iron-studded front door. "It's exactly what I expected."

A hulking abomination of dark gray stone topped with a turret that looked to be an instant away from crumbling into Loch Dunvegan. Neat rows of windows dominated the façade, but there wasn't a flicker of life behind them. They were dark, blank, unblinking, a dozen suspicious eyes scrutinizing every poor fool that made the mistake of approaching the front door.

"The seat of Rory MacLeod, in all its dubious glory." Keir squinted up at the weather-beaten front door. "Grim old pile, isn't it?"

"Grim enough. If I'd been MacLeod, I'd have let it tumble into the sea long ago, and good riddance. Seems a fitting end to such an infamous place."

"It's not the castle itself that's infamous." Keir frowned as he took in the lopsided turret. "It's the inhabitants."

"It's both." It wasn't a kind assessment, but whatever slender thread of kindness he'd been clinging to had disintegrated in the downpour they'd encountered in Strathcarron this morning. "MacLeod was a notorious smuggler, and his three daughters are witches. It doesn't get any more infamous than that."

"Witches." Keir snorted out a laugh. "There's no such thing as witches. Don't tell me you believe all the wild rumors about the MacLeod sisters."

"There's a grain of truth to every rumor."

"And all but that one grain is nearly always a load of bollocks." Keir gave him a cheerful slap on the back.

Cheerful, for God's sake.

A man couldn't be expected to be cheerful with icy water dripping down the back of his neck and his boots squelching with every step, but Keir tended to remain jovial no matter what miseries befell him.

It was bloody irritating, was what it was.

The dousing they'd endured should have been more than

enough to knock the smile off the man's face. Highland downpours were a misery of a thing, especially in the fall, but even that resounding soaking had been no match for Keir's good humor.

Callum didn't suffer from the same affliction. He'd always been an impatient, sour-tempered fellow, and he didn't see any reason to stop now. "Ballantyne better have a damned good reason for dragging us all the way up here," he grumbled, as they resumed their trek up the graveled drive to the door.

Ballantyne's summons couldn't have come at a worse time. He had no business traipsing about on the Isle of Skye, hundreds of miles away from his clan, his boots overflowing with rainwater, but whatever trouble Ballantyne had gotten himself into this time must be dire. He never would have called them here otherwise.

Perhaps he'd been bewitched. If ever there was a man apt to fall victim to a bewitching, it was Ballantyne.

"I daresay he does." Keir gave a careless shrug. "I don't know why you're so put out. Don't you have the least bit of curiosity about the MacLeod sisters? I'm looking forward to meeting the young ladies at the heart of such spectacular rumors. It isn't every day a man has the chance to meet a witch."

Witches, of all ridiculous things. "You just said there's no such thing as witches."

Keir shrugged. "There are plenty of people in Scotland who insist otherwise. Not me, mind you, but plenty of others."

"All that proves is that Scotland is awash in superstitious fools."

The MacLeod sisters were *something*, yes—the fantastical rumors about them were proof of that much—but he'd wager his last penny that witchery had nothing to do with it. No doubt they were the usual, run-of-the-mill charlatans, but perhaps with better acting skills.

"They're not witches. They're just three troublesome chits with nothing better to do with their time than play at—"

"Callum." Keir laid a hand on his arm, halting him on their way up the drive, and nodded toward the front door. "Look."

He glanced up, his steps slowing.

A young lady was standing in the open doorway at the castle's entrance. She'd appeared out of nowhere, as if born of the air itself, just like . . .

Well, like a witch. "Where the devil did she come from?"

"The castle, I presume." Keir came to a stop beside him. "She must be one of the sisters."

She was dressed in a dark green gown with a bulky dark blue cloak thrown over the top of it, the rough linen nearly drowning her, and she had a long, reddish-gold braid hanging down her back. "She looks like a housemaid."

Keir shook his head. "I don't think so. Ballantyne said the sisters live here alone."

Whoever she was, she was watching them approach, her small frame rigid and her brow furrowed with . . . was that dread?

"What's the matter with her? Why is she looking at us like that?"

"I haven't the faintest idea. She must know who we are, mustn't she? Ballantyne would have told them we were coming."

One would think so, but that wasn't a welcome expression on her face, or even a curious one. No, she was gaping at them with such abject horror he glanced behind them, expecting to encounter something awful, indeed.

A fire-breathing dragon, perhaps, or a mob of pitchfork-wielding villagers? There was no love lost between the MacLeod sisters and the villagers of Dunvegan, according to Ballantyne.

But there was nothing behind them. The drive was deserted.

"She doesn't look as if she's expecting us," Keir murmured. "I don't like to frighten her. Perhaps we'd better wait for Ballantyne to appear and make the introductions."

Where *was* Ballantyne? Shouldn't he be here to meet them?

They waited, locked in a strange sort of stand-off with the

red-headed girl, who'd made no move to go back inside, or meet them on the drive. She appeared to be frozen, one slender hand resting on the door-frame, her face as pale as death.

The three of them stood there, none of them moving, and eyed each other over the empty expanse of the drive between them.

Waiting was the proper thing to do—the gentlemanly thing—but he wasn't inclined to stand about in his wet boots while this bedraggled-looking chit mustered up the courage to squeak out a greeting.

"Enough. I'm going ahead." If the girl fell into a hysterical swoon, then so be it.

"Callum, wait."

But he didn't wait. He strode forward, his eyes on the girl, who was shrinking back with every step he took toward her, her thin shoulders hunching. When he was a dozen paces from the front door he opened his mouth to offer a greeting, but before he could get a word out, an unholy shriek shattered the silence.

It was a battle cry. Not the first he'd ever heard. Clan Ross had been in their fair share of skirmishes with neighboring clans. It was bloodcurdling enough, and fairly trembling with rage, but the voice was much higher than one would expect, with a shrill edge to it.

It was a woman's voice, but it wasn't the girl in the doorway who'd uttered it. She was still frozen where she stood, one trembling hand over her mouth, her wide eyes dark smudges in her pale face.

Beside him, Keir was shouting something, but before he could decipher it, or even stir a step, something crashed into him, nearly knocking him down. It wasn't heavy, but before he could react it scrambled up his back and wrapped an arm around his neck.

"What the devil?" He tried to throw it—*her*—off, but she clung like a burr.

"No. Don't move, Callum." Keir's voice had gone quiet, but

there was a thread of urgency in it that made Callum freeze where he stood.

That was when he felt it.

The cold press of a blade against the vulnerable stretch of skin just below his jaw, where his pulse beat, and blood rushed through his carotid artery.

"We don't care for strangers here at Castle Cairncross," a voice said near his ear. If there'd been a tremor in it, he might have made another attempt to toss her to the ground, but it was calm, matter-of-fact. "You shouldn't be here."

"We don't mean you any harm." Keir held up his hands. "We were invited to—"

"I didn't invite you. You've made a mistake, coming here." The blade moved against his flesh then, just the tiniest shift in the angle, but it was enough.

A trickle of warm blood slid down his neck.

Then, as if the spill of his blood wasn't warning enough, she added, "A fatal mistake."

Chapter 2

A bloody murder was unfolding in the castle's front drive.

There weren't many things worse than a pair of enormous smugglers strolling up to the front door of her castle, but her sister slitting one of their throats without blinking an eye was one of them.

Five months ago, such a dramatic turn from the concerning to the unimaginably dreadful would have shocked Freya, but since her father's passing, this was the way of things at Castle Cairncross.

Just when she was sure things couldn't get any worse, they *did*.

"Sorcha?" Freya kept one eye on the two men as she sidled down the drive, one hand out toward her sister. "Let's not act hastily, dearest. We don't know who these men are. They may not be smugglers at all."

"No?" Sorcha didn't release her victim but pressed the blade against the oozing cut she'd already carved into the man's neck. "Perhaps not, but you can be sure they're some manner of blackguard."

She could hardly argue that point, could she? Only wicked people with ill intent ever came to Castle Cairncross these days. She'd never seen any of the smugglers who'd come before, not face-to-face. None of them had ever made it as far as the castle's door, but in the dozens of nightmares she'd had about them, they all looked just like the man under Sorcha's blade.

She was close enough now to see his eyes, and they were . . . dear God.

His gaze met hers, and she suppressed a shudder. To be fair, a man wasn't at his best with a knife-wielding hellion on his back, but his eyes chilled her to the bone. They were the same icy gray as Loch Dunvegan in the dead of winter, when there wasn't any sun in the sky to lighten the dark roil of the water.

If there was ever a man with a villain's face, it was this man. If the other one had been half as terrifying, she might have let Sorcha do her worst, but he was fair-haired and blue-eyed, and blessed with a most angelic face.

He was quite the prettiest man she'd ever seen, but weren't the prettiest men always the worst scoundrels? The clouds scudding across the sky above them were pretty, too, but they were still harbingers of doom.

Yet doubt niggled at her. There was something not right about this, and the last thing she and her sisters needed was to add a murder to their already dire circumstances.

"Wait a moment, Sorcha. If these men have come with ill intent, then why would they approach from the drive? Anyone watching from the castle could see them coming well before they reach the door."

"How should I know? Stupidity, perhaps?"

Oh, no. Sorcha was at her most mulish. Nothing was more difficult than reasoning with her when she was in such a state. "For pity's sake, Sorcha. Surely we're obliged to ask them why they've come here before you butcher this man in cold blood!"

"Very well, then." Sorcha shifted her blade, and another trickle of blood inched down the man's neck. "You have five seconds to persuade me you're not another one of the villains after my father's treasure before I spill your blood all over the front drive."

The gray-eyed man let out a growl. "Enough."

Every hair on Freya's neck rose in alarm, but the warning came too late. His arm lashed out, and before she could take a step, hard fingers closed around her wrist and tugged. She stumbled, and before she had a chance to regain her footing she was trapped against a chest as unyielding as a stone wall.

One impossibly long, hard arm wrapped around her waist, and the other snaked around her neck, pressing against her windpipe. "Keep still."

She should have screamed. The instant his cold fingers touched her wrist she should have writhed and struggled and lashed out with every bit of strength she possessed, but to her everlasting shame, the scream that swelled in her chest died with a whimper before it made it to her lips.

Either of her sisters would have fought the man with everything in them, but she'd never been as brave as they were. She went cold with panic, the strength in her limbs deserting her and leaving her as limp and unresisting as a rag doll in his arms.

Black spots danced at the edges of her vision, but this was no time to succumb to a maidenly swoon. Sorcha was still perched on the man's back, with the dirk still pressed to his throat. She had to persuade her sister to release him before the thin rivulets of blood on his neck became a deluge.

"I—I'm all right, Sorcha. He isn't hurting me." She wasn't all right, and he was hurting her, his arm like a vise around her neck, but this situation would go from bad to worse in a heartbeat if Sorcha lost her head.

"Release her at once!" Sorcha hissed, each word heavy with menace, but the tremor in her voice gave her away. "Let my sister go, or I swear I'll tear off a strip of your flesh!"

The man ignored Sorcha's threat, and as cool as you please turned and presented his back to his friend, with Freya still clutched against his chest. "A bit of help, if you would, Keir."

"If you insist upon it." The second man wrapped a burly arm around Sorcha's waist and plucked her off his friend's back like one would a burr stuck in a horse's tail. "Although I confess I'm rather curious to see what she'll do next."

Sorcha, who'd never taken kindly to being manhandled,

squirmed and kicked to get free, but the man had the good sense to keep her arms securely pinned behind her back. "Easy there, lass. We're not going to harm you."

As soon as he was free, the first man—Callum—pressed the fingers of one hand to the cut on his throat, his other arm still tight around Freya's neck. He frowned down at his bloody fingers before turning to Sorcha. "Damned hellion. One accidental slip of your wrist, and you might have killed me."

Sorcha, far from being intimidated, let out a harsh laugh. "If I had spilled your blood, it wouldn't have been an accident."

"Shall we try this again?" The fair-haired man raised one hand in a placating gesture, the other one still holding Sorcha's wrists. "I'm Keir Dunn, Laird of Clan Dunn, and this gentleman here is—"

"*Gentleman?*" Sorcha spat, whirling around to face the man. "He's holding my sister against her will! He's hurting her!"

"He wouldn't have needed to do either if you hadn't pressed a blade to his throat." Mr. Dunn nodded at his friend. "That's enough, Callum. Let the lady go."

He didn't let her go, but the arm around her neck eased slightly. "I'll let her sister go as soon as that vixen puts her blade on the ground."

"What the devil is going on here?"

The familiar voice rang out over the drive, and Freya sagged against her captor, relief threatening to take her knees out from under her. It was Cat and Lord Ballantyne. They'd returned from the village, and not a moment too soon.

But a brawl in the front drive of Castle Cairncross still had the power to shock some people, because Cat and Lord Ballantyne didn't rush forward to save them. They were frozen in place, their mouths hanging open.

"What's going on, Ballantyne? Let me see." Keir Dunn, the fair-haired man, nodded at Sorcha. "This young lady here tried to gut Callum like a pig, and this other lady appears to be moments away from a swoon. I confess it's not quite the greeting we expected."

The threat of a throat-slitting penetrated Cat's shock, and she came tearing down the drive, Lord Ballantyne on her heels, both shouting at once. Lord Ballantyne stopped a few paces away from the melee, his hands up in a placating gesture. "These gentlemen aren't smugglers, Miss Sorcha. They're friends of mine from Kildary. I asked them to come here."

"My goodness, Sorcha!" Cat took the dirk away from Sorcha, her eyes going wide when she noticed the blood smeared on the edge of the blade. "What have you done?"

Lord Ballantyne strode forward and cupped Freya's elbow in his hand. "If you'd be so good as to unhand Miss Freya, Callum?"

The man glanced down at her, a flare of surprise in his gray eyes, as if he couldn't recall quite how she'd gotten there, then he released her so suddenly she stumbled a little. Even as she cursed herself for a coward, she scrambled backward, away from him, her heart pounding as if it were one beat away from bursting from her chest.

"These gentlemen are Lord Ballantyne's friends," Cat was saying to Sorcha, her tone reproachful. "He—that is, *we*—invited them to come here."

Freya stared at her sister. "Did it occur to you to inform us of this, Cat?" She didn't often get angry, but her cheeks were heating rather alarmingly, and her fists were clenched so tightly her fingernails bit into her palms.

Cat flushed, her teeth worrying at her lower lip. "Of course it did. That is, I didn't know they were coming until about an hour ago, but—"

"For God's sake, Cat!" Sorcha threw her arms in the air. "Don't we have enough trouble as it is without adding two blackguards to it?"

"They, ah, well, the thing is . . ." Cat's gaze darted between

Sorcha, Freya, and Lord Ballantyne. "Perhaps I'd better take my sisters inside. Where we can discuss this in private."

"No." Freya crossed her arms over her chest. She wasn't going anywhere until they had the whole of it. "I don't like this, Cat. Why are these men here?"

"More importantly," Sorcha added, "when are they leaving?"

"They're, er . . . they're not." Cat drew in a deep breath. "I am. That is, Lord Ballantyne and I are leaving tomorrow morning."

"Leaving?" The word echoed in Freya's head as if Cat had shouted it, but it emerged from her lips in a hoarse whisper. "You're *leaving* us?"

Dear God, had she ever sounded more pathetic?

"Yes." Cat rushed forward and took her hands. "But for a few weeks only, dearest."

"A few weeks! But where will you go?" Tears stung her eyes—silly, foolish tears that threatened to spill over onto her cheeks, and she turned away from the two strange men, horrified at the thought of those hard gray eyes witnessing her weakness.

Cat squeezed her hand. "To Ballantrae Bay, to see Cormac Donigan."

"Cormac Donigan?" He was their father's former business partner, but Rory and Cormac had parted ways years ago. "But why?"

Cat glanced at Callum Ross, then took Freya aside, lowering her voice. "If anyone knows what's become of Rory's treasure, it's Cormac Donigan. The smugglers won't stop coming if they think the treasure is here. We need to find it if we're ever to have any peace, Freya."

Every villain and blackguard in Scotland believed the treasure was hidden at Castle Cairncross. If Cat and Lord Ballantyne could find it . . . well, it wouldn't solve all their problems, but the smugglers would cease tormenting them.

They wouldn't be forced to flee Castle Cairncross, then.

It was a chance. A bleak one, but a chance. "Do you really think Cormac Donigan will know where—"

"No! It's a mad scheme, Cat. If you insist upon going to Ballantrae Bay, then go, but you may take these two with you." Sorcha jerked her chin toward the two men. "Goodness knows we don't want them here."

No, they didn't. Of course they didn't. Callum Ross had grabbed her, *threatened* her. The idea of such a man invading the sanctuary of her beloved castle made bile rise in her throat. A thousand objections to their presence here rushed to her lips, but she couldn't make them leave her mouth.

As much as she wanted to, she couldn't agree with Sorcha.

The truth was, they needed Lord Ballantyne's friends. If—no, *when*—another lugger came—they couldn't be here at the castle alone. To pretend otherwise was mere foolishness and would spell their doom. "Sorcha—"

"No," Sorcha repeated through gritted teeth. "The last thing we need at Castle Cairncross is another pair of scoundrels."

Freya glanced at the gray-eyed man, who was watching the scene unfold with cool detachment, and another involuntary shudder tripped down her spine.

Callum Ross was a cold-blooded brute, but the devil you knew was far better than the dozens of devils they didn't. Every villain in Scotland was eyeing Castle Cairncross. Sooner or later, another lugger would come. It was only a matter of time before one of the boats made it to the shore, and once it did, they'd be overrun.

God help them, then.

"We can't keep on as we have been, Sorcha. This business with Father's treasure needs to come to an end." She took care to keep her voice soft, coaxing. "I don't like this either, but if another lugger should come—"

"Then we'll drive them off, just as we did the last three!"

"And the next one? Will we drive them off, too? And the one after that?" She shook her head. "No, Sorcha. We just managed to drive off this last one, and they grow bolder with each attempt. The day is fast approaching where we won't be able to frighten them off, and then what will become of us?"

"Please, Sorcha," Cat added softly. "There's no other way."

Sorcha said nothing. The six of them stood there in the drive in silence, a ludicrous tableau, until at last Sorcha turned, and without a word marched down the drive, and vanished into the woods beyond.

Freya watched Sorcha go, her heart in her throat. It wasn't an outright rebellion, and thus, more than she'd hoped for. It was as close to an agreement as they were likely to get from Sorcha.

As for Callum Ross . . . she risked one more glance into those cold eyes and took a few hasty steps backward, away from him.

She'd simply stay out of his way.

It was a large castle. With a little luck, she'd never have to lay eyes on the man again.

"I see the rumors about the MacLeod sisters weren't exaggerations." Callum threw himself into one of the dusty leather chairs across from the fireplace in the drafty study Hamish had led them to, his grim gaze on the glass of port in his hand.

Hamish opened his mouth, presumably to agree that Sorcha MacLeod was a hellion of the first order, and her sisters not much better, but what emerged wasn't agreement, nor was it the apology it should have been.

In fact, it sounded like a strangled laugh.

Callum stared at him. "Do you find this amusing, Ballantyne? Forgive me, but I fail to find any humor in some deranged chit tearing a chunk of flesh from my throat."

"No, of course not. It's just the expression on your face was . . . well, it isn't often you're caught so completely off guard, Callum. But of course, it's not at all amusing. I do beg your pardon. Perhaps I've had a touch too much port."

"Perhaps I haven't had enough." Callum tossed back the last dregs and set the glass aside with a thump. "I daresay you'd find Sorcha MacLeod's antics less diverting if her blade had been pressed to *your* neck."

"I won't argue that point. I didn't find it all agreeable when Catriona poisoned me with a handful of deadly monkshood."

Deadly monkshood? What the devil?

He glanced at Keir, who was staring at Hamish with his brows aloft. "Catriona MacLeod *poisoned* you?"

"It was an accident." Hamish grabbed the bottle of port from the sideboard and dropped into the chair across from Callum.

Keir snorted. "How does someone accidentally poison a man with deadly monkshood?"

A small smile crossed Hamish's lips. "It's a long story, and one not worth telling."

"What the devil are you smiling at, Ballantyne? One of the MacLeod sisters tried to behead me, and another tried to poison you, and you're grinning as if you find it charming." God above, had the man lost his wits? "It seems they're every bit the witches the rumors claim them to be. They've certainly bewitched you."

At that, the smile slipped from Hamish's lips. "They're not witches. Bloody hell, Callum, if you knew how much damage those rumors have done them—" He broke off with an exhaled breath. "I didn't call you to Skye to argue over whether or not the MacLeod sisters are witches."

"Ah, now we're getting to it." Keir drained his glass and held it out for Hamish to refill it. "Why did you call us up here, then? That blasted note you sent was about as illuminating as a cave drawing."

Hamish didn't answer right away but sat there turning his glass in his hand.

Callum seized the bottle of port, poured a measure into Keir's glass, then topped off his own. "Well, Ballantyne?"

"You heard Catriona. She and I are leaving Castle Cairncross tomorrow. The only way to stop this business with Rory

MacLeod's treasure is to find it and put an end to the rumors once and for all."

"And? What has that got to do with us?"

"We can't leave her sisters here alone, Callum. Another lugger will come, and that's to say nothing of the villagers of Dunvegan, who don't look upon the MacLeod sisters with friendly eyes. At this point, the villagers may be more dangerous than the smugglers. I need you here to keep watch over Freya and Sorcha MacLeod."

"So that's it, then." Callum dropped his empty glass onto the side table. "You summoned us all the way to Skye to babysit a pair of redheaded hellions."

"No. I summoned you to Skye to *protect* them. I grant you Sorcha's a bit, er . . . unpredictable, but Freya's no hellion. She's a quiet, unassuming young lady."

"Freya?" Callum glanced at Keir. "Who the devil is Freya?"

Hamish rolled his eyes. "You did notice there were three sisters, did you not? Freya is the middle sister. If you recall, you were standing on the front drive with her not ten minutes ago."

"For God's sake, man. Freya was the lady in the green dress with the blue cloak over it," Keir added. "One would think you'd remember her, given the way you manhandled the poor lady."

Green dress? Oh, right. That tiny wisp of a girl who'd appeared at the castle door when they'd first arrived. The one who'd stood about wringing her hands while her demonic sister tried to behead him. "Yes, yes. I recall her now. Not much use today, was she?"

Keir cast him an incredulous look. "Because you frightened the wits out of her, Callum! She nearly fell into a swoon."

Had she? That was a pity, but he never would have grabbed her if her mad sister hadn't leapt on him. If Freya MacLeod had lost her wits, she could blame her sister for it.

"Freya's a bit timid, but make no mistake, Callum. If it

hadn't been for her, there would be a pool of your blood soaking into the drive right now." Hamish drew a finger across his neck. "Sorcha MacLeod doesn't listen to many people, but she does listen to Freya."

"If she's so adept at managing that wild sister of hers, what do you need with us?" Callum rested a booted foot on the worn ottoman in front of him, a sudden exhaustion seeping into his limbs. "Surely they're able to take care of themselves."

Hamish leaned forward, his elbows on his knees, and fixed his gaze on Callum. "They're as capable as any young ladies I've ever met. Each one of them is cleverer than the last, but a pair of young women are no match for hardened smugglers intent on storming their castle, no matter how clever they are."

Keir drained his glass. "What do smugglers want with the MacLeod sisters?"

"It's not the sisters they're after, it's Rory MacLeod's treasure. Every damn cutthroat from Ireland's east coast to the Orkney Islands thinks it's hidden here at Castle Cairncross, and they'll stop at nothing to get it."

Callum snorted.

Rory MacLeod's infamous treasure. He knew all about it, of course. He'd heard the rumors, just as everyone else had, about how MacLeod had found the lost Jacobean gold and made away with a fortune in coins and jewels.

He hadn't believed a word of it. Rory MacLeod had been a legend in the annals of Scottish smugglers before he died some months ago, and fantastical rumors had followed him like children after the Pied Piper.

Some of the rumors were true, and some weren't. He would have put Rory's alleged treasure into the latter category, but Hamish had been chasing that lost gold for months now, and if it had led him here to Castle Cairncross, then . . . well, perhaps there was more truth to it than he realized. "How many have come?"

"Three. Two luggers before I arrived, and a third just a few nights ago. The sisters drove the first two off, and we managed to keep the third one at bay, as well, but—"

"But their luck won't hold out forever." Keir dragged a hand through his hair. "It's only a matter of time before one of them succeeds in gaining the castle."

"Exactly." Hamish nodded. "It's a miracle they haven't succeeded already, but as I said, the MacLeod sisters are clever. Even so, it would be the height of recklessness to leave Freya and Sorcha here alone."

Three luggers, in three months' time? Someone believed the rumors to be true, then.

Unless, of course, this was all an elaborate ploy orchestrated by the MacLeod sisters. Hamish had said they were clever. What could be cleverer than fooling a wealthy English marquess into saving your hide? "Has it occurred to you, Ballantyne, that Catriona MacLeod is leading you on a merry chase?"

"A dozen times since I arrived in Dunvegan, but I saw the last lugger myself. In any case, that was before . . ." A small smile drifted over Hamish's lips. "Well, let's just say I have every reason to believe Catriona MacLeod is telling me the truth."

Oh, good Lord. He knew that smile. Hamish had smiled in just that same ridiculous way when he'd fancied himself madly in love with the barmaid at the Slippery Eel in Edinburgh.

"These reasons of yours, Ballantyne. They wouldn't have anything to do with the fact that Catriona MacLeod happens to have the face of an angel, would they?"

"Noticed that, did you, Ross?" Keir raised an eyebrow at him.

Yes, he'd noticed. He was a man, after all, and he wasn't blind.

"Surely her face hasn't anything to do with this." Keir raised an eyebrow at Hamish. "Ballantyne here isn't so foolish as to lose his head over a pair of green eyes, are you, Ballantyne?"

Hamish gave them another of those enigmatic smiles. "My reasons are my own."

"There's your answer, Keir. He *is* foolish enough."

"My feelings for Catriona MacLeod have nothing to do with either of you. Now, do you agree to remain at Castle Cairncross and keep an eye on Freya and Sorcha MacLeod as I've asked, or shall I fetch another bottle of Rory MacLeod's port, and keep pouring until the two of you feel more cooperative?"

Keir gave a careless shrug. "I'll stay. Callum?"

He couldn't conceive of a more foolish errand than this one. He'd come all the way from Kildary to Dunvegan when he could ill afford to leave his clan to guard a pair of silly chits who were old enough to take care of themselves.

If it had been anyone but Hamish who'd begged the favor of him, he would have refused on principle, but as it was . . .

Hamish and Keir were his oldest friends. He had few enough of those, and he wasn't a man who refused a friend when they asked a favor of him.

No matter how ridiculous it was.

"I'll stay, but that's no reason for you not to fetch more port, Ballantyne." He held up his empty glass. "I hope that's not the last bottle.

A crumbling castle, and a pair of redheaded vixens who may, or may not, be witches?

There wasn't enough port in the world for that.

CHAPTER 3

Freya's brilliant plan to avoid Callum Ross was a resounding success. She hadn't laid eyes on him since that awful scene in the front drive on the day he arrived at Castle Cairncross.

Which had been . . . yesterday. Still, more than a day had passed since then. Whole hours in which she'd escaped the sight or sound of him. Of course, she'd spent nearly all those hours in her bedchamber, but a lady must take her successes as they came.

Now all she had to do was get through the next three weeks. That would be easy enough, surely? It was only twenty-one days. Why, that was hardly any time at all.

Just five hundred and four hours. It would be over before she knew it.

Never mind that she'd spent hours this afternoon pacing her bedchamber before she'd worked up the nerve to venture to the top of the staircase, and then she'd darted down it as if the hounds of hell were on her heels.

She plucked glumly at one of the pianoforte keys. Five hundred and four hours of peeking around every corner and scurrying up staircases every time she caught a glimpse of him. She'd only ended up in the music room because she'd fancied she heard footsteps behind her.

She didn't even play the pianoforte, for pity's sake. God above, what a dreadful coward she—

"There you are, Freya. I've been all over the castle, looking for you." Sorcha burst through the door of the music room, a cloud of dust swirling into the air as she slammed it closed behind her. "Why are you hiding in here?"

"Hiding? What a ridiculous notion, Sorcha! Why should I be hiding?"

Yes, two strange, enormous men she'd never laid eyes on until yesterday had invaded her castle, and yes, the more terrifying of the two of them had grabbed her and nearly suffocated her with his massive paw around her throat. And yes, they'd both been watching her every move like a pair of hawks hunting a mouse ever since, but that didn't mean she was hiding.

She wasn't *hiding*. She was merely . . . dusting the pianoforte.

"I beg your pardon." Sorcha paused in front of a window, a watery beam of gray sunlight washing over her. "I need, ah, a small favor from you."

"A small favor," Freya repeated flatly. Oh, this didn't bode well. Sorcha's favors were never small, and they invariably led to trouble. The last favor she'd done for Sorcha had ended with a small fire. The hem of her best cloak had been singed beyond redemption, but perhaps the less said about that, the better.

She eyed her sister. Sorcha was dressed in an old, dark gray riding habit Catriona had outgrown years earlier, the elbows worn thin with use, and atop her head sat an old black felt hat of their father's. A gnarled walking stick she'd fashioned from a thick branch of a fallen pine tree completed this odd costume.

Odd, but familiar. It was the usual costume she wore when she went tramping about in the woods. For anyone else, a sedate stroll through the trees was an innocent enough pastime, but Sorcha *wasn't* anyone else. She was Sorcha, and too much like their father for anything she did to be entirely innocent.

"It won't take any time at all, I promise you," Sorcha said in her best wheedling voice. "I'll be back before you've even had a chance to—"

"No." Freya cut her off before she could get another word past her lips. "It's out of the question, Sorcha."

"For pity's sake, Freya! There's no need to make such a fuss. It's just a quick errand."

"A quick, harmless errand." Freya snorted. "You always say that, and it's never true."

"But I mean it this time! I'll be back before you've even had a chance to miss me." Sorcha offered her most ingratiating smile.

Well, it wouldn't work. Not this time. They'd both promised Cat they wouldn't venture beyond the castle grounds, but Sorcha had never excelled at observing boundaries. "No, Sorcha. Nothing good will come of it, and you know it as well as I do."

Nothing good, and likely a great deal of bad, particularly if Sorcha intended to go into the village. Between the smugglers haunting the waters of Loch Dunvegan—the MacLeod sisters' fault—and the rumors of witchcraft taking place inside the castle—also the MacLeod sisters' fault—they had few friends left in the village these days.

Few friends, and dozens of enemies, all of them eager to put the MacLeod sisters in their place.

Sorcha wasn't the sort to keep her mouth closed if she was challenged. She loved her sister, but Sorcha was stubborn, willful, and alas, it must be said, occasionally a bit too, er . . . forceful.

Blade-to-a-man's-neck forceful.

"Come now, Freya. Don't tell me you're going to allow those two. . . ." Sorcha waved a hand toward the entryway. "Those two lairds to keep us prisoners in our own home!"

"Shame on you, Sorcha. It was Catriona who forbade us from leaving the castle, not Laird Ross or Laird Dunn, and you know it as well as I do."

"Yes, well, Catriona isn't here, is she?"

No, she was off on a treasure hunt with Lord Ballantyne, dash it, and it would be weeks before they returned. How was she meant to keep Sorcha out of trouble for weeks on end?

Really, Cat's faith in her was utterly misplaced. It was all quite distressing.

"As for those two lairds, if they aren't our jailors, then why are they guarding the door?" Sorcha kicked at the pianoforte bench, a pout on her lips. "The *only* door, now."

Indeed, and she had Lord Ballantyne to thank for making it more difficult for Sorcha to sneak out whenever she pleased without a word to anyone. He'd secured the cellar and kitchen doors with nails and heavy planks of wood.

There was one way into Castle Cairncross now, and one way out, and that was through the front door. It did feel a bit like a prison, but a lady didn't want her enemies strolling into her castle whenever they pleased.

"Please, Freya! I need your help to make a clean escape. There's no chance of my getting out the door and down the drive with that *man* pacing the entryway like a guard at Newgate."

"Which man?" The one with an angelic face? Or . . . the other one?

She swallowed, her fingertips finding the pulse fluttering at her throat. Every time she recalled the pressure of that thick arm against her neck, her breath went all fluttery and shallow, as if it were still there.

"How do I know? One laird looks much like the other to me."

Honestly, only Sorcha could mistake one of those men for the other. One of them was a handsome, fair-haired gentleman, and the other was . . . well, it was like confusing an angel with Satan himself. "For pity's sake, Sorcha. They look nothing alike."

Sorcha wrinkled her nose. "It's the bigger one, I think. I need you to lure him out of the entryway so I can get out."

"Lure him! You want *me* to lure Callum Ross?" Sorcha may as well have asked her to dive from the top of the turret into the freezing waters of Loch Dunvegan and resurface with a thrashing fish caught between her teeth.

"Of course, you. Who else, if not you?"

"But how?" How did one distract such a brutish man? Throw raw meat at him? "I haven't got a single thing to say that Callum Ross would find the least bit entertaining. It's not as if I can discuss my embroidery with him or instruct him in the finer points of lace tatting."

He wasn't at all the sort of man a lady could engage in polite chitchat.

"Not the lace, no." Sorcha thought for a moment, then a sly smile curved her lips. "I know just the thing."

Dear God, that smile. She hardly dared to ask. "What?"

"You can cause a commotion in another part of the house."

"A commotion? What sort of a commotion?"

"A noise, or some minor disturbance, like glass shattering, or a scream, or an accident. A fall, perhaps? Not a real one, of course, but . . . oh, I know! You could feign a stumble at the bottom of the staircase, and pretend you've twisted your ankle."

Oh, no. She didn't like the sound of this. "How does my twisting an ankle get you out the front door?"

"Don't you see? He'll be obliged to assist you to a settee in the drawing room. As soon as he's turned his back, poof! I'll be down the stairs and out the door in a trice!"

"Poof?"

"Yes. Poof!" Sorcha snapped her fingers. "Just like that. It's the perfect plan."

"It's *not* the perfect plan. For one, Callum Ross doesn't strike me as a gallant, heroic sort of man. He'll likely just leave me in a heap on the floor. Secondly—"

"Nonsense. Even he isn't such a savage as to leave an injured lady lying in a heap on—"

"*Secondly*, I'm not much of an actress, and if I feign a fall, there's a good chance I might truly injure myself." Even if her ruse worked, he'd have to assist her into the drawing room, and that would almost certainly mean she'd have to touch him . . .

Blast it, there was that odd shivery sensation fluttering in her belly again, unfamiliar, and unwelcome.

Sorcha gave the floor a hard rap with her walking stick. "As always, Freya, you underestimate yourself. You're a MacLeod, aren't you? You can do whatever you set your mind to. Mother always said—"

Freya groaned. "Not this again."

Her mother used to say that for all Freya's sweet, quiet nature, there was a tempest inside her, a deep source of strength that she needed only to draw upon in times of doubt or fear.

This tempest, alas, had never seen fit to present itself, despite doubt and fear being her near constant companions these past few months. But there was no use arguing with Sorcha once she'd made up her mind. She'd go off on her errand today, either with or without Freya's help, and there was sure to be a dreadful scene over it.

She despised scenes. They made her stomach queasy.

"Please, Freya?" Sorcha folded her hands under her chin, and gazed at Freya with wide, beseeching green eyes. "Please? I promise I won't ask you again."

Perhaps there was a bargain to be struck here. "Very well. I'll do it, but first I'll have your word that you won't leave the castle again until Cat and Lord Ballantyne return."

"What, the entire time? But it could be weeks!"

"Those are my terms. Take them or leave them."

Sorcha huffed out a breath. "Fine. I promise it."

"And you have to promise to return to the castle before dark."

"Yes, yes, all right. Thank you, Freya!" Sorcha pressed a kiss on her cheek. "I swear you won't regret it."

"See that I don't." But of course, she *would* regret it. She always regretted it, and now she'd spend the next several hours worrying herself to a frazzle until Sorcha returned. But if it kept her sister safely inside the castle walls for the next five hundred and four hours, it would be well worth it.

Anyway, it was too late now. She'd agreed to it, and Sorcha was already hurrying toward the door. "I'll just pop up the back staircase and wait on the landing while you entice him away from the door."

Entice him? She'd never enticed anyone in her life. Certainly not a gentleman, and Callum Ross was the last man in existence she would have chosen to start with.

It might have been different, if he'd been another sort of man. The ordinary sort. But there was nothing ordinary about him. Not his size, not his unsmiling lips, and not his cold gray eyes.

Why, she may as well attempt to lure a hungry fox out of a hen house.

"Wait, Sorcha." She hurried to the door, her cowardly heart turning somersaults inside her chest. "Perhaps this isn't such a—"

But it was too late. Sorcha was already turning the corner at the end of the hallway.

Dash it. Now what? How was she going to find a way to entice Callum Ross away from the front door?

She peeked around the corner. There he was, pacing from one end of the entryway to the other like a soldier marching across the battlefield.

Or an executioner, seconds away from hacking off someone's head.

It wasn't that he was such a giant of a man, or even his stern, forbidding countenance. She'd seen forbidding men before. Her own father had been a big, broad-shouldered man, and a smuggler to boot, with a glint in his green eyes that hinted at something wild lurking just below the surface.

But Callum Ross, with that thick mane of dark hair and his grim, unsmiling mouth was nothing like her father had been. Rory MacLeod had been a vibrant man with a booming laugh and a wide, wicked smile. She had dozens of lovely memories of him, but her favorite was of rushing down the stairs to greet him when he returned from one of his adventures and screaming with laughter as he tossed her into the air, then caught her again, his strong arms wrapping around her.

For all his faults—and there had been many—he'd been warm and alive.

Callum Ross was her father's opposite in every way. He was as still and cold as a corpse, as silent as a cipher, and his mouth was such a stern, harsh line, it looked as if his lips would crack into a thousand pieces and drop right off his face if he even attempted a smile.

He was the most frightening man she'd ever encountered.

At least, he frightened *her*. Sorcha wasn't afraid of him. Sorcha wasn't afraid of anything. If only she had some of Sorcha's fearlessness, and Sorcha some of her reticence, everything would be a great deal easier.

At the other end of the hallway, Callum Ross's heavy tread echoed throughout the entryway. Back and forth, from one end to the other without pause.

Short of doing herself an injury, how in the world was she meant to distract such a man?

Think. There must be a way. She just had to think.

She turned to the window and gazed out at the woods that surrounded all but the eastern side of Castle Cairncross. A great many of the leaves still clung to the trees, but the storm yesterday's clouds had promised was coming. It would be upon them soon enough, leaving the branches as bare as the bones of skeletons.

It had gotten colder as the storm neared, and she wrapped her arms around herself to ward off the chill. A hot cup of tea would be welcome right now—

Why, of course! She could invite Callum Ross to have some tea in the drawing room. Surely even gigantic, dour Scottish lairds with arctic gray eyes appreciated tea?

Dear God, just thinking of those eyes made a shiver dart

down her spine, but it was too late to revert to her usual cowardice. She'd promised Sorcha.

The tea would have to do. There was nothing for it but to send a quick prayer up to the heavens that she didn't make an utter fool of herself.

Chapter 4

The mouse had found her way out of her hole.

Freya MacLeod had been scurrying around the main floor of the castle for the last half hour, peeking around corners and darting into crevices as if searching for a delectable bit of cheese.

God only knew what she was up to. She'd kept a careful distance from him so far, but she wasn't as stealthy as she thought she was. If he were the sort of man who could be easily spied upon, he wouldn't be at Castle Cairncross right now.

He'd noticed the nervous glances she'd cast his way, but he hadn't paid her any mind. She'd either work up the courage to approach him, or she wouldn't. It made no difference to him, either way.

He wasn't here to make friends with the MacLeod sisters.

He remained still as a soft patter of footsteps came up the kitchen staircase and continued toward the entryway. He didn't move a muscle when she peeked around the edge of the banister, or even when she worked up the courage to edge closer to the door, nor did he blink when she came to a stop behind him.

He waited. The grandfather clock chimed the four o'clock hour, then ceased, leaving them in silence, aside from the soft click of the pendulum as the minutes ticked by.

One, two, three minutes passed, but she didn't take another step or breathe a single word. It was absurd. Was he meant to stand here for the rest of the afternoon, pretending he didn't see her?

A sharp command to get on with whatever it was she'd come for hovered on the edge of his tongue, but he bit it back. The girl was anxious enough. If he dared to glance in her direction, it might send her into a fit of hysterics.

Anything was preferable to that.

He'd just about given up on her when at last, she cleared her throat and let out a timid squeak. "Laird, er, that is, Mr. Ross?"

He drew in a slow, silent breath and turned to her, and God above, she looked like she was on the verge of a swoon.

She was carrying a tea tray with an array of dishes knocking into each other atop it. Her fingertips had gone white from the death grip she had on the edges of the tray. Her eyes were downcast, and her lower lip was bitten raw.

A shame, really. She had a pretty mouth, plump and pink, with a shallow groove at each side of her lips that hinted at the possibility of dimples. He couldn't be certain of that, as he'd never seen her smile, but he was rarely wrong about dimples.

Not that he was likely to ever see hers. She had little to smile about, and in any case, her dimples were no concern of his. He didn't have any business thinking about Freya MacLeod's mouth, or her dimples, or any other part of her.

Nor would he, if she'd simply leave him alone. That he'd noticed her mouth at all wasn't a welcome realization, and when he spoke, his voice was harsher than he intended. "What is it?"

Another squeak burst from her lips. "I, er . . . I beg your pardon. I just . . . I thought . . ." She trailed off and resumed abusing her lower lip with the edges of her teeth.

Good Lord. They'd be here forever at this rate. "What do you *want*?"

He tried to speak gently, but he wasn't a gentle man any more than he was a patient one, and his words carried the same harsh edge as when he issued a stern command to his hunting dogs.

Predictably, she took a hasty step backward. "I, ah, I thought you might like to have some tea, my lord. That is, my laird," she corrected hastily, a blush flooding her cheeks. "Um, I mean, Laird Ross."

Tea. For the past five hours he'd been standing in this entryway and listening to that grandfather clock tick off the minutes without either of the MacLeod sisters offering him a single refreshment.

Not that he cared. He didn't give a damn about tea.

So why had Freya MacLeod developed a sudden and pressing concern for his hydration? She and her sister had kept well out of his way since he and Keir arrived yesterday, but now here she was, wobbling tray in hand, when it was obvious she didn't want to suffer through tea with him, any more than he did with her.

Curious, that. Suspicious, even.

If she'd been a different sort of lady, he might have suspected her of some scheme or other. If she'd been anything like her younger sister Sorcha, for example—a termagant if there ever was one—he would have made it his business to find out what mischief she was plotting, through fair means, or foul.

But this wee little mouse? She wouldn't dare.

"No, thank you." He turned back toward the door. "I don't care for tea."

It was a clear dismissal, but instead of scampering off like a proper little mouse, she lingered. "I have some lovely Dundee cake, and orange marmalade that I make myself."

He jerked around to face her again. "I don't care for cake, either."

In truth he was fond of cake, especially Dundee cake, but not fond enough to endure what was sure to be an excruciating half hour of sipping tea with Freya MacLeod. She could hardly work up the nerve to look at him, and he didn't have time for a silly young lady who was frightened of her own shadow.

"Oh. I, ah . . . very well, then." She shifted awkwardly from one foot to the other, the tea tray still rattling in her hands, but just when he was certain she was about to dart back down the kitchen stairs, her chin rose in an unexpectedly defiant gesture, and then—

"Oh! Oh, no!"

She lurched forward, the tray slipped from her hands, and everything—the teapot, the cups and saucers, the Dundee cake and marmalade and the lady herself went sailing into the air, and—

"Damnation!" He managed to catch her under her arms before she toppled head over heels onto the stone floors, but there was no saving the dishware, which crashed to the floor in an explosion of silver teaspoons, shattered porcelain, hot tea, and a pot of sticky orange marmalade that somehow survived intact and rolled across the hallway like a billiard ball from the tip of a cue.

"Are you hurt?" He set her upright onto her feet, but when he released her arm she swayed, and let out a cry of pain.

"My ankle! I—I . . . oh, dear. I think I've twisted my ankle."

God above. For such an allegedly biddable chit, Freya MacLeod was turning out to be a great deal of trouble. "Can you put your weight on it?"

"I think so."

"Try it. I've got you."

He held her steady, but she let out another cry when she attempted to stand on the injured foot, a spasm of pain crossing her face. "Ouch! Oh, dear. If you'd be so good as to help me to one of the settees in the drawing room, I—"

She broke off with a gasp as he braced one hand on her back, slid the other behind her knees and swept her up into his arms. "My goodness! Mr. Ross! What are you doing?"

"What do you think? I'm carrying you to the drawing room." He lifted her higher against his chest and made a valiant effort not to notice the sweet scent that clung to her—fragrant black tea and orange marmalade—or the press of her soft curves against him.

"I don't need you to . . . I insist you put me down at once!"

"Quiet."

As rescues went, it wasn't the most gallant or the most gracious, but he managed to get her into the drawing room and lay her down onto one of the worn settees. He sat down beside her, but not right beside her, of course. An ocean of faded blue silk cushions remained between them—and he reached for the hem of her skirt. "Let me see your ankle."

She sucked in a sharp breath and jerked her feet away from him, her cheeks flushing scarlet. "I will not! You can't just . . . a proper gentleman does *not* breach a lady's hems, Mr. Ross."

"That depends entirely on the lady, Miss MacLeod."

"That comment does you no credit at all, Mr. Ross. As for my hems, they are sacrosanct. I must insist they remain unmolested."

There was nothing amusing about the situation, but she looked so outraged, with her pert nose in the air and that prim frown on her face that he choked back a laugh. "Forgive me, but a proper gentleman does breach a lady's hems if there's a chance there's a broken bone underneath them."

"It's not broken. I just wrenched it a little, that's all."

"There's only one way to be sure. Come, Miss MacLeod, there's no need to be so missish. If you've broken a bone, I need to know about it." He nodded at her foot, which was still tucked underneath her skirts.

She huffed, but after a bit of offended flouncing about, she offered him her ankle, taking care to tuck her skirts modestly around every bit of exposed leg. "Yes, all right. Don't touch my skirts, if you please."

"I wouldn't dare." He took the injured limb in his hands and turned it carefully this way and that, but there was nothing to indicate she'd broken it. There were no protruding bones and no swelling, and not so much as a scratch or any redness to the skin. "It appears to be perfectly fine."

"As I said." She jerked her foot out of his hand, tucked it back under her skirt and edged away from him until she was perched on the opposite side of her cushion, as far from him as she could get. If he reached a finger in her direction, he hadn't the least doubt she'd burst into flight and scurry back to whatever mouse hole she'd emerged from, despite her injury.

Their conversation died a quick death once they'd settled the question of her ankle, and they sat there staring at each other, neither of them speaking. The silence grew heavier with every passing moment until at last she cleared her throat. "I, ah . . . I understand from Lord Ballantyne that you, he, and Mr. Dunn have been friends for some time."

So, they were to have a polite conversation now, were they? How tedious. But silence, it seemed, was too much to hope for. "Yes."

"Your fathers were friends, I think?"

He did his best not to think about his father, and he certainly wasn't going to discuss him with Freya MacLeod. "Yes," he answered shortly, and perhaps a touch rudely.

But she didn't seem to notice. She sat quietly, plucking at her skirts, her gaze straying to the window behind them. Her profile was arresting, with her high cheekbones, a dainty upturned nose, a gently rounded chin, and fine, creamy white skin.

And that hair . . . when men waxed poetic about a woman's crowning glory, this was what they meant. She wore it bundled in a tight, untidy knot, the thick coil resting at the back of her neck. It was not flattering, with every stray lock scraped away from her face the way it was, and secured by what must be dozens of hairpins, but the haphazard style did nothing to hide the beauty of those lustrous, red-gold tresses.

Not that he thought her beautiful. That is, she was pretty enough, if one admired tiny, pale, timid, redheaded lasses.

He did *not*.

Still, it was odd he'd overlooked her yesterday. Of course, he'd had a dirk pressed to his neck at the time, but even so, short of an actual slit throat, hers wasn't a face a man failed to notice.

Or perhaps it wasn't so odd. She was doing everything she could to hide herself.

It wasn't just the severe hairstyle, but her clothing, as well. Her gown appeared to be several sizes too large for her, and she'd added a fichu and kerchief, piling one piece atop another until she was drowning in layers of fabric. The colors were drab, too—dark grays and browns on a lady who was, perhaps more than any other lady he'd ever seen, meant to wear bright, dramatic shades.

And that pinafore, for God's sake. What was a lady of her age doing in a girl's pinafore? Unless . . . did she wish to be mistaken for a dull, colorless chit of no more than fourteen or fifteen years of age?

If so, she was doing a fine job of it.

Yes, that was it. The hair and clothing weren't an accident. Miss Freya MacLeod was trying to fade into the background. But *why*? God knew he was no expert on the whims and foibles of young ladies, but he had yet to come across one who went so far out of her way to escape notice.

Especially not one with that face.

It didn't make any *sense*, and now he was curious, damn it, when the last thing he needed was to become curious about some lady he'd never lay eyes on again once he left this godforsaken castle—

"It grows dark," she said suddenly. As if on cue, the grandfather clock on the second-floor landing chimed the five o'clock hour. "It's later than I realized," she murmured, her gaze still fixed on the window.

She remained still, but there was something watchful in her

face as she peered out at the darkening sky, and a strange tension in her body. “Are you well, Miss MacLeod? Does your ankle pain you?”

“No, not at all.” She let out a little laugh and untucked herself from the settee. “I only wrenched it a bit. It feels much better.”

He said nothing, and for an instant, her eyes met and held his. It was the first time she’d looked directly at him since he’d arrived, and he felt it . . . God, he felt it everywhere.

She had the greenest eyes he’d ever seen, a fresh, tender green, and as clear and innocent as the first shoots of snowdrops after the winter frost. But for all their sweetness, there was a depth to them, and a flash of something he hadn’t expected in such a fainthearted lady.

A hint of fire.

“If you’ll pardon me, Mr. Ross, I believe I’ll see to the mess in the entryway, and then perhaps I’ll go lie down for a while.” With that vague excuse she rose to her feet, offered him an awkward little curtsy, then fled the drawing room.

He turned, frowning at the door through which she’d just vanished.

What was that all about?

He turned toward the fire, shaking his head. Damned if he knew what had come over her. Perhaps he’d gotten too close to her hems, and it had sent her scampering around the corner like a pickpocket with a handful of coins.

If she’d been anyone other than who she was he would have been suspicious enough to go after her, but Freya MacLeod, a scheming vixen? No. If ever there was a lady less given to misbehavior than she was, he had yet to encounter her.

Such a docile, quiet little thing wouldn’t dare get up to any mischief.

This was a terrible idea. A dreadful, awful, foolish, risky idea.

Freya crouched in the shadows to one side of the staircase, her heart fluttering in her chest, and peered out at the long drive leading up to Castle Cairncross.

There wasn't a single tree to hide behind. It was as empty as a drive could be and seemed to stretch to infinity. How had she never noticed how exposed it was before? There was nothing but forest for miles around, yet there wasn't so much as an obliging shrub or twig to hide her as she scurried down the drive.

Really, was a twig too much to ask?

She peeked around the edge of the staircase, but there were no lairds to be seen. Mr. Dunn had retired upstairs some hours ago, presumably to sleep, as he'd been awake for a good part of the night, pacing the entryway.

As for Callum Ross, he hadn't yet realized he'd been duped, but he would, and sooner rather than later. This was her only chance. There was nothing for it but for her to gather what little courage she possessed and seize it before it was gone.

She sucked in a deep breath and crept from her hiding place to the front door, snatching up the cloak she'd left draped over the banister yesterday.

There. That was one step over with. Only another three or four hundred more to go before she reached the end of the drive. The woods were directly beyond it. Once she passed the tree line, she'd be invisible to any large, outraged lairds who happened to glance out the window.

She could manage a few hundred steps, for pity's sake. She wasn't such a coward she couldn't even walk down her own front drive. Really, it wasn't as if she were doing anything wrong. A lady was allowed to take a walk. Why, ladies all over Scotland did it every day, and none of them fell into a panic over it.

Of course, none of those ladies had been accused of witchcraft.

Still, there was no help for it. No good would come of letting

Sorcha run wild. So, she threw her shoulders back, straightened her spine, and with a final furtive glance down the hallway, she turned and darted out the door, pausing only to close it quietly behind her and mutter a quick prayer that she wasn't making a dreadful mistake.

Fleeing the castle without a word to either of her captors—er, that is, her protectors—wasn't the way to earn their trust or endear her to them.

Why, even now Sorcha might be tramping through the forest, on her way back to the castle. There was no evidence that the smoke she'd seen through the window rising in a thin gray curl from the west side of the village had anything to do with Sorcha.

Even so, her steps quickened on the pathway, because somehow, Sorcha was in the middle of whatever new catastrophe was unfolding. She knew it as surely as if warning bells were clanging in her ears. The skin on the back of her neck only ever puckered as it was when something was amiss.

The only question now was, how bad would it be this time? Would it be a minor infraction, like the time Sorcha threatened to cast a spell on Mrs. MacDonald when the nosy old woman accused her of consorting with the devil in the dark depths of Dunvegan Woods?

Sorcha had been dragged off to the magistrate that time, and it had taken a pretty piece of coaxing for Cat to get her released. It had been an ugly incident, one that hadn't improved their reputation amongst the citizens of Dunvegan, but no weapons had been brandished, and no threats had been made.

Or would it be like three days ago, when Sorcha had leapt on the laird of Clan Ross's back, pressed a knife to his throat and threatened to spill his blood all over the front drive?

If only she could lie to herself! It would make everything a great deal easier.

Because she already knew the answer. She could sense it in

the same way she could sense an impending storm even when the sun was shining, and the skies were clear blue. It was like a cold finger tracing down her spine, the threat of impending disaster, and that curl of smoke she'd spotted from the drawing room window did little to ease her mind.

Where there was smoke, there was a good chance Sorcha was nearby, fanning the flames.

She glanced into the sky as she hurried along the pathway, damp seeping through the flimsy soles of her slippers. She hadn't dared take the time to put on her boots.

Not with Callum Ross mere steps away.

The sky had turned its usual winter gray as the light faded, and the smoke was nearly invisible against that leaden gloom, but . . . was it thicker now? Had those filmy wisps turned into clouds? Or worse, billows?

Billows of smoke were concerning, indeed.

She stopped several paces from the edge of the woods, a chill gripping her like a cold hand around her neck. It was as dark as night under the thick canopy of entwined branches. Once she ventured inside, she'd hardly be able to see at all, and would be at the mercy of whatever dangers awaited her.

Sharp branches, exposed tree roots, disgruntled woodland creatures . . .

Her sisters adored these woods, much as their mother had done when she was alive. There were few things that gave Cat more pleasure than foraging in the woods for plants with medicinal value.

As for Sorcha . . . well, no one knew quite what Sorcha got up to in the woods. She'd always been cagey about her comings and goings, but whatever it was she was doing, it took up a good deal of her time.

Freya did *not* love the woods. She was the only one of her sisters who regarded them with a creeping sort of horror. It wasn't surprising, really. Of all the generations of MacLeods who'd lived at Castle Cairncross, she was the only one who'd turned out to be a coward.

But there was nothing to do for it this time but plunge ahead. That worrying curl of smoke was coming from the direction of the village, and the woods stood between her and it.

There was no way to go, but forward.

Chapter 5

"For God's sake, Callum, what have you done to Freya MacLeod?"

Callum turned from the fireplace to find Keir standing in the doorway of the drawing room, his brows drawn down in an uncharacteristic scowl. "Done? What do you mean? I didn't do anything to her."

Aside from breaching her hems, but that didn't count, as it hadn't been at all titillating.

"No?" Keir raised an eyebrow. "Then why did I just see her scurrying down the hallway like a criminal fleeing the gibbet?"

"I haven't the vaguest idea. The lady is afraid of her own shadow. How should I know what I said? She appeared out of nowhere an hour or so ago, babbling some nonsense about Dundee cake and orange marmalade, and insisted I take tea with her."

"Tea? I don't see any tea."

"No, but I daresay you saw the remains of the tea on the floor of the entryway. She stumbled and dropped the tray."

"No. I came down the back staircase. But how strange. And you didn't say anything to frighten or offend her?"

"Not that I'm aware of, no, but I doubt it would take much to send Freya MacLeod into an attack of the vapors." Perhaps he'd sat too close to her on the settee or examined her ankle with too much enthusiasm. God only knew what had set the girl off.

Keir dropped onto one of the worn settees. "It didn't seem odd to you that she sought you out this afternoon?"

"It did, in fact." It wasn't as if he'd endeared himself to Freya MacLeod, grabbing her as he had in the drive yesterday. She'd given him a wide berth ever since, only to appear out of nowhere this afternoon and invite him to tea.

And it hadn't been until he'd refused her invitation that she'd stumbled . . .

But there was nothing in that, surely.

Except there'd been that odd little thrust of her chin, right before she'd dropped the tea tray, and that expression in her eyes just before she'd fled the drawing room, that flash of fire, and now he thought of it, hadn't she kept glancing over his shoulder, toward the window?

He turned to Keir, suspicion sneaking up on him. "You said you saw her hurrying down the hallway just now. Did she seem to be favoring her right foot, by any chance?"

Keir frowned. "No. She appeared perfectly able-bodied to me."

"How curious." Quite a miraculous recovery, that.

"You must have said something to her, Callum. Keep in mind that we're here to keep the ladies safe, not frighten the wits out of them."

"I assure you, I didn't." He hadn't exchanged more than a dozen words with her, and all of them so banal he could scarcely remember them now. "Nothing that would send a lady of any sense into a headlong flight down the hallway."

A headlong flight on an injured ankle, an ankle without a hint of redness or swelling . . .

Something was wrong here. Perhaps he'd been too hasty, dismissing Freya MacLeod as he had. Her family was renowned for their trickery, after all. Wasn't it possible she was wilier than she appeared to be?

"Nothing that might offend a lady of delicate sensibilities?"

Keir pressed. "Did you glower at her? One of your glowers could send a timid lady fleeing for safety, and I've rarely come across a lady as timid as Freya MacLeod."

Timid, was she? She'd appeared so at first glance, yes. As little as an hour ago he'd dismissed her as a spiritless, docile little thing, and the least diabolical of the three MacLeod sisters, but now . . .

Now, he wasn't so sure. "Perhaps she's not quite as timid as we think."

"It's a pity about the tea." Keir rested one booted foot on a nearby ottoman. "A thick slice of Dundee cake sounds like just the thing."

"Never mind the cake. That stumble of hers, Keir. She claimed to have hurt her ankle, but I'm beginning to suspect she feigned the entire thing."

"Why would she? What does Freya MacLeod have to gain from feigning an injury?"

What, indeed? Something told him they were about to find out. "I can't be sure, but something's amiss. I'm certain of it."

Keir didn't appear to hear him. He was staring out the window across from the settee, his eyes wide. "Ah, Callum?"

"Perhaps she's every bit the hellion her sister is, and we didn't see it."

"Callum, I think—"

"She claimed she was going to her bedchamber to rest, but—"

"She hasn't gone to her bedchamber." Keir jerked to his feet and strode across the drawing room to peer out the window.

"What? How do you know?"

Keir rapped a knuckle against the glass. "Come and see for yourself."

Callum rose and strode to the window, squinting through the glass in the direction Keir was pointing. At first, he didn't notice anything amiss, but just as he opened his mouth to ask, he saw her.

It wasn't terribly late, but the evenings came on quickly this far north, especially in the winter, and Castle Cairncross was surrounded by thick wood on three sides, with the village of Dunvegan on the fourth.

The towering pines and oaks cast long shadows over the drive, and with darkness descending, Freya MacLeod was nearly indistinguishable from her surroundings in her dark blue cloak, the hood drawn up to cover her bright head.

"Where the devil does she think she's going?" He turned from the window and met Keir's gaze. "You don't think she'd attempt to go to the village?"

The woods were potentially treacherous, but the town posed far more of a threat, as the villagers, with few exceptions, did not look upon the MacLeod sisters with a friendly eye. They were so unfriendly, in fact, that Hamish had warned them not to permit either of the sisters to venture into the village unaccompanied.

Or at all, if it could be helped.

She wouldn't risk going into the village alone, this close to sunset. Not without a good reason. What, then, had prompted this sudden flight into the darkness?

There was only one answer that made any sense. "When was the last time you saw the other chit? Sorcha?"

"I haven't seen her since I retired to my bedchamber earlier this morning. Did you see her this afternoon?"

"Yes. She was up on the roof then, tending to those birds of hers."

But that was an hour or two ago. Good Lord. There was no telling the mess Sorcha MacLeod could get into in several hours, and as for Freya, she wasn't as innocent as she appeared, despite those wide green eyes.

She hadn't hurt her ankle at all. When he'd refused the tea, she'd feigned a stumble and a twisted ankle to get him away from the door, so Sorcha could sneak out of the castle!

The devious little chit had tricked him, and she'd done a damn good job of it, too.

As it turned out, Freya MacLeod *would* dare. She *had* dared, and now she was nearly at the bottom of the drive, only a few steps away from vanishing into the woods.

Not such a timid little mouse, after all.

The hair on the back of her neck was prickling.

She hadn't made it more than a dozen steps before that telltale prickle made her stop in her tracks. Her neck only ever prickled that way when someone was watching her.

Had one of the men seen her from the window? If so, which one? Were the eyes following her blue, or a deep arctic gray?

God, not the gray. The blue would be bad enough, but the gray . . . so cold, those eyes. Even his long, thick lashes couldn't hide the glint of ice there.

But his hands were warm. So warm, she'd swear she could still feel the touch of his fingers against the bare skin of her ankle, as if he'd branded her. She'd been so startled at the brush of those warm fingers against her skin she'd nearly kicked him in the chest.

Silly of her, really. Despite his cold eyes, Callum Ross was a human being. Presumably his blood pumped through his veins in much the same way hers did. Still, human or not, he wasn't the sort of man a lady wanted chasing her through a dark wood.

She ventured a glance behind her, just to see if—

Oh. *Oh, no.*

She froze, her feet rooted to the pathway. The front door of the castle was open, and on the top step stood Callum Ross, with Keir Dunn next to him, and they were both watching her as she hovered at the edge of the woods.

Both pairs of eyes, gray and blue, yet it was Callum she couldn't look away from, Callum who sent her heart into a frenzy, beads of sweat blooming on her hairline.

She'd never encountered a more frightening man in her life.

Even from this distance he looked like a giant. His head with those wild dark locks was nearly as high as the door frame, and his shoulders as wide, and as she stood there, poised on the edge of flight he was staring right at her, that cold gray gaze of his penetrating the cage of her ribs like a shard of ice embedded straight into the pulsing muscle of her heart.

Dear God, that glower. It was darker than the deepest corner of Dunvegan Woods.

He opened his mouth and shouted something, his deep voice echoing among the trees, but it was too late now. She'd made her decision, and there was no going back.

The only way out of this was through it.

So, she turned and fled toward the woods without a backward glance, but there was no outrunning the burning sensation on the back of her neck, as if that frigid gray gaze held the power of a thousand winters.

One step, another, a half dozen more, and she was nearly there . . .

She was panting by the time she plunged through the tree line, the woods closing behind her like a door slamming shut. She ran blindly then, the sharp edges of the branches snatching at her as she passed, tearing at her cloak, the tree roots at her feet threatening to trip her with every step, and send her headlong into the shrubbery lining the pathway.

Was she headed west, toward the smoke?

She hardly knew, but a wise lady didn't stop to assess her direction when two furious lairds were on her heels. She'd just have to hope instinct would take her the right way, and that despite the great disparity in the length of their legs, that she would manage to outrun her pursuers.

If she could only find Sorcha before they reached her, all would be well.

Or as well as they could be, considering she'd be obliged to spend the next five hundred and two hours trapped in the castle with an enraged Callum Ross.

She plunged through the trees, not daring to look back. Despite her aversion to the woods, she knew them a good deal better than either of the men pursuing her. If she could only keep her wits about her, she'd find her way to the village while they were still blundering through the trees.

She ran as fast as she could through the darkness, her chest squeezing with each of her gasping breaths, fancying she could hear the heavy tread of men's boots behind her with every step, but after a lifetime of stumbling blindly along the pathway, the gloom began to give way to the fading light.

She didn't stop until she emerged from the woods onto the top of what served as the High Street in Dunvegan. By now twilight had fallen, and the street was deserted, the shop doors closed and locked. All but Baird's Pub, which was doing a brisk business, as always.

A wave of dizziness washed over her, and she braced her hands on her knees as the bread and cheese she'd had for luncheon threatened to come back up in a hot burst of sickness, but after a few deep breaths the nausea receded, and thank goodness for it.

There was no time to cast up her accounts.

She could smell the smoke now, the heavy, acrid scent of it stinging her nostrils and invading her lungs. It was farther to the west than it had looked from the castle, well past the edge of the village.

But no, surely not. That didn't make any sense, unless . . .

Unless that curl of smoke didn't have anything to do with Sorcha, after all. The only thing that lay that far to the west of the village was Clyde Stewart's farm, and her sister had no reason to go there.

Did she?

Mr. Stewart lived there alone. He'd lost his wife some ten years earlier, and he had no children. He was a strange man, the sort she took care to keep well away from.

But the smoke was coming from that direction, the hazy cloud hovering directly over what could only be Mr. Stewart's property.

Dash it, what should she do? Should she trust Sorcha would find her way home on her own, or should she go on toward the Stewart farm? She couldn't think of a single piece of business Sorcha could have with Clyde Stewart, but one could never tell with Sorcha.

It must be nearly six by now. The storm was coming closer with every minute, and the sky was darkening with ominous clouds. Sorcha had sworn she'd return to the castle before dark, and while it wouldn't be the first promise she'd broken, it felt different this time.

In the end, all that mattered was that Sorcha was still missing, and this was no time to dally, with her pursuers on her heels. She allowed herself one deep, calming breath before she stepped onto the High Street and crossed over to the side opposite Baird's Pub, keeping to the shadows as much as she could. The last thing she wanted was to draw the attention of the men who frequented that establishment.

Or anyone else, for that matter. She couldn't be seen rushing about the village at this time of day. It looked suspicious, a MacLeod sister wandering about alone in the dark. If anyone happened to see her, they would assume the worst. They always did, when it came to her and her sisters.

As much as she might wish otherwise, she wasn't like every other lady in Scotland anymore. Or *any* other lady at all, come to that. She was a MacLeod, and being a MacLeod carried certain risks these days.

Why had she let Sorcha leave the castle this afternoon? She should have known better than to agree to such a reckless scheme. She might have foreseen it would come to this. Bad luck seemed to be forever on their heels no matter what they did, but these were just the sort of foolish antics that made it easy for it to catch them.

But no one accosted her, or even seemed to notice her as she made her way toward the apothecary's shop at the opposite end of the High Street, taking care to keep her steps slow and measured—

"Freya?"

The voice was soft, a whisper only, but it seemed to have come from the darkness itself, and she jumped, her heart shooting into her throat. "Oh!"

But it was only Glynnis Fraser, the apothecary's sister, and the one friend they still had left in Dunvegan. "Glynnis, my goodness." She sagged against the side of the shop, her hand over her chest. "You startled me."

"Oh, dear. I am sorry." Glynnis hesitated, her brow furrowing. "Are you looking for Sorcha?"

Her heart gave an anxious leap under her palm. "Yes. You've seen her, then?"

Glynnis nodded. "Yes."

"Thank goodness!" Sorcha couldn't have gotten far, then. That was welcome news.

But her relief was short-lived, the hope rushing through her freezing to ice in her veins at Glynnis's next words.

"She came down the High Street a little over an hour ago. I thought she must have returned to the castle by now, but then I saw you pass by the window." Glynnis frowned. "She had a cart with her, with one of her birds in a box inside it."

"One of her sparrowhawks? That is strange." Sorcha was as protective of her birds as a mother with a newborn baby. "What in the world could she be thinking, dragging one of her precious birds halfway across Dunvegan?"

Glynnis gave a helpless shrug. "I don't know what she's up to, but I thought it was odd, so I watched to see which direction she went. She headed directly west, toward Clyde Stewart's farm on the outskirts of town."

"I don't understand. It doesn't make any sense." They weren't at all acquainted with Clyde Stewart. What reason could Sorcha have to visit him, of all people?

"No." Glynnis shook her head. "It doesn't."

They stood there for a moment, staring at each other, a dozen unasked questions hanging between them, but neither voiced them. There was no point.

Only Sorcha knew the answers.

Freya attempted a smile, but her cheeks felt numb, and her mouth too wide for her face. "I'd better go then and fetch her before she gets herself into trouble."

"Yes, I think so."

But she hadn't gotten more than half a dozen steps past the shop before Glynnis's voice stopped her. "Freya?"

She turned back to find Glynnis hovering in the doorway in the faint glow from the lamp inside the shop, wringing her hands. "Yes?"

"Hurry."

Chapter 6

Freya MacLeod, the timid, docile MacLeod sister, the one Hamish had promised wouldn't cause them a moment's trouble, had just *ignored* him.

For one moment it had looked as if she was going to give up this nonsense and return to the house. She'd paused when he shouted her name, but instead of scurrying back up the drive like the biddable chit she was meant to be, she'd whirled around and vanished into the trees in a swirl of dark green skirts.

"She's a bit slippery for such a quiet, unassuming young lady, isn't she?"

Callum glanced at Keir, who was grinning like a fool at the empty space at the edge of the woods where Freya had been standing only moments before. "I don't know what you're grinning about. Don't tell me you find this amusing."

Keir shrugged. "Nothing wrong with a lass with a little spirit, eh?"

Nothing at all, provided *he* wasn't the one who'd been tasked with guarding her.

He should have known she wasn't as tame as she appeared. It was always the quiet ones who caused the most trouble. At least with the youngest sister, he knew better than to expect her to do anything other than whatever she pleased, but this middle sister . . . just when he'd decided he could put her out of his mind, she'd gone feral.

It would only be a temporary burst of defiance, however. He'd known ladies like Freya MacLeod before, and their fits of independence never lasted long. If the girl was foolish enough to head into the village, they'd soon chase her back out again.

She'd be back before long, but it wouldn't be soon enough. They'd have to go after her. Hamish had made it clear that permitting either of the sisters to leave the castle unattended was as risky as poking at a hornet's nest with a sharp stick.

The last thing they needed was a swarm of enraged villagers descending on the castle.

He turned to Keir, one eyebrow aloft. "We'll see if you're as impressed with her spirit after a chase through the woods."

A chase, and a drenching. No sooner had the girl vanished into the trees than it began to rain. Not a gentle, soothing rain, either, but a cold, heavy Scottish drizzle that was threatening to turn into a downpour before it burned itself out.

"Stealthy little thing, isn't she? I never saw her slip out the door."

"Stealthy? Is that what we're calling it?"

She was sly, yes. Cunning, certainly. A schemer, and a liar? Yes, she was those too, with that feigned stumble of hers, and her imaginary twisted ankle. For all her sweet face and soft voice, Freya MacLeod was as much of a menace as her younger sister.

The only difference between them was Freya was sneakier about it.

"Dunvegan's a quiet village." Keir followed him as Callum marched down the drive. "What could be so urgent she felt the need to go charging off into the dark like some sort of avenging angel?"

Angel? Freya MacLeod was no angel. A green-eyed demon was lurking behind that sweet smile.

Damned if he knew why she'd run off, and he cared even less.

Her reasons didn't interest him. All that mattered was that they got her back. Once they did, he'd see to it she didn't escape a second time, even if it meant locking her in her bedchamber. "We'll find out soon enough."

She was long gone by the time they reached the woods, but the ground was already damp from the rain, and there was a clear set of footprints in the middle of the pathway.

Such tiny footprints could only belong to one person, and it looked as if . . . he squatted down to get a better look at them. "Is she wearing *slippers*?" Had the girl lost her wits? It was October in the Highlands, for God's sake. Her feet would be soaked in an instant.

Keir crouched down beside him to study the prints. "It looks like it. She must have run right out the front door after I passed her in the hallway, without taking the time to change into boots." Keir rose to his feet, his expression grim. "I don't like this, Callum. Something feels off. We'd better hurry."

They tracked her footprints until they lost them among the fallen leaves covering the forest floor, but by then it was clear she was headed toward the village.

One day. He and Keir had been here for a single day, and already both MacLeod chits had run off to the only place in Dunvegan they'd been warned not to go.

But there was no sign of her when they emerged onto the High Street. "Now what? From here, she could have gone anywhere."

"There's a pub." Keir nodded at a small wooden building on the opposite side of the street. It was a ramshackle place, the peeling white-washed outer walls stained with mud. A lopsided sign hanging on a pole outside the door proclaimed it to be Baird's Pub.

It was no place for a lady. "She wouldn't go in there." He couldn't make much sense of Freya MacLeod. She didn't seem reckless, nor would he have said she was a fool, but perhaps he was giving her too much credit.

She'd fled the castle alone, at night, just as a storm was coming, hadn't she?

Keir looked at him as if he'd lost his wits. "Of course not, but you can be sure if she came down the High Street, every single man in that pub would have noticed her. She's not the sort of young lady a man overlooks."

"I didn't notice." He hadn't noticed that cloud of red-gold hair, either, or the almost-dimples at the corners of her lips. "I didn't come to Dunvegan to gawk at Freya MacLeod's face."

Her face, or any other part of her. And if it took him more effort than he'd anticipated to keep his eyes to himself, he wasn't going to admit it to Keir.

He'd never hear the bloody end of it if he did.

Keir snorted. "Bollocks. You're as susceptible to a lovely face as the rest of us."

"I hardly even looked at her face." Her eyes, though. For one unguarded instant, he'd gazed directly into those startling green eyes, and now every time he closed his own eyes he saw hers again, as if they'd been burned into his eyelids.

He couldn't get them out of his head.

Maybe the MacLeod sisters *were* witches, just as the rumors claimed. Maybe Freya MacLeod had bewitched him, entranced him with her green eyes.

It was reason enough not to look at her again.

"You're a hard-hearted, ill-tempered sort, Callum, but you're not blind, and neither are the men inside Baird's Pub. Come, we're wasting time."

Callum followed Keir across the street and into the pub. The dozen or so men inside stared at them as they made their way toward the barkeep, who was running a filthy cloth over the scarred wooden bar top.

"Did you happen to see a lass pass by a short time ago?" Keir asked. "A young lady, with red hair?"

"Mayhap I did." The barkeep looked between them, his eyes narrowing. "What do ye want with her?"

Keir held up his hands. "We're not going to harm her. She's, ah, a friend of a friend of ours. We've come to Dunvegan to keep an eye on her."

"That so?" The barkeep looked them up and down again. "Yer doing a bloody poor job of it then, aren't ye?"

A sharp retort leapt to Callum's lips, but Keir cast him a quelling look, and he bit it back. It was best to leave it to Keir. He was far more persuasive.

"As I said, we don't mean her any harm." Keir nodded toward the front window, which offered a clear view of the High Street. "Did you see her?"

The barkeep hesitated, but Keir had one of those reassuring faces that made people confide in him. "I'm not sure which way she went." He leaned over the bar, lowering his voice. "But the other sister—the wild one, Sorcha? I saw her making her way toward Clyde Stewart's farm earlier this afternoon. Mayhap her sister's gone after her. Wouldn't be the first time."

"Stewart's farm," Callum repeated. Uneasiness flared in the pit of his stomach. Hamish hadn't mentioned anything about Clyde Stewart, or his farm. "Who is he?"

"Widower who lives to the west of the village, over the next hill. He's been alone out there since his wife died some ten years ago. Keeps to himself, does Stewart."

A widower, living alone on a remote farm? What kind of business could Sorcha MacLeod have with some lonely old widower? Damn it, he didn't like this. He didn't like it at all, and judging by the hard expression on Keir's face, he didn't, either.

"I don't like it," the barkeep said, as if he'd read Callum's mind. "There's no call for those MacLeod girls to be out there. Stewart's a strange one, ye ken? Not trustable, like."

"We ken." Keir's voice was grim. He dug into his pocket and tossed a few coins onto the bar top. "For your trouble, friend."

"Ye'd best hurry. The youngest sister, Sorcha has been out there for some time."

Callum glanced at Keir. "How long?"

"Two hours or so. Maybe more." The barkeep slapped a hand over the coins, slid them across the bar top, and in a flash, they disappeared into his apron pocket. "Ye mark my words, friends. No good ever came of Sorcha MacLeod lingering anyplace. No good at all."

Neither he nor Keir spoke as they made their way out of the pub and onto the High Street, but as soon as they were out of earshot, Callum turned to Keir. "What the devil are those two chits up to? Hamish never said anything about Clyde Stewart, or—"

"Callum." Keir pointed at the sky over the western edge of Dunvegan. "Look. Just there."

The rain pelted Callum's face as he raised his head and squinted into the dark sky above. "What? I don't see—"

But then, in the next instant, he did.

A thin cloud of gray smoke, nearly indistinguishable from the gloomy sky above could be seen over the tops of the buildings lining the High Street. As they watched, the wisps grew thicker, until dark puffs were billowing into the sky above the tree line.

There could be only one explanation for a cloud of smoke that size.

Something was on fire.

The hills that lay between Dunvegan and Clyde Stewart's farm were a wilderness of jagged rock and thorny gorse. It took Freya nearly an hour to stumble across it, and she lied to herself the entire way.

She told herself that the fears spinning in frenzied circles in her brain were unfounded, that it was something else, that it couldn't be as bad as she was imagining it was.

But alas, telling the same lie again and again didn't turn it into the truth.

Some small, frightened part of her had known what she'd

find the moment she saw that curl of smoke in the sky, but as she crested the shallow rise above the farm, she still wasn't prepared for the scene that met her eyes.

The once peaceful valley below her had turned into a fiery nightmare.

Clyde Stewart's stables were on fire.

There were flames everywhere, the brilliant orange spikes shooting into the sky and setting the entire night alight. She squeezed her eyes closed, a prayer on her lips, but when she opened them again the fire was still there, the furious roar of it echoing in her ears.

Sorcha was down there, amidst all that destruction.

She lurched down the hill, her legs shaking, but as she neared the burning stables a wall of unbearable heat rushed toward her, and she staggered backward, shielding her face with her arms as the flames shot higher, and impossibly higher still, painting the dark sky above with streaks of orange light.

How could this be happening? Where was Sorcha? She wasn't . . . oh, dear God, she wasn't inside the burning stables, was she?

No. Please, no—

"Freya!"

The familiar voice reached her over the roar of the fire, bringing with it a wave of relief so powerful her head swam with it, and her wobbly knees threatened to collapse from underneath her.

But there was no time for that. She had to get to Sorcha, *now*, and get her away from here. She stumbled forward again, but the angry heat from the fire was like a living, breathing thing, snatching at her clothes, her hair, her skin.

Every instinct screamed at her to run in the other direction, away from the scorching heat, but she pushed blindly forward, toward the opposite side of the stables, her hand raised to protect her eyes.

But it did her little good. The heat—dear God, she'd never

felt anything like it. It was unbearable, as if it were melting her skin to her bones. One step, two, a dozen . . . her feet were moving, but somehow she wasn't gaining any ground.

She was no closer to Sorcha than she'd been when she began. Hadn't Sorcha been directly across from her? Oh, she couldn't see! Her eyes were streaming from the smoke, the fire an orange ball of blurred flames.

If she could just get through to the other side . . . if she ran, perhaps she could make it?

But even as she darted forward a shower of sparks shot into the air and came down again atop a mound of hay piled near one side of the stables. A warning shout leapt to her lips, but she'd hardly drawn a breath before the sparks caught. The flames devoured the hay in an instant, and the blistering heat shot through her like a bolt of lightning, as if the flames were inside her, under her skin, burning her from the inside.

There was no way for her to get to Sorcha! The heat was too great, and the smoke was suffocating, as if the fire had leapt down her throat and reduced her lungs to burning cinders.

Sorcha's mouth opened, and a sound emerged. A shout, a shriek, a panicked wail. It was all those things, and at the same time none of them.

It wasn't a sound she'd ever heard emerge from her sister's lips before.

Her body had gone numb with shock, rooting her feet to the ground, but that wail jerked her loose from the fog of panic holding her in place, and she took another dozen halting steps forward.

She could do this. She was closer to Sorcha now, so close, just on the other side of the stables. If she could make it around the outside wall, perhaps she could—

"No, Freya!" It wasn't just a shriek this time, but a frantic tumble of words.

Through the sparks, smoke, and burning flames, her eyes met her sister's, and that was when she knew it was hopeless.

Sorcha was brave, the bravest person she knew. She always had been.

But now, the green eyes that met Freya's were glassy with panic.

"No! Run, Freya!"

Run? Leave her sister here, alone? No, she couldn't, she *wouldn't*—

But Sorcha was still shouting, trying to tell her . . . something. She blinked against the smoke billowing around her, coating her tongue with the acrid taste of ash and pulling tears from her stinging eyes, but she could just make out Sorcha standing opposite her, waving her arms toward the woods behind her.

Sorcha was shouting something, but Freya couldn't hear her. She couldn't hear anything now but the howl of the flames, and her own ragged breath in her ears. She couldn't see, she couldn't *think*—

"Go! Now, Freya! I'll find you!"

Sorcha's voice was faint now, drowned out by the shriek of the fire and the groan of thick wooden beams giving way. The stable roof was going to go. It was only a matter of time before it collapsed inward in a burning heap of charred wood.

Sorcha screamed something else, something about the castle, but Freya couldn't make out her sister's words over the roar in her ears. Was it the shriek of the fire deafening her, or was the roar inside her head?

She could no longer tell.

Had Sorcha said to run to the castle? That she'd meet her at the castle?

She tried to shout back—to tell Sorcha they'd find each other in the woods, or at the castle—but fear and panic had her by the throat now, its relentless grip pressing hard against her windpipe, and she couldn't gather a breath, couldn't utter a word.

Then in the next instant, it was too late. Without warning,

Sorcha turned and ran for the woods, her skirts flying out in an arc behind her.

In the blink of an eye, she was gone.

Freya tried to run, to get to the woods and leave the wailing fire behind her, but her body was strangely frozen, her feet tethered to the ground. She had to go, *now*, but her brain had gone sluggish, and she could only stand there, staring dumbly at the fire, the violent glow of it tearing a gaping hole into the dark sky.

She couldn't move. She couldn't *move*.

The leaping flames danced crazily before her eyes, and it was as if there was a spell holding her where she stood. How long would she have remained there, helpless, if a shout hadn't pierced the haze of panic surrounding her?

Until she became a part of the fire itself?

The shout came from behind her. It was dark, so dark, despite the flames lighting up the sky. Even when she turned away she could see them still, the indistinct streaks of violent orange light dancing in front of her eyes, but something was moving toward her from the direction of the village—a large, dark shape with arms and legs and raised fists.

Men, running. Half a dozen of them, or perhaps more, running toward the burning stables.

Toward *her*.

Had Sorcha seen them coming? Was that why she'd run?

Her sister wasn't to blame for the fire. She knew this down to her marrow, in the deepest part of her, in the same way she knew the sun would rise and set again, and the tides of Loch Dunvegan would advance and retreat, the invisible currents churning beneath the surface in an endless rhythm.

She knew her sister, perhaps better than she knew herself.

Sorcha was quick-tempered, and fierce in defense of her family. And she was angry. Angry at Rory for dying and leaving them alone. Angry at the villagers for turning their backs on them when they most needed friendship, and angry at the smugglers for stealing their peace.

But willfully, maliciously destructive? No. Never.

Yet it wouldn't matter. The truth had long since ceased to make any difference. Glynnis wouldn't be the only one who'd seen Sorcha pass through the village on her way to Mr. Stewart's farm. The men who spent every afternoon drinking in Baird's Pub would have seen her, as well.

By now, everyone in the village would know she and Sorcha had been here—that they'd been on Mr. Stewart's land while his stables burned to the ground, and if someone should have been hurt, or worse, killed . . .

The citizens of Dunvegan wouldn't side with the wicked MacLeod sisters. One way or another, they would be held responsible for this.

It was already happening.

The men were getting closer, their shouts echoing through the night, even over the relentless shriek of the fire.

Run. She had to run, just as Sorcha had told her to do. There was no time to hesitate, no time to lose. In another few minutes they'd be on her, and then . . . dear God, she didn't want to think of what they'd do to her, then.

Yet even as the frantic command was echoing in her brain, she hesitated, staring at what had once been Clyde Stewart's stables, now a hulking black mass of burned wood, only the heaviest beams still in place, looming like a skeleton over the charred, smoking remains.

There was another shout, a man's voice, dark with fury.

Her name, her father's name was in his mouth.

MacLeod.

And she was grateful to him, whoever he was, because it was the sound of her own name that made her move at last, that one word that shook her loose from the trance she'd fallen into.

That one word sent her whirling around, her feet flying over the fields to the east of the stables, in the opposite direction Sorcha had gone, even as everything inside her howled with despair at leaving her sister.

But it had to be this way, just in case . . . just in case . . .

In case these men came after them. They'd have a better chance at escape, if they separated.

No, not a better chance.

It was their only chance.

CHAPTER 7

Amidst the leaping flames, the billowing smoke, and the choking stench of burning wood, Callum never took his eyes off Freya MacLeod. Not when a shower of sparks lit the pile of hay to one side of the stables alight, and not when the timbered roof collapsed.

"Do you think Sorcha MacLeod had a hand in this?" he asked Keir, his gaze still locked on the dark outline of Freya's slender form.

"No." Keir didn't hesitate, and there was no doubt in his voice.

"You sound certain." Surprisingly so. At best, the girl was dangerously unpredictable. At worst, she was violent, and he had an oozing gash on his neck to prove it. Was it so difficult to imagine she'd set a fire?

"I am certain. Sorcha MacLeod is a fierce lass, and protective of her family, but this?" Keir jerked his chin toward the fire. "Reckless destruction? No."

Callum wasn't as sure. Attacking a stranger with a blade was reckless enough, but this wasn't the time to argue the point. What did it matter, now? If he'd been doing what he'd promised Hamish he would, it would never have come to this. He'd been the one tasked with watching the door this afternoon.

This was his fault, and his fault alone.

Hamish had warned him it was dangerous for the MacLeod

sisters to leave the castle. He'd promised his friend they wouldn't suffer any harm. He'd failed to keep that promise, and this was what had come of it.

But it stopped here. When Freya MacLeod turned and fled into the woods—and she would, soon—he'd be after her in a heartbeat, although whether he could do a damn thing for her now remained very much in question.

The damage had already been done.

In the span of a few hours, Freya and Sorcha had managed to get themselves into one devil of a mess. If the MacLeod sisters hadn't already worn out their welcome in Dunvegan before this, then they certainly had done so now.

Fires tended to do that. Particularly deadly ones.

"We need to act, Callum." Keir was watching as the villagers advanced on Freya, his face grim. "Now, before it's too late."

"I'll see to Freya. Go after Sorcha." The fire had reached a frenzied pitch, and he had to shout into Keir's ear to make himself heard over the shriek of the flames. "Find her, and whatever you do, keep her away from the castle. It's not safe for her there."

Keir didn't waste time or breath replying. He darted off into the woods after Sorcha, his white shirt a blur as he ran through the darkness. In an instant, he reached the tree line, and in another blink he vanished into the darkness, swallowed by the trees.

There was nothing to do then but wait for Freya to make her move. He squinted at her, his eyes aching from the heat and smoke. She stood motionless, staring at the burning stables as if she couldn't quite believe what she was seeing.

But she'd realize soon enough she was in danger. Even now the villagers were closing in on her, their shouts growing louder as they neared the stables. She had no choice but to flee into the woods, just as her sister had done.

It was the only chance she had of losing them.

But she remained still far longer than she should have, seemingly lost in a trance as the enraged villagers drew ever closer. What was she doing? Did she not realize the danger she was in? Once those men caught up to her, they wouldn't pause to listen to her explanations.

Now. Go, damn it. Run.

Yet she didn't run. She stood there frozen as precious seconds slipped by, and the mob closed the distance between them, their shouts becoming more frenzied as they bore down on her.

He tensed, every muscle pulling tight as he charged toward her. He was closer to her than the mob of villagers, but not by much. There was no time to think, and not a moment to waste. In another instant they'd be upon her, and it would be too late.

But he never reached her. There was still half a field's length between them when she bolted. Not toward the western edge of the woods as Sorcha had done, but in the opposite direction, her red-gold braid flying out behind her as she disappeared behind the tree line.

The woods were the safest place to go, the easiest place to lose herself. Once she melted into the darkness, it would be nearly impossible for the men to find her. She zigzagged west, running for the tree line, her chest burning with effort, her wheezing breaths in her ears drowning out every other sound.

She ran wildly, blindly, the canopy of leaves above her shutting out the glow from the fire, the branches grabbing her as she passed, tearing long, jagged rents into her cloak.

But she didn't stop, even when the heel of one of her slippers caught on a tree root and flew off her foot. She stumbled forward, the ground rushing toward her, but somehow, she righted herself again and kept on, dodging the fallen branches torn from the trees by the storm.

If she could reach the castle, she'd be safe. All she had to do was make it as far as the castle, and all would be well.

She seemed to run forever, an eternity, her bare foot throbbing from the rocks and sharp sticks she trod on as she flew through the woods, but at last she made out the turret of Castle Cairncross ahead of her, outlined against the sky.

Thank God. Thank *God*.

Just a little farther now. If she could only make it a little farther . . .

In the next breath she was there, the drive that led up to the castle emerging just past the edge of the tree line. When her foot hit the gravel she stumbled with relief, landing hard on her hands and knees, but she was up again at once and darting toward the door, an unhinged laugh on her lips as she recalled the circumstances of her leaving the castle earlier this evening.

Had she really thought being chased by Callum Ross was the worst thing that could befall her? How foolish, how stupid of her to think for even a moment that things couldn't get worse than that.

It could always get worse. So much worse . . .

Ever since her father's death five months ago things had gone from bad to worse, until some fresh nightmare was upon them with every day that passed. Smugglers, missing treasure, and now Catriona was gone, and Sorcha . . .

God, what of Sorcha? Why had she gone to the Stewart farm in the first place? What could have made her do something so foolish, so reckless?

They were questions without answers.

She reached the entryway of the castle moments later and staggered up the steps, her heart beating out of her chest in time with each of her ragged breaths as she ran through the door, slammed it behind her, and collapsed against it.

"Sorcha?" Her voice was thin, hoarse, rough with the smoke she'd taken into her lungs and her frantic dash through the woods. "Sorcha, are you here?"

There was no answer. Only the echo of her own words.

Where was she? She'd said to come here to the castle, hadn't she? Or had she said *not* to come here? She couldn't think, couldn't remember—

But soon enough, she had her answer.

They were coming up the drive, shouting as they ran. The villagers, a dozen or more of them now, a wild mob of furious men with torches in their hands.

They were coming for *her*.

Her, and Sorcha. Someone must be made to pay for the destruction to Stewart's property. And if Mr. Stewart himself should have been hurt, or God forbid, killed . . . well, someone would have to pay for that, too.

Who, other than the MacLeod sisters? And where else could a mob of enraged men find a MacLeod sister, other than at Castle Cairncross?

She should have remained in the woods. She should have hidden herself among the trees and waited for Sorcha to come for her. That's what her sister had been trying to tell her—that the woods were the only place that was safe for them.

Oh, dear God. She'd made a dreadful mistake.

And now it was too late. The men were coming, their torches bright spots of flame in the darkness, the indistinct rumble of their voices becoming clearer as they moved up the drive toward the entrance of the castle.

She hovered for an instant in the shadows by the front door. If only she could keep still, perhaps they'd pass right by her? She was good at stillness, at not drawing attention to herself, at disappearing into the background while remaining in plain sight . . .

No. It wouldn't work this time. Not when they were coming for her.

Now. She had to move *now*, before it was too late.

But where? The front entrance was the only way out of the castle. Even the kitchen door that led to the stables was blocked. Oh, why had they done something so foolish as to cut off all but one pathway to escape?

They'd thought they'd be safe if they could keep anyone from getting inside the castle. It hadn't occurred to them that the day might come when they'd be desperate to get *out*.

Safety, as it turned out, was nothing but an illusion.

The heavy bootsteps were drawing closer, the torchlight flickering against the windows.

She was nearly out of time.

The staircase stretched out before her, the outline of the grandfather clock on the landing just visible in the gloom, the upper floors beyond that swallowed by the darkness.

She was moving before she made any conscious decision to do so, her feet, still wet from the rain, silent against the worn carpet of the stairwell. Up and up, her harsh breaths echoing in her head as she fled toward the alcove, and from there up the stairway that wound around the inside of the turret.

She paused when she reached the roof, blinking away the rain that fell onto her face. No, not here. There was no place to hide, and nowhere to run. If they came upon her here, she'd be trapped.

Fear pierced her chest at that thought, rooting her feet to the floor and threatening to steal her reason, but she mustn't panic now. Not when she'd made it this far. She closed her eyes and drew in a long, deep breath, clenching her hands together to stop them shaking.

The single moment of stillness cleared the fog from her brain.

Her father's study. Yes, of course! It was tucked into the back of Cat's workroom, the door half-hidden behind a heavy cabinet, with just enough room for a smallish lady like herself to squeeze through the gap.

There was a good chance the men chasing her would never notice the door, and if they did . . . well, if they did, her father's dirk was hidden in one of his desk drawers. Whether she'd have the courage to brandish it was another question, one she prayed she wouldn't have to answer tonight.

She darted through the arched doorway and into Cat's workroom, then hurried toward the far side of the room, where the cabinet stood against the wall. At least, so it appeared, but there was a door hidden behind the cabinet, invisible to anyone who didn't already know it to be there.

She slid behind the cabinet and fumbled for the study's door-knob, her fingers closing around the cold iron just as the tread of footsteps on the stairs reached her.

Dear God, they were inside the castle.

For an instant she froze like a trapped animal, every instinct screaming at her not to move, to remain as still as possible, but she fought off the panic and slipped through the door, closing it with a quiet click behind her.

She wasn't trapped. Not yet.

Her father's desk was under the one window in the room. There was no light, the storm having chased the moon behind dark, heavy clouds, and the desk was a great, hulking thing looming in the darkness.

She stumbled forward, her hands shaking as she pulled open the middle drawer, and yes! Thank goodness, it was still there.

Her cold fingers closed around the hilt of the dirk. Even while she prayed she wouldn't have to use it she snatched it up, then fell to her knees, crawled underneath the desk, and pressed herself into the farthest corner, tucking her legs underneath her and making herself as small as possible.

Then, she waited.

And waited, and waited . . .

There was no way to tell how much time passed as she huddled there in the darkness, the dirk clutched in her fist.

Ten minutes, half an hour, a lifetime?

There was no sound. No voices, and no thud of footsteps approaching.

No flicker of light from an approaching torch.

Had the men given up then, and left the castle? Or had they searched the roof and the workroom, and not noticed the door?

She had no way of knowing. Perhaps they'd given up the chase, or perhaps they were ransacking the bedchambers right now. Turning over tables and chairs and poking into every corner and crevice of her home, the one place in the world she still felt safe.

Until tonight. Now they'd stolen that away from her, too.

Before long she was shivering, the cold of the stone floor beneath her seeping through her sodden skirts. She drew her legs more tightly against her chest, but soon enough her teeth were chattering.

Yet there was nothing for it but to remain where she was throughout the night. If no one found her before daylight came, she could venture from her hiding place and go search the woods for Sorcha.

But not before then.

How many hours would it be before sunrise? She couldn't hear the chime of the grandfather clock from here. There was nothing but cold and darkness and the pounding of her heart in her chest.

If she could only remain awake until sunrise, all might yet be well.

Or as well as it ever would be again.

But as the minutes dragged by her eyes grew heavy, and her eyelids drooped. She struggled to keep them open, to remain awake and alert, but her body, exhausted by cold and fear and her wild dash through the woods, betrayed her.

Her head fell back against the desk, her vision blurring, and her fingers going lax around the dirk.

Chapter 8

For such a small lady, Freya MacLeod could run, even in those ridiculous slippers.

He'd lost sight of her amongst the trees, but in the end, there was no escape for her. He'd catch up to her soon enough, either in the woods or at the castle, yet still he ran as if the devil were on his heels, into the thick copse of trees now as dark as midnight, the branches reaching into the sky shutting out the orange glow from the fire.

He was so intent on catching up to her, it was some time before he noticed the rumble of dozens of footsteps behind him.

Damnation. The village men were charging through the woods now, and there was no question where they were going, with their torches held high and their shouts echoing among the trees. They were on a witch hunt, and they were headed straight for Castle Cairncross to find themselves a witch.

Whether Sorcha had set fire to Stewart's stables or not no longer mattered. From what Hamish had told him, the citizens of Dunvegan had been looking for a reason to chase the sisters out of the village for weeks now.

Now they had one, and the truth was nothing compared to a man's thirst for vengeance.

Except it wouldn't be banishment from the village now. No, it would be far worse.

The MacLeod sisters' chances had run out.

But as luck would have it, a rabble of infuriated, torch-wielding men couldn't make their way through a dense wood with any speed, and he easily outpaced them, reaching the edge of the drive leading up to the castle while they were still bumbling through the trees.

Even so, there was no time to lose.

The castle loomed over him as he ran, his mind a blur of whirling thoughts. If Freya MacLeod had any sense at all, she would have bolted the front door behind her. It would be no easy task to get inside the castle.

Or out of it again, come to that.

No *easy* way, no, but there was a way. They'd barred the doors, yes, but yesterday morning, after Hamish and Catriona had left for Ballantrae Bay and Keir was watching the front door, he'd poked into every corner of the lower level of the castle and had found just what he was searching for.

Castle Cairncross had a postern gate. It was nothing but a crumbling hole now, dusty and disused, but it let out into a private courtyard that was invisible from the outside of the castle. It was a tight fit, but he could squeeze through it if he had to.

Except when he reached the castle door and grasped the knob, it turned easily in his hand.

God above, was the girl mad? She must have heard the villagers coming after her. Did she not realize the danger she was in? At best, that mob would drag her to whatever dirty hole stood for a prison in Dunvegan, toss her inside, and bolt the door behind her until the next assizes.

At worst, they . . . no, he wouldn't think of it.

Hamish would have his head if a single red-gold hair on Freya MacLeod's was disturbed. She'd lied to him, yes. She'd schemed her way right out the front door, despite knowing it wasn't safe, but he'd fight tooth and nail against that mob to keep them from putting their hands on her.

He slipped through the front door, closing and bolting it behind him, then paused in the entryway. It was dark and deserted. He opened his mouth to call for her, but then closed it again. There was a greater chance the village men would hear him than that she would answer.

There wasn't a sound to guide his steps. The entire castle throbbed with silence.

She was here, though. He could sense her, hiding somewhere in the darkness, waiting and listening. But where? There were dozens of nooks and alcoves into which a small slip of a thing like Freya MacLeod could tuck herself, and she knew this castle inside and out.

He might search for hours, and never find her.

But he had to try. He had to reach her before the men from the village found her, and then . . . well, he didn't bloody know what he'd do once he discovered her, but he'd decide on that later. He had to find her first.

As for where she might have hidden herself . . .

Hamish had said something about the roof, hadn't he? Yes. He'd mentioned that Freya spent a good part of her time on the roof of the castle, studying . . . something. Rain? Or variations in temperature? He hadn't paid much attention, as it all sounded like nonsense to him.

But the roof was as good a place to begin his search as any.

Freya jerked awake a short time later, the darkness still pressing against her, her head swimming with grogginess. Where was she? It was so cold, and her body was so heavy, as if she were being held to the floor with a great weight.

It came back to her in fits and starts, confused images flickering against her eyelids of sparks shooting into the night sky, the glow of torchlight and angry male voices shouting, and . . .

Sorcha, fleeing into the woods, and Mr. Stewart's stables a writhing mass of flames, and the men from the village coming up the drive toward the front door of the castle, their torches glowing in the darkness, and . . .

Had it been a nightmare? She squeezed her eyes closed, her heart *pounding*.

Please let it have been a nightmare.

But any hope she might have had that she'd dreamt it vanished in the next moment at the squeak of a door hinge.

A chill seized her, the pounding of her heart deafening in the silence.

It was no nightmare. She was under her father's desk, hiding from an angry mob of villagers from Dunvegan who believed she or Sorcha had set fire to Mr. Stewart's stables.

And now one of them had found her.

The dirk. What had become of the dirk? She'd fallen asleep with it in her hand. She patted the floor around her, and . . . yes! Thank goodness it was there, beside her. She snatched it up, the brass handle slippery in her clammy hands, then went as still as she could, her breath held.

But there was nothing, not a sound to be heard. Perhaps she'd dreamt—

Squeak.

No. This was no dream. She'd heard that squeak dozens of times before. It was the hinge on the door of her father's study, and then the unmistakable click of the door closing.

Someone had found her hiding place.

Could it be Sorcha?

Before she even had a chance to mutter a quick prayer that it be so, her hopes were dashed. Footsteps approached, and they were far too heavy to be Sorcha's. The steps crossed from the door to the window, the heels of a pair of boots ringing against the stone floor.

He—for it was a man, and a big one, with that heavy tread—didn't say a word.

She huddled against the back of the desk with the dirk clutched in both her hands and did her best to control her breath as the boots moved away from the window, the footsteps coming closer.

He paused when he reached the desk. It was as dark as a dungeon, so dark he didn't cast a shadow, but she could see his boots from where she was hidden, the heels and toes splattered with mud.

Those boots. There was nothing distinctive about them—they were the same black leather gillies worn by men all over Scotland—but for one thing.

The size. They were massive, the bit of the laces she could see straining against the muscled calves they attempted to contain. She'd only ever seen one pair of boots that size, and there was only one man she knew of who could fit into—

"Oh! No, don't!" She scrambled backward as an enormous hand appeared, but the desk was already against her back. There was no place for her to go.

The hand found her ankle, grabbed hold of it, and tugged.

"Let go!" She struggled for purchase, but the sides of the desk and the worn stone floor beneath her were smooth, and there was nothing to grab on to. She kicked out, but the rough fingers around her only tightened, and then she was being dragged, her skirts riding up her thighs as Callum Ross hauled her out from under the desk.

"Don't—"

"Quiet." A large hand came down over her mouth. "Not a word."

This time, there was no chasing away the panic. On some level she recognized it was far better that he'd been the one to find her rather than one of the village men, but alas, her wits had deserted her.

Her mind went blank, the panic shutting off all rational thought as if a lantern had been snuffed, leaving nothing but pure animal instinct, and she reacted as any trapped animal would.

She struck out, raising the dirk and bringing the edge of the blade down across his knuckles. And thus, the question of whether she'd have the courage to defend herself with a weapon was answered.

She did. She *had*.

He snatched his hand back, a low grunt leaving his lips, staring at the blood welling from the gash and falling in dark red drops onto the stone floor.

But even an open, bleeding wound wasn't enough to stop Callum Ross from dragging her from her hiding place. She was whisked across the floor as if she weighed no more than a feather, and the next thing she knew, he was kneeling over her, so close she noticed for the first time the thick ring of black that surrounded the pale gray of his irises.

"You've gotten us into one devil of a mess, Freya MacLeod."

He waited, those cold gray eyes pinned to her face. But for what? For her to speak, to plead with him, or burst into tears?

She had no tears. Not for this.

She gazed up at the giant of a man looming over her, his knees pinning her to the floor, his brow lowered in his usual scowl, and she said nothing, because what was there to say? The worst thing she could ever imagine had happened. There were no words for that.

At last, those stern lips parted, and he broke the spell. "I'm trying to help you, Freya."

"I—I don't want your help! I don't want anything from you."

"I'm all you've got, lass." His face was inches from hers. "Stop fighting me."

But she couldn't stop. While he still held her, his fingers as unrelenting as an iron trap around her ankle, she continued to writhe and thrash like a rabbit caught in a snare. "Let go of me!"

He didn't reply, only waited while she struggled, kicking out at him until at last she exhausted herself. He reached for her then, and to her everlasting shame, she curled in on herself, shrinking back.

But he merely took the dirk from her hand and set it aside, out of reach. Then, to her shock, he released her ankle, muttering a curse as he glanced down at his bleeding hand. The cut was a deep one, right across his knuckles, but he only pulled a handkerchief from his pocket, wrapped it around his mangled hand and tied off the ends.

"Here. Put these on." He snatched up a pair of black half boots from the top of the desk and shoved them into her hands.

She stared down at them. "These aren't mine. They're Cat's. They're too big for me."

"They'll have to do. We need to leave here. Now." He didn't wait for an answer, but reached down, caught her upper arm and hauled her to her feet.

"Leave here?" What, leave Castle Cairncross? "You're mad! I'm not leaving here without my sister!"

He released her so suddenly she stumbled against him. "You can leave here with me now or take your chances with that mob of village men. Those are your choices, lass. Which will it be?"

Choices? But those were no choices at all! "I can't leave Sorcha here to face them alone!"

"You can, and you will. Keir will take care of Sorcha. We need to get away from Dunvegan." Despite her protests, he was already dragging her through the door of her father's study and into Cat's workroom. "It's not safe here anymore."

Not safe? This was her *home*. How could it not be safe?

But of course, she knew how. Those men with their torches, the way they'd chased her through the woods, the viciousness with which they'd spat her name.

MacLeod.

It all crashed down on her, then. The fire, and the villagers, and Sorcha's headlong flight into the woods. In the space of a few hours, everything had fallen apart. With Sorcha gone, she had no one on her side, no one to help her but—

Callum Ross. Dear God, she was at the mercy of Callum Ross.

The man she'd just stabbed with her father's dirk.

She'd *stabbed* him, and now she had no choice but to depend on him to keep her safe.

This wasn't happening.

It was a nightmare, nothing more, much like all the other nightmares she'd had since her father's death, and the luggers started coming.

It was easier to think so, easier to keep repeating this lie in her head as Callum Ross hurried her down the back staircase, through the kitchens and into the stillroom, where he half led and half dragged her toward a rough opening that had once served as the castle's postern.

The cobwebs clinging to the crumbling stone caught in her hair as he helped her through it into the small courtyard beyond. She stopped, staring at the mossy stone wall in front of her. "How will we get over the wall? It's too high."

Callum came through the opening after her, his broad shoulders touching the sides of the hole. He had one of the kitchen chairs in his hand. He propped the back of it against the stone wall to steady it, then jumped on top of it and held out his arms to her. "Come. Quickly, Freya."

Leaping into Callum Ross's arms was the last thing she wanted to do, but what choice did she have? The men from the village were still outside, their shouts echoing in the night as they tried to breach the castle's front door.

So, she took his hands, and he hauled her up onto the chair. "I'm going to lift you high enough so you can grab the top edge of the wall. Get yourself over as quickly as you can, then drop down on the other side and wait there for me."

She nodded, gritting her teeth as his hands closed around her waist. Then she was in the air, her feet dangling for an instant before she dragged herself upward until she was sitting atop the narrow stone cap that ran across the top of the wall.

The ground looked as if it were miles away, but Callum was already scaling the wall behind her. Unless she wanted to share her ledge with him, she had no choice but to jump.

A cry lodged in her throat, but before it could escape she was in the air again, the ground rushing toward her. She landed on her bottom on the other side, and sat there in a daze, the wind knocked out of her, but then Callum was there, hauling her upright with a hand on her arm.

He turned her to face him. “Listen to me carefully now, lass. I’ve a horse lodged at the inn in Dunvegan. We need to fetch him, but they’ll be looking for us. It’s not safe to go through the woods, so we’ll have to go over the rocks that skirt the loch. We need to move quickly, and quietly. Do you understand?”

“I—I understand.”

“Good. Let’s go.” They crept around the eastern edge of the castle, the villagers’ angry voices fading behind them as they flew toward the cliff’s edge far above the loch. There was a pathway of sorts through the rocks, but it was a narrow, treacherous thing, and strewn with debris from the storm.

Freya stumbled blindly along, the rain lashing at her face, doing her best not to look down at the churning waters below them. Callum remained behind her, his hand around her upper arm keeping her steady.

The walk seemed to take hours, her energy flagging with every step, but at last they reached the Merry Maid Inn.

Callum didn’t bother with the proprietor. He took her directly to the stables, where he saddled the largest black horse she’d ever seen, crooning to the beast in soothing tones as he worked.

Then once again, his large hands closed around her waist, the warmth of them seeping through the layers of her clothing and lifted her onto the horse’s back. He wasn’t gentle, but he wasn’t rough, either. He was businesslike, as if he were in the habit of tossing young ladies about and arranging them to his liking.

He swung up behind her and hauled her against a chest as hard and massive as the castle’s stone turret. A protest rose to her lips, but before she could gather her breath to utter it, he removed his heavy woolen cloak from his shoulders and draped it over hers.

Then he set the horse in motion with a brisk slap of the reins.

She looked back only once and could no longer see the turret of the castle jutting into the sky.

This isn't happening. It isn't . . .

But she couldn't fool herself forever. Reality, alas, had a dreadful way of catching up to you, in all its ugliness. It had caught up to her now, and it was uglier than she'd ever imagined it could be.

When sleep came, she let it pull her into its arms. It was easier, this way.

It was so much easier, not to think at all.

Chapter 9

By the time they reached Drynoch, Callum's hand was bleeding again. His white cotton handkerchief was glued to his fingers with clots of fresh, dark red blood.

It hurt like the devil, too.

Rumors, lies, and exaggerations dogged the MacLeod sisters, just as Hamish had said, but one thing was certain: dirks, blades, or sharp objects of any kind were best kept out of their devious clutches.

It hadn't been luck or chance guiding Freya's hand when she'd sliced him open last night.

Chance wasn't that kind, and no one was that lucky.

She'd known exactly what she was doing when she'd brought that blade down on his hand. She angled it just right to ensure the deadliest edge of it came down right across his knuckles.

The chit had damn near sliced his fingers off.

His digits remained miraculously intact, thankfully, but she'd reduced his hand to a pulpy mess of shredded flesh, and he was reminded of it with every twitch of the reins between his fingers.

Someone had taught her how to handle a dirk. Her father, most likely. He'd never encountered Rory MacLeod in the flesh, but if the rumors about him were true, then Rory wasn't a man one wanted to tangle with. As for his daughters, they were every inch the vixens one would expect such a man to sire.

Only a fool risked turning his back on a MacLeod, unless he

fancied having a dirk buried between his ribs. Even Freya, with those innocent green eyes and the gold threads in her hair that made her look like an angel, had turned out to be handy with a blade.

God only knew what other tricks she had tucked up her sleeve. One would never guess it to look at her, but the lass was full of surprises.

Awful things, surprises. He'd never understood why people were so fond of them. Surprises started as secrets, were fed on lies, and ended unpredictably. There was nothing enjoyable about that.

But if it hadn't been for Freya's bravery last night, they would never have made a clean escape from Dunvegan. They'd been in a tight spot last night—as tight a one as he'd ever been in—but the girl had kept her wits about her.

When he dragged her out from under that desk he'd braced himself for incoherent sobbing, at best, and at worst, dramatic swooning. Neither had happened. She'd stabbed him with a dirk, yes, but if he'd been in her place, he would have done the same. He understood that impulse to strike out, that animal instinct to survive. Respected it, even.

She remained calm afterward, too, even as a mob of enraged villagers tried to batter down the front door of her castle. She'd done just as he'd told her to do, without a word of complaint. She'd scampered up that courtyard wall without the least hesitation, then dropped down to the ground without a wince. Then she'd scampered over that devil of a pathway above Loch Dunvegan as if she spent every day balanced on a cliff's edge.

In half boots a size too large for her, no less.

But the tempting curves she was hiding under the shapeless dresses she wore? That was a less welcome surprise. There wasn't a man alive who'd choose to ride with a cock stand, but after hours in the saddle with her sweetly rounded arse nestled between his thighs, his body had overruled his head.

She mumbled something in her sleep, turning her face into his neck, and he tightened his arms around her, settling her more firmly against his chest.

Not because he wanted her closer. He *didn't*. He wasn't some romantic hero, clasping his lady tenderly in his arms. He had needs just like any other man did, of course, and he saw to it those needs were satisfied, but there wasn't any reason to linger over the business.

Tender caresses, endless kisses, sweet words, and displays of affection?

No.

He didn't *cuddle*, damn it, and he wasn't going to start with the lass who'd stabbed him, but given their situation, he had little choice in the matter. He had to keep his arms around her if he didn't want her tumbling off his horse. He'd gone to too much trouble to get her out of Dunvegan to let her break her bloody neck now.

Hamish was already going to have his head, as it was.

Besides, it was cold and wet, the dampness seeping into his bones. The rain was still falling, and for all Freya MacLeod's murderous tendencies, the warm, solid weight of her against his chest wasn't entirely unpleasant.

She smelled like rain, and the woods, and something else, something sweet he couldn't name. Vanilla, or honey? Not that he'd sniffed her, of course, but her head was tucked under his chin, and the wisps of red-gold hair that had escaped her braid were tickling his nostrils.

It wasn't as if he *wanted* to smell her. He'd even tried breathing through his mouth, but as the night wore on, he gave up and let his chin rest against the top of her head.

After riding throughout the night, they'd at last reached Kyleakin. From here they'd cross Loch Alsh and leave the Isle of Skye behind. From the Kyle of Lochalsh on the other side, it was another three-day ride to Kildary.

If the journey went as well as he hoped, they'd arrive at Balnagown Castle before the end of the week.

And once they did, then what? Freya wasn't going to appreciate being detained in Kildary for the next few weeks, and she wasn't going to be the only one.

There would be no warm welcome awaiting her at Balnagown Castle.

What was he meant to do with her? Lock her in a bedchamber until he received word from Keir that the danger had passed, or until Hamish returned to Dunvegan? He hadn't any blessed idea, but there wasn't a damned thing he could do about it. He'd promised Hamish he'd keep her safe, and the safest place for Freya MacLeod was as far away from Dunvegan as he could get her.

Whether she'd ever be able to return to her home wasn't for him to say. It would depend on whether Sorcha MacLeod had set that stable on fire. If she had, then God help her.

God help her, even if she hadn't.

The villagers hadn't been in a forgiving mood last night. If they caught either of the MacLeod sisters now, they'd fit their necks with a pair of nooses first and ask questions only after they swung.

But none of that was his concern. He'd sworn to protect her until Hamish returned from his travels, and not a single moment longer than that. He'd wash his hands of her at the first opportunity, and never spare her another thought once he had.

"Sorcha?" Freya twitched against him, and he tensed.

She hadn't awoken, but sleep wasn't any protection from the nightmares playing in her head, because a moment later she jerked again, whimpering.

"Quickly, Sorcha. Run . . . the woods? No, *don't*—"

She broke off with a gasp, but there was such agony in that last word, such anguish that he tightened his arms around her instinctively, bracing his forearms against the sides of her body, so slight and vulnerable against him.

He didn't trust her. She proven last night that she was a schemer and a liar, and a bit too handy with a blade for his comfort. She might be the least dangerous of the three MacLeod sisters, but that was like saying she was the least venomous of a nest of venomous snakes.

But no one deserved to go through a nightmare alone. So, he pressed her closer against his chest, praying she wouldn't wake and produce a hidden dirk from within the voluminous folds of that ridiculous cloak she wore, and slash open the knuckles of his other hand.

There's nothing wrong with a lass with a little spirit, eh?

Had it only been hours since Keir had asked him that? It seemed impossible, but not even a whole day had passed since he and Keir had stood in the doorway of Castle Cairncross and watched as Freya MacLeod disappeared into the trees.

Look at where all her spirit had gotten her.

Spirit could be a dangerous thing, for a woman. He needn't look further than his own mother for proof of that.

Spirit could get a woman cast out of her clan. Or burned at the stake.

The lady in his arms was a witch, by some people's reckoning. A dangerous creature, clever and cunning, with the power to summon the wind and thunder, and able to conjure rain and lightning with a magical flick of her slender fingers.

Pure absurdity. As clever as Freya MacLeod undoubtedly was, she was no witch. But neither was she the harmless chit she appeared to be.

An hour passed, then another. Freya shuddered in his arms, another whimper falling from her lips, but then sleep took her again and she burrowed into him the way a terrified child might after suffering through a nightmare.

But she was no child, and he was no one's savior. If the last twenty-nine years of his life hadn't proved much, they had proved that. He couldn't even save himself.

What had Hamish been thinking, asking him to watch over the MacLeod sisters? Keir, yes. It made sense to ask Keir. But him?

No. Love must have driven Hamish into temporary madness.

Freya didn't stir again, but lay quietly against him, her long, dark golden eyelashes resting against cheeks as pale as the flickering rays of white sunlight just peeking through the clouds.

Her nightmares had passed, but they'd return soon enough.

For now, it was best if she slept.

There was no peace awaiting Freya MacLeod once she opened her eyes.

The night was too dark. If it hadn't been so dark, she would have found her way back to Castle Cairncross by now.

Back to Sorcha.

It was what she told herself as the distance between her and her home grew by inches and ells, by falls, furlongs, and miles. If the darkness hadn't been so impenetrable, the night so cold, the stars so absent, she would have fled Callum Ross's protection. She'd be like Sorcha's sparrowhawks, soaring over the land, steady and unafraid, her talons at the ready and her sharp, yellow predator's gaze fixed on her castle's turret.

But when she untangled herself from her nightmares, they'd left Dunvegan far behind. For as long as she could remember Castle Cairncross's awkward turret jutting into the sky had been her guiding star, but she could no longer see it. It was gone, along with everything else that spoke to her of home.

Nothing was familiar. Not the chest pressed against her back, or the saddle swaying beneath her. Not the clop of the horses' hooves striking the road, the occasional cottage they passed or the flat gray water she glimpsed through the trees.

Even the sky looked different here.

Wherever they were, it wasn't anywhere she'd been before. All her comforting lies vanished then, like the mists swirling over the water at the first glow of sunrise.

She straightened upright, putting a sliver of space between

her back and Callum Ross's chest. It had been ages since she'd been on a horse, and it wasn't comfortable, sitting upright in the saddle, but a lady didn't lounge on a gentleman as if he were a settee.

Especially not *this* gentleman.

She cleared her throat. "Where are you taking me?"

Silence. The minutes ticked by, but still, he didn't answer her. Either her voice had been lost in the rising wind around them, or he didn't intend to give her the courtesy of a reply.

But just when she'd given up, he muttered, "To Balnagown Castle, in Kildary."

Balnagown Castle? She never heard of it, but hadn't her father mentioned Kildary, once or twice? Or had it been Kiltearn? Killilan? She must have mistaken the name, because the village he'd told her about was only about thirty miles northwest of Inverness.

Yes, she'd certainly confused the name. Inverness was more than a hundred and thirty miles from Dunvegan. It was impossible he was taking her as far away from her home as—

"Stay here, lass."

His voice was so low, so quiet she felt it more than heard it, a low rumble against her spine, his warm breath stirring the wisps of loose hair at the back of her neck and making her shiver.

He was a man of few words, but then perhaps a man with such a cold, forbidding stare as his had no need of words to persuade people to do his bidding. He was the sort who issued orders, and expected they'd be obeyed. The sort who told someone to stay where they were and found them precisely where he'd left them when he returned.

It didn't take more than a glance at Callum Ross's severe dark eyebrows and stern lips to see that. He gave the commands, and everyone scrambled to obey him.

It was pure foolishness to imagine she was an exception. She wasn't, and he knew it as well as she did. Otherwise, he would have taken some measures to prevent her from leaping from the horse's back and disappearing into the sparse wilderness along the banks of the loch.

If she'd been braver than she was, a lady with a steel-edged spine like Sorcha, she might have led him a bit of a chase. It wouldn't have done her any good in the end, of course. There was no place for her to go, or any means by which to get there, and she wouldn't get far with her feet sliding about inside Cat's boots with every step.

Unless she chose to turn horse thief. Why, she could snatch up the reins right now, turn the horse's head back toward Dunvegan and leave Callum Ross far behind.

What was a bit of horse thievery, in comparison to arson?

But he'd catch her, somehow. She couldn't say how he'd manage it without a horse, but he wasn't the sort of man who'd let his quarry slip through his fingers.

Still, if she had at least attempted a respectable escape, she'd have no reason to reproach herself for being such a coward.

But she did just as he'd told her to do. She sat atop the horse, clutching the edges of his coat with numb fingers as the one chance she'd had at escape since they'd left Dunvegan faded with every scrape of the horse's hooves under the frozen dirt beneath them.

She remained where she was, the still waters of some loch or other spread out before her, the gray water blending into the gloomy clouds in the sky above, her brain a dull, sluggish thing in her head, and waited for whatever fate would befall her.

It seemed too much effort to do anything else.

He wasn't gone for long. Soon enough there was a crunch of boot heels on the frozen ground behind her, then an incredulous voice said, "Who's this, then?"

It was the shock in the voice that roused her and made her turn to look.

A tall, gangly lad with wild dark hair had stopped in the middle of the road and was staring up at her with an expression of pure astonishment.

She stared back at him, curious. He was just a boy—or, no, he wasn't quite a boy anymore, but he was not yet a man, either. He was suspended somewhere between the two, at the mercy of long, ungainly limbs that yet only hinted at the strapping man he would someday become.

He gaped at her for a moment longer, dark eyes wide, before turning to Callum. "Yer bringing someone to the castle?"

Callum didn't deign to offer the lad more than a grunt in response, and a terse, "Fetch the boat, Brodie."

He didn't speak harshly, but the command had the boy nearly tripping over his long limbs. "Aye, Ross."

"Sit, stay, fetch . . ." she muttered to herself as poor Brodie scrambled to obey. They were all mere pawns to Callum Ross's king, to be manipulated according to his whims. It was a lowering thought—

Wait. Had he just ordered the lad to fetch a *boat*?

She gazed out at the gray water curling along the edge of the shore, and from there to the small white cottages that lay like sleeping sheep along the coastline behind them, then turned to Callum. "Where are we?"

He was watching Brodie, who was manfully attempting to drag a small fishing boat from the tall grasses a few paces from the water, and didn't spare her a glance. "Kyleakin."

Kyleakin! If they were in Kyleakin, that meant the gray expanse of water in front of her was Lochalsh, and the village she could just glimpse on the other side of the water was Kyle of Lochalsh, on the mainland.

Only then did it truly sink in what was happening.

He was taking her off Skye! Away from her home, her sister, and everything she knew and loved. It wouldn't take more than an hour to reach the shores of Kyle of Lochalsh.

One hour, and her home and her sister would truly be left far behind.

Dear God, Sorcha. What had become of her last night? Had she gone back to the castle to search for her, only to find it dark and empty? Sorcha would have been frantic, once she realized Freya wasn't there.

Ah, she couldn't bear to think of it.

Was it possible Sorcha hadn't made it back to the castle at all? Those men who'd chased her through the woods last night must also have chased Sorcha. Her sister knew those woods better than anyone, but she was one small lady, and there'd been more than a dozen men in that mob.

Had they caught her? Or had she made it back to the castle, only to find them waiting for her? What had Sorcha been doing, out at Mr. Stewart's farm? She and her sisters knew better than to trust any of the men in Dunvegan.

One question after another spun through her head until she was dizzy with them, but there were no answers for her. She was going in circles, only to find herself at the same dead end, every time.

That was where this would end, if she allowed Callum Ross to take her away from Skye. She'd agreed to leave the castle last night, yes—she'd had no other choice—but she'd never agreed to *this*.

If she left Skye now, she might never find her way back again.

Meanwhile, the boat was waiting.

Some strong emotion seized her then, something that was both fury and panic at once. It kindled like flames in her breast, and the timidity that had kept her quiet began to singe and curl at the edges. How had she ended up here at the water's edge, one short boat ride away from abandoning her sister, and leaving Skye behind her?

"Come on, lass. Down you go."

If Callum Ross had chosen any other time to seize her waist and attempt to drag her from the saddle, things might have gone differently. Another moment, and the spark of rebellion might have died a quick death, but as it was, those massive paws closing around her waist set the spark aflame.

What happened next was . . . well, she didn't plan it.

It just *happened.*

"No!" The word tore from her throat, raw and bloody, and before she even realized she'd opened her mouth, other words came tumbling out after it, a veritable barrage of them, each one louder than the last and throbbing with fury. "Release me this instant, you . . . you . . . barbarian!"

Barbarian? Goodness, where had that word come from? Surely, that wasn't the word she'd meant to say?

The boy, Brodie, must have been as shocked as she was, because he froze, dropping the rope that tethered the boat to the shore. "She just . . . did she just call you a—"

That was as far as he got. His voice was drowned out by the deafening shriek that rushed like a streak of flames from her lips. "I'm not going to your blasted castle! I'm not going anywhere with you!"

But no one was as shocked as Callum Ross.

He must have been dumbfounded indeed, because the man who hadn't so much as flinched when she'd feigned a stumble and sent a whole tea tray's worth of dishes crashing to the floor, the man who'd eluded a torch-wielding mob and taken the blade of a dirk to his knuckles without so much as a twitch . . .

He *dropped* her.

Or, well, not dropped her, precisely, but his hands went slack around her waist. It was only for an instant, no more than the time it took for her to draw a breath and release it again, but it was enough.

Enough time for her heel to connect with his stomach.

"Oof!" His breath left his lungs in a startled whoosh, and Cat's half boot flew off her foot and went sailing into the shrubbery at the water's edge like some exotic black bird.

Brodie watched it fly in an arc over his head, his mouth falling open.

If there'd been any softness to Callum Ross's midsection, she might have gotten further than she did, but alas, landing a kick to the layers of muscle there was rather like kicking a stone wall.

Still, it was enough. A bit of writhing and a squirm of her hips was all it took.

For one moment, one glorious instant, she was free. She might have remained so if she hadn't been missing a boot on one foot and hadn't just crushed the toes of the other on Callum Ross's torso. And that was to say nothing of his arm, which was not only as muscled as his stomach, but longer than any man's arm had a right to be.

But like so many rebellions before it, hers was doomed to failure.

She didn't make it more than a half dozen steps before that long arm curled around her waist. With one dizzying lurch everything tilted underneath her, and the ground disappeared from under her feet. The world tipped on its side, then went upside down in a blur of brown packed dirt road and gray sky.

It wasn't until her forehead bounced against the broad plane of his back that she understood what had happened.

He'd thrown her over his shoulder! Of all the savage, barbaric—

"See Titan's taken care of," he called to Brodie, nodding at his horse as he strode toward the water's edge with her bouncing against his back as if she weighed no more than a rag doll.

She was gasping for breath by this point, stunned by the quickness with which he'd scooped her up, and rather flabbergasted at her own daring.

"Give me the rope. Quickly lad, before she bolts again."

Bolts! He meant *her*. He was talking about her as if she were his horse!

How had it come to this? She hadn't done anything wrong, yet she was being dragged away from her sister and her home as if she'd committed some unspeakable crime.

The panic that was never far away from her came crashing

down on top of her with a vengeance then, stealing the breath from her chest. Every rational thought flew from her head as the panic gripped her, writhing like a serpent in her belly.

Slow, even breaths. If only she could manage a half dozen breaths, she could keep it at bay, and all might yet be well.

One, two, three . . . yes, that was better.

And it was, but not for long. Her lungs rebelled on the fourth breath, freezing to a halt in her chest. She dug her fingernails into her palms to shake the panic loose, chase it away, but it was no use. It had her in its grip now, and it was squeezing, squeezing . . .

There was no way to escape it. It was sucking her down into the cold darkness, just as it had done once when she was a child and went swimming in Loch Dunvegan with her sisters. One moment she was splashing in the cool water, and the next the tide had caught her, and the water was closing over her head.

This was just like that had been, a slow, numb descent, her lungs clamoring for air, her chest burning.

She couldn't catch her breath. *She couldn't breathe—*

An arm pressed into her side, warm and impossibly hard. "Easy, lass."

It was the low rumble of his voice that brought her back to herself. Or no, not his voice, but the vibration of his back against her chest when he spoke. It was oddly comforting, that deep rumble, the one comforting thing she'd discovered about the man, like the hum of the carriage seat beneath her when she used to ride to Uiginish with her mother and father and sisters, to stroll around the point on a sunny day.

How had he known? Had he sensed her panic, the way her body had gone rigid against his? She opened her mouth to ask, but then closed it again without saying a word.

It didn't matter. Perhaps there was some kindness in him, but she couldn't afford to trust Callum Ross. He'd taken her from her castle, the only home she'd ever known, and from her sister, and given the chance, he'd take her farther away still.

He was a kidnapper, or, well, a napper of young ladies. Was there such a thing?

What did it matter? She had no choice in this, any more than she did anything else. In the five short months since her father's death, she'd become powerless, a burden to be passed from one hand to the next at the whim of men who knew nothing about her hopes, her fears or her dreams.

First the smugglers, then the villagers, and now Callum Ross.

And she was at his mercy.

Chapter 10

Callum didn't make a habit of manhandling young ladies.

Freya MacLeod was the first he'd ever scooped into his arms and tossed over his shoulder like a sack of flour, and she would be the last.

She'd gone limp against him, her chest jerking with each of the labored breaths sawing in and out of her throat. If she hadn't been gripping the back of his shirt in both her fists, he would have thought she'd fallen into a swoon.

For all her rumored timidity, she hadn't yet succumbed to one.

The fiery stables burning to the ground right before her eyes, the mobs of villagers maddened with rage chasing her through the woods, and a flight through the dark night with a man she hardly knew and had no reason to trust?

She'd weathered it all with admirable bravery.

But she was frightened now. He was holding her close enough he could feel the tremors running through her. She was shaking in his arms, still but for the involuntary shudders wracking her body.

Clutching such a slender, fine-boned slip of a lady while she shivered with panic was like trapping a butterfly in his hands, the edges of its fluttering wings tickling his palms.

Wasn't he behaving just like the barbarian she'd accused him of being? He didn't like Freya MacLeod thinking of him as a brute, but it was a bit late for that. He hadn't precisely endeared himself to her after that incident in the front drive of Castle Cairncross.

He didn't regret what he'd done that day. Not exactly. No gentleman wanted to grab a lady as he'd grabbed her, but neither did he fancy a slit throat. Sorcha MacLeod hadn't left him much choice, but he wasn't proud of it, nor would he forget it anytime soon.

He'd done what he had to do, but the horror on Freya's face when he'd grabbed her arm, the way her green eyes had gone wide, then darkened with terror . . .

It was shameful, a man of his size forcing a wee lass to do his bidding, but there was only one solution to the problem he and Freya now found themselves in, and that was for them both to get into the boat and leave Skye far behind them.

But she didn't seem to recognize how much danger she was in, even after a mob of rabid villains had tried to drag her heels first out of her castle. If Freya MacLeod had any idea how to keep herself safe, he hadn't seen any evidence of it. So, he'd have to see to her safety himself, just as he'd promised Hamish he would.

Of course, at the time he hadn't had the least idea what he was promising, but a man didn't go back on his word, no matter how troublesome it became to keep it.

God knew Freya MacLeod was proving troublesome enough. Whoever would have thought one small lady could wreak such havoc? One would never think it to look at her, but for all her daintiness, Freya MacLeod was chaos wrapped in green skirts and a dark blue cloak.

"You can put me down now, Mr. Ross. I give you my word that I won't bolt."

Put her down? He'd put her down, all right. Directly into the boat. He marched toward it, prepared to drop her into it and leave Skye before anything else could go awry, but once he'd dislodged her from his shoulder and was holding her against his chest, she stopped him with a hand on his arm.

"Wait, Mr. Ross. Just listen to me."

She pleaded so prettily, but that was the problem. One glance into those guileless green eyes and a man could lose his wits. He'd made the mistake of listening to her when she approached him in the entryway yesterday with that tea tray, and this was where it had gotten them.

She'd already lied to him once. He wasn't such a fool as to give her the chance to do it again. "There's no point, Miss MacLeod. There's nothing you can say that will make any difference."

"Please, Mr. Ross."

She'd been clutching at his arm, a sleeve of his shirt caught in a death grip, but she released it now, and after a brief pause, she rested her hand against the back of his. The weight of that small, warm palm against him, the plea in the gesture, the gentleness of it was his undoing.

Damn it. He was going to regret this.

He gave the boat one last glance, then lowered her to the ground with a heavy sigh. "Very well, Miss MacLeod. What is it?"

She stood before him, her skirts flapping against her legs in the brisk wind coming off the water. "I can't get into that boat."

"You can, and you will." Did she still not see that she had no choice?

"No, I mean . . ." She avoided his gaze. "I—I'm afraid."

"Of boats?" Freya MacLeod, who'd braved the dark woods, a scorching fire, and a mob of enraged villagers, was afraid to get into a boat? "There's nothing to be afraid of, Miss MacLeod. The boat is perfectly safe."

"It's not the boat. It's . . . I'm afraid to leave Skye." She met his gaze for an instant, then her eyes darted away from his again. "I'm afraid if I leave Skye, I'll never find my way back to it again."

Not find her way back to Skye? What did that mean? Did she imagine he was going to keep her forever? "I'm not kidnapping you, Freya. You are aware of that, aren't you?"

"It's not . . . you don't understand. My sisters and I . . . ever since my father died, I—I keep losing things . . ." She trailed off, biting her lip.

It wasn't much of an explanation. It would have been easy enough to dismiss her fears—to scoop her up and deposit her in the boat, yet he hesitated. Her words resonated deep inside him, like a chord vibrating after the string was plucked.

The trouble was, there was a part of him that understood how losing things could make a person desperate. If you lost enough of what mattered to you, you'd cling to whatever you had left with raw, bloody hands.

But that didn't change anything. Not this time. It was on the tip of his tongue to say so, but then . . .

Her chin wobbled.

It was just a tiny wobble, there and then gone again in a heartbeat. Had he missed it, he would have bundled her into the boat without a qualm, but as fate would have it, he saw it, and once he saw it, he couldn't help but see *her*.

A small, pale lass in a damp, bedraggled dress, her hair a tangled mess with a leaf or two from her run through the woods caught among the heavy tresses. There was a long, shallow cut on her right cheek where a branch had struck her, the hems of her skirts were caked with mud, and she smelled of smoke and scorched wood.

Her cloak was stained with blood. *His* blood, from when she'd stabbed him with the dirk.

He glanced down at his knuckles, at the grubby bandage wrapped around his hand, the smeared blood like streaks of dark rust on his handkerchief.

The sight of it should have been enough to dull any sympathy he had for her, but he must have lost his wits somewhere between Dunvegan and Kyleakin, because all he could see was her hunched shoulders, and the dark violet circles under her eyes.

None of this was her fault. She and her sister should never have left the castle in the first place, yes. It had been foolish and reckless, but aside from that, neither of them had done anything wrong. Certainly nothing that justified the villagers' hostility toward them.

The MacLeod sisters were a bit odd, yes. They were as clever and cunning as their father had been, and utterly devoted to each other and their castle, but there was no crime in any of that. There was no crime in anything they'd done—not that he could see. There was no proof that either Freya or Sorcha had anything to do with that fire.

That mob of villagers from Dunvegan had come after them for who they *were*, not for anything they'd *done*.

Freya had been through a nightmare last night. The fire, the village men chasing her, her sister's disappearance—in the space of single night, her every fear had come true. Yet she hadn't given up or dissolved into hysterics. He hadn't seen a single tear or so much as a wobble of her chin, until now.

I'm afraid. It couldn't have been easy for her to admit that to him. Her reluctance to admit to fear, to even dare to feel it was . . . well, he understood that, as well. Damn bad luck, that, as it made it much harder for him to dismiss her.

He could hear her out. He couldn't do much for her, but he could do that.

"You can't return to Dunvegan right now. You realize that, don't you?" That mob would have her head on a platter as soon as she set foot inside the village limits. "There's likely someone watching Castle Cairncross even now."

"Yes. I expect there is."

She bit her lip again, and he knew she was thinking about her sister. "There's no reason for you to think you won't ever be able to return home again. Once your eldest sister and Lord Ballantyne are back in Dunvegan—"

She shook her head. "It may be too late by then."

Too late for Sorcha, she meant, though from what he'd seen of Sorcha MacLeod, if she didn't wish to be found, she wouldn't be. "I'm not sure what else we can do."

She drew in a deep breath. "My father died four months ago, Mr. Ross. Do you know how many luggers have come to Castle Cairncross since then?"

"Ballantyne mentioned three."

"Yes, that's right. Three luggers, each of them loaded with smugglers. It would have made sense for us to leave the castle and save our skins, but we didn't do that. Do you know why?"

"No." If it had been him, he'd have been relieved to have an excuse to abandon the old pile, and good riddance to it. "Why?"

"Because Castle Cairncross is our home. We knew if we left it, we might never be able to return to it again. We didn't want that." She paused, watching him, then added softly, "Don't you see? It's still my home. Nothing has changed."

"I beg your pardon, but everything has changed." The villagers had made up their minds that Freya and Sorcha MacLeod were going to be held responsible for that fire. That they hadn't set it didn't matter at all. With so many voices raised against them, they were almost certain to be found guilty of arson.

What better way to rid Dunvegan of its witches?

It was enough to see them both hang, and if Clyde Stewart had perished in the blaze? There may never be another MacLeod at Castle Cairncross ever again.

Perhaps she was right, and she wouldn't ever be able to return to her home, but it was too late to do anything about it now. The damage had already been done. "I don't understand,

Miss MacLeod. You've already acknowledged that you can't return to Castle Cairncross. At least, not yet."

"I'm aware of that, Mr. Ross, but—"

"What are you proposing, then? If I had a castle on Skye, it would be at your disposal, but as it is, I don't see what choice we have but to leave Skye behind, at least for now. There isn't any other—"

"I don't need a castle, Mr. Ross." She glanced at Brodie, who was still standing by the boat, watching them with wide eyes. "A cottage would do very well."

A cottage? Where were they going to find an obliging cottager willing to turn over his home to . . . his gaze wandered over Brodie's shoulder to the cottage on the bluff behind him.

Oh. *Oh*.

"Perhaps Brodie would be kind enough to allow me to stay in his cottage for a night or two."

"I don't see what that would accomplish." A few extra nights on Skye weren't going to solve Freya MacLeod's problems.

"I thought you might be willing to return to Dunvegan and see if you can find my sister." She pressed her folded hands to her bosom. "I realize it's asking a great deal of you. If I could go myself, I would, but they'll be looking for me."

"No, Miss MacLeod. It's out of the question. It's not safe for you to be left here alone with Brodie. You're not that far from Dunvegan." Given the MacLeod family's notoriety, it wouldn't take long for news of the fire to spread. By the end of a few days' time, everyone from Trotternish to Kyleakin would be trading the story of it over pints at the pub.

It was possible someone here might recognize her. God knew her red hair didn't help.

"But—"

He held up a hand to hush her. "Even if I agreed to leave you here, Miss MacLeod, I'd be recognized in Dunvegan. Mr. Dunn and I stopped by Baird's Pub last night when we were out searching for you. A dozen men overheard me tell the barkeep we were staying at the castle at Lord Ballantyne's request. Everyone in Dunvegan must know of it by now."

"I see."

Her face fell, all the hopeful light going out of it at once, like a cloud blocking the sun, and the next thing he knew, his mouth was opening, and words were coming out of it. "But perhaps Brodie could go in my place."

What was he saying? It was safer for them to leave Skye at once. No good would come of a delay, but it seemed he was willing to overlook it if it meant keeping Freya MacLeod from withering like a fresh spring flower trampled under a boot heel.

What was happening to him?

"Could he, indeed?" She reached out, her fingers landing lightly on his forearm. "I would be so grateful to you, Mr. Ross! And to Brodie as well, of course."

She gave the lad a beaming smile over Callum's shoulder, and Brodie blushed up to the roots of his hair. Good Lord. The poor lad was no match for Freya MacLeod.

He glanced down at her pale fingers against the darker skin of his forearm. Did she even realize she was touching him? He bloody did. Every inch of his body had leapt to attention at the light brush of her fingers against his skin.

He cleared his throat. "What if Brodie can't find out anything about your sister? What then, Miss MacLeod?"

Her face clouded, and her hand fell away. "If you and Brodie do me this favor, then I give you my word I will accompany you to Balnagown Castle without a single complaint, regardless of whether there is word of my sister, or not, and I will remain there until such a time as you deem it safe for me to return to Dunvegan."

Compliance. That was what she was offering him. It wasn't necessary that she was agreeable—he could compel her cooperation—but he didn't care for the idea of dragging this wee lass all the way to Kildary without her agreement.

He wasn't a barbarian, no matter what she might think.

"Dunvegan is a day's ride from Kyleakin, and it will take Brodie another day to return, and that's assuming everything goes well." He nodded at the tiny, whitewashed cottage. "We can't risk anyone seeing you, so you'll be confined to the cottage for three or four days, Miss MacLeod, perhaps more. It's hardly luxurious accommodation."

"I don't care about luxury, Mr. Ross. I only care that my sister is safe."

"Very well, then. I'll have a word with Brodie." He strode toward Brodie, who was pretending he hadn't heard every word they'd just spoken.

"I'll do it," Brodie said, before Callum could get a word out. "I don't like to see the lady in such distress," he added, with a courtly bow for Freya MacLeod.

Dear God. The boy was a rogue in the making. "Good lad, but keep in mind this is no romantic adventure. Don't pass through the village of Dunvegan on your way there. Keep an eye on Cairncross Castle, but don't approach it. Stick to the woods, and if anyone questions you, keep your mouth closed."

"Aye, Ross. Shall I put the boat away, then?"

"I suppose so." He turned back toward Freya, who was standing at the edge of the water, the wind tossing her red curls about her face.

Four days alone in a tiny cottage with Freya MacLeod, without a thing for them to do but sit and stare at each other.

What could possibly go wrong?

The cottage was tiny, but that was hardly surprising. From the outside it appeared no larger than a doll's house, and yet . . .

She glanced behind her, where Callum Ross was standing in the open doorway, his thick arms propped against the frame and his enormous body blocking all but the most determined rays of the morning sun.

There wasn't a cottage in Scotland that didn't become

smaller when he stepped into it. Everything seemed to shrink around him, until there wasn't a corner of the place that wasn't filled with his presence.

One might say what they liked about Callum Ross—that he was brutish, sullen, and silent—but he wasn't a man one could ignore, and she was trapped in this tiny, one-room cottage with him for several days, without a single thing to do to distract either of them.

Dear God. Perhaps she should have let him take her to Balnagown Castle, after all. "This is, er . . ." She waved a hand at their surroundings. "Snug."

He let out a sound that may have been a snort, or a grunt. She couldn't tell which. "Brodie doesn't need much space."

"No, I suppose not."

He abandoned his place in the doorway and entered the cottage, his heavy boots thunderous against the worn wooden floorboards, and closed the door behind him, plunging them into a dim gloom that did nothing to calm her nerves.

She took another step away, instinctively putting space between them, but there was nowhere for her to go. The cottage was composed of a single room, the only furnishings a small table with two chairs, a worn settee with a trunk beside it, and a basin and pitcher atop a length of board in what must have passed for the kitchen.

"You'd best rest now, lass." He gestured toward a small, neatly made bed against the far wall.

Sleep did sound heavenly. It had been two nights since her head had touched a pillow, and her limbs were heavy with exhaustion. With any luck, she'd sleep for four days, and wake to the sound of Brodie returning to the cottage.

"You're certain Brodie won't mind the intrusion?" One's bed was rather personal, after all.

He was poking at the fire, coaxing it into a blaze. He didn't turn, and he spared her only another grunt in reply. It was much like the last grunt he'd given her, but she chose to interpret it as a gracious invitation to make herself at home in Brodie's bed.

She nearly groaned as she sank down onto the edge of the mattress.

It was soft, and piled high with thick, clean bedding. Why, she could just tuck herself into the nest of blankets and let oblivion take her. Sleep was the only way she'd be able to forget the nightmare that had unfolded at Castle Cairncross last night.

There was only one problem.

Callum Ross. How in the world was she meant to fall asleep with him only ten feet away from her? He was the same man who'd grabbed her on the castle drive and pressed his forearm against her throat.

The man who'd kidnapped her, for pity's sake!

Except . . . oh, very well. He hadn't kidnapped her, precisely. He *had* dragged her out from under her father's desk and spirited her away from her castle and the sister she loved, but he'd done it for her own good.

But that was the trouble with things that were done for one's own good. One never appreciated them, even when they should.

She'd gone with him willingly, though. It couldn't properly be called a napping if she'd agreed to go with him. Except she hadn't just agreed, had she? She'd scaled one of the castle walls, risked a broken neck on that treacherous pathway above Loch Dunvegan, then ridden fifty miles on the back of his horse without a murmur of complaint.

There'd been no napping. She was well and truly in this thing, and there was no sense in pretending otherwise, and since she was facing uncomfortable truths . . .

Callum Ross could have simply abandoned her to her fate. He could have saddled his horse and ridden out of Dunvegan without a backward glance, leaving her to face that mob alone. He'd made a promise to Lord Ballantyne he'd keep her safe, yes, but he'd never agreed to risk his life for her, and anyway, people broke promises every day.

But not Callum Ross. He'd kept his word.

Some might even say he'd saved her life last night.

She lay on her back for a bit, staring up at the ceiling, then peeked over the edge of the blanket she'd wrapped around herself.

He was stretched out on the settee, the cushions sagging under the muscular bulk of him. It was far too short for him, however, and his legs were hanging over the edge of the arm.

He looked dreadfully uncomfortable, but it wasn't as if he could share the bed with her. She squeezed her eyes closed and gathered the edge of the blanket tighter around her neck, then turned her nose into the fold of cloth and drew in a deep breath.

It smelled nice, like leather and rain, and just a touch of smoke—

Smoke? She struggled out from under the blankets and bolted upright, glancing down at herself. God above, she was still wearing Callum Ross's coat. That scent she'd just dragged greedily into her lungs, the scent she'd found so comforting, was *him*.

A flush rose from her chest into her cheeks, flooding them with heat.

But it didn't mean anything. Of course it didn't. It didn't mean a single thing that she'd just burrowed into his coat like a contented mouse into a dry bed of straw. She was just confused, that was all. Confused, and so exhausted her mind was playing tricks on her.

Still, it didn't seem right she should keep his coat when he didn't have a single blanket, and she had half a dozen of them all for herself. She might not like or trust the man, but she couldn't quite reconcile keeping his coat with her conscience—

"For God's sake, lass. What's wrong *now*?"

His deep voice broke the silence, and she glanced over to find him watching her, his brows lowered in a dark scowl. What had she done to earn the scowl this time? Breathed too enthusiastically? "What do you mean? There's nothing—"

"Is the bed not to your liking? Are the blankets insufficient?" He opened one eye and peered at her through the gloom. "Is the cottage too hot, or too cold, or the waves rushing against the shore with too much enthusiasm?"

Odious man. To think she'd been concerned about his comfort! Why, it would serve him right if she kept his coat and left him to freeze.

Except he'd done her a good turn, sending Brodie off to Dunvegan. She wouldn't get a wink of sleep if she had to think about him shivering on that settee.

She threw the blankets aside, rose to her feet and marched across the room, removing his coat as she went, and ignoring the chill that drifted under the neck of her gown.

"What is it?" He glanced warily up at her as she paused beside the settee, but he didn't bother getting up.

"Here." She held out his coat. "You'll need this."

Something flickered in his gray eyes, but he made no move to take the coat from her. He remained where he was, staring up at her until she let out a huff, reached over the back of the settee, and draped the coat over him.

There. It wasn't much, but it would have to do.

She marched back over to Brodie's bed, tugged the blankets over herself, and burrowed deep into them, squeezing her eyes closed. Yes, that was much better. He might scowl all he liked now, and she wouldn't have to see it.

For the next few hours, she could forget Callum Ross even existed.

It wasn't long before her body relaxed against the mattress, her limbs growing heavy, but just as she was on the edge of unconsciousness a deep voice murmured, "Sleep well, lass."

CHAPTER II

Callum jerked awake, his toes frozen, a crick in his neck and his stomach grumbling with hunger. He blinked against the light, the grogginess falling instantly away from him as he sat up.

A cool afternoon light was coming through the window. It was harder to tell in the winter when the light was so flat and gray, but it looked as if it were mid-afternoon.

He hadn't slept for long, then.

Something had roused him. A noise. A repeated, rhythmic thump followed by an odd dragging sound, like a foot sliding across the floor.

Thump, drag, thump, drag . . .

No wonder he'd woken with an aching head.

There could only be one culprit. God above, did the girl never sleep?

He glared at her over his shoulder. "Cease that pacing, if you please, Miss MacLeod. You're making my head pound."

One last thump echoed in his skull before she came to a stop behind the settee. "Oh, dear. Did I wake you? I beg your pardon, Mr. Ross."

"I don't see how you could have failed to wake me with that deafening thumping you're making. And what is that maddening dragging sound? It sounds as if you're lugging a dead body around behind you."

"A dead body? How absurd. Where would I get a dead body?"

Where, indeed? "I shudder to think, Miss MacLeod."

"It's not a dead body, but a bare foot." She lifted the hem of her skirts an inch. On one dainty foot was a half boot a size too large for her. The other foot was bare, her pink toes curling against the floorboards. "Cat's other half boot is in the shrubbery outside."

Of course it was. Where else would it be? Not on her foot, certainly. That would make too much sense.

He let out a beleaguered sigh. "Wait here. I'll fetch it."

He took more time than he should have poking through the shrubbery, but he finally found the blasted boot half buried among some thorny brambles a few paces away from the shore of Lochalsh. He plucked it up and returned to the cottage, the boot dangling from his fingers by the laces.

"Here. Either put this one on or take the other one off." He'd go mad if he had to listen to her thump and drag herself across the floor for the next three days.

"Thank you." She stepped into the boot, pulled the laces as tight as she could, then resumed marching from one end of Brodie's tiny cottage to the other, pausing every now and then to glance out the window, as if she expected Brodie would come riding up at any moment with her sister perched on the back of his horse.

She was sure to be disappointed. At the very least it would be another day before Brodie could possibly return, and that was assuming he didn't find anything of interest to keep him in Dunvegan.

As for Sorcha MacLeod, if she was still in Dunvegan, he hoped she had the good sense to stay well hidden, but it seemed unlikely. Good sense and Sorcha MacLeod didn't appear to be on speaking terms. She had wonderful survival instincts, though. The girl was thoughtless and reckless, but she was a fighter.

He'd wager his last penny that Keir and Sorcha MacLeod

were a long way from Dunvegan by now. Keir was no fool. He knew a lost cause when he saw one, and as far as Dunvegan was concerned, the MacLeod sisters were a lost cause.

He dropped down onto the settee, passing a hand over his eyes. The cut on his knuckles was oozing again, and the dressing was filthy and damp, but exhaustion was tugging at him. It could wait until he'd had another hour or so of sleep. He rolled onto his back, stretched his legs out as far as the settee would allow, and threw his arm over his eyes to block out the light.

Just another hour or so, and he'd be back to himself again. He drew in a deep breath and closed his eyes.

There, that would do. Yes, that would do quite nicely—

Thump, thump, thump . . .

"For God's sake, Miss MacLeod." He jerked upright again, his arm falling away. "Can't you keep still? You're making my head spin with that endless marching."

And thumping. Mustn't forget the thumping.

"I do beg your pardon, Mr. Ross, but we've been trapped inside this cottage for ages." She huffed, throwing her hands in the air. "I don't know how you can lie there with such equanimity. I feel as if the walls are closing in on me."

"It's only been a few hours." If she took another turn around the room, he'd go mad. She'd been at it since she woke, and the thud of her footsteps against the floorboards was echoing in his skull.

Good God, what was he going to do with her for four days?

The thudding stopped. "I'm sorry. I'll just look out the window, then."

"Good." He fell onto his back and stared up at the ceiling, waiting for sleep to take him, but his eyes remained stubbornly open.

Damn it, now it was too bloody quiet.

He struggled upright again, stifling a sigh. He'd promised Hamish he'd keep her safe. That was all. He'd never promised he'd keep her entertained, but here they were. "What do you do at home to keep yourself occupied?"

It was a predictable enough question, but she gave him an odd look, then turned abruptly away from the window to sit on the edge of the settee. "I read, and draw. I chat with my sisters and make orange marmalade. Not all that much, really. Nothing useful, in any case."

It had been the wrong question to ask, somehow. He wasn't sure why—it was an innocent question—but she'd gone still and was gazing into the fire with a forlorn expression on her face.

Damnation. He preferred the pacing.

"Brodie doesn't have any books?" He didn't ask about drawing paper or pencils. That was too much to hope for.

"Only the Bible, and a battered copy of Defoe's *Captain Singleton*." She sighed, dropping her chin onto her hand. "I don't fancy either."

"The Defoe would keep you occupied." Though it was a bit bloody for her tastes, perhaps.

"I don't care for books about piracy."

"But your father was a smuggler." The line between smuggling and piracy was an exceedingly thin one. He would have said this was a nearly universal opinion, but the flat look Miss MacLeod gave him said otherwise.

"A smuggler, yes. Not a pirate." Her chin rose. "My father didn't engage in extraneous violence, Mr. Ross, nor did he turn smuggler for his own gain."

"No. I suppose he didn't." One could say what they liked about Rory MacLeod, but he'd never been a common thief. There were some who claimed he was a hero. Callum wasn't one of them, but if Rory had been into smuggling for the money, Castle Cairncross wouldn't be crumbling to dust.

Rory had never been a wealthy man, and by the looks of things, he'd left his daughters destitute enough.

"Brodie does have a pack of playing cards," she offered after a moment, breaking the silence between them. "We could have a game."

"A game? You want to play cards with me?" She must be bored indeed if she was willing to overlook their differences for a paltry game of cards.

She made a great show of looking around. "Yes, with you, Mr. Ross. In case you didn't notice, we're here alone."

Oh, he'd noticed. He'd done nothing but notice since they'd stepped over the threshold three hours and twenty-six minutes ago.

"Well, then? Would you like to have a game, Mr. Ross?"

He didn't like it. Cards bored him. They were for aristocrats who had time and money to waste. Still, it would help to pass the time, and it would keep her from wearing a hole in Brodie's floors with all that pacing. "If I must."

"Really? Wonderful!" She let out a little squeal, jumped up to fetch the cards from a small wooden box on a shelf by the front door, then hurried back to the settee.

He sat up, taking care to leave a respectable length of cushion between them. "What game do you choose?"

"Whatever you like. Maw, perhaps? Or One and Thirty?"

"Those are wagering games, Miss MacLeod. Do you have any money?"

"Money?" Her face fell. "No, but perhaps we could play for something else?"

"Like what? What do you have that I might want, Miss MacLeod?"

Was that . . . it almost sounded like . . . good God, was he *teasing* her? How the devil had that happened? He wasn't a flirt, and neither was he a rogue. He wasn't charming enough to tease young ladies, particularly young ladies he didn't like that much.

He was as bored as she was, it seemed. There was no other explanation for his uncharacteristic, er . . . playfulness?

Dear God, the very word made him blanch.

"My sisters and I play for secrets." She gave a casual shrug, as if it made no difference at all to her whether he agreed to play or not, but she was nibbling on her lower lip, something she only did when she was plotting.

It was disturbing that he knew that about her, and a pity he hadn't realized it sooner. If he had, she wouldn't have made it out of the castle two nights ago. She'd nearly bitten her lip bloody when she'd pretended to sprain her ankle, the devious little chit.

"Secrets? Have you a great many secrets, Miss MacLeod?"

"Not a great many, no, but I have a few. Everyone has secrets, Mr. Ross."

He couldn't argue with that. Some of them had a great many more than a few.

"Mine aren't particularly interesting ones," she went on. "It's a pity you didn't kidnap Cat or Sorcha instead. They both have dozens of secrets, and each one more scandalous than the last."

"I didn't *kidnap* you, Miss MacLeod. I promised Lord—"

"Yes, yes. You promised Lord Ballantyne you'd look after me." She waved this away with a flick of her fingers. "I'm aware of that, Mr. Ross, but you must acknowledge that from my perspective, it feels very much like a kidnapping. Now, are we playing, or not?"

She gave him a hopeful look, and despite himself a grin tugged at his lips. Whatever had given Hamish the idea that Freya was the biddable sister? "We're playing. Shall we begin with One and Thirty?"

She cocked her head, considering it, then dealt them each two cards with their faces down, and a third one face up. "I prefer Bone Ace, if you're amenable. Look at that! You have three clubs to my queen of diamonds. You owe me a secret, Mr. Ross."

He stared down at the playing cards spread out atop the

trunk. "Why, Miss MacLeod, do I feel as if I've just stumbled into a notorious gaming hell?"

She gave him a demure smile. "I couldn't say."

By God, the chit was a card sharp. "I find that hard to believe."

"You may believe whatever you like, Mr. Ross, but it doesn't change a thing." She tapped a finger against her lip. "Now, what sort of burning secret can I compel you to divulge?"

"I don't have any secrets, Miss MacLeod."

It wasn't true, of course. He had dozens of them, each one deeper and darker than the last, but he didn't want Freya MacLeod in his head. She'd already worked her way under his skin, and that was bad enough without her getting a peek into his thoughts.

"As I already said, Mr. Ross, everyone has secrets." She leaned back against the settee and fixed him with that sharp green gaze. "But if yours are so dark and deep you'd rather not reveal them, we can play for truths instead."

She had an answer for everything. "Truths?"

"Yes. Whoever wins the hand may ask the other a question, and he—or she, as the case may be—must answer it truthfully."

"I see. But what's to stop me from lying to you?" She didn't know him well enough to distinguish his lies from his truths.

"Your own moral compass, Mr. Ross." She cast him a shrewd look, her eyes narrowed. "I'll know it if you lie. Your face will give you away."

Doubtful. He was an accomplished liar. "Very well. Ask your question."

She considered him for a moment. "All right, then. How long have you known Lord Ballantyne?"

That was her question? How dull. "That's hardly a secret, Miss MacLeod."

"We're not playing for secrets, Mr. Ross. We're playing for truths. Even so, you don't seem all that keen on sharing, so I thought we'd start slowly, and build up from there. Your answer, sir?"

It was a harmless enough question, considering what she might have asked him. "Since I was a child. So many years that I can't recall a time when I didn't know him."

"Your fathers were friends, I think?"

"Yes." A smile twitched at his lips. Wily chit. "But that's two questions, Miss MacLeod."

"So it is." She flipped over the two cards that were still face down, frowning when she turned over a six of clubs, then a nine of hearts. "Fifteen, dash it."

He turned over his own cards. "The king of spades, and the ace of clubs. That's twenty-one, Miss MacLeod. Now it's your turn to share a truth. Did you really twist your ankle the other day in the entryway?" He already knew she hadn't, but he wanted to hear her say it.

"No," she answered at once. "I feigned the entire episode, from the stumble to the injury. I rather regret smashing that teapot, if it's any consolation to you. It was one of my favorites."

"Ah, I thought as much, and you confess the truth without even a hint of a blush on your cheek. Have you no shame, Miss MacLeod?" He was certainly teasing her. Awkwardly and rather stupidly, yes, but teasing, nonetheless.

"That's two questions, Mr. Ross. You'll have to win another round to get your second answer." She gathered up the discarded cards and dealt them out, an impish smile twitching at her lips, but it vanished an instant later when she turned up a four of clubs to his queen of hearts. "Blast it."

"This game is more fun than I anticipated. My earlier question has already been asked and answered. You have no shame."

Her eyebrows flew up. "That's rather a hasty conclusion, I think. How have you reached it?"

"No blush, Miss MacLeod. It tells me all I need to know, and since I already have the truth, I reserve the right to ask a different question."

She let out a heavy sigh. "These underhanded tactics do you no credit, Mr. Ross, but very well. What is your question?"

"Why did you sneak out of the castle?" He'd wondered about it, more than once. She knew how dangerous it was, so why had she risked it?

"You're no longer asking for a truth, Mr. Ross." She toyed with the cards, not looking at him. "Now you're asking for my secrets."

He was, and that he wanted rather desperately to hear her answer meant he should never have asked the question at all. He shouldn't want to know Freya MacLeod's secrets, or anything else about her.

But it was too late now. "The question stands, Miss MacLeod."

He knew she'd gone to fetch her sister, of course. That was the truth of it, but like so many truths there were a dozen secrets hiding beneath it.

Still, she hesitated. "You've changed the rules of the game during the play, Mr. Ross. If we're to play with secrets, then I should be permitted to offer up a secret of my own choosing, as penalty."

"I don't see why. When the game began, I wasn't permitted to choose my truths. Anyway, it's far more diverting to play this way, don't you think?"

"It's more dangerous, certainly," she murmured, gathering up the cards.

"Danger is always diverting, Miss MacLeod. But you haven't answered my question. I'll have your secret, if you please."

"I'm afraid you've just wasted your question, Mr. Ross. It's no secret. Indeed, you already know the answer. I left the castle to go after Sorcha. She has a troubling habit of making the villagers . . . uncomfortable."

Uncomfortable? That was putting it in the most agreeable

terms. Half of Dunvegan believed the MacLeod sisters were a trio of wicked, redheaded witches.

It was absurd, of course, but a good number of the villagers believed it, and they especially believed it of Sorcha, who seemed to encourage rather than attempt to dispel their fears. "Does your sister make the villagers uncomfortable because they think she's a witch?"

Her hands went still on the cards.

It wasn't his turn. He had no right to ask her the question. He wouldn't blame her if she refused to answer him.

But that wasn't what she did. She was quiet for some time, but then she said, "It's not just Sorcha, Mr. Ross. There are those who think all three of us are witches. To hear them tell it, Cat spends her days brewing poisons in a witch's cauldron, and Sorcha can command the animals."

How curious, that she'd left herself out. "What of you, Miss MacLeod? What powers are you meant to have?"

"It's too ridiculous to even mention it."

"No doubt, but indulge me, if you would."

"For pity's sake. Since you insist, they think I can control the weather."

"The weather," he repeated. No, surely not.

"Yes. According to the rumors, I can summon thunder and lightning and control the wind and the rain with a twitch of my magical fingers. I did warn you it was ridiculous."

She had, but this? Good God. "Where did they get such an idea?" Surely anyone dull-witted enough to believe such a thing must lack the creativity to invent it.

"There was a sudden squall the night the first lugger sailed into Loch Dunvegan. Such squalls are common, but once the rumors of witchcraft started, the squall took on a mythical quality. It became a part of the narrative and was added to the tally of our sins."

"Ah, I see. Then you've been aware from the start that the villagers view you and your sisters with suspicion."

"They haven't been subtle about it, Mr. Ross. Of course I'm aware."

"But you went after your sister anyway, even knowing what they think of you. At night, alone. Weren't you afraid of what might happen?"

"Afraid?" She laughed, but there was no humor in it. "I'm always afraid, Mr. Ross. Every hour of every day."

Her answer bothered him, but why should it? He hardly knew her. Freya MacLeod's secrets and fears were no concern of his.

"Then why?" He tried to clamp down on the words, to catch them between his jaws and grind them down before he could say them, but they were out of his mouth before he could stop them. "Why did you go after her?"

She continued to busy herself with the cards, still avoiding his gaze. "You don't have any sisters or brothers, do you, Mr. Ross?"

"No." He had his mother. That was all. "Although I'm curious why you'd assume such a thing. Am I so transparent as that?"

"Transparent? You, Mr. Ross, are deceptively transparent, in the same way Loch Dunvegan is. It appears clear enough at first glance, but the truth lies far below that, invisible to the eye. The surface matters very little. It's what's invisible that makes it what it is."

That was . . . uncomfortably specific. "Very poetic, Miss MacLeod, but you didn't answer my question. Why would you assume I don't have siblings?"

"Because if you did, you never would have asked such a question." At last, she met his gaze, the cards in her hands forgotten. "There are different levels of fear. Have you ever noticed that? The truth, Mr. Ross, is that I *was* afraid to go after Sorcha that night, but I was more afraid of what might happen to her if I didn't."

She shrugged, as if this answer was the only one that made

any sense, as if it were obvious that love would always overrule fear, every time. It wasn't true. He'd seen men give up everything—their names, their legacies, and even their families—out of fear.

And here was this tiny bit of a lass, braver than all of them.

"Are you afraid of me, Freya?" Damn it, where did that question come from? He hadn't meant to ask it. How many times did he have to remind himself that her fears and hopes, her truths and secrets and worries had nothing to do with him.

He didn't even want to know the answer. He should stop this game, now. He'd only learn more about her if they kept on with it, and he already knew too much.

Already felt too much . . .

It wasn't a good idea to know her. There wasn't any room in his life for Freya MacLeod. There was hardly any room in it for him anymore.

But he'd asked the question, and it hung there, suspended between them.

"I was. That first day at the castle . . ." She trailed off, shaking her head.

It was no more than he'd expected, but her answer pierced him still, as if she'd plunged that dirk through his breastbone.

"But I'm not afraid of you anymore. Not since . . ." She glanced up at him, the blush that had been missing before now staining her cheeks.

He leaned forward. "Since?"

"Since you found me under my father's desk."

"You *stabbed* me, Miss MacLeod."

"I did, yes. I, ah, I beg your pardon for that. I thought you were one of the villagers who chased me through the wood. When I realized it was you, I was . . . relieved. I don't pretend I wanted to leave Castle Cairncross, Mr. Ross. I didn't." She met his gaze. "But I was glad you'd come for me. I realized then that I was no longer afraid of you."

She didn't seem to expect an answer. She gathered his cards

up, added them to the pack, and replaced the deck in the wooden box.

"Are we finished playing already?" He tried to keep his voice light, to offer her a smile, but something heavy had sprung to life between them, and he could see by the way she dropped her gaze again that she felt it, too.

"I think it's best, don't you?"

This was what came of telling secrets. "Perhaps it is."

They sat there for a moment, neither of them speaking a word, until he rose and crossed to the window to gaze out at the waning gray light. It must be nearly teatime, by now. "Are you hungry, Miss MacLeod? I can prepare tea for us."

"No, thank you. I find myself fatigued. I believe I'll see if I can sleep a bit more." She rose, but halfway across the room she turned back to him. "It was good of you to play cards with me, Mr. Ross. I know you didn't want to."

With that, she retreated to the bed, and buried herself in the blankets until not even the tip of her nose was peeking out, leaving him standing there, staring after her.

Why had he ever imagined she'd be the easier of the two younger MacLeod sisters? She wasn't as violent as her sister, no. She hadn't tried to behead him, after all. She wasn't the villainess Sorcha was, but she was . . . complicated.

Timid one moment, and too brave for her own good the next.

And sweet—that coaxing voice of hers could charm a bird from its nest—and yet for all the honey dripping from her tongue, there were barbs there, as well.

Thorny, sharp ones.

There was no rhyme or reason to Freya. She was one thing at one time, and in the next instant, the precise opposite of that thing. It made him wonder about her, and the last thing he needed was to be wondering about Freya MacLeod.

It would be far better for them both if he never thought of her at all.

Or looked at her. Or touched her.

He turned back to the window and listened to Brodie's clock tick off the quiet minutes one by one until her breaths turned deep and even. He crept closer to the bed, taking care not to wake her with the thud of his boots against the floor, and peered down at the unmoving pile of bedclothes in the middle of it.

All he could see was a mess of sheets and blankets, but he heard the soft sigh of her breath over the murmur of the waters of Lochalsh washing against the rocks at the edge of the coastline, and he caught a glimpse of a red-gold curl peeking out from under a thick blue blanket.

It would do him no good to become preoccupied with Freya MacLeod. Once he delivered her safely back into Hamish's keeping, he'd wash his hands of her.

Until then, another long, empty day stretched out before them tomorrow.

Chapter 12

Freya didn't suggest a game of cards the following day, nor the day after that.

There would be no more secrets or truths shared between them. Whatever madness had made her suggest it the first day had passed, and it was just as well.

Really, it was a great relief. Why, she couldn't be more thankful that their brief and ill-advised sojourn into intimacy had passed. It wouldn't do her any good to discover too much about Callum Ross.

It was better this way. Safer.

Why was she so despondent, then? It should have comforted her. Since her father's death and the arrival of the first lugger she'd wished for safety above all else, but it turned out Aesop had been right about wishes. One should be careful with them.

The Greeks were always right about such things.

But was there such a thing as too much safety? Wasn't safety in its most extreme form just another type of cowardice?

There was certainly such a thing as too much silence. If today had proved nothing else, it had proved that. Brodie had been gone for nearly three days now, but it felt as if it had been a lifetime, and now another long, torturous evening stretched out before them.

What was a lady meant to do with so much time? She'd slept, dined on the tea, bread, and cheese that Callum had produced from somewhere, and read the first hundred or so pages of *Captain Singleton* before tossing it aside in disgust.

What a dreadfully tedious book. Fate truly had cursed her, leaving her to fill all the endless hours with nothing to distract her but *Captain Singleton* and Callum Ross.

She despised the first, and the second . . .

She didn't despise him anymore, and that was a great pity, as it would be far easier if she did. Perhaps then she wouldn't mind that he hadn't said more than a dozen words to her in the past four hours.

She sneaked a quick peek at him. He was standing at the window watching the light fade from the sky as the sun dropped below the horizon. It was apparently the most fascinating sight he'd ever witnessed, because he'd been gazing at it for the past hour, his back to her.

She *may* have developed a worrying habit of peeking at him every now and again over these past few days. Out of curiosity, of course. Nothing more than that. Well, that and boredom. It wasn't as if she had anything better to do.

Very little had happened in the three days since they'd arrived at the cottage, yet somehow, everything had changed. Even the air between them felt charged now, heavy and crackling with portent, as if they were both waiting for something.

She'd caught him watching her half a dozen times today, but goodness only knew what he was thinking. He had the most inscrutable face she'd ever seen, like a pane of shattered glass, with a thousand distracting cracks running in every direction.

Every time she caught him staring, he turned abruptly away.

This was all her fault. It had been her idea to play cards—her idea to use truths as currency. It had seemed harmless enough at the time, but she should have left well enough alone. What had she been thinking, suggesting such a thing? She might have known truths would become secrets soon enough, and secrets . . . well, they were dangerous things, weren't they?

Revealing, that is.

If ever there were an idea she should have kept to herself, it was that one. She must have been mad, revealing herself to Callum Ross as she'd done. He wasn't one of her sisters, for goodness' sake.

She took up the discarded *Captain Singleton* again, but soon enough she was peeking at him over the top edge of her book.

Despite his complaints about her pacing yesterday, he'd spent the better part of the afternoon marching from one end of the cottage to the other, like an animal an instant away from bursting through the bars of his cage.

A lion, or perhaps a bear. Something of that sort. Something large and exceedingly sturdy.

He wore only his breeches and a loose white linen shirt, having stripped off his coat and waistcoat, and abandoned them in an untidy bundle on one of the kitchen chairs.

It was all rather shocking, really. She'd never seen a gentleman in just his shirtsleeves before. Well, that wasn't quite true. She'd seen Lord Ballantyne in a state of undress, but it didn't count because he'd been unconscious at the time, on account of Cat having poisoned him with monkshood.

There'd been nothing titillating about Lord Ballantyne's, er . . . dishabille.

But Callum Ross in just his shirtsleeves? That was a sight that was equal parts titillating and distressing. He was . . . well, there was no sense in pretending, was there? He was an exceptionally well-proportioned man, with his broad shoulders and a pair of long, muscular legs, set off to perfection by the tight fit of his breeches.

There wasn't an inch of padding anywhere as far as she could tell, and she'd made a thorough study of the matter over the past three days.

Her gaze drifted lower, pausing to admire his trim waist before drifting lower still, to his, er . . . his backside. She'd never paid any attention to a gentleman's backside before, but it must be said that *his* backside had earned a considerable amount of her attention today.

Far more than was ladylike.

That was the titillating part.

Whoever would have guessed a backside could prove so fascinating? Not she. Was the fact that she'd never given a man's backside a moment's attention merely from a lack of exposure to backsides, or was it that Callum Ross had a more, er . . . distracting backside than every other gentleman she'd ever encountered?

She already knew the answer.

There was no denying the obvious. He was attractive.

That was the distressing part. What sort of lady ogled the backside of the man who'd kidnapped her? Except he hadn't truly kidnapped her, blast him. He'd rescued her, and at rather grave risk to himself.

She dragged her gaze away from him, her cheeks heating. Dear God, even another go at *Captain Singleton* would be better than leering at Callum Ross and thinking thoughts she had much better not be thinking.

This was all the fault of that blasted card game! This had been ever so much easier when she found him terrifying, but there was no going back now. Apparently, once a lady noticed a gentleman, she couldn't *unnotice* him.

Someone should have warned her.

She'd do well to forget all about Callum Ross, and his backside. His front side as well, for that matter. She snatched up the book and trained her gaze resolutely on the page, picking up where she'd left off earlier. Captain Singleton and his crew had just landed on the continent of Africa.

Surely, Mr. Defoe had something interesting to say about Africa?

But alas, no. After endless pages of description of the animals Captain Singleton and his crew hunted, killed, and then ate, the pages began to blur before her eyes. She didn't fight it when the book slipped from her hands but laid her cheek against the settee and drifted off to sleep.

She hadn't been dozing for long when the squeak of the cottage door opening woke her. She sat up, rubbing her eyes.

The window was now dark. The sun had set at last.

Callum was standing in the open doorway. Oh, no. Was he leaving her here alone? Sneaking away, while she was sleeping? She could hardly blame him if he was. Goodness knew she'd caused him enough trouble.

It was that dratted card game! Prying into his secrets must have been the last straw for him. She struggled upright, her heart lurching into her throat. "Mr. Ross? Where are you going?"

"You're awake." He gave her an oddly formal nod. "I won't be gone for long. I thought I'd have a quick swim in Lochalsh."

"Oh." Now that he said it, she saw he had a length of rough towel in one hand, and a homemade bar of soap in the other.

He wasn't leaving her then, thank goodness. Relief rushed over her, but there was dismay there, too. Since when had Callum Ross become so indispensable to her? Only five days ago she'd despised the very sight of the man.

"You mean to say you're going to . . ." She waved a hand at him in a sweeping gesture that incorporated his every inch, from the top of his head to the toes of his boots. "To swim without clothing on?"

Dear God. There'd be a riot if the matrons of Kyleakin got a look at his bare backside.

His eyebrows shot up. "Well, it wouldn't be nearly as satisfying to bathe with my clothing *on*, would it? My boots, in particular."

His boots? He was worried about his boots, and not the miles of smooth, bare skin he was about to unleash on the unsuspecting population of Kyleakin?

"You needn't be worried about my modesty, Miss MacLeod," he added, a grin twitching at his lips. "There's a deep pool hidden amongst the trees nearby obscured on one side by an outcropping of rock. It's protected, and it's dark enough now that no one will see me."

"A swim in a deep pool, hidden amongst the trees and rocks?"

My, that did sound tempting. Heavenly, in fact. Between the fire, the escape from Castle Cairncross, and the mad dash from Dunvegan to Kyleakin, her body was sticky with dirt, sweat, and grit. "Isn't it dreadfully cold, though?"

Not cold enough to dissuade him, it seemed, because he merely shrugged. "I don't intend to linger over it."

"No, I don't suppose so." She scratched the back of her neck, which was suddenly itchy. No doubt it was all the filth from the road. Her scalp was coated with it, her fingernails crusted with it, and every time she turned her head she caught the acrid scent of smoke from the fire at Stewart's stables. It was embedded in her hair, her clothing. "Is it very far away?"

"No. Only a fifteen-minute walk from here." He crossed his arms over his wide chest, eyeing her with one of his inscrutable expressions, although if she had to take a guess, she'd say he was caught somewhere between suspicion and amusement.

"A bath sounds delightful." She eyed him back, waiting. Surely, he wouldn't be so cruel as to scurry off to his own bath, and deny her the same opportunity?

Except he was that cruel, because the next words out of his mouth were, "I can see what you're plotting, and you may put it out of your mind at once. You can't come with me, Miss MacLeod."

She crossed her own arms, glaring back at him. "Whyever not? What's the harm in it?"

"It isn't proper."

Proper? Surely they'd left "proper" behind them by now? If a lady couldn't indulge in a little impropriety under these trying circumstances, when could she? "It's proper for you to strip down to nothing for a bath, but improper for me to do so?"

Perhaps "strip down" wasn't the best way to phrase it, as it conjured up an exceedingly inappropriate mental image of him tearing his clothing off.

"Yes. That's precisely the case." He was looking at her as if she'd lost her wits. "You're a young lady, Miss MacLeod. Young ladies don't bathe unclothed in the out-of-doors."

For pity's sake. After everything that had happened—the fire, the chase through the woods, the mob of villagers with their torches, and his bloody knuckles—he'd made up his mind to insist on the strictest propriety in *this*?

She tossed her blankets aside, rose to her feet, and faced him with her hands planted on her hips. "What nonsense. You just told me it was private. That the darkness and the trees and rocks would hide you from the neighbors' prying eyes. Will they not hide me, as well?"

"You . . . I . . ." He dragged a hand through his hair and muttered, "It's not the neighbors' prying eyes I'm worried about."

What did that mean? If he wasn't concerned about the neighbors, then who . . .

Oh. *Oh*.

Heat sparked through her, the flush of it rising from her chest into her cheeks, but now he'd tempted her with thoughts of a bath, she couldn't let it go.

Really, this was all his own fault. "Please, Mr. Ross?" She folded her hands under her chin. "I won't remove my clothing. I promise it."

He raised an eyebrow. "You're going to bathe with your clothes on? How do you propose to do that?"

"I won't bathe. I'll just . . . wade. There won't be a need for me to remove any of my clothing then. Only my boots. Does that satisfy your sense of female propriety?"

"No, but I can see there's no point in arguing with you." He strode over to the stand that held Brodie's washbasin and plucked up another length of toweling from the shelf underneath it. "Here. Take this."

"Thank you!" She darted across the room, took the towel from him, and followed him out the door before he could change his mind.

"This way." He took her down a rough pathway that led behind the cottage and into a stand of trees, away from the shores of Lochalsh. "Stay close, Miss MacLeod. It's dark, and it will get darker still as we get deeper into the woods."

She followed close on his heels, and it was a good thing, because the darkness was as thick as it was in Dunvegan Wood. The inky blackness pressed against her, so penetrating all she could see was the dull glow of his white shirt in front of her as they made their way down a series of connected pathways.

Left, then right, then left again, and under a low gathering of branches. Sunlight was a stranger to this quiet place, the moss so lush the ground was like a carpet of furred green under their feet.

She heard the water before she saw it, a gentle splash some short distance ahead of them, but she was not prepared for the sight that awaited her when at last the trees opened, and they emerged on the edge of a small, deep pool, the black water reflecting a slice of moon visible in the night sky above them.

"My goodness, how pretty," she breathed in a whisper, because such an ethereal place deserved a hushed voice. "It's a bit like the fairy pools in Glenbrittle." She'd only been there once, years ago, but she'd never forgotten it.

Callum didn't reply, but for the first time since she'd laid eyes on him the day he'd come marching up Castle Cairncross's drive she could read what he felt on his face, because he was taking no pains to hide it.

Admiration, even reverence for the beautiful place spread out before them. There was a stillness to him she'd never seen before, a peacefulness in his expression that was . . . well, it was a flattering look on him. Far better than his usual scowl and the care and worry that had drawn a line between his brows.

"Do you see the weeping willow tree, just there?" He nodded

toward a tree a few paces to their left. It was a large one, perhaps the largest willow she'd ever seen, with long, graceful branches drooping down low enough some of them trailed in the water.

"I do, indeed. I don't see how I could miss it. It must be lovely in the summer, when the leaves are green." They were a dark golden brown now, and still rather pretty, but subdued.

"The pool is shallower on the other side of the willow, but more than deep enough for wading. That's all you intend to do, isn't it, Miss MacLeod? Wade, that is."

"Yes, yes, of course." She waved an impatient hand at him. She'd already said so, hadn't she? Though now she was here, she was far more tempted to swim than she had been before she saw the pool.

"Good. That's your wading pool, then, on the other side of the willow. I'll remain here, on this side, and allow you your privacy."

And preserve his own, too, of course, but it wasn't as if she was going to peek at him, as tempting as it might be. Although now the idea was in her head . . . no, no, it wouldn't do, the mystery of his bare backside notwithstanding.

A lady didn't *peep*, for pity's sake.

"Fifteen minutes only, Miss MacLeod," he called, vanishing into the darkness on his side of the willow. "You'd best make haste."

Miss MacLeod did not make haste. Not if he could judge by the playful splashing coming from the other side of the willow, and the long, satisfied sigh that followed.

Only Freya MacLeod could find a way to wade *seductively*.

His cock rose to attention, searching for the source of that delightful sound. He pressed the heel of his hand hard against it, willing it to deflate, but after three days trapped in a tiny cottage with little to do but gaze at *her*, the troublesome organ persisted.

Stubborn appendages, cocks, but a plunge into the icy water would discourage it quickly enough. With a low curse, he stripped off his shirt and breeches, tossed them over a branch near the side of the pool, and jumped in, gasping as the freezing water closed over his head.

God above, but it was *cold*. So cold it snatched the breath from his lungs and sent his blood rushing through his veins. The water quenched his ardor, but it was a temporary reprieve only.

It didn't matter what she was doing. Even the most mundane tasks—sleeping, eating, reading—took on a new eroticism when Freya MacLeod engaged in them. He kept still when she slept so he could listen to the soft, steady rise and fall of her breath. If she drank a cup of tea or ate a bit of bread, he became mesmerized by her mouth, and his lips quirked in a helpless grin whenever she rolled her eyes over *Captain Singleton*.

She was stealing his wits with one breath, one bite, one page at a time.

It was maddening. *She* was maddening, and the devil of it was, she wasn't even trying to catch his attention. She hadn't the least idea how alluring she was, or how tempting he found her.

Which, of course, only made her more so.

Unless he hadn't been as stealthy as he thought. She'd caught him staring at her a few times, but where another lady might have preened, she seemed more baffled by it than anything else.

But not nearly as baffled as he was. How had this happened? He'd hardly noticed her that first day at Castle Cairncross. He'd overlooked her so thoroughly Hamish had been obliged to remind him there was a third MacLeod sister.

There was no overlooking her now. No looking past her, either, and with each day that passed Brodie's cottage seemed to grow smaller, the walls closer, the space between him and Freya narrower, and narrower . . .

Another splash came from her side of the willow, then another one, louder this time and followed by a laugh that was pure joy, a laugh that floated through the swaying branches of the willow, a laugh he felt as surely as a warm palm caressing his cold flesh, leaving a trail of fire in its wake.

She was utterly enchanting, damn her.

He stifled a groan. It had been a mistake, bringing her to the pool. She was altogether too close, and he was altogether too naked, but it took a stronger man than him to resist the plea in those big green eyes.

The sooner they returned to the cottage, the better. He wouldn't find much relief there, but at least he'd be dressed, and his cock tucked chastely into the tight confines of his breeches. "You have five more minutes, Miss MacLeod."

The splashing stopped. "Is that all? It feels as if we just got here."

"Five minutes." He snatched up the lump of soap and began a vigorous scrubbing, the flesh of his arms and chest burning under the punishing assault. "And not a bloody minute longer," he muttered to himself, like the bad-tempered devil he was.

He ran the soap over the rest of his body, between his toes and between his legs. His cock had given up the fight and retreated, and just as well. Perhaps it would do the gentlemanly thing and stay there until he returned Freya to Hamish.

He scrubbed the past four days of dirt and grime from his hair, dunked his head under the water, then surfaced and gave a vigorous shake, sending water droplets in every direction.

There was a great deal of splashing coming from the other side of the willow. Far too much splashing for a lady who'd promised she'd only wade. "What are you doing over there, Miss MacLeod? Because from here, it sounds like you're swimming."

The splashing stopped. There was a long pause, then, "Swimming? No, indeed, Mr. Ross. Of course not. I promised I wouldn't."

She'd promised, yes, but perhaps she was as susceptible to temptation as he was. He'd soon find out. He rose from the pool, shivering, and made quick work of drying himself and donning his clothes.

He half expected to find a soaking wet water nymph on the other side of the willow, but when he emerged from the branches he found Freya standing on the bank of the pool, fully clothed, and with a demure smile on her face. "Look at the sky, Cal—er, I mean, Mr. Ross. You can see Cassiopeia."

"Who?"

"Cassiopeia, Queen of Ethiopia. She was Andromeda's mother." She pointed at the sky. "Just there above her and to the left is Ursa Minor."

He followed the gesture and drew in a sharp breath. Millions of stars were suspended in the velvety darkness above them, more stars than he'd ever seen before, as if someone had tossed a handful of diamonds into the air, and they'd remained where they landed, winking and twinkling with joy at their sudden freedom.

"Cepheus is to their right," she murmured. "Do you see that sort of elongated triangle? That's Cepheus. He was Cassiopeia's husband, and Andromeda's father."

He gazed into the sky, trying to find the shapes she pointed out amidst the infinite pinpricks of light. "How do you know so much about the stars?"

"My father taught me when I was a girl." She turned to him, the moonlight catching the golden strands hidden amongst the red of her hair. "Did no one ever teach you about the constellations?"

They hadn't. No one had ever taught him much of anything. His mother had done the best she could for him, but she was a midwife and had been gone a good deal of the time, earning their bread. He'd spent much of his childhood alone.

"Draco is just there, to the left of Cassiopeia, above Ursa Minor. See his tail?" She traced the shape with her finger. "He was a dragon, but I've always thought he looked more like a serpent, with that long, pointed tail."

"I don't know how you can find him, with so many stars."

She was quiet, but he felt her shift beside him, the warm weight of her gaze like fingertips stroking his skin. "The North Star, Mr. Ross. If you ever get lost, search for the North Star. You can find all the constellations from there."

He turned to her, so pale and beautiful with the starlight on her damp skin. He traced his finger from the soft skin behind her ear down her neck, chasing an errant drop of water glittering in the moonlight and catching it on his fingertip. "What's this, Miss MacLeod?"

She had gone swimming, the minx.

"Don't tell me you broke your promise." He traced his fingertip over the hollow at the base of her throat, leaving a damp trail across her skin before touching the loose hair at the end of her braid. "Ah. Wet, just as I thought. Shame on you, Freya."

But there was no anger in his voice. He'd intended it as a mild scold, but it came out low and throaty, a caress more than a reproach.

"I—I beg your pardon." She gazed at him, her eyes deep, mysterious shadows in the perfect oval of her face. "It seems I'm not as good at resisting temptation as I imagined."

He stared at her for a long moment, his throat working. He had no right to touch her, no right to kiss her, but here, under the stars with the moonlight shining down on them like a blessing, there was nothing in the world that could stop him from tasting her.

Surely, Fate brought them here. Who was he, to argue with Fate?

He touched his palm to her cheek and drew her closer, closer, until his mouth was hovering over hers, only a breath away from her parted lips.

"Neither am I," he whispered, just before his mouth found hers.

Chapter 13

It was a moment made for a kiss.

Here, in the moonlight with Callum, with the slender branches of the willow tree sighing around them, Freya couldn't have denied him any more than she could deny the moon its glow, or the stars their shimmer.

Who was she, to argue with Fate? Because somehow they'd been destined to find themselves in this magical place, his lips finding their way to hers.

"Freya." He cupped her cheek in his broad palm, his voice a husky whisper.

He touched her with a gentleness that should have been impossible in such a big, rough man—a gentleness she hadn't sensed in him until this strange, hushed moment between them, his fingertips careful as they brushed the sensitive shell of her ear. A shiver coursed through her, her breath catching as his hand drifted lower. He explored her as if he'd imagined touching her everywhere, learning every aching inch of her skin.

Then slowly, oh so slowly he drew closer and pressed a small, chaste kiss on one corner of her mouth, then the other. His skin was cool from the water, but his mouth was warm, the imprint of his kiss lingering like a brand on her skin.

And dear God, how could such a small kiss make her heart pound with such frantic abandon? Her blood was racing, her heart throbbing as if she'd been running through Dunvegan Wood for miles.

"Freya," he murmured again, both a plea and a warning in his voice, his breath hot against her ear. His hand dropped away, and he stood before her quietly, waiting.

Waiting for her. Whatever she decided, he'd accept it. She could turn him away, and he'd go without question. She *should* turn him away.

That's what a proper young lady would do. The magic that surrounded them—the moonlight and the stars twinkling above them—didn't change the rules of propriety. A respectable young lady didn't kiss a gentleman she hardly knew, and one she wasn't sure she trusted.

But what had propriety ever done for her? She'd been plagued by smugglers these four months and more. People who'd once been her friends had turned on her. Half of Dunvegan believed her to be a witch. She'd lost her father and both of her sisters, and she'd been driven from her beloved castle.

She'd lost her home.

All her restraint, all her prudence hadn't saved her from any of it. For months now, she'd been tiptoeing through her life, startling at every shadow in her path and quailing at every sound.

She'd locked herself up inside her castle and shut herself away from the world, and for what? None of it had kept her safe. It had only made her lonely. And she was tired, so tired of losing things. Just this once, she wanted to take something for herself.

She didn't turn Callum away. Instead, she reached for him, letting her curious fingertips wander over the back of his neck. The ends of his hair were wet still, and droplets of cold water fell on the back of her hand.

"Do you want this, Freya?" He drew back, his gray eyes lost in the shadows of the willow branches moving across his face. "Do you want me?"

She did. She did want him.

She'd never kissed a gentleman before, yet she knew the ache in her lower belly, the insistent tug between her legs was desire.

Because she'd dreamed of this, hadn't she? In the privacy of the darkened cottage, burrowed deep into the blankets on Brodie's bed, hadn't she imagined how Callum's lips might taste, and imagined the slide of his skin under her fingertips?

She had. A dozen times over, in dream after dream, some waking, and some sleeping. Ever since they arrived at the cottage, she'd fallen asleep to the imagined brush of his lips over hers, his hands in her hair, his warm palm against her throat—dreams so real they were more like memories.

Impossible, yes. She couldn't remember something she'd never had.

But she could have it now. All she had to do was reach out and take it.

What good ever came of fighting against fate? It would have you in the end, one way or another, and she didn't *want* to fight this. She wanted to sink into it, just as she'd sunk into the pool of water beside them, and let it envelop her.

"Yes." Tentatively, her hand trembling, she reached for him and lay her hand against his cheek, a secret thrill rushing through her at the prickle of his emerging beard against her palm. "Please, Callum."

He went still, but then the tight control that had been holding him back snapped loose. A low groan fell from his lips, and then he was there, close against her, pressing soft, sweet kisses to her temples, her eyebrows, and even the tip of her nose.

And then . . . then he returned to her mouth, and dear God, had anything ever felt as good as the wicked tip of his tongue teasing at the seam of her lips, urging her to part for him?

She didn't think. She didn't reason. She simply gave herself over to it, opening her lips to him even as her cheeks burned. "I've never . . . I don't know how to . . . like this?" Goodness, was this how gentlemen kissed?

"Yes, Freya." He chuckled, the warm drift of his breath

against her mouth tearing a sigh from her throat. "Just like that."

He eased her against the slender trunk of the tree at her back and pressed closer, the long length of his body so tight against hers she could feel the strength in him, the tenseness in his muscles, the heat and desire he held ruthlessly at bay as he touched her with the care one took with something that was precious to them.

He stroked his thumb over her cheekbone before sliding his rough palm down her neck, his fingers lingering at the pulse point fluttering there. "May I kiss you here?"

"Yes." She rose to her tiptoes, a desperate whimper on her lips. God . . . dear God, she'd never imagined a kiss from a man could taste so sweet and so wild at once, like the wild cherries that grew in the hedgerows at home.

She'd always loved those cherries, the way the sweetness lingered on her tongue.

She twined her arms around his neck and pressed closer, and it was strange that she could be so much smaller than him, yet their bodies could align so perfectly. It was as if she had been made for him, his hard angles fitting her soft hollows like a hand sliding into a glove.

"So pretty." He traced the outline of her mouth, catching her lower lip between his thumb and forefinger and giving it a gentle, teasing tug before leaning close and pressing a soft kiss there. His tongue lingered for an instant, probing at that tender skin until her fingers tightened in his hair, a wordless plea falling from her lips.

It didn't make sense, that inarticulate plea, but he understood it, and it seemed to release something in him, to free the desire he'd been holding in check, his big body trembling with the effort. Then his mouth was on hers, more demanding this time, his tongue hot and slick and devastating as he conquered every inch of her mouth, filling all the lonely places she'd never known were inside her until he touched them, and made them his.

He groaned as she met his every stroke, every caress of his tongue and lips, so sweet she wanted to lose herself in it, drown in it. Her heart fluttered with it, her head swam with it, her knees weakening with every touch of his fingers, every caress of his tongue.

And after all she'd endured—the smugglers, the fire, the wrath of the villagers—would it be his kiss that would make her swoon, at last?

He kissed her, then kissed her again, their tongues twining, his hands sinking into her hair as he plundered her, his hot tongue stroking and teasing into every recess of her mouth, searching for every hidden corner of sweetness there.

And he found them. He found them all, and it was so heady, his kiss, the wicked, tempting glide of his tongue against hers. How had she never known a man's kiss could steal her breath, her thoughts, her reason?

Or was it only Callum's kisses that tasted so sweet? Each brush of his tongue was like kindling laid on a fire, until the sparks between them caught and burst into a flame, setting every part of her alight.

"God, Freya." He dragged his hands down her back to her hips and held her there as his mouth played over her throat, his tongue tracing her pulse point before his hot lips slid lower, dropping kisses onto her collarbones and the tops of her breasts.

A sensuous languor spread through her, moving from the depths of her quivering belly into her chest, her nipples stiffening with the slow heat of it. Her eyelids felt heavy, her eyes dropping closed under the weight of them.

"Callum." A whimper tore from her chest. "Please, I . . ." Dear God, she didn't even know what she was begging for.

But he did. He knew, and he gave it to her, gave her everything, his big hands moving in restless strokes over her hips as he caught her soft sighs and whimpers on his tongue. "So sweet, Freya. The sweetest thing I've ever tasted."

Sweet? No. There wasn't a word for what this was. There

were only sounds—his deep groans and her wordless pleas, their breath mingling—and sensations—the heat of him against her, his strong thighs pressing into her belly, the desire pulsing deep inside her.

This was madness. Pure madness, his mouth on hers, and like all madnesses it would have to stop.

Soon, soon, soon . . .

But not yet. No, not yet.

She nipped his lower lip, her teeth sinking into the plump flesh, teasing and goading him at once, because she wanted more—she wanted everything—the rough drag of his hands over every inch of her, the heavy weight of his body on top of hers, and . . . and . . .

She didn't know! She understood what happened between a man and a woman. Her sisters had explained it to her, but they'd never explained *this*, the desire that set her alight, the searing heat that arose in the wake of his every caress, the emptiness he'd awakened deep inside her, an emptiness only he could fill.

There was no explaining this. There was only feeling it.

Her desire made her frantic, a wildness surging inside her with such fury she didn't recognize herself. She didn't know this Freya, the strong, fearless Freya she became when she was in his arms, a woman who took what she wanted with no hesitation, and no apology.

She pressed her lips to his neck, licking up the drop of water she found there before taking his earlobe into her mouth and sinking her teeth into it.

"Ah!" The sharp cry fell from his lips at her tiny bite, another groan rumbling in his throat as she moved her hands over the powerful line of his back, tracing his spine and then sliding lower, and lower still until she was cupping his backside in her palms.

"Freya." He tore his lips from hers and pressed his face into the arch between her shoulder and neck, his panting breath hot against her skin. "We shouldn't . . . we can't—"

But they could. They *were*.

"No. Don't stop, Callum." She hardly recognized her own voice, the huskiness of it, the breathlessness, the low, pleading note throbbing there, but surely she'd sink lifeless to the ground if he stopped? "Not yet."

He growled against the quivering skin of her neck, tightening his fingers around her waist and pressing her more firmly against the tree trunk at her back. "You want my touch? Tell me. Tell me you want me, Freya."

"Yes." She arched her back, pressing closer, her breasts brushing against the hard wall of his chest. "I want you, Callum."

Desire. Yes, that was what this was, the sensation swelling in her belly and between her legs, the tingling at the tips of her breasts. This was what it was to want a man.

How had she ever thought she could give this up?

But she had. What man, after all, would ever want her, a lady rumored to be a witch, in his bed? No man she could think of, or even one she could imagine. So, she'd given up on desire before she'd ever had a chance to taste it.

Yet here he was, holding her in his arms, when he was the last man in the world she ever thought she could want. That her first taste of desire should be with him—*for* him—was . . . well, desire was a strange thing, wasn't it?

A few short days ago she could never have imagined such a thing, could never have imagined kissing him, touching him—but it was right, somehow, as if this moment between them, this madness here in the moonlight with him—had been written in the stars since the beginning of time.

How could it feel like this, otherwise? How could she want him so much, with everything inside her, every beat of her heart?

He wasn't hers. He could never be hers. She knew that. Of course she knew. She'd known it from the start, even as she welcomed his kiss, his touch. But she hadn't known that it could feel like *this*. Like she was dying and coming to life at the same time.

How could she?

Would it feel like this with any man? Or was it only him?

What if it was only Callum, and she never found her way into his arms again? What then? What if this was her one chance to ever feel this way, and the memory of this kiss had to last her an entire lifetime?

She couldn't give it up. Not yet.

He clasped her face in his hands and gazed down at her, a shock of his silky dark hair tumbling over his forehead. "We can't . . . this isn't the place, Freya. I should never have. . . ." He broke off, shaking his head. "We should go back to the cottage now."

Her fists loosened in his damp shirt, cold reality chasing the delicious fog of desire that had enveloped her.

He was right, of course. Yes, they should go back.

She stepped away from him, a chill rushing through her at the loss of his heat. Perhaps he saw it on her face, because he caught her hands, pulled her close, and pressed a chaste kiss to her forehead. "I beg your pardon, Freya. This was . . . a mistake."

A mistake. That was plain enough, wasn't it? He didn't want her.

She withdrew her hands and gave him a shaky smile. It hadn't felt like a mistake to her. It had felt utterly and inexplicably right, but he hadn't been as affected as she had.

But then he must have kissed dozens of young ladies. There was nothing special about her. She simply happened to be here, that was all. She might have been any young lady. Aside from his rumpled hair and kiss-reddened lips, he was every inch the stern, distant Callum Ross again, the man with the cool gray eyes and unsmiling mouth.

Meanwhile she was still trembling, her knees wobbly and weak under her skirts.

A moment made for a kiss . . .

And it had been. But it had been *only* a moment.

"There's no need to beg my pardon, Mr. Ross." She attempted a smile, but it felt stiff on her face, so she gave it up, turning away to fetch her towel and what was left of the lump of soap he'd given her. "Shall we go back to the cottage now?"

He didn't move. "I don't think you understand. I—"

"It's quite all right, Mr. Ross. No explanations are necessary. I'd like to return now, if that's agreeable to you. I'm rather cold, with my wet hair."

He gazed down at her without speaking, but after a few awkward moments of staring at each other, he nodded. "Of course. We'll return the same way we came. Stay on the pathway and follow me."

Well, he'd made one devil of a mess of that, hadn't he?

He could see what she was thinking. Freya was no dissembler. He could read her as easily as he could a page in a book.

Her every thought, her every feeling was there in her face, her eyes.

Confusion, anger, embarrassment, and finally . . . shame.

He'd made her *ashamed* of herself. Ashamed, after she'd kissed him with such sweetness his throat was still aching with it. He'd never felt less alone than he had in the brief moments she'd been in his arms.

And this was how he'd repaid her for it.

She thought he didn't want her. He'd been panting over her only moments ago, delirious with desire for her, but she was an innocent, young and naïve.

What did Freya MacLeod know of a man's desires?

Not a blessed thing.

But he had no such excuse. He'd known what he was doing when he'd taken her into his arms and kissed her, and he'd done it anyway. Even now it was taking every bit of willpower he possessed not to take her lips again, to hold her in his arms and kiss her until she understood how badly he wanted her.

But it was better this way. Freya MacLeod wasn't for him.

Except she had been, for just those few stolen moments. When he'd been holding her against him, she'd been entirely his. She'd trembled so sweetly then, soft pleas and whimpers falling from her lips.

But it was a moment out of time, one never to be repeated. Nothing could come of this madness between them, and he wouldn't hurt her, not for the world.

She'd been hurt enough.

So, he pressed forward through the trees, the soft shuffle of her footsteps behind him. It was the longest walk of his life, but at last they reached the end of the pathway and emerged from the wood.

He saw the light as soon as they broke through the trees.

"Wait." He held out his arm to stop Freya from moving forward, watching as the light bobbed in the darkness. Someone with a lantern in their hand was moving about near the cove behind the cottage, where Brodie kept the small fishing boat he used to ferry passengers across Lochalsh.

"What is it?" Freya asked, a hint of breathlessness in her voice.

He nodded toward the lantern light. "There's someone out behind the cottage, near the boats."

"It must be Brodie, mustn't it?"

It stood to reason, yes, but the thread of uncertainty in her voice echoed his own doubts. If it was Brodie, why hadn't he entered the cottage? What was he doing at the cove, messing about with the boat?

Unless it wasn't Brodie.

"Who else would it be, but for Brodie?"

"Nobody we want to see. Just wait, lass. We're about to find out."

Whoever it was had turned away from the shoreline, the lantern light still bobbing with their every step as they made their way back toward the cottage.

"Get back." He caught Freya's arm and urged her backward,

into the shelter of the trees. It was almost certainly Brodie, but he didn't have a weapon to hand, so it was best to be cautious.

They stood and listened to the thud of the man's boots as he hurried from the cove back toward the cottage, until at last he was close enough the muted rays of the lantern revealed Brodie's familiar features.

"It's all right." He seized Freya's hand and urged her out from under the cover of the trees. "It is Brodie."

But it wasn't all right. He knew it as soon as he got a closer look at Brodie's face. The lad was tired, but that was hardly a surprise. Kyleakin to Dunvegan and back in three days was a hard ride, but it wasn't the lines of exhaustion marking his youthful friend's face that had Callum stopping in his tracks.

It was the fear.

"Brodie?" He lurched forward, tugging Freya along behind him, suddenly unwilling to leave her by herself even for a moment. "What is it? What's happened?"

"Callum. Thank God." Brodie hurried toward them. "I thought they'd somehow gotten past me when I found the cottage empty."

"They?" Freya's fingers dug into his arm. "Who are *they*?"

Brodie glanced at him, a warning in his eyes, but Callum nodded. Whatever it was, Freya had a right to know about it.

"There are men following me." Brodie let out a breath. "Wily ones, too. I didn't notice them until I'd gotten past Luib."

"Who are they?" But he already knew enough. The men, whoever they were, hadn't followed Brodie from Luib.

They'd followed him from Dunvegan. Nothing else made sense. Somehow, these men had not only worked out that there was a connection between him and Brodie, but they also knew Callum had Freya MacLeod with him.

And now they were coming after her.

"Thief-takers. Two of them." Brodie cast a stricken glance at Freya. "The villagers of Dunvegan got a reward together on behalf of Clyde Stewart. There are villains crawling all over Dunvegan and the surrounding area, looking for Miss MacLeod, and Miss Sorcha MacLeod."

Villains, indeed. Thief-takers were cunning, ruthless, and notoriously corrupt. They were the worst sorts of scoundrels, and they'd follow Freya to the end of the earth if they believed there was money to make from catching her. No good would come of one of them getting their greedy hands on Freya or Sorcha.

But that wasn't even the worst of it.

There was only one reason a pair of thief-takers would chase Freya from Dunvegan all the way to Kyleakin, a journey of nearly forty miles. No one bothered to come so far in pursuit of an innocent lady.

"Clyde Stewart. Is he—"

"Missing. Presumed dead. His body hasn't turned up, which is curious, given he's believed to have perished in the fire, but the good citizens of Dunvegan don't seem to be bothered by that small detail."

Callum heard what Brodie wasn't saying. Freya and Sorcha were wanted for the murder of Clyde Stewart, with or without his body. It wouldn't hold up legally, but that wouldn't stop the thief-takers the villagers had sent after Freya.

"I saw the two scoundrels who followed me here at Baird's Pub on the High Street a day ago. I recognized them again when they turned up in Luib. They've been behind me since then, and not far behind, neither."

"They chased you all the way from Dunvegan?" Freya's voice was faint, and all the color had drained from her face.

"Aye." Brodie glanced at her, then shifted his gaze to Callum. "You haven't got much time, Callum. You and the lass need to get into the boat and get away from Skye, now."

"Wait." Freya released Callum's arm and took a step toward Brodie. "My sister, Brodie. Is there any word of my sister Sorcha?"

"No. They haven't been able to find her. She's still missing, and Mr. Dunn with her."

"Thank God," Freya whispered, even as she sagged against

him, her face as pale as a ghost in the dim light from the lantern. "Thank God."

Callum laid a hand on her arm, steadying her, then turned back to Brodie. "What about Castle Cairncross? Has anyone been there?"

"No, not that I saw. I watched for a day and night, and didn't see anyone come or go. The place is deserted."

"And the villagers, Brodie," Freya asked. "Are they—"

"I beg your pardon, Miss MacLeod, but there isn't time for this." Brodie cast an anxious glance toward the road that led down to the shoreline. "You need to go. If the thief-takers catch up to you on this side of the Loch—"

"They won't." Brodie was right. They needed to leave, *now*. Once they crossed Lochalsh, they'd be safe enough. Their pursuers would have to wait until the morning to secure another boat. By the time they got across, he and Freya would be long gone, and the thief-takers would have no way of knowing which direction they'd taken.

They'd lose themselves in the Highlands quickly enough. He'd make sure of it.

"Take Miss MacLeod down to the boat, and see her settled, Brodie. I'll fetch our things from the cottage and meet you down there." He didn't wait for her reply, but ran up the pathway to the cottage, gathered their belongings, and ran back down again.

Freya was seated on the wooden plank at the front of Brodie's tiny fishing boat, her hands braced on either side of her, her knuckles white. She was as still as a statue, and so pale his chest tightened at the sight of her.

"Here, lass. Take this." He draped her cloak around her shoulders and pulled it snugly against her throat. "It's two miles across Lochalsh to the other side. It'll take an hour or so for me to row us across, and it's going to be cold, so keep your cloak buttoned, all right?"

She nodded, her green eyes huge in her white face. If she was ever going to fall into a swoon it would be now, but she had enough presence of mind to reach out and take Brodie's hand. "Thank you. I won't forget the kindness you've shown me."

Brodie blushed up to the roots of his hair, but he gave her hand an awkward pat. "You take care of yourself now, Miss MacLeod."

She nodded, then turned to Callum. "I'm ready."

Before he climbed into the boat, Callum took Brodie aside. "Those men from Dunvegan," he began, speaking in a low voice so Freya wouldn't hear him. "If they should try and harass you—"

"Let them try." Brodie's chin hitched up, and his dark eyes turned fierce. "They can't do anything to me. I haven't done anything wrong."

No, he hadn't, but neither had Freya. It didn't matter much to a thief-taker whether their quarry was guilty, or not. "You may want to go up to McCrory's place for the night, just the same. You'll be safer there with him and his brothers."

Brodie scoffed. "I don't need McCrory's protection. I can take care of myself, Callum."

"I know it, but I'd feel better if you went. I don't want you to come to any harm, lad."

Brodie huffed and rolled his eyes, but he nodded. "Fine. I'll go to bloody McCrory's."

"Good man." Callum squeezed his shoulder, then climbed aboard the boat, seating himself on the center plank, facing Freya. "I'll see Angus brings the boat back over to you tomorrow."

"Good enough."

Callum took up the oars, but he hesitated before putting them into the water. "You've done us a good turn, Brodie. I'm in your debt."

Brodie snorted. "You were in my debt before this." He waved his hand toward the open water of the loch. "Now go, while you still can."

So, they went, the loch as smooth as glass, the moonlight catching the drops of water coming off the oars as he took them away from Skye.

Away from Dunvegan, and Castle Cairncross.

Freya stared straight ahead as he rowed them across Lochalsh, her gaze fixed on the shores of Kyle of Lochalsh in the distance.

In the hour it took for them to reach the other side, she never spoke a word.

Chapter 14

Kildary, Scotland

It shouldn't have been as easy as it was to leave the Isle of Skye behind.

There should have been a squall as they crossed Lochalsh, with dark clouds above them and roiling waters below. There should have been lashing rain and violent winds that threatened to turn the boat over and send them tumbling into the sea.

Something. It was the first time she'd ever left Skye, and it shouldn't have happened with so little sense of occasion. It wasn't right that she could leave her home and her sisters behind with no more fanfare than lacing up her boots or brushing her hair.

They reached Balnagown Castle on the evening of their third day of travel. There was a significant distance between the Kyle of Lochalsh and Kildary—nearly eighty-five miles—and Callum had taken a circuitous route to confuse any thief-takers who'd decided the bounty on her head was worth a chase through the Highlands.

The journey should have taken longer than it did, but Fate had been on their side, the fickle creature, much as she had been when they'd crossed Lochalsh. Fate, who'd declined to interfere in her family's favor these past months, had made quick work of Freya this time.

Balnagown Castle was not what she expected. That she'd expected anything at all was rather a surprise. After three days traveling on horseback with nothing but a silent Callum Ross to distract her, she hadn't thought of much of anything aside from the increasing ache in her backside.

And Sorcha. She'd thought of Sorcha, and Cat, and Cairncross Castle.

Her home had never been as far from her as it was now, and the loss of it was an ache inside her, an empty, throbbing ache where her heart had once been.

But when she caught her first glimpse of Balnagown Castle as they approached, she sat up with a gasp.

This was the seat of Clan Ross, one of the most powerful clans in Scotland? This was the home of Callum Ross, a man so grave, so solemn he looked as if he'd emerged fully grown from one of those horrid, Gothic castles, like Athena from Zeus's head.

He should have been the product of dark gray stone with sharp, pointy turrets and a foreboding slab of thick, iron-studded oak in place of the front door.

A castle like Castle Cairncross, in fact.

But this? No, surely not. "*This* is Balnagown Castle?"

For the first time since they'd left Strathpeffer this morning, Callum spared her a glance. "Do you see another castle about, lass?"

Her eyebrows rose. My, someone was a bit touchy about his castle, wasn't he? She considered her companion from her place in the saddle. He'd dismounted and was standing in the neatly graveled drive with a scowl on his face so fearsome it was a wonder it hadn't chased the birds from the trees.

And trees there were, each more picturesque than the last, what was left of their summer leaves fluttering in the breeze. The white stone castle was nestled amongst all this perfection with such flawless symmetry one could almost believe the hand of God himself had placed it there.

There were turrets and battlements, and all manner of castle-like appendages, but it was more of a manor house than a proper castle, despite the tower rising from its center. There was a lovely wilderness on the eastern side of the castle, and beyond it, formal gardens with a view of Balnagown River to the north. From there, lush parklands stretched out in every direction, as far as she could see.

Why, even the sky itself didn't dare frown on such a place. It arched overhead, the blue of the day giving way to the setting sun. It tinted the sea of puffy white clouds a brilliant pink as it sank below the horizon.

It was nearly winter in Scotland, and winter meant rain, but dark, dreary rain clouds wouldn't do for Balnagown Castle, it seemed. Never in a thousand years would she have imagined a man like Callum Ross could come from a fairy-tale castle such as this.

"It's delightful, isn't it?" Indeed, she'd never seen a prettier place in her life.

"Delightful," he repeated, his tone flat, as if it were the last word he'd use to describe it, and his brow lowered even farther, if such a thing were possible. "If you like," he muttered, adding a grunt for good measure.

God above, that scowl. He'd been wearing it for the better part of the last day, and she was weary of the sight of it. He was spoiling the vision in front of her with that derisive twist of his lips, and that grunt didn't help, either.

If she never heard that blasted grunt again, it would be too soon.

She hadn't wanted to come here, and she didn't wish to be here now. During their three days of travel, she hadn't once ceased thinking of Sorcha and the threat of the thief-takers hanging over her head, but for the first time since they'd left Dunvegan behind, her heart lifted.

Just a touch. A lovely castle didn't solve any of her problems—

they'd all be waiting for her when she left here—but it was difficult to believe anything dreadful would befall her in such a place as this.

It was too beautiful for that.

Perhaps all might yet be well. Callum was a grunting, stone-faced menace, to be sure, but he *was* a man of his word. He'd return her to Dunvegan when the danger had passed, and Cat and Lord Ballantyne would see to it that no harm would come to Sorcha.

They would, because anything else was unthinkable.

Her home wasn't lost to her. Not yet.

But until she could return to it . . . well, perhaps she'd make a friend or two here. It had been so lonely at Castle Cairncross these past few months, ever since the smugglers started coming. Surely, only the most agreeable people lived in such an enchanting castle as—

"Hell and damnation. What the devil are you doing back here so soon?"

Her head jerked up. A man was standing in the open door of the fairy-tale castle. He was nearly as big as Callum, and had the same dark hair, but despite his handsome face, he was hardly the prince such a castle deserved. His arms were crossed tightly over his chest, and a scowl dark enough to rival Callum's sat on his lips.

A scowl he made no effort to hide.

It deepened as he took in Freya, carving a groove into his forehead and the sides of his cheeks. He was a young man, about Callum's age, or perhaps a little younger. Certainly not more than twenty-seven years or so, but his cold expression made him look older.

He abandoned his slouch against the doorframe and strolled down the steps, joining them in the drive. "You made quick work of your business in Dunvegan. We didn't expect you for another few weeks, at least."

"Plans change."

It was hardly an explanation, but Callum didn't elaborate. He left it there, the insultingly short reply making it clear he didn't intend to explain himself.

"So I see." The man came toward them, taking in Freya with a pair of watchful blue eyes as he came closer. "Who's the lass?"

"My name is Freya MacLeod," she said, before Callum could speak. "I'm the daughter of Rory MacLeod, of Clan MacLeod," she added, lifting her chin as she spoke her father's name.

The man's blue eyes widened slightly. He'd recognized the name.

It wasn't surprising. There weren't many people in Scotland who hadn't heard of the infamous smuggler Rory MacLeod, but if this scowling gentleman was surprised to find a MacLeod in his front drive, he got over it quickly enough. "Is that so? And what are you doing at Balnagown Castle, Freya MacLeod?"

What, indeed? It was a simple enough question, but one without an easy answer. She'd spent the past three days wondering how she'd account for her presence when they arrived here, but alas, she hadn't come up with a satisfactory explanation. Only some creative stories, all of which were designed to hide the ugliest parts of the truth.

Lies, in other words, but she'd always been hopeless at lying, and when she opened her mouth, the truth tumbled out. Or a version of it, at any rate. "Certain, er . . . unexpected circumstances made it necessary for me to leave my home in Dunvegan. Mr. Ross took me away and brought me here."

The man's eyebrows rose. "What, you mean to say he *kidnapped* you?"

It had felt that way to her at the time, and goodness knows Callum had been high-handed enough about the business, but despite how cross she was with him, she couldn't bring herself to hurl such an accusation.

Not because of the kiss they'd shared, of course. Why, she'd hardly given their kiss a single thought these past few days. No, she wasn't such a fool as to let a handful of sweet words and a few careless kisses cloud her mind.

But because Callum hadn't had any other choice but to take her away from Dunvegan, and to claim otherwise was a lie. "No, I don't mean to say that at all." She held the man's eyes. "I went with Mr. Ross willingly. It wasn't a kidnapping."

It had been a rescue, and a heroic one, at that. He hadn't done it for her, but because of the promise he'd made to Lord Ballantyne, but in the end his reasons didn't make a bit of difference.

Not to her.

If he hadn't been the one to find her that night, if it had been one of the men from the village who'd pulled her out from under that desk . . . a shudder raced down her spine and the hairs on the back of her neck stood upright.

They would have found her, one way or another. That night, or perhaps the following day. They wouldn't have given up until they did. They would have torn the castle apart, and perhaps not only the castle. They might have torn her apart right along with it, but for Callum, and that was what she told the man with the angry blue eyes. "Mr. Ross saved my life."

It had been nothing less than that, and she wouldn't ever forget it.

"That's our courageous laird." The man's lips curled. "Ever the hero, eh, Callum?"

She glanced at Callum, startled by the bitter note in the man's voice, and found those disconcerting gray eyes on her. She had the oddest sensation that he could see through her, right through her skin to her blood and bones, and the pounding heart hidden inside her breast.

He contemplated her for a long moment, his gray eyes unreadable, then just as quickly dismissed her. "It wasn't a kidnapping, although in the end, perhaps it amounts to much the same thing."

She frowned at him. It wasn't the same thing at all, and she opened her mouth to say so, but Callum had already turned away from her, and from that point on, he ignored her entirely, instead turning his attention to the man.

"My mother is here, James?"

The man's lips tightened. "Aye, she's here."

"Good. Fetch Willis to see to the horse, and summon Mrs. Doherty as well, to assist Miss MacLeod." Callum didn't wait for a reply, but tossed the reins to James, who reached instinctively to catch them.

Everyone obeyed Callum Ross's orders, it seemed.

Whether they wished to, or not.

Callum reached for her then, closed his hands around her waist, and without so much as a by-your-leave, lifted her down from the horse, depositing her in the graveled drive in her too big half boots, keeping one hand wrapped around her upper arm.

Her right foot had fallen asleep, and her legs threatened to buckle beneath her after such a long time on horseback, but she disentangled herself from his hold and straightened her shoulders.

What in the world was happening? Instead of the welcome Callum should have received, a strange tension crackled between the two men. James was still scowling, his hands now clenched into fists around the reins, and Callum had gone rigid beside her.

But she had little time to wonder about it, because Callum was already marching her toward the arched front door, leaving James in the drive, staring after them.

It was such a pretty place. With its gleaming white stone and the lush greenery of the land surrounding it, it looked like something out of a storybook.

But with her every step toward the door, her uneasiness grew. For all its beauty, there was something amiss at Balnagown Castle.

* * *

"What I don't understand, Callum, is why you brought her *here*."

God above, here it came. That hadn't taken long, had it? His arse had hardly had a chance to touch his seat before James burst through his study door and threw himself onto one of the chairs in front of the desk.

"By all means, James, make yourself at home."

James arched an eyebrow. "Did you suppose I'd do otherwise, Callum?"

"Damned if I know what you're going to do anymore, James."

He thought he'd known, once, but then he'd thought they were friends once, too. Good friends, even, but that had been when he and his mother had first arrived at Balnagown Castle, nearly a year ago.

God, was that all? It seemed like a lifetime had passed since then.

As it turned out, he and James *hadn't* become friends. Whatever feeble chance there'd been of it had withered on the vine a few months ago, and it had yet to recover.

He didn't know what they were now. Not friends, but not quite enemies, either.

He stared at the glass in his hand. Only a moment ago it had been filled with a generous measure of whisky, but now only a few drops of amber liquid remained in the bottom of the glass.

"Well, Callum? What were you thinking, bringing Rory MacLeod's daughter here? Don't we have trouble enough?"

We? Was the trouble theirs now? Just before he'd left for Dunvegan just over a week ago, James had made a point of letting him know his problems were his, and his alone.

He downed his second glass of whisky in one swallow and resisted the urge to reach for the bottle again. "What would you have had me do with her, James? Toss her into Loch Dunvegan?"

"No, of course not, but surely there must have been someone there who could look after her. Some friend of the family?"

"Not according to Ballantyne."

James snorted. "Ah, Ballantyne. Of course. I might have known he had a hand in this. You should know better than to trust an English aristocrat, Callum."

"Ballantyne's been a good friend to me." Callum met James's gaze. "Loyal."

His point wasn't lost on James, but he didn't rise to the bait, instead snatching up the bottle of whisky and pouring himself a generous measure.

Just as well, really. God knew there was nothing to say that hadn't already been said a dozen times over. They drank in silence, and for a few moments Callum could almost convince himself it was just the same as it had been when he'd first come here.

"Pretty girl, Miss MacLeod." James tossed back his whisky and set the glass on the desk. "What did she say her first name was, again?"

"Freya." Freya MacLeod. Her name was going to haunt him well after she returned to Dunvegan. Whoever would have thought such a tiny lass could throw his life into such disarray?

He reached for the bottle again, even as the whisky he'd just downed was still burning his throat. It was going to take more than a few wee drams to erase the memory of sharing a saddle with her these last three days, her curved bottom nestled snugly between his thighs.

If ever there was a lass who could drive a man to drink, it was Freya MacLeod.

"Too damn pretty, by half." James was watching him, his

blue eyes seeing in an instant everything Callum was trying to hide. "If she'd been plain it might not matter, but that face? That face is going to cause trouble, Callum."

That face, those eyes, that hair, those lips, and that was to say nothing of that shapely bottom. "Do you think I don't know that, James? The girl's life was in danger. There was no way I could leave her in Dunvegan."

If there had been a way, he'd have found it.

"Tensions are high amongst the clan members right now, Callum. I don't need to tell you that things are . . . delicate."

Delicate. That was a polite way of putting it. A more appropriate word would be "disastrous." "No, but you're telling me anyway, aren't you?"

He rose, abandoning his empty glass on his desk, and wandered over to the window. His back ached like the devil, an after-effect of keeping himself relentlessly upright in the saddle, so no, er . . . unfortunate parts of his anatomy happened to brush against any part of Freya MacLeod's.

"What are you going to tell Lorna?" James reached for the bottle and poured himself another dram. "Or are you pretending you didn't notice how attractive Freya MacLeod is?"

"I admit she's not entirely unpleasant to look at." If one admired long, thick red hair, green eyes the same shade as new spring leaves, and smooth, pale skin.

All that, and an arse like a work of art.

God, he needed another whisky.

"Not entirely unpleasant?" James snorted. "High praise, indeed. And here I thought you'd try and convince me you never spare a glance for any other ladies since you became betrothed."

"I'm not betrothed." He wasn't, not yet, but he may as well be. The thing was as good as done. But of course he'd noticed Freya. Any man with eyes in his head would notice her.

"Perhaps not yet. I don't know what you're waiting for. Alistair Niven made his wishes perfectly clear. Why don't you just get on with it?"

James knew well enough why he wasn't yet betrothed to Lorna Niven, despite her father's final wishes.

Because he didn't love her. Not the way a man was meant to love the lady he married.

And because James *did*.

For all that he spoke casually, James couldn't hide the pain in his voice. Callum heard it, as surely as he saw the bleakness in his friend's eyes.

Former friend, that is. He'd made a mistake, telling James about the betrothal. No one else at the castle knew of it aside from Lorna, not even his mother. But in a weak moment he'd confided the truth to James, and that confession had marked the beginning of the end of their friendship.

Callum turned away from the window. "You know why."

James had been staring into his empty glass, but now he looked up, his gaze meeting Callum's. A long silence unfolded between them, but what was there left to say? Alistair had made his wishes plain, just as James had said.

Despite the man's good intentions, Alistair had made a bloody mess of everything.

Finally, James looked away with a shrug. "The marriage is what's best for the clan."

Was it? Alistair Niven had certainly thought so, but Callum wasn't so sure. Marriages were one way to bridge the divide between feuding clan members, and had been for centuries, but the chasm that had separated Clan Ross since Culloden was as deep as it was wide.

"We've got another problem, as well," James added, setting his empty glass down on the edge of the desk.

Of course they did. There was no end to the problems. "We?"

James rolled his eyes. "Yes, *we*. God knows you'll cock it up if I leave it to you, if you haven't already."

Callum smothered a sigh and returned to the chair behind his desk. In some ways, it would be a great relief if he did cock it up, and beyond the fixing of it. "What's the problem now?"

"I should think that was obvious. You've spent the past week alone with Freya MacLeod—a lady not lacking in personal charms—traveling here from Dunvegan. At a guess, I'd say Lorna isn't going to be pleased about it."

Right. *That*. Lorna wasn't the sort of lady to rush to conclusions—she was far too sensible for that—but it was a delicate business and destined to become more so. "I don't know what you'd have me do, James. I promised Ballantyne I'd look after Freya. I wasn't going to leave her in Dunvegan to be torn apart by that mob that was after her."

"Mob? What did that little slip of a thing do to get a mob after her? It can't be because of her father. Rory MacLeod is much beloved by the Scots, especially on Skye."

"It's nothing to do with Rory. Not entirely, although the villagers didn't care much for the swarm of smugglers invading Dunvegan's shoreline after he passed."

Whether that treasure would ever be found, or if there even was such a treasure, was anyone's guess. Ballantyne seemed to think there was, though, and he trusted his friend's judgment.

Or he would have, if Hamish didn't happen to be madly in love with the eldest MacLeod sister, Catriona. Love made a man stupid, and Ballantyne had been besotted with the lady. He'd thought his friend was a damned fool at the time, but that was before he'd kissed Freya MacLeod.

It made more sense now.

"Smugglers?" James's eyes went wide. "Good Lord. How do the smugglers come into it?"

Callum propped his feet on top of his desk, heedless of the dust and mud on his boots. He was too exhausted to care. "It's a long story, and it's not mine to tell." God knew the less that was said about that business, the better.

Especially the part about the MacLeod sisters being suspected of witchcraft. He'd rather keep that information from his mother, whose protective instincts would rush to the fore if she found out about the, er . . . alleged witchery.

He couldn't blame her for it. As a midwife, she'd battled similar suspicions, but this business was already complicated enough, without her interference.

"Freya's here now," he went on. "There's nothing I can do about it but do my best to make sure her presence causes as little fuss as possible before she can be safely returned to Ballantyne's care."

James settled back in his chair, his narrowed gaze on Callum's face. "Is that all, then?"

Callum let out a mirthless laugh. "Isn't that enough?"

"I was just wondering if you were going to confess to the rest of it." James shrugged, but his shrewd blue eyes were flinty.

"I have no idea what you're talking about."

"No?" James leaned forward.

Damn it. He knew that look. It didn't bode well for him. "No."

"I'm talking about the fact that you're besotted with Freya MacLeod. Not that I blame you. There's no denying the lady is fetching."

"I'm not *besotted* with her." That is, he did spend quite a lot of time thinking about her. Watching her, too. It was difficult to tear his gaze away from her. He'd dreamed about her last night, as well, about those stolen kisses under the willow tree.

But none of that meant he was besotted with her. He desired her, yes, just as he had other ladies before her. There was no denying she lingered in his mind in a way none of the other ladies had, but that was only because they'd hardly spent a minute out of each other's company over the last week.

But besotted? The very idea was absurd.

"Very well, Callum, if you say so, but I suggest you stay as far away from Miss MacLeod as you possibly can while she's here. Lorna's not a fool."

No, she wasn't. But *could* he keep away from Freya? Could he live here in the same castle with her without talking to her, or gazing at her, or God forbid, kissing her again?

It was going to be a long, torturous few weeks.

Perhaps he'd have that third drink, after all. He snatched up the whisky bottle, poured the last of it into his glass, and swallowed the whole of it in one go.

James watched, a small smile on his lips. "I hope we've got plenty of whisky."

Chapter 15

Freya had lived more of her life these past nine days than she had during the entire year.

Nine days. It had been nine days since Callum Ross arrived at Castle Cairncross. Nine short days since he'd come marching up her front drive as if her castle belonged to him, and nothing had been the same since then.

Nine days, and in that time she'd witnessed a fire, lost a sister, been chased through the woods by a vengeful, torch-wielding mob, stabbed a laird, and been kissed for the first time.

And what a kiss it had been!

That one kiss had destroyed all her peace. She couldn't say whether that made the kiss a good one or a bad one, having never been kissed before, but it had certainly been a momentous one.

She touched her fingertips to her mouth. Every time she thought about that kiss her lips tingled, as if Callum were still kissing her, their breath still mingling. It was almost as if his lips had left an indelible imprint on her own.

After such a thrilling week, one would think a lady would fall asleep the instant her head touched the pillow and that she'd remain that way throughout the night with nary a twitch, but she'd woken hours ago to a still silent castle and darkness outside her bedchamber window.

Living, as it turned out, was apt to rob a lady of her sleep.

Her mind, the troublesome thing that it was, had insisted upon reliving the events of the last nine days, both the good and the bad, and once her busy brain had started to turn, her eyes had refused to close again.

She lay on her back atop the soft, comfortable bed Mrs. Doherty, Balnagown Castle's housekeeper, had taken her to yesterday evening, and daydreamed away the hours until the sun rose, chasing away the darkness outside her window and ushering in the cool morning light.

Last night, she'd dreamed of . . . nothing. Nothing of any consequence.

And if a few hazy fragments were still floating in her mind—a pair of gray eyes reflecting the moonlight, a big, rough hand toying with a lock of her hair—well, a lady couldn't control her dreams, could she?

That was the lovely thing about dreams. One might commit all sorts of scandalous acts in a dream, and escape accountability for every single one of them.

But her dreams had fled in the morning light, as all dreams did, taking sleep with them.

She tossed the covers aside, rose from the bed, and made her way to the window. Her bedchamber was at the back of the castle, where the land dropped down in a steep, grassy slope to a wooded valley below. From here she could see the blue ribbon of Balnagown River winding through the hills and valleys of Easter Ross.

It was nothing like the view from her bedchamber window at home. Loch Dunvegan was magnificent, but even on those days when the water lay as still as a sheet of glass it was a fierce and dramatic sight to behold, one dominated by gray light and tempestuous waves crashing against jagged rocks.

It was breathtaking, but it had none of Balnagown Castle's serenity.

It soothed something inside her, something so small and so deeply buried she hadn't realized it was agitated until it ceased fluttering. What must it be like to wake every morning and find nothing but calmness outside your window?

The valley would be a lovely place to walk, especially in the spring when the green of the new season overtook the drab winter brown.

She gazed out at the slender band of blue water winding through the trees until her stomach began to grumble. There was no sense in putting it off, was there? She'd have to go downstairs eventually, if only to keep from starving.

It wasn't that she was afraid to face Callum, of course, it was just . . . well, the kiss made it all a bit awkward. What did a lady say to a gentleman who'd kissed her so thoroughly?

If she knew the answer to that question, the ride from the Kyle of Lochalsh to Kildary wouldn't have been as silent as it was. In those two and a half days of hard riding, she and Callum hadn't exchanged more than three dozen sentences.

Perhaps less.

Neither of them had breathed a word about the kiss.

It was as if it hadn't happened. Or it would have been, if there hadn't been something new between them now, a heavy, pulsing awareness so tangible it was almost as if she could dig her fingers into it, clutch it in her hands.

But while she'd spent the entire two and a half days of their journey bouncing between nervousness and giddiness, Callum hadn't seemed to even notice the tension between them.

Perhaps kisses were different for gentlemen? Yes, that must be it. He'd likely already put it out of his mind. For him, it must have been a small, insignificant thing. No doubt he'd forgotten all about it. Why, he probably kissed ladies like that all the time, and never gave it a second thought.

If he could get past it, then so could she. It was just one kiss, after all, but if it hadn't been her first kiss, she likely would have put it out of her mind by now, too. It wasn't as if it had meant anything to her.

Right, then. She'd just march downstairs, greet Callum as

coolly as she would a distant acquaintance, and see if there was any breakfast to be had.

She turned away from the window, squaring her shoulders, but a few steps from the bedchamber door she caught a glimpse of her reflection in the looking glass above the dressing table and stopped.

She couldn't go downstairs like *this*.

She was still wearing the night rail Mrs. Doherty had given her yesterday. That esteemed lady had cast a scandalized glance at the limp, creased dress she'd been wearing since she left Dunvegan, and snatched it up and made away with it.

But she hadn't yet brought anything in its place. Aside from Cat's cloak, which had somehow escaped Mrs. Doherty's hawkish gaze, she didn't have a stitch of clothing to her name.

She plopped down on the edge of the bed, the bravery of only moments ago deserting her. What if they'd all forgotten she was here? What would she do then? It would be dreadfully awkward if she appeared in the breakfast room in her filthy cloak and—

"Miss MacLeod?" A low knock sounded at the door. "Miss MacLeod, are you awake?"

She froze, darting a stricken glance at the bedchamber door. They hadn't forgotten her, then. A wave of shyness came over her, and for one wild moment she had an absurd urge to dart into the clothes press, or scurry under the bed.

"Miss MacLeod? I've come to take you down to the dining room for breakfast."

Oh, dear. Now she'd have to go down, wouldn't she?

As if in answer, her stomach let out another urgent growl.

She rose from the bed, gathered the neckline of her night rail snugly around her neck, and tiptoed toward the door. Her hand hovered over the knob, but then she grasped it and threw it open with a touch too much force before her cowardliness could get the better of her.

"Oh!" The lady on the other side of the door took a step backward, blinking in surprise. "I see you are very much awake, after all."

"I—yes." For pity's sake, why could she never act normal around strangers? "I beg your pardon."

"Why, don't be silly, child. You've no need to beg my pardon for anything." The lady cocked her head, studying her for an instant before giving a decisive nod. "Well, well, it's just as I suspected. You're a wee bit out of sorts, aren't you?"

"Perhaps a little, yes."

"Ah, well, it's not surprising, after such a long journey." For her part, the lady didn't seem at all surprised to find the laird had brought a stray young woman to their castle. Perhaps he made a habit of adopting waifs.

And kissing them.

"I'm Aila Ross." The lady paused, then added, "Callum's mother."

His *mother*? Callum hadn't said a word to her about his mother being here. Although now she thought of it, he hadn't said much of anything at all about Balnagown Castle, or its inhabitants.

It was a bit odd, but Callum wasn't a chatty sort of gentleman.

"Well, never mind. You'll settle in soon enough. Might I come in?" Mrs. Ross held up her arm. Several day dresses, a shawl, and a few other bits and pieces were draped over it. "I've brought a few things for you."

"Yes! Yes, please do come in." Freya opened the door wider and stood back. "This is so kind of you."

"It's nothing at all, lass." Mrs. Ross swept into the bedchamber and laid her bundle of clothing on the bed. "Callum said there wasn't time for you to fetch anything from Dunvegan to bring with you."

"Er, no." What else had Callum told his mother about Dunvegan? Had he mentioned that she'd been driven out on the point of a pitchfork? Or close enough to it, in any case.

Aila Ross cast a measuring eye over Freya, then plucked a green day dress from the pile. "Shall we start with this?"

Freya fingered a fold of the green dress. It had been ages since she'd had a new dress, and this was a lovely spring green one, with a darker green ribbon trim at the waist and the hem of the skirt. It was a fine garment, made of soft, thick cotton. "It's very pretty."

Mrs. Ross held the dress up in front of her. "Yes, I think it will do nicely. It looks as if it will fit, and the color is very nice with your green eyes and red hair." She pressed the gown into Freya's hands. "The dressing room is just through there. Go ahead and change, and I'll fasten the buttons for you."

Freya took the dress and did as she was bid, quickly exchanging her borrowed night rail for the borrowed gown, then reappeared in the bedchamber, awkwardly smoothing the skirts.

"Oh, yes. That will do." Mrs. Ross beckoned her closer. "Come here, and I'll do up your buttons for you."

Once again, Freya did as she was told, and stood quietly as Aila Ross fastened the row of tiny buttons at the back of the dress, then turned her around with her hands on Freya's shoulders. "There! My, don't you look pretty. Your hair, though . . ." She tsked, shaking her head.

Freya's hand shot to her head, a despairing groan leaving her lips when she felt the tangle of curls. "I must look a fright."

"Not at all, Miss MacLeod." Mrs. Ross gave her a kind smile, steered her over to the dressing table, and pressed her gently down into the chair in front of the looking glass. "It just wants a little brushing, that's all."

Freya peeked at Mrs. Ross from under her lashes as she ran the brush through her hair.

Callum looked very much like his mother. Mrs. Ross didn't have his intense gray eyes—hers were a soft, dreamy blue—but they both had the same thick, dark hair, and there was a similarity to their features, especially around the jaw and mouth.

Although Mrs. Ross smiled more than Callum did. At least, she smiled at Freya as she brushed out the tangled locks of her hair, but she didn't hurry through the task. She worked through each curl with her fingertips before attempting to untangle the strands with the brush.

How long had it been since someone had brushed her hair for her?

Years.

Her mother had taken great pride tending to her daughters' thick red curls. After she died, Cat had helped her for a time, expertly wielding hairpins and brush to tame the red-gold ringlets until Freya was old enough to do it herself.

She watched Mrs. Ross's hands in the mirror, her graceful movements as she started at the root and dragged the brush down, down, down until she reached the final upturned curl at the end of each lock of hair, then set it over Freya's shoulder before starting on the next one.

Then, to her utter shame and humiliation, tears sprang to her eyes.

She wasn't going to start weeping, was she?

Nothing in the world could be more awkward than giving way to the tears pressing behind her eyelids, all because Aila Ross was kind enough to brush her hair? But try as she might, her eyes were blurring with them, and her nose was stinging, and . . .

Mrs. Ross's hand stilled, the brush going lax between her fingers. She didn't speak, but she met Freya's eyes in the mirror, then deliberately set the brush aside, and laid her hands on Freya's shoulders. "Callum tells me that you've had, ah . . . quite a trying time of it this past week."

Freya sniffled, but after some effort, she managed a watery, "Yes. My sister Sorcha is—"

That was as far as she got before she broke off, because the truth was, she hadn't the first idea how to finish that sentence. "I don't know where she is."

Dear God, what must Mrs. Ross think of her? She'd shown up at this delightful castle looking half wild without a stitch of clothing to her name, and now she'd burst into tears over her lost sister.

But if Mrs. Ross was scandalized, she hid it well. "You poor thing. Callum said that there was some sort of trouble in Dunvegan. A gentleman's stables caught on fire?"

"Yes, and we—my sister Sorcha and I—happened to be there at the time, and the villagers think we had something to do with it." A flush rose her in her cheeks, and she dropped her gaze to her lap.

She had nothing to be ashamed of. She hadn't done anything wrong, but even so the shame always seemed to be there, lurking just under the surface.

"That is unfortunate, Miss MacLeod, but why would they blame—"

"Because they think we're witches," Freya blurted, then slapped a hand over her mouth, the reflection of her green eyes in the looking glass wide with horror.

Of all the things she might have said, why had *that* been what spilled from her lips? Mrs. Ross was sure to be horrified by that confession. She'd be well within her rights to bludgeon Freya with the hairbrush, then order her from Balnagown Castle at once.

"Witches?" Mrs. Ross lifted one dark eyebrow. "How curious that Callum didn't mention that."

No, he wouldn't have, would he? No clan wanted to welcome a witch into their midst, and if the witchery weren't bad enough, she was also suspected of arson and murder! She'd brought a world of trouble down upon Clan Ross simply by her presence here.

"I believe they used to say the same about your mother. About the witchcraft, I mean." Mrs. Ross's voice was calm, conversational even, and there wasn't a hint of accusation in the blue eyes that met Freya's in the mirror. "I recall there being rumors about it."

"M-my mother?" Had she misheard? She *was* terribly out of sorts, but she would have sworn Mrs. Ross had just said—

"Your mother, yes. She was a Murdoch, wasn't she? I grew up in Ayrshire, Miss MacLeod. The Murdochs were our neighboring clan."

"D-did you know her?" Was it possible fate had smiled on her at last, and she'd happened to stumble across an old friend of her mother's? Goodness, her heart was pounding! It seemed too good to be true, but perhaps—

"No, I'm afraid not." Mrs. Ross squeezed her shoulder. "But I saw her once or twice. She had the most beautiful green eyes, just like yours. There were all sorts of wild rumors about the Murdoch women, back then."

"Then, and now." She and her sisters were MacLeods, not Murdochs, yet the rumors persisted and had done so for generations.

"Yes. It's a sad fact that women with extraordinary abilities are often regarded with suspicion. As a midwife, I've faced similar unfounded accusations."

"You're a midwife? I didn't realize." It wasn't any wonder, then, that Aila Ross understood her so perfectly. She was a peculiar woman herself!

"I am, indeed." Mrs. Ross put the hairbrush aside, and her gaze met Freya's in the glass. "I've never put much stock in rumors, Miss MacLeod, and I don't intend to start now."

She said no more about witches, but in those few words, she'd said everything.

"Freya." Freya reached behind her and laid her hand over the hand still resting on her shoulder. "Please, you must call me Freya."

Mrs. Ross smiled. "And you must call me Aila."

* * *

Callum had spent half the morning pacing his bedchamber preparing for the moment Freya would enter the breakfast room.

It wasn't enough time.

When she appeared in the doorway he went still, the cool, detached greeting he'd rehearsed freezing on his lips.

She was wearing a green dress. Of all the dresses his mother could have found for her, why did she have to choose one that made Freya look like a spring flower?

He hastily lowered his gaze to his breakfast plate, but it was too late. The memory had already been seared into his brain.

"Callum. Here you are. Chocolate for me this morning, Bell." His mother nodded to the footman, then took her usual place at the table, in the seat across from his. "Freya, would you prefer tea or chocolate this morning?"

"Tea, please." Freya hesitated, but then slid into the seat next to his mother's. "Good morning, Mr. Ross."

"Miss MacLeod." He offered her a polite nod, then jerked his attention to his coffee cup, which he was clutching with such enthusiasm he'd opened the gash on his knuckles again. "I hope you slept well."

"I don't know that she did." His mother passed a teacup to Freya. "She's a bit out of sorts, I'm afraid, but I daresay some tea will set her to rights."

She did look paler than usual. Her cloud of red-gold hair had been brushed back away from her face and fastened into a thick coil at the back of her neck. It wouldn't have been a flattering look on any other lady, but everything, it seemed, flattered Freya. The severe style emphasized her smooth, creamy skin, delicate features, and big green eyes.

A man could lose himself in those eyes.

But the violet smudges underneath them spoke of a sleepless night, and just like that, his every protective instinct roared to life. It was all he could do to stop himself from snatching her up, rushing her off to his bedchamber, and taking her to bed.

His bed. He'd lay her down in the soft sheets, brush her hair back from that exquisite face, and spend hours kissing those petal pink lips, and then—

No! Damn it, he was losing his wits.

He tore his gaze away from her with a wrench that made his neck crack and devoted his attention to pushing his cold eggs about on his breakfast plate. His appetite was gone, a casualty of his unhealthy fixation with a lady who wasn't his, and never would be.

"I thought I might have a walk this morning, while the weather holds." Freya took a small sip of her tea, then returned the cup to the saucer. "I'm curious about Balnagown Castle. I've never come across one quite like it before. It's as lovely a place as I've ever seen."

"It's pretty, is it not? A walk is just the thing for you, Freya. The fresh air will put the roses back in your cheeks. I daresay Callum would be pleased to take you on a stroll through the gardens this morning."

"I did notice a pretty little folly when we were coming up the drive, situated beside an ornamental pond. We don't have any follies at Castle Cairncross, and I've always admired them. I'd quite like to have a closer look at it, if—"

"I'm afraid that will be impossible. I won't have time." His tone was curt, but taking Freya MacLeod on a romantic stroll through the gardens was out of the question. He may as well slice open the knuckles of his other hand as subject himself to such misery. "I have a great deal of correspondence to see to this morning."

"Well, no matter." His mother waved this away. "This afternoon will do well enough. Or perhaps after tea, if the weather holds."

"No. I beg Miss MacLeod will excuse me. I'm not available this afternoon, either. I've promised to take Lorna for a ride."

Silence followed this declaration, one that dragged on for so long he reluctantly abandoned his contemplation of his coffee cup and glanced up.

His mother was frowning at him, and the tentative smile had vanished from Freya's lips. She gazed at him for a moment, the confusion clear in her eyes, but then she looked hastily away, devoting all her attention instead to spooning sugar into her tea. But her shoulders had gone rigid, and when she set her spoon aside, her hand was trembling.

He'd hurt her feelings. She was taking pains to hide it, but her gaze remained downcast, and aside from two dull spots of red in her cheeks, what little color she'd had when she came into the breakfast room had drained from her face.

It was a hell of a way to find out that hurting her feelings would feel like trampling a daisy underneath his boot heels.

Brutal, and unforgivable.

But necessary, for all that it made him feel as if his heart was no longer an organ of flesh and blood, but a cold, heavy stone sinking in his chest, but squiring her around the estate would only encourage his preoccupation with her.

Beyond fulfilling his promise to Hamish, Freya MacLeod wasn't his concern. If he repeated it enough times, perhaps he'd start to believe it.

He had to. The sooner he accepted it, the better it would be for them both.

She didn't belong here. She'd be gone soon enough, and life would go on as it had before he'd ever laid eyes on her. Before he'd gone to her cursed castle, and chased her through the woods, and discovered that the middle MacLeod sister, the one everyone overlooked, had a whole world of secrets hidden underneath her placid exterior.

Before he'd *seen* her and heard her. Before he'd felt her soft curves against him, and her mouth had parted shyly under his. Before he'd fallen into a kiss unlike any he'd ever experienced before. A kiss he'd felt not only in his lips but in his belly and his fingertips and the center of his chest, as if a shower of sparks had exploded under his breastbone.

"I beg your pardon." He jumped to his feet, the coffee sloshing over the edge of his cup and pooling in his saucer. "Excuse me, Mother, Miss MacLeod. I have a meeting with my land steward this morning."

"Well, then, I suppose you'd better go, hadn't you?" His mother gave him a thin smile. "I daresay Gordon will be pleased to escort Miss MacLeod on a walk through the gardens this afternoon."

Callum was halfway to the door, but he stopped in his tracks. "Gordon?"

"Yes, Gordon. Your secretary? You do remember Gordon, don't you?" His mother took a dainty sip of her chocolate. "He'll make an admirable escort. Unless you have some objection to him, Callum?"

"No, of course not." No objection at all, if he put aside the fact that Gordon smiled too much, was a flirt and too charming for his own good, and hadn't the first idea how to behave like a proper gentle—

"Yes, I think Gordon will do very well. Do make sure you allow him time away from his duties this afternoon, Callum. He's a charming young man, and he has ever so many amusing stories about Balnagown Castle! He'll make an ideal escort for you, Freya." His mother patted Freya's hand. "I daresay you'll find him utterly delightful."

Chapter 16

"You see before you, Miss MacLeod, the fruits of three centuries of industry."

"Three centuries! My goodness." Freya made all the appropriate gushing sounds, turning to her escort with a beaming smile. "How remarkable, Mr. Corbett."

Gordon Corbett, her escort for the afternoon, gestured with an extravagant wave of his hand toward the castle. "Would you ever imagine, looking at it now, that Balnagown Castle was once a humble tower house?"

"No, indeed. I don't see how anyone could." Anyone unfamiliar with Scottish history, that is, as a great many of the fine old castles dotting the countryside had begun as humble tower houses.

She didn't say so, however. She wouldn't dream of insulting Mr. Corbett, who'd been kind enough to devote several hours of his time to showing her around the estate this afternoon.

He'd proved himself to be every bit the delight Aila had promised he would be.

He was nearly as delightful as Balnagown Castle itself.

Tedious historical facts aside, it was one of the prettiest places she'd ever seen, and it was especially so this afternoon, with its creamy stone gleaming in the sunshine. The façade glowed with the pale winter light, as if it knew it was being admired and was preening like the belle of the ball.

"But alas, Miss MacLeod, there's a dark side to Balnagown's history, much as there is to every other castle in Scotland. I wouldn't dream of misleading you into believing otherwise. I'm afraid it's very dark, indeed." He gave her a roguish waggle of his eyebrows. "Murders, mayhem, that sort of thing."

"Murders? Dear me."

"Wicked doings, Miss MacLeod. Wicked doings, indeed."

"How dreadfully unfortunate, Mr. Corbett." She gave a mournful shake of her head, but a grin was twitching at her lips. He was tremendously entertaining, and handsome, too, with his fair hair gilded a pale gold by the sun and a pair of merry dark eyes that danced when he smiled.

It was almost enough to make her forget that awful breakfast this morning.

Almost.

Yet despite the sunshine, the beautiful grounds, and her good-humored and knowledgeable escort, a dark cloud had been hanging over her since her regrettable encounter with Callum in the breakfast parlor.

She'd done what she could to dispel it, devoting all her attention to Mr. Corbett and laughing at his antics, yet it persisted in hovering there still, stealing her pleasure in an otherwise lovely day.

Callum had hardly spared her a glance this morning, and that scowl of his had been even darker than usual. So dark, in fact, it had quite put her off her morning toast and tea.

But perhaps her low spirits weren't so surprising. She was hundreds of miles from her home, with no idea when she'd ever be able to return to it again, and Sorcha was never far from her thoughts. It was more than enough to make any lady despondent.

Yes, that was certainly it. It had nothing whatsoever to do with Callum. Why, she'd hardly noticed his coldness to her this morning. She didn't need Callum Ross's attention, for pity's sake. She hadn't thought twice about the way he'd so coolly rejected her company today, and with so little attempt at civility.

No, she hadn't spared Callum Ross a single, blessed thought since then.

It would likely be several weeks before she could safely leave Balnagown Castle behind her, and she wouldn't spend them mooning over him, just because they'd shared a few innocent kisses.

Mostly innocent, and rather more than a few, but what difference did it make?

She could hardly even remember them now. They were just kisses, nothing more. Gentlemen kissed ladies every day, and Callum's kisses were doubtless much like every other gentleman's kisses. There was no need to become so preoccupied with something that mattered so little.

"These wicked doings, Mr. Corbett." She wrenched her attention back to her escort and offered him another bright smile. "Surely nothing too terribly wicked could happen in such a pretty castle as this?"

He blinked down at her, his gaze lingering on her lips, but he recovered quickly and returned her smile with a cheeky one of his own. "Yes, scandalously wicked, but I don't like to shock you, Miss MacLeod."

"I'm a MacLeod, Mr. Corbett. We don't shock easily." If smugglers, rumors of witchcraft, and the thief-takers that were on her heels hadn't ended her, she was sure to survive whatever dastardly tales Mr. Corbett might relate.

Criminals, murders, beheadings . . . she'd hardly bat an eye over any of it.

"Ghosts, you know, Miss MacLeod." He lowered his voice. "Two of them, and both rather ghastly, I'm afraid."

Ghosts? Was that all? Every castle in Scotland had a ghost or two, including Castle Cairncross. Her father used to delight in telling them stories of his great-aunt Margaret MacLeod, who was said to haunt the third-floor corridor outside the family bedchambers, clad only in her night rail and lace cap. "Ghastly or not, you must tell me about them now, Mr. Corbett, or I'll suspect you of being a dreadful tease."

"Well, I can't have that. Very well, then. The ghost of a murdered Scottish princess is believed to haunt the hallways of Balnagown, but never fear, Miss MacLeod. She's a friendly ghost who bestows a gentle smile on all who encounter her."

"She sounds lovely, and not at all ghastly."

"I daresay she is. I've never seen her myself, but those who have say she has beautiful red hair." He gave her a sly grin. "And even more beautiful bright green eyes."

Goodness, he was a rogue, wasn't he? "I see. Tell me, Mr. Corbett. If you happened to be walking with a fair-haired, blue-eyed lady, would this ghostly princess resemble her, instead?"

"Certainly not." He glanced down at her, his dark eyes twinkling. "What do you take me for, Miss MacLeod?"

"A flirt, Mr. Corbett, and an accomplished one, at that."

He threw his head back in a laugh. "Not a bit, I assure you. Now the second ghost is a good deal more shocking. I do hope you don't run into *him*, as he's terribly wicked. He's called Black Andrew, and he's said to wander the red corridor at night. If you should find yourself in that part of the house and hear heavy footsteps following you, I advise you to—"

He broke off at the rumble of approaching hooves, and they both turned to see two riders coming toward the castle. As they drew closer a strange fluttering began in her belly, as if a dozen butterflies had taken up residence there.

One of the riders was tall and dark-haired, and sat upright in the saddle, his wide shoulders straight and his hands relaxed on the reins.

Well, there was no mistaking *him*, was there? It should have been impossible to identify him from this distance, but no other gentleman rode with such easy grace as he did. Goodness knew she'd spent enough time in the saddle with him to know that.

"Ah, here comes the laird, and Miss Lorna with him."

Miss Lorna. Hadn't Callum mentioned that name at the breakfast table this morning? He'd said something about having made a promise to take her riding this afternoon.

It looked as if he'd kept it. Which was all just as it should be, of course. He might ride with whomever he pleased. It was no concern of hers.

But as Callum and his companion came abreast of them, the butterflies fluttered away, and in their place a dark heaviness settled in her belly, as if she'd swallowed a stone.

Miss Lorna, whoever she was, was an accomplished rider. She rode as if she'd been born to the saddle, her shoulders back and her bearing proud. She had admirable control over her mount, maneuvering him with smooth confidence that made it a pleasure to observe her.

A pleasure for someone else, that is. It wasn't pleasure rushing through her veins or gnawing a hole into the pit of her stomach. No, it was something much darker than that, something bitter and angry that felt suspiciously like . . .

Jealousy. Dear God, what an ugly emotion it was, like poison rushing through her.

All at once, she wanted nothing more than to disappear. To run for the castle, or sink into the ground, or—oh, she didn't care! Anything would do, if it meant she could avoid the introduction that was bearing down on her.

Her fingers tightened on Mr. Corbett's coat sleeve. "Should we walk on? I'm curious to see this red corridor Black Andrew haunts."

"Indeed, but shall we stay and greet the laird and Miss Lorna first? It looks as if they're coming this way."

"It does, doesn't it?" Blast them, yes, they were unmistakably headed in this direction, and the stone in her belly sank deeper with every inch they advanced. It was plain to see Miss Lorna was a beauty, with lovely olive skin and thick dark hair coiled at the back of her neck, just underneath the brim of her smart riding cap.

"Miss Lorna is close to your age, I think, Miss MacLeod. I daresay you'll find her agreeable. Everyone loves her."

Did they? How utterly delightful. Mr. Corbett may as well sink a blade in her belly and be done with it. "I'm sure they do."

"Mr. Corbett! How do you do?" Lorna offered him a cheerful wave as she and Callum reached the pathway at an easy canter and brought their horses to a stop. "This must be Miss MacLeod. How do you do? I'm so pleased to make your acquaintance, Miss MacLeod. Welcome to Balnagown Castle."

"Thank you. You're very kind, Miss . . ."

"I am a goose, am I not? I'm Lorna Niven." She offered Freya a friendly smile. "Callum mentioned he'd brought a lady back with him from Dunvegan, but he didn't tell me much else."

No, he wouldn't have, would he? "Er, well, there's not much to tell, really."

A lie, and an egregious one, but she was hardly going to admit to this beautiful, elegant lady that she'd been driven from her home by an outraged mob who suspected her of witchcraft.

"He can be disappointingly discreet when he makes up his mind to it," Lorna added, with a playful smile at Callum. "It's quite irritating."

Discreet, was he? Yes, he'd have to be, considering what had happened between them at Brodie's cottage. Not that it mattered to her. It didn't, but one would think a gentleman who was, er . . . well, whatever Callum was to Lorna Niven, would refrain from kissing another lady.

But perhaps Callum wasn't a gentleman at all.

Yet for all the ugliness rushing through her, she had no reason to suspect him of anything underhanded. Not really. That is, it was plain to see he knew Lorna Niven very well. A lady didn't tease a gentleman as Lorna teased him otherwise.

But that didn't mean there was a *tendre* between them.

She glanced at him, then looked quickly away, a pinch in her chest. This morning's scowl was nowhere in evidence now, and to add insult to injury, he was unfairly handsome today. The exercise and fresh air had whipped bright color into his cheeks, and his silky dark hair was charmingly disheveled, drat him.

Those who had something to hide had every reason in the world to be discreet. But had Callum really hidden anything from her?

Perhaps the better question was, had he revealed anything to her? Because now she thought of it, he'd told her surprisingly little about himself, and nothing at all about his life at Balnagown Castle.

He'd certainly never mentioned Lorna Niven's name, not in the entire four days they'd been alone at Brodie's cottage. They'd had nothing but time on their hands, yet he hadn't breathed a single word about her.

It was a telling omission.

She'd asked for the wrong secrets during the card game, it seemed.

But he hadn't just kept Lorna Niven's existence from her. He hadn't said a word about his mother being here at Balnagown, either. It could be that he was innocent of any wrongdoing. This was all pure speculation on her part, and that while the green goblin of jealousy was coloring her every thought.

But if he wasn't innocent, well . . . there was nothing handsome about a liar, and all the silky dark hair tossed in artful waves around his face didn't change that.

Either way, she felt like an utter fool, mooning over that kiss as she had. Had he been laughing at her while she was going on about how she was no longer afraid of him, and how grateful she was he'd been the one who'd found her hiding under her father's desk?

Just the thought of his amusement made her cringe. The truth was, she hardly knew Callum, and it might be better if she never did.

Balnagown was a large castle. Perhaps she'd do well to keep her distance from him.

". . . promised to take Miss MacLeod to see the red corridor," Mr. Corbett was saying. "This brave lady has expressed a wish to visit Black Andrew's haunting grounds."

"Are you quite certain you wish to do that, Miss MacLeod?" Miss Niven asked. "I've heard he's a shocking sight. I've never seen him, but I recall a guest of my father's leaving the castle in the middle of the night after hearing Black Andrew's ghostly footsteps. He was quite shaken."

"Miss MacLeod claims to have no fear of ghosts. She insists she doesn't find them in the least shocking." Mr. Corbett smiled down at her. "We'll see if she's telling us the truth soon enough."

"I assure you I am, Mr. Corbett. I never lie." She couldn't resist a glance at Callum then. He was watching her, his face so expressionless she might have believed he was utterly unaffected by this conversation if it hadn't been for his eyes.

Something was swirling in those pale gray depths, something turbulent.

"As for ghosts, I don't find them shocking. I've always found living people to be a great deal more so." She raised her chin and looked pointedly away from Callum. "Shall we, Mr. Corbett?"

"Yes, indeed." He drew her arm more securely through his and gave her a roguish grin. "Never fear, Miss MacLeod. If Black Andrew should appear, I'll defend you with my life."

Lorna laughed. "Bravo, Mr. Corbett."

"See to it your heroics don't interfere with your duties, Corbett." Callum bit off each word through gritted teeth. "We've those letters to see to later this afternoon."

Both Lorna and Mr. Corbett glanced at him, clearly surprised, but after an awkward instant of silence, Mr. Corbett nodded. "Of course."

Callum said nothing more. But then he was good at that, wasn't he?

"It was a pleasure to meet you, Miss Niven." She inclined her head to Lorna, but she took no leave at all of Callum and marched off on Mr. Corbett's arm without sparing him a single glance.

It would be just as well if they didn't run into Black Andrew in the red corridor.

In her current mood, she'd frighten the life out of him.

He wasn't going to go chasing after Freya MacLeod. Damn it, he *wasn't*.

Corbett appeared content enough to act as her escort, and Freya couldn't have been more pleased to have him, with the way she'd strolled off on the man's arm without so much as a backward glance.

Which was just as it should be, of course. Wonderful, even. It wasn't as if he'd wanted to play chaperone for her today. God knew he was relieved to have the chit out of his way.

If she was clinging to Corbett's arm with a bit more enthusiasm than was strictly appropriate, then so be it. And if that absurdly bright smile she'd just bestowed upon him would only encourage the man's flirtatious tendencies, it wasn't his place to say so.

It was nothing to do with him.

Except he *had* promised Hamish he'd keep an eye on her. Hamish was sure to disapprove of Freya wandering off alone with a notorious flirt, and neither was Hamish likely to excuse that inviting smile she'd given Corbett, or the flutter of her eyelashes as she gazed up at him.

Hamish wouldn't like any of this. In fact, Hamish would have been furious over that entire encounter. Utterly, blindly furious.

Hamish, that is.

As Hamish's surrogate in all things related to Freya MacLeod, it was incumbent upon *him* to see to it she didn't get herself into any difficulties with her careless behavior.

Well then, there was only one thing to do, wasn't there?

Chase Freya MacLeod.

He took the stairs two at a time and reached the guest wing on the third floor just when she was about to enter her bedchamber. "Wait, Miss MacLeod. A moment, if you please."

She turned, her eyebrows aloft. "Yes? How may I help you, Mr. Ross?"

Good God, but her voice was as cold at Balnagown River in the middle of February, and her eyes were as flinty as a pair of jade stones.

There would be no inviting smiles for *him*, then. "Just a word of caution, Miss MacLeod, to take care how you behave with Gordon Corbett. He's likely to take all your charming pleasantries as encouragement."

"I beg your pardon." Her eyebrows ticked up another notch until they disappeared into her hairline. "My behavior toward Mr. Corbett was in no way inappropriate."

Her voice had cooled to arctic levels, and her lips had gone so tight she might have spat a diamond through her teeth. If he'd had his wits about him he might have seen those eyebrows as the warning they were and taken steps to avoid an impending fit of feminine outrage.

But he was well past that.

His wits had deserted him in almost the same instant he'd first laid eyes on Freya MacLeod, and God knew they were nowhere to be found now. "Indeed, it was, and I think you know it. You were purposely flirting with him."

"*Flirting?* Why, how dare you? You're mad. I was doing no such thing, although if I was flirting with him, I don't see how it's any concern of yours."

"Of course it is. Hamish has charged me with keeping an eye on you, if you recall, and I don't think he'd approve of the blatant display I just witnessed."

She gaped at him for a moment, her mouth open, but then her chin shot up. "Blatant display! I haven't the faintest idea what you're talking about, Mr. Ross, but I warn you to watch what you say, or you'll find yourself on the receiving end of a blatant display you won't soon forget."

"There's no use denying it, Miss MacLeod." He leaned his hip against the doorframe and crossed his arms over his chest. "I saw it with my own eyes."

"Why, of all the arrogant, high-handed nonsense! I don't know what you think you saw, Mr. Ross, but I can assure you, it wasn't flirting!"

She stamped her foot, her green eyes glittering with fury, and some distant part of him vaguely recognized he had no right to speak to her in such a way, but that feeble voice of caution was no match for the rest of him.

When, after all, had logic ever won a battle against seething, raging jealousy?

Never. Not once, in all of history.

"No?" He took a step toward her, until he was so close the tips of his riding boots brushed her skirts, and her back was against the door. "I see. Then you simper and flutter your eyelashes at every gentleman?"

"*Simper!*" Two bright spots of color appeared in her cheeks. "I . . . you . . . for pity's sake, Mr. Ross, you've quite lost your mind! I've never simpered in my life!"

She looked a great deal like her sister Sorcha when she was in a temper. So much so that it was a bit worrying, but he'd gone too far now. Any thread of control he'd had had snapped at the sight of Freya's dainty fingers curled around the sleeve of Corbett's coat.

Anyway, she didn't have a dirk to hand, so his limbs were safe.

But his mind was another matter. He was losing it, bit by bit.

Or else he'd already lost it, just as she'd said, because he was opening his mouth again, and words he'd much better have kept to himself were tumbling out. "For God's sake, Freya! Do you think I didn't notice that Corbett was looking at you like you were a sweetmeat on a silver tray?"

"If he was, it's nothing to do with me! For your information, Mr. Ross, I don't flirt with gentlemen I've only just met."

He braced his arm on the door above her head and leaned closer, and the scent of fresh air and the hint of black tea that clung to her tickled his nose. "But you kiss them, don't you, Freya?"

Good Lord. He'd done it now, hadn't he? If there was ever a wrong thing to say to a lady, that was it, but how could he regret the deepening flush in her cheeks, the dark green flash of fury in those eyes?

She was glorious. He couldn't tear his gaze away from her.

"I didn't kiss you, Mr. Ross. If you recall, *you* kissed *me*."

"So I did." He leaned closer and lowered his head until his lips were a breath away from her ear. "But you kissed me back, didn't you, Freya? Not chaste kisses, either, but deep, wet, dizzying kisses. What would you say if I told you I'd dreamed about those kisses over and over again since that night under the willow tree?"

She stared up at him, her chest jerking with each of her short, shallow breaths. "I'd tell you not to worry over it, as I'm sure you'll forget them soon enough. I'm not the first lady you've kissed, Mr. Ross, and neither am I fool enough to believe I'll be the last."

"You seem certain of that." Far more so than he was.

Freya wasn't the first lady he'd kissed, no, but every other kiss paled in comparison to the one he'd shared under the willow with her, just as every other lady paled in comparison to her.

Not one of them had ever haunted his dreams as she did.

"I am certain. Do you deny it's the truth, Mr. Ross?"

He shouldn't deny it. He didn't have any promises to offer Freya MacLeod. Yet the words he should have said, the words that might have released her from this strange spell that held them together, wouldn't come.

Instead, he touched his fingertips to her chin, raised her face to his, and told her the truth. "I hardly know anymore, Freya."

For an instant their eyes held. Her smooth, pale throat moved in a swallow, and it was all he could do not to rest his palm against that delicate column so he might feel the movement, trace her fluttering pulse with his fingertips.

But she didn't give him a chance. She jerked her chin away from his hand and turned toward her bedchamber door, reaching for the doorknob. "I don't wish to discuss this with you any longer, Mr. Ross."

He caught her wrist in a gentle grip before she could turn the knob, and for an instant—only an instant—he pressed his face against the back of her neck and allowed himself a moment to breathe in the scent of her hair.

Sunshine, fresh winter air, and *Freya*.

It was only a moment, only a breath. It wasn't enough, but before he could fill his lungs with the dizzying scent of her again, her bedchamber door opened, and she slipped through it without a backward glance.

And he was left alone in the corridor, standing there staring at a closed door.

Which was no less than he deserved.

CHAPTER 17

Freya didn't slam her bedchamber door.

It was a small triumph, but she'd seize it, nonetheless. There was some paltry measure of satisfaction in it, and goodness knew she had little reason to congratulate herself over this business with Callum.

A lady must take what she could get.

What a dreadful scene! How had she and Callum gone from those dizzying kisses under the willow tree only days ago to shouting at each other in the corridor where anyone who happened to be strolling nearby could have overheard them?

She sagged against the door behind her, brushing away the tears that threatened with an angry swipe of her hand. What did Callum mean, accusing her of flirting with Gordon Corbett? She'd enjoyed Mr. Corbett's company this afternoon, but even if she'd wanted to flirt with him, she wouldn't know where to begin.

She'd never flirted with a gentleman before.

But it was a week for firsts, it seemed. Flirtations, kisses, shouting matches with an enraged laird. Goodness only knew what tomorrow would bring. Perhaps she'd remain in her bedchamber until she could return to Dun—

"Miss MacLeod?" There was a soft knock on the door behind her. "Freya? It's Aila Ross."

Dash it. She swiped at her cheeks again, catching on her fingertips the one errant tear that had escaped. Callum Ross didn't deserve her tears. Only a fool would weep over such an ill-tempered, scowling, high-handed scoundrel like him.

"Freya? I know you're in there."

She pasted a smile on her lips and opened the door. "Good afternoon, Aila. Thank you for arranging for Mr. Corbett to escort me today. He's as charming as you promised, and quite knowledgeable about—"

"What happened between you and Callum, Freya?"

Oh, *no*. This just went from bad to worse, didn't it?

It wasn't enough that she'd kissed Callum, but now she would be obliged to confess her sins to his mother! Aila Ross was sure to blame her for all of it.

This was dreadful. How had she gotten herself into such a tangle?

"I beg your pardon for asking." Aila stepped into the bedchamber and closed the door behind her. "I happened to be coming out of my bedchamber, and I'm afraid I overheard you and Callum arguing. I confess I'm quite shocked. Callum isn't a perfect man, but he's no rake, to steal kisses from innocent young ladies."

Freya held back a snort. If a gentleman who stole kisses from innocent young ladies could be called a rake, then Callum had behaved very much as a rake would.

She could hardly say so to Aila, however. There wasn't a mother alive who wanted to believe her son was a seducer of innocents.

But she was no better than Callum. She'd behaved like a perfect fool, sighing over his pretty words and devastating kisses under the willow tree, and this is what had come of it. All this, over a few stolen kisses! For pity's sake, ladies kissed gentlemen every day without falling into hysterics over it.

"It, ah . . . it was an accident."

Aila's lips twitched. "Callum kissed you by accident?"

"Er, well, no. A mistake, rather. It was a mistake." She perched on the edge of the bed, silently cursing her wobbling knees. They were always the first to go.

Aila hesitated. "It, ah—forgive me, Freya, but it was only a kiss, was it not?"

"Yes, of course! There was no, er . . ." There was no delicate way to finish that sentence. "It was just a kiss."

Well, half a dozen kisses, but certainly no more than that.

But wasn't that awful enough? She'd exchanged half a dozen kisses with a gentleman she hardly knew, and who believed her to be a flirt. Did he suppose she'd been flirting with him the entire time they'd been alone in Brodie's cottage?

Was that why he'd kissed her?

Worse, *had* she been flirting with him, without realizing it? It was all so awful, the blasted tears she'd chased off earlier returned, and she covered her face with her hands.

"My dear girl." Aila sat down beside her on the bed and laid a gentle hand on her back. "I will not make excuses for Callum's behavior, but I will say that he's had a difficult year, and hardly knows which way is up anymore."

What did that mean? Oh, she didn't want to know!

"It's a long story, but I'm willing to tell it to you, if you're willing to listen."

Freya sniffled. "Yes, all right. If you think it will help."

Very well, then. Perhaps she *did* want to know.

"I hardly know where to start. I suppose the only place is at the beginning." Aila's hand continued to move in soothing circles over Freya's back. "Did Callum tell you he didn't grow up at Balnagown Castle?"

"No. But isn't Balnagown Castle the seat of Clan Ross?" She'd assumed Callum had been raised at Balnagown, but now she thought of it, he'd never said so.

He hadn't said much of anything about his past.

"It is, yes, but there was a disagreement amongst the clan during the height of the Jacobite Rebellion, and like many clan disagreements, it became complicated. A deep rift developed between the two factions, one that has yet to fully heal."

"I see." It was a common story. Many of the clans had been torn apart by the Jacobite Uprising and had yet to heal the wounds that had been left behind.

"Malcolm Ross, Callum's father, was a staunch supporter of Bonnie Prince Charlie, but there were other members of the clan who were loyal to King George II. Malcolm was the Laird of Clan Ross in the spring of 1746. He fought at Culloden, and many members of the clan made the decision to fight alongside their laird." Aila drew in a deep breath. "Not a single one of them returned to Kildary."

Freya's throat worked, but what did one say in response to such a tragic loss? There were no words. Instead, she reached for Aila's hand and held it between hers.

"As you can imagine, the clan was devastated. Many of them held Malcolm responsible. They blamed me as well, and before long it became impossible for me to remain at Balnagown Castle. Callum was only an infant, and doesn't remember that time, but the years that followed were challenging, and his memories of our struggles are quite vivid."

Aila didn't elaborate further, but there was no need. It was no small thing, to be cast out by one's clan. Great hardship must certainly have followed, and loneliness.

Pitiless, aching loneliness.

"The clan chose Alistair Niven as the new laird," Aila went on. "He was a dear friend of Malcolm's, and a good man."

"Lorna Niven's father."

"Yes. He passed away in February. It was Alistair's dearest wish to see the clan reunited, so when he felt his health failing, he called me and Callum back to Kildary. We returned to Balnagown Castle late last year."

As recently as that? They'd been back for less than a year. "I daresay it's been difficult for you."

"It has, yes. Alistair's dying wish was to see Callum made Laird of Clan Ross. Alistair believed making Callum the laird would correct the wrong done to our family and hoped it would heal the rift and unite the clan. Perhaps it will, in time, but for now, there are those who don't approve of Alistair's choice. It's been difficult for Callum."

"Ah, I see." This explained the strangely cold reception they'd received the day they'd arrived at Balnagown Castle. That gentleman who'd greeted them—James—must be one of those who didn't want Callum to lead the clan.

"It's only right that Callum should become the laird, just as his father was before him, but I don't have to tell you, Freya, that what is right and what is easy are rarely the same thing. Those things that make sense in the abstract often become muddled in real life. People are messy. They have a stubborn way of taking something simple and making it complicated."

Goodness knew that was the truth. One needn't look any further than the villagers of Dunvegan for proof of that, but it seemed shortsighted indeed for anyone to object to Callum becoming the laird.

That is, he *was* a trifle brusque. There was no denying that, and perhaps a little frightening at first glance, although now she'd known him for a little while, it seemed ludicrous that she'd ever been afraid of him.

She'd been put off by his eyes at first, yes—such an unusually pale gray—but one grew accustomed to them, after a time. They were rather remarkable eyes, really, with those long, thick eyelashes.

Despite his flaws, Callum was a strong, proud, protective, and ethical man. She'd only known him for a week, but anyone could see he was a man of his word. If he hadn't been, she wouldn't be here now.

She'd be locked in the magistrate's cellar in Dunvegan.

At best. At worst, her head would be mounted on a pike outside Baird's Pub.

Good Lord, what a thought. When had she developed such a ghastly imagination?

But the point was, Callum had promised Hamish he'd keep her safe, and he'd done just as he promised, despite it proving costly for him to do so.

He was just the sort of man a clan should want as their laird.

"Callum doesn't make it any easier on himself, of course." Aila gave her a rueful smile. "But I don't have to tell you that, do I? I daresay you noticed how stubborn he can be, after a week spent in his company."

Stubborn? My, yes. He made Sorcha look accommodating, and that took some doing. She hadn't thought there was a person in existence as stubborn as Sorcha until she'd encountered Callum Ross.

It wouldn't do to say so to his mother, however. "He, ah, does seem accustomed to having his own way."

Aila laughed. "How polite you are, Freya! But it's quite all right, you know. I'm his mother, and I know he's as stubborn as a mule."

"I can't argue with you there." Freya gave her a grateful smile. "Thank you for explaining all this to me, Aila."

"Of course, dear. Now, I'll leave you to rest." Aila rose from the bed, but she paused on her way to the door and took up the old, dark blue cloak Freya had left draped over a chair this morning.

Cat's cloak. It was a cold day, and she'd chosen to wear the warmer dark green one Mrs. Doherty had brought her before her walk with Mr. Corbett this afternoon.

"My, this cloak has seen better days." Aila frowned at the streaks of dirt and the rusty red stains on the shoulder and the back of it. "I can't think why Mrs. Doherty didn't take it to be laundered along with your dress. I'll take it down with me, shall I?"

"No!" Freya leapt up from the bed and without thinking, snatched the cloak from Aila's hands.

Aila blinked at her. "Very well. I needn't take it if you prefer, Freya."

"I beg your pardon. It's just . . . it's my sister Catriona's cloak, and I can't . . . I don't want . . ."

She trailed off, heat rushing into her cheeks. How could she explain that she couldn't bear to part with it? That as childish as it was, the cloak felt like her last link to her home and her family, and she wanted to keep it exactly as it was?

"It's quite all right, Freya. I understand." Aila squeezed her hand, then went to the door and slipped into the corridor, closing it with a quiet click behind her, leaving Freya alone.

She returned to her perch on the edge of the bed, a dozen thoughts spinning through her head. None of what Aila had told her excused Callum's kissing her, but it did give her some insight into the turbulence swirling around him. Such uncertainty could drive a man to do something he wouldn't otherwise.

Like kiss a lady he hardly knew, and didn't like all that much.

It could drive a lady to something she might not do otherwise, as well.

Like kissing him back.

The moonlight and stars hadn't helped, either. If ever there'd been a moment made for a kiss, it was that one. Why, the heavens had practically demanded it.

A kiss that, in the end, meant little.

But it was a moment she'd never forget. The way his eyes had darkened, and the heat swirling in those gray depths right before he took her mouth . . .

She'd never felt anything like that kiss before. Even just the memory of it made a shiver of pleasure dart up her spine.

Her first kiss. Likely her last, too.

But it had been a strange, suspended moment, one unconnected to what had come before it, or what would come afterward.

A moment out of time.

She wasn't destined for Callum Ross, and neither was he destined for her. A moonlight kiss, no matter how breathtaking, didn't change that.

She shivered, despite the cheerful fire crackling in the grate. There was a cold place inside her that the warmth couldn't touch, and it ached with loneliness. She took up Cat's cloak and wrapped it around herself, clutching the worn folds tightly against her neck.

It smelled of Cat, of black licorice and comfrey, and of Dunvegan Woods—rain and damp earth and thousands of pine needles littering the forest floor.

It smelled of home.

She'd find her way back to Castle Cairncross, one way or another, and would return to her old life. Her old, dull, quiet life of sitting on the roof of her solitary turret, watching the clouds skim across the sky, and scribbling in her notebook.

Goodness, how lonely it sounded! But it had been enough for her, once.

Surely, it would be so again.

A gentleman exercised moderation in all things.

It had been a favorite saying of his father's—or so his mother had told him. She'd repeated it often enough when he'd been a younger man, restless, angry, and hot-tempered. It had fallen on deaf ears at the time, much as her other cautions and reprimands had.

But it had embedded itself in his mind, nonetheless, and there it had stayed. The words of a father he'd never known, spoken in his mother's voice.

Moderation in all things, and particularly this one.

When he'd at last escaped to the privacy of his study after dinner tonight, he'd gone straight to the sideboard and the whisky bottle, but when a man wanted a glass of whisky as badly as he did tonight, he shouldn't have one.

A single glass could lead to an entire bottle in the blink of an eye.

He poured half a glass of port instead, and he'd been standing by the window nursing it ever since, watching as evening fell over Balnagown Castle.

Evening, at last. Today had begun badly, grown worse as each minute ticked by, and had lasted an eternity.

Simper. That was what he'd accused Freya of, wasn't it?

Flirting, simpering, fluttering your eyelashes . . .

The words chased themselves around in circles inside his head, the unfairness of them striking him deeply in the center of his chest.

But it wasn't even his words that were the worst of it.

It was everything else. The catch in her voice when she'd spoken to him, her anger, the flush of it in her cheeks. Worst of all, the hurt in her eyes when she'd turned away from him, the sheen of the tears there.

Tears she'd refused to let fall.

But perhaps it was better this way. Better if she despised him.

Better for her, that is, because to be despised by Freya MacLeod, to be the object of her scorn was . . . there were no words for it.

It was like the time he'd been kicked in the chest by the mule they'd kept when he'd been a boy. One moment he'd been standing upright, trying to dislodge a stone from her hoof, and the next he'd been on his back in the muddy stable yard, his lungs frozen on an indrawn breath, and his chest on fire.

He brought his glass to his lips and sipped, the rich, smoky taste of the port sliding over his tongue as twilight advanced, and the sky above the castle turned a subdued violet.

This, then, was what had become of the kisses he'd stolen from her. The kisses he'd been holding so close to his chest he could no longer distinguish them from the beating of his heart.

It ended here.

The study door opened behind him, followed by the soft

patter of footsteps over the carpet, but he didn't turn from the window.

He already knew who it was.

Neither of them spoke. Aside from the ticking of the clock on the mantelpiece the study was silent. He drew in a long breath, waiting.

"A gentleman, Callum—"

"Exercises moderation in all things." Despite his dark thoughts, his lips twitched. "It's port, Mother, not whisky, and only half a glass."

"I suppose that's all right, then."

Silence fell once again, the soft ticking of the clock becoming louder the longer it dragged on, until he couldn't bear it, and turned away from the window to face his mother.

"Freya—that is, Miss MacLeod—has retired for the night?"

"Not yet, no. She was a trifle restless after dinner, so I suggested she take a brief walk through the garden. It's a beautiful evening."

Was it? He hadn't noticed.

"I left her on the front drive, gazing up at the sky," his mother went on, when he didn't speak. "She's familiar with the constellations. Did you know that?"

"I did. She told me all about Cassiopeia, and the North Star."

If you ever get lost, Mr. Ross, search for the North Star.

He'd always thought Balnagown Castle was his North Star, but now . . . now, he was no longer sure. Maybe he'd only wanted it to be.

"I know about the kiss between you, Callum. I overheard you arguing about it this afternoon. You should be more careful. Anyone who happened to be near the staircase might have heard you." His mother paused. "I explained the circumstances of the lairdship to her."

He'd been staring down at his glass, but he looked up now, surprised.

But perhaps he shouldn't have been. His mother was fair-minded to a fault, but she was as partial as any other mother. She would do what she could to see as little blame as possible fell on him.

A useless endeavor, in this case. No explanation could excuse his behavior. "What did she say?"

His mother shrugged. "She listened."

"I never should have—" He broke off, an unfamiliar heat in his cheeks.

He should never have what? Looked at her? Touched her, or kissed her?

Yes, all those things, but he wasn't going to discuss it with his mother. Instead, he said only, "I suspect your explanation made little difference."

"You're quite wrong, Callum. It made a great deal of difference to her."

The taste of the port went sour on his tongue. "The circumstances of the lairdship don't excuse my kissing Freya, or my behavior this afternoon."

His mother had never been one to prevaricate, and she didn't now. "No, it doesn't, but neither are you the wicked scoundrel you seem to think you are."

He returned his gaze to his glass, the dark red liquid at the bottom swirling with a turn of his hand. The truth was, he was every bit the scoundrel his mother claimed he wasn't, and a liar, besides.

That night under the willow tree, he hadn't given Lorna or his impending betrothal a second thought. He'd forgotten all about it. That night, all his thoughts had been for Freya.

When he'd seen her there, her pale skin gilded silver in the moonlight . . .

Well, it no longer mattered. He would be betrothed to Lorna soon enough, and it did him no good to dwell on a moment that would never be anything more than that.

"How does Lorna do?" his mother asked suddenly. "I imagine she was a bit surprised to find you'd brought a young lady back with you from Dunvegan, particularly a lady as attractive as Miss MacLeod."

Lorna? Why should his mother ask about Lorna?

Unless . . . did his mother know about the betrothal? It wouldn't be surprising. She seemed to know everything that happened at Balnagown Castle, and she and Alistair Niven had been good friends.

But if she did know, surely she would have said something to him?

He gave her a sharp look, but she only gazed innocently back at him, her expression giving nothing away.

As for Lorna, if she had been offended by Freya's sudden appearance at Balnagown Castle, she'd kept her misgivings to herself. "Lorna is as she always is. We came upon Gordon and Freya in the garden this afternoon, after our ride. Lorna welcomed Freya to the castle with her usual grace."

"Yes, that does sound like her." His mother gave an approving nod. "She has a lovely temperament."

"Yes." Lorna was as easygoing a lady as he'd ever encountered.

It should have made them a perfect match, yet somehow it . . . didn't.

He did love Lorna. Even more, he liked and admired her, and there was no denying she was beautiful, but his feelings for her were distinctly brotherly. Yet he hadn't hesitated to agree to her father's request—the lairdship, in exchange for marriage to Lorna. It had made sense at the time, but that was before . . .

Before Freya MacLeod. God knew he'd never seen her coming.

But he'd made Alistair a promise, and he wasn't a man who broke his promises.

"What are your feelings for Miss MacLeod, Callum?" His mother's voice was hesitant. "Forgive me, but I think it's rather important."

"I'm not sure." It was a ridiculous reply, but true, for all that. "She's . . . I can't explain it."

Damned if he knew how he felt about Freya. He desired her, yes. He wanted her, more than he'd ever wanted any woman. A mere glance from those green eyes made his entire body burst into flames.

He'd desired ladies before, of course. He knew what it felt like. Passion and desire were simple, straightforward emotions, after all, and in his experience, fleeting ones.

Nothing like the miasma of tangled emotions roiling in his chest.

But what he felt for Freya wasn't just desire. No, it was something else entirely.

Something *more*.

He had a fierce, consuming need to protect her, but he couldn't be certain whether she'd inspired that feeling or whether it arose from the promise he'd made to Hamish.

It was a mystery he hadn't yet solved.

Or perhaps his protectiveness was just a natural result of her circumstances.

She'd been chased by a mob, for God's sake. Blamed for a fire she hadn't set, and that was just the start of it. If Clyde Stewart didn't turn up, she could be taken up for a murder she hadn't committed. Her father's death had left her destitute, and the target of every smuggling scoundrel in Scotland, and if they didn't get her, then the thief-takers on her trail would.

What man of proper feeling wouldn't wish to protect her?

If that weren't all baffling enough, there was affection there, as well, and something else, something softer than affection that he'd never experienced before. Something akin to . . .

Tenderness. Tenderness, of all things.

There had been ladies before Freya, but none of them had ever been to him what she was.

As for what else he felt for her, there were too many emotions to name. He didn't even *know* the names for most of them. She perplexed him and amused him. She occasionally irritated him, and always intrigued him.

There was only one thing he understood beyond a doubt. His feelings for her were powerful. If he'd known he could experience such emotions, he would never have made that promise to Alistair Niven.

He hadn't made the promise because he wanted to be the laird of Clan Ross. But he'd wanted to be part of something, to belong somewhere. He and his mother had spent so much of his childhood by themselves, untethered to anything, or anyone.

"Callum?" His mother was watching him, her brows furrowed as if she was confused, but he knew better. She likely understood the emotions pouring through him better than he did.

Some of the tightness left his chest as he stared back at her. His childhood had been a lonely one for them both, but he'd always had her, and having Aila Ross as his mother had been no small thing.

In that way, fate had smiled on him.

But now . . . well, perhaps she was smiling on him again, or perhaps she was merely toying with him, as a cat does with a mouse right before it deals the killing blow.

"Whatever it is you feel for Freya will become clear." She cocked her head, considering him. "Or perhaps it won't."

He snorted, but once again, his lips twitched. "Thank you, Mother. That's tremendously enlightening."

She laughed. "I beg your pardon. I wish I could be more helpful."

"You could refrain from suggesting that Gordon Corbett escort Miss MacLeod around the grounds again." When he'd come upon them on the garden pathway today, Freya had been laughing as if she hadn't a care in the world, her cheeks pink and her eyes bright.

He liked Gordon Corbett. Gordon was a decent fellow, and a damned good secretary, but that hadn't stopped him from wanting to seize the man by the neck and drag him away from Freya.

"Jealous of Gordon, are you, Callum?" His mother raised an eyebrow. "That *is* telling."

Callum opened his mouth to deny it, then snapped it closed again.

He was jealous, damn it. And Freya wasn't the only one who deserved his apology.

Gordon did, as well.

"As I said, Callum, I left Freya in the garden, without Gordon or anyone else anywhere about. She's alone, and you owe her an apology. I believe you called her a flirt earlier this afternoon?"

God above. Was there anything his mother didn't know? "I may have, yes."

"Ah, just as I thought. An apology is in order, then." His mother rose to her feet and strode to the door, turning back to him when she reached it. "I suggest you go and offer it to her now."

Chapter 18

There were no stars to be seen in the sky tonight. Cassiopeia had vanished, taking Cepheus and Draco with her, and the North Star was shrouded by the heavy clouds hovering over Kildary.

Instead of the winking silver lights, the sky was tinted a thick, murky green. It was a disturbing shade, and a rare one—one that hinted at trouble. It only occurred when there was a great deal of water trapped inside the clouds.

That green could only mean one thing.

Another storm was coming, and it would be a bad one, with violent gusts of wind and torrential rains, enough of it there was a chance Balnagown River would swell until it overflowed its banks.

If they were lucky, that is. If they were unlucky, they'd have more than rain to contend with. Freya had seen that shade of green before. On one memorable occasion there'd been hail after a green sky, sharp, stinging pellets of it raining down on Dunvegan.

At least, it began as pellets. By the time the storm had reached its full fury, balls of hard ice had pummeled the ground, some of them as wide as her palm, and as solid as her fist.

Twelve people had died on Skye that day.

There was no reason to suppose they'd be any luckier in Kildary, but Aila would see to it the clan was prepared for the worst. She'd seek Aila out before she retired to her bedchamber tonight and warn her about the impending storm.

But not yet. Not yet.

For now, she'd remain where she was, alone in the small rose garden Aila had taken her to this evening. There were no flowers to be seen now, just the bare canes, the rose blossoms having been neatly pruned for the winter, but it was a lovely, quiet place.

She drew in a deep breath of the chilly air and burrowed deeper into Cat's cloak, burying her cold hands in the pockets. She'd have a short walk, then return to the—

Wait.

There was something inside one of the pockets, something small, stuffed tightly into the corner, near the pocket's seam.

She brushed it with her fingertips. It felt like . . . a scrap of paper?

She pulled out the tiny, crumpled ball, smoothed it out against her palm, and stared down at the rough drawing, a startled laugh catching in her throat when she found her own face staring back at her. "What in the world?"

Of course! It was the silly sketch she'd drawn while she'd been lazing about on the roof, the day Callum and Keir Dunn had come to Castle Cairncross.

Goodness, how long ago that day seemed now.

She traced the lines of the sketch, the fierce eyes and dark, slanted eyebrows, the curl of a wicked grin on her lips, and the lightning bolts shooting from her fingertips.

It was her face, but not her face at the same time.

Her face, but better.

At least, that's what she'd thought when she'd drawn it, but now . . . well, it wasn't all that different from her real face. Her features were a bit exaggerated, yes, especially her eyes and mouth. The sketch made her look less like dull Freya MacLeod, and more like some fierce, avenging angel dropped down from the heavens, her lightning bolts at the ready.

But there was no mistaking that it was her.

Perhaps there'd never been anything wrong with her face to begin with.

There'd never been anything wrong with *her*.

Yet her smile faded as she stared down at this other, wilder Freya, with the power of the elements in her fingertips. She wasn't the fierce lady in the sketch—not entirely—but neither was she the lady who'd made this drawing, all those days ago.

She was neither of them, and both of them at once.

There was a part of her that was still the quiet middle sister, the one who was afraid of her own shadow. The one who'd never been much like the rest of the MacLeods, or the Murdochs, for that matter.

She was like a redheaded child that appeared from nowhere in a family of brunettes. The child who didn't quite fit. She'd always been that child, but in her family it wasn't her red hair that made her different. All the MacLeods had red hair.

It was her cowardice.

At least, she'd always thought of it that way. She'd never said so aloud, not in those words, but if she had, her sisters would have expelled every breath in their lungs arguing with her.

They'd never seen her as a coward. Only she had.

After Aila had left her alone in her bedchamber this afternoon, she'd spent hours gazing out the window, telling herself she was the same Freya she'd always been.

The middle sister. The quiet one. The coward.

She'd succeeded in lying to herself, for a time. She was an expert at it, after all.

But lies were ephemeral things, apt to change as circumstances did, and now, standing here alone in the garden with the eerie green sky above her, she saw it for the lie it was.

She could never again be the girl who'd sat atop her turret rooftop and watched the world pass by her at a safe distance, as if these last few weeks had never happened.

She would never again be able to find contentment in such a lonely existence as that.

There was no going back to her old life now. How could there be, when she was no longer the lady she'd once been? After all that had happened—the fire, Sorcha's disappearance, and the mob of villagers bent on vengeance—something fundamental had shifted inside her.

It wouldn't ever shift back again, and there was no pretending it would.

It had been easy enough to lie to herself, once. Perhaps it still would be if it weren't for Callum Ross.

It wasn't that he'd changed her. How could he? No one could change another person. Not really. True change could only come from inside you.

She'd changed *herself*.

Yet at the same time, it never would have happened without him.

Her entire existence had been upended before Callum had ever come along, yes. Since her father's death her life had collapsed, piece by piece, like a child's puzzle scattered across the floor. Lies had turned out to be truths, and truths lies, and everything had been turned inside out until she no longer recognized it anymore.

It had changed her. Of course it had. No one could lose so much and come out unscathed on the other side.

Unscathed, but whole, and no one was more surprised at it than she was. Whoever could have guessed that fear, heartache and loss could change one for the better?

Not she. Yet it had happened, all the same.

How many times had her sisters scolded her for underestimating herself? How many times had they insisted that she was remarkable, like all the Murdoch women who came before her?

As many times as she'd refused to believe them.

Even the villagers of Dunvegan, who despised her as a witch, had given her more credit than she'd ever given herself.

But her sisters had been right. She was, every inch of her, her mother's daughter.

There's a tempest inside you . . .

It had taken its time making itself known, but it had been there all along, just waiting for the right moment to burst out of her, hair wild and lightning bolts at its fingertips.

She might still be waiting, if it hadn't been for Callum.

It wasn't anything he'd said to her. If wasn't as simple as uttering a few words. If it had been that easy, her sisters would have stumbled over the right words dozens of times over by now.

No, it was more than that.

It had taken her some time to figure it out, but in the end, it came down to one thing.

Callum had believed in her. He hadn't been the first, no. Her sisters believed in her, far more than she'd ever believed in herself, but it had been Callum's hard, implacable conviction that she could do whatever she set her mind to that had made the difference.

He didn't give way to doubt, and he hadn't let her give way to it, either. When he found her under her father's desk the night of the fire and told her they had to leave Castle Cairncross at once, she'd responded as she always did to anything that frightened her.

Which, admittedly, had been most things.

She'd told him she couldn't do it. That she couldn't leave her sister, her castle, her home.

I can't, I can't, I can't . . .

And he, with all the conviction of a high-handed, arrogant laird who believed himself right in every instance, had looked her in the eye and told her . . .

You can, and you will.

The miracle of it was that she *had*. She'd scrambled over the top of that wall outside the stillroom at Castle Cairncross like a monkey climbing a tree, jumped ten or more feet down to the other side, then managed that treacherous pathway over Loch Dunvegan without a word of complaint.

She'd ridden from Dunvegan to Kyleakin, and from there to Kildary.

He'd helped her, yes. He'd been there with her every step of the way, and not once since then had she ever uttered the words "I can't" again.

And then, she'd kissed a laird.

For all her meekness, all her misgivings, all her mistrust in herself, she'd made up her mind to have that kiss, and once her mind had been made up . . .

She'd seized it. With both hands, and without hesitation.

It might not have made such a difference, if it had been just a usual sort of kiss.

But it hadn't been. It had been a tender, passionate joining of mouths that had made her heart pound and set her blood alight as it rushed through her veins.

She never could have imagined such a kiss as that, but she hadn't needed to imagine it. She'd only had to make up her mind to *take* it.

All this time, it had been as simple as that. Not easy, no. As Aila had said this afternoon, the right thing and the easy thing were rarely the same.

That was true of the simplest things, too.

How could she go back to her lonely rooftop, after such a realization as that? How could she go back to merely drawing life, instead of living it?

She couldn't. Even if it had been possible, she wouldn't.

Despite what she'd always believed, she'd never been destined for that life.

As for what would happen next, there was no telling, was there? But something new awaited her. It would come, one way or another, but it wouldn't be Callum Ross. For her remaining time here, she needed to keep as much distance between them as she could.

Because if she didn't . . . if she didn't . . .

She'd be leaving Balnagown Castle with a broken heart.

And there it was, the sad truth of it. Her heart was in danger, and she couldn't afford to lose even the smallest piece of it. She'd need every bit of heart she had to get through whatever awaited her in Dunvegan.

But until then, she'd do what she did best.

She took one last look at the sketch, then crumpled the bit of paper in her hand and stuffed it back into her pocket. Above her, the clouds skimmed across the green sky, the strange color deepening as the light shifted.

It would be a day at most before the storm would come. Perhaps by tomorrow evening. Even now the chill was descending, the goose bumps rising to the surface of her skin underneath the thin wool of Cat's threadbare cloak.

It was well past time to retire to her bedchamber. She'd find Aila, warn her about the storm, and then make her way to her bed. She turned toward the castle, the faint crunch of her boot heels on the graveled pathway loud in the silence, but she hadn't taken more than a few steps before a tall shape detached itself from the surrounding darkness.

The gloom was too thick for her to make out his features, but that never seemed to matter with Callum. Somehow, she always knew him, regardless of the darkness or the distance between them.

What was he doing out here in the garden at such a late hour?

Unless . . .

Had he come here for her?

He stepped into the glow from the window behind them, and the faint light fell across his face. The straight nose, those stern lips, and finally, when he was close enough he could have touched her, his eyes, the pale gray deeper tonight, like tarnished silver.

How much time would pass, after she left here, before those eyes ceased to haunt her?

Would they ever?

Neither of them spoke. The minutes ticked by as he joined her on the pathway and they stood there together, side by side. It wasn't an uncomfortable silence, but it was a deep one, as if thousands of words were crouching in the darkness, waiting to leap into existence the moment they were spoken aloud.

"No stars tonight," he said at last, and it seemed prophetic somehow, that he should say the very thing she'd been thinking only moments ago, as if Fate herself had put the words in his mouth.

But that was a nonsensical fancy only. There was nothing prophetic here, just two people standing in a dearth of moonlight, neither one of them looking at the other.

"No North Star." He did turn to face her then, his eyes dark, mysterious pools lost in the shadows falling across his face. "How does one find their way, Miss MacLeod, when there is no North Star in the sky?"

It felt, somehow, as if he was asking something else, something other than the question he'd voiced, but that was just another fancy of hers. "You can determine the position of the North Star by the other constellations. The Southern Cross, or Orion, perhaps."

"And if none of the stars are visible? What then?"

"Then I suppose you get lost." She smiled, but it felt unsteady on her lips, as if it were trembling there. "It's not such a terrible thing to be lost, is it, Mr. Ross?"

He didn't answer right away, but stood quietly, his gaze back on the sky above them. "Not always," he said at last. "Not if you're found again. There's a certain joy in finding what one's lost, is there not, Miss MacLeod?"

"Indeed, especially those things one doesn't realize they've lost until they find them again. But you don't need the North Star for that. Anyone who can follow the rise and set of the sun can find themselves again."

His low laugh reached her through the gloom, and a prickle

of awareness ran down her spine. "Of course, but so can anyone with a compass. Yet there's a certain beauty in the celestial method. A certain romance to it. Don't you think so, Miss MacLeod?"

Did he consider himself a romantic, then? A lover of beauty? She wanted to ask him. Her mouth opened, the words hovering on the edge of her tongue, but she closed it again without speaking. It wasn't a question a lady asked a gentleman while they stood under the sky alone, at night. It would sound as if she were flirting with him, and a flirtation with Callum Ross was no way to protect her heart.

He didn't seem to expect an answer. At least, he didn't prompt her for one. Instead, he fell silent again, his gaze still on the sky. A moment passed, then another, each one quieter yet somehow heavier than the one before it.

Finally, he drew in a breath. "The sky is a strange color tonight. I don't think I've ever seen it as green as it is now."

"There's a storm coming. Rather a bad one, I think."

"When?"

"I can't say, exactly, but sometime tomorrow, likely later in the afternoon. It may bring hail with it. Someone should see to it the cottagers are prepared."

"You expect it will be as bad as that?"

She turned her gaze back up to the sky, and the green-tinted clouds rushing across it. "I do, yes. I hope I'm wrong, but green skies like this are a harbinger of storms to come."

He nodded. "I'll ride out to the cottages tomorrow morning."

That was her duty discharged, then. There was no reason for her not to go up to her bedchamber now, and dozens of reasons why she shouldn't remain here with him, alone in the darkness. "Very well. I'll bid you good night, then."

"Wait, Freya."

Freya. Not Miss MacLeod, but Freya. She'd already taken a step away from him, but with that one word he held her suspended, her traitorous heart pounding.

She paused, her feet stilling on the pathway. "Yes?"

"This afternoon, in the corridor outside your bedchamber. I never should have . . ." He paused, dragging a hand through his hair. "It was wrong of me, to accuse you of flirting with Gordon Corbett, and I beg your pardon for it."

It had been wrong of him, yes, and it had hurt her feelings. She hadn't realized how much until her chest loosened at his words. "Your apology is accepted, Mr. Ross, and I beg your pardon for calling you arrogant and high-handed."

His brows drew together. "You didn't call me arrogant and high-handed."

"I assure you, I did." Her lips gave a traitorous twitch. "Good night, Mr. Ross."

Once again she turned to go, and once again, he stopped her. "Wait, Miss MacLeod." He bent over and picked up something that had fallen on the gravel drive and held it up. "Is this yours?"

It was her sketch. "Yes. It must have fallen out of my pocket."

She held out her hand for it, but he didn't give it to her. Instead, he carefully opened the crumpled bit of paper. He stared down at the drawing for some time, then looked back up at her. "Why did you crumple it up?"

"Because it's destined for the bin." When he said nothing, only continued to stare at her, she added, "As you can see, it's not a good likeness."

"On the contrary. It looks just like you, Freya."

Of all the things he might have said, it was, somehow, just the right one.

"I've never seen the lightning bolts, of course." He was still gazing down at the sketch. "Just as well, really. They're rather terrifying."

A surprised laugh fell from her lips. "I've never seen them either, but I'm looking forward to their arrival."

He chuckled, and they stood there for a moment, gazing at each other before they both looked away at once.

She should go, scurry up to her bedchamber before something . . . untoward happened.

Another kiss, perhaps.

But that wasn't what she did. She remained where she was, so close to him she might have reached out and touched him, the smooth slide of his warm skin under her fingertips.

Only moments ago, she'd promised herself she'd keep her distance from Callum Ross.

Yet somehow they found themselves here again, the strange green light above them and the night surrounding them, with all the unsaid words still suspended between them.

He'd only come in search of her because he owed her an apology.

That was what Callum told himself as he'd made his way from his study to the barren gardens on the east side of the castle, but as soon as he saw her, he knew it for the lie it was.

He hadn't come in search of her because his mother had insisted on it, or because he owed her an apology for the ridiculous accusations he'd flung at her this afternoon.

He'd come for her because he couldn't *not* come for her. Because somehow, he seemed to be destined to always find his way back to Freya MacLeod.

She was standing on the pathway, her slender figure limned by a lantern in the window behind her, but her face lost in the shadows. She was very still, her head turned away from him, and he paused, drinking in the sight of her.

She'd turn soon, and see him, and the moment would be lost.

"No stars tonight," he murmured, revealing himself at last.

She turned then, a smile trembling on her lips, and said . . . something. Something about the stars, and the sunrise and sunset, and the strange green hue of the sky. She told him there was a storm coming, that the green sky portended it.

They spoke of being lost, then being found again.

He offered her his apology.

Didn't he? He thought so, but the words fled his mind as soon as he'd said them.

They didn't matter. Only Freya mattered.

Freya, with her lovely face and soft green eyes. Freya, whose maddening kisses had changed everything. But she seemed anxious to be free of him, and he couldn't blame her.

What had he ever done, to earn her trust?

Yet he couldn't let her go, either. He couldn't bear it.

And so, he remained still, his body rigid with the effort it took not to call her back to him as she turned to make her way back to the castle.

But Fate decided otherwise when something fell from her pocket. "Wait, Freya." He reached down and picked it up.

It was a sketch. A rough one, clearly done in a hurry.

A sketch of her face. Wide green eyes, dark winged eyebrows and the mischievous smile he'd seen once or twice before, a slight upward quirk at the corners of her lips, and her soft, pink lower lip with that wicked curve.

And . . . a laugh rose to his lips.

Lightning bolts, shooting from her fingertips.

He gazed down at the sketch, resisting the urge to trace her lips.

". . . not a good likeness."

Not a likeness? Did she think the sketch didn't resemble her? But how could she, when every line, every curve, every bit of shading was the essence of her? Sweet, mischievous, powerful, witty, and a little bit wicked, all at once.

"On the contrary. It looks just like you, Freya."

The air around them went still, the darkness pressed closer, and for one aching moment it enveloped them, wrapping them up in its arms.

Then she stirred, breaking the spell. She took a step toward him, rose to her tiptoes, and pressed a chaste kiss to his cheek. "Thank you, Callum."

Then she was gone, melting into the shadows beyond the light spilling through the window, leaving him with the green-hued sky above him, her drawing still clutched between his fingers, and the imprint of her lips on his skin.

Another kiss. Except this kiss wasn't like the kiss they'd shared under the willow tree.

This kiss felt like a goodbye.

Chapter 19

By the following morning, the faint tinge of green that had stained the sky the evening before was gone. The ethereal hue was visible only in the darkness. It came as if out of nowhere, then vanished again as soon as the sun dipped below the horizon, leaving one to wonder whether they'd seen it at all.

But as mystical as it appeared, it was science, not prophecy.

The green color was a product of the orange glow of the waning sunset illuminating the blue water droplets inside the clouds, and Freya had seen it enough times to know there was no magic in it. That green meant the same thing, every time. The storm would come. Even now the clouds were turning darker, the ominous gray deepening.

She'd been watching them for hours.

The breakfast hour had come and gone, but she hadn't ventured downstairs. One of the housemaids had come with a tray of tea and toast, but it sat untouched on a small table, the tea gone cold.

She wasn't hiding, of course.

Her bedchamber window happened to offer the best view of the sky, that was all. Still, there was only so long a lady could bear to linger in her bedchamber without going mad. Even now the walls seemed closer and the air staler than it had been an hour earlier.

How she missed her beloved turret! She could tuck herself

out of sight on the roof as snug as a mouse in a hole and enjoy the fresh air without anyone knowing she was there.

It made the perfect hiding place for—

No. Not a hiding place. She wasn't *hiding*, dash it. Not then, and not now.

But if she did wish to go outside, she'd better go now, before the heavens unleashed the fury that was swelling in the banks of clouds rolling across the sky over Kildary.

She'd have a quick walk only, just long enough to fill her lungs with fresh air, and she'd remain close to the castle. She strode toward the bedchamber door, taking up the thick, dark green cloak Mrs. Doherty had brought, but she paused at the sight of Cat's blue cloak draped over the back of a chair, where she'd left it last night.

It was silly, of course. The wind would make quick work of Cat's poor, ratty old cloak, sneaking into every tiny tear, every loose seam. The green one was much warmer, and yet . . .

She snatched up the blue cloak. It would do well enough for a brief walk. She slid her arms into the sleeves and fastened the cloak snugly around her neck, but she left the hood down.

Cowering under a hood was too much like hiding.

Perhaps she *did* scurry down the staircase like a fox fleeing the hounds, and she *may* have allowed herself a sigh of relief when she found the entryway deserted . . .

But that was her affair, and no one else's.

She wandered the garden pathways for some time, avoiding the rose garden and instead retracing the steps she and Mr. Corbett had taken the day before, but she soon grew bored with walking in circles, and wandered deeper into the grounds, passing the kitchen garden and the dairy as she meandered along.

It grew darker as the clouds advanced, and the wind picked up, plastering the skirts of the cloak against her legs. An earthy odor filled her nose, and the air around her crackled with portent.

There was no rain yet, but she kept one eye on the sky, and

the other on the castle. It wouldn't do to wander too far, and be caught out when the rain—

"... made it back to the castle in good time."

The lady's voice interrupted her musing, faint but unmistakable.

It sounded like ...

Oh, no. It was.

Lorna Niven was coming out of the stables, the ribbons of her riding hat dancing wildly in the wind. Her head was turned away from Freya as she spoke to someone behind her.

Callum appeared in the stable doorway an instant later. They proceeded down the pathway together, walking side by side, so close their shoulders brushed.

They must be returning from the cottages. Callum had said he'd ride out this morning to warn them of the approaching storm and must have invited Lorna to accompany him.

Whatever Miss Niven was saying to Callum was making him smile.

It wasn't as if she *planned* to evade them. Her feet made the decision for her.

Such a humiliating act of cowardice was unworthy of her, but Callum's smile as he gazed down at Lorna was ... well, she simply couldn't make herself face them right now.

She darted left, off the pathway toward a small copse of towering oaks a dozen paces away, her cheeks heating with shame as she ducked behind the tallest of them. God above, she was every bit the quivering mouse she'd always been, but if she must sacrifice her pride to protect her heart, then so be it.

She waited, her breath held as Callum and Miss Niven made their way down the pathway toward the castle. As soon as they'd rounded the corner by the dovecote and were out of sight she flew toward the stables without looking back.

By the time she reached the stable door she was panting, but she wrenched it open and darted inside, dragging it closed behind her before falling back against it and pressing a hand to her chest. Under her palm, her heart was thrashing about in a frenzy, as if it were about to leap from her rib cage and fall to the dusty floor at her feet.

Her head landed against the door behind her with a dull thump. What a fool she was. If she expired right here, she'd have no one to blame for it but herself.

Yet there was no denying the relief sweeping through her. As it turned out, forcing oneself to make polite chitchat with the man one had exchanged a dozen secret kisses with was an awkward thing, and best avoided.

She hadn't yet visited the stables, in any case, and she'd been curious about them. The roof was visible from her bedchamber, and it was a massive timbered affair, the heavy beams a pleasing, dark honey brown from three centuries of weathering.

Inside, it smelled of leather and fresh, clean hay. A few raindrops began to fall, their soft patter hitting the roof above her. If she didn't fancy being caught in a downpour she'd have to return to the castle soon, but there was time yet.

She wandered farther inside, peering into the corners as she went.

It was dim, but not as dim as she would have expected. She followed the pale light into the main part of the stables. Wide stalls lined the walls on both sides, and each one had its own half-moon–shaped window behind it.

How handsome it was! But then a lovely castle must have lovely stables.

She wandered about for a bit, stroking a velvety nose here and there and murmuring to the horses as she went, until she reached the last stall in the row. Callum's horse Titan was inside it, calmly helping himself to some hay.

"Hello there."

The horse lifted his head, his liquid dark eyes on her. She

edged closer, bracing a hand on a thick beam beside the stall so she might see over the top of the tall door. It was spacious inside, as befit a horse of Titan's stature, with an abundance of clean bedding hay arranged neatly along the side of the wall.

"My, that is a snug bed you have." Titan knickered a response, and she ran a hand over his sleek, muscular neck. "There, you're a handsome gentleman, aren't you?"

She crooned to him for a bit, but it wouldn't do to linger too long. The wind had risen even in the short time she'd been here, and the rain would follow soon enough.

But just as she was turning toward the stable door, ready to make her way back to the castle, a movement caught her eye, and she paused.

What in the world? The beam on which she'd been resting her hand was *moving*.

She stepped closer, peering at it in the dim light. "My goodness. Where did you all come from?"

A caravan of determined spiders was marching along in a dark parade of furry bodies and scrambling legs as thin as threads.

There was nothing unusual about spiders in a stable, of course, but there were so many! Dozens of them—no, not dozens, but hundreds of them were scurrying busily about as if on some sort of spidery mission.

Where had they all come from?

She peered up into the rafters, and above her, she could just make out the silky threads of spiderwebs tucked into the corners where the beams met. Some of the spiders were coming from there, while others had made their homes in the deep cracks in the weathered wood.

They were all moving in the same direction.

Down, toward the floor.

How curious. The spiders were abandoning their webs.

She didn't know much about spiders. Insects, animals, and most particularly birds were more Sorcha's area of expertise.

She and the spiders had come to an unspoken truce years ago. They kept to their part of the castle, and she kept to hers.

It was a mutually agreeable arrangement, spiders being, upon the whole, averse to being crushed under careless feet, while she was averse to eight-legged crawly things creeping up her skirts or into her sleeves.

Or worse, into her hair.

There wasn't a lady alive who wanted spiders in her hair.

She'd encroached upon the spiders' territory this afternoon, however.

Wasn't there an old wives' tale about spiders abandoning their webs being a harbinger of bad weather? When the spiders fled their homes and moved closer to the ground, it was meant to be a sign that a storm was approaching.

It was true that spiders were remarkably attuned to weather changes because of their ability to detect minute shifts in the air currents, and here were the Balnagown spiders, already taking refuge from whatever fury the sky would unleash on Kildary.

She'd never put much stock in old wives' tale, but such tales became old for a reason. There was often a grain of truth in them.

If the spiders had the right of it, the storm would come soon enough.

Above her, the dust motes danced in the pale beam of light streaming through the window, the filaments of the broken spiderwebs swaying in the breeze.

She rose once again to the tips of her toes and peeked through the window over Titan's back. There wasn't much rain yet, but the sky was gray, the clouds marching furiously across it.

How interesting. It seemed the spiders were in the business of predicting storms, just as she was. She'd have to pay closer attention to their comings and goings from now on.

She leaned closer, until her nose was only an inch or so from the beam. "You're all in a great hurry." She watched their tiny legs scrambling about. "It's going to be quite a storm, by the looks—"

"Are you *talking* to the spiders?"

Freya whirled around, her hand flying to her chest, her heart beating a wild tattoo under her palm. "God above! You nearly scared the life out of me."

The child—for it was a child, not more than nine or ten years old, with fair hair that was nearly white—blinked at her. She was sitting cross-legged in the corner of one of the stalls, stroking something white and fluffy nestled in her lap. "I've been here the whole time."

"Yes, well, you might have made your presence—*achoo*!"

She gulped in a breath, a violent sneeze erupting in a rush from her throat. She got a face full of dust for her trouble, the fine grit coating her throat and setting off a coughing fit that had tears streaming from her eyes. She slapped a hand over her mouth, wheezing and choking her way through the assault on her lungs.

"You didn't swallow a spider, did you?"

"Not that I'm aware of, but I thank you for putting the thought into my head." Dear God, she could almost feel dozens of hairy spider legs tickling her throat. "What have you got there? Is it a cat?"

The girl gave her the disgusted eye roll only children of that age could produce. "No. It's a lamb."

"Is it, indeed?" Freya crept closer. It wasn't fluffy, after all, but woolly, its tiny, downy head resting on the girl's knee and the rest of him—or her—nestled in a tight ball in the child's skirts. "It's quite small for a lamb, isn't it?"

"She's only a few days old. She's the littlest one, and I won't take her back, no matter what you say." The girl curled a protective hand around the lamb's head, her chin jutting out. "Her mama won't feed her."

"Oh, dear. How awful." Freya moved a few steps closer. "Is there nothing that can be done for her?"

"My papa says no, and that she's best left alone." The girl looked up from the tiny creature nestled in her lap, her stubborn, upthrust chin now wobbling. "But I couldn't do it! I couldn't bear to just leave her to die."

"Why, of course you couldn't." Freya knelt in the straw beside the girl and reached her hand out. "May I stroke her?"

The girl nodded, and Freya ran a hand over the lamb's head. It was hardly bigger than her palm, the fur as soft as the finest cotton. "Goodness, she is very tiny, isn't she? But she seems well enough for the moment."

"I gave her some milk." The girl plucked a glass bottle from the straw next to her and held it up. "I think she was very hungry, because she drank it all up, and right quick, too."

"I daresay she was. You're taking good care of her."

They sat there quietly for a little while, stroking the lamb's head in turn as the rain pattered on the roof, then Freya broke the silence. "What's your name?"

"Maisie. It's really Mairead, but I hate it."

"Do you? I think it's pretty."

"It means pearl," the girl said glumly. "What's yours?"

"Freya. It means 'noble lady,' of all ridiculous things. Particularly so for me, as I don't have a single drop of noble blood. I can't imagine what my parents were thinking, but then they named my sister Sorcha, and that means 'brightness' or 'light.' "

"Does it not suit her?"

"No, not really. That is, she's quite dazzling, but not in a luminous, shimmering sort of way. She's more of a . . . er, blazing, burning sort of bright, and I don't think that's how the Gaels intended it."

Maisie considered this, then declared with all the arrogance of a ten-year-old child, "But that's the best kind of bright."

So it was. It was a timely reminder, straight out of the mouths of babes. Freya's nose began to sting, and a hot pressure pressed against her eyes, but she managed a wobbly, "I think so, too."

They continued to stroke the lamb in companionable silence, but the wind rose another notch while they sat there in the hay. It was time she returned to the castle, but somebody must be looking for this child, and she wouldn't leave her here alone.

"Where did you come from, Maisie?"

"The cottages."

Well, that was vague enough. Children were cagey creatures, and this one more than most. She was rather like Sorcha, in fact.

Freya opened her mouth to see if she might pry more information out of the girl, but before she could say a word, Maisie announced, "I ran away."

"Ran away? You mean, your parents don't know where you are?"

"No." Maisie gave her a disgusted look. "That's what running away means, Freya."

"So it does. But hadn't you better go back before the storm comes? I daresay your parents will be looking for you."

"I'm never going back! My mama and da were going to let Cream Puff *die*!"

Cream Puff was the lamb, presumably. "I'm sure they didn't mean to—"

"So, I ran away, and I took Cream Puff with me, and I'm never going back. Never!"

God above, the child was a sheep napper. "I think—"

"And I took this with me!" Maisie held up the baby's bottle. "It's my brother's, but I stole it, and I'm not sorry, neither!"

A sheep napper, a snatcher of baby bottles, and utterly unrepentant, too. Why, Maisie was more like Sorcha with every word out of her mouth. "No, er, of course not, but you can't—"

"I'm not going back." Maisie gathered Cream Puff protectively against her chest. "You can't make me."

No, indeed. If Maisie was anything like Sorcha had been at

this age, then no one could make her do anything, but perhaps she could *persuade* her. She did have quite a lot of experience persuading stubborn, willful young ladies to do her bidding.

"How far away is your cottage, Maisie?"

"Not far. Just over the rise." Maisie waved a careless hand toward the south side of the stables. "But it doesn't matter, because I'm not going back."

"What if I came with you? I may be able to persuade your da to let you take care of Cream Puff." If Maisie's da was anything like hers had been, he'd be so relieved to have his child back safely, he'd agree to anything.

Maisie ran a gentle hand over Cream Puff's head. "Do you think you can?"

"Yes. I'm as persuasive a lady as you'll ever find. If he refuses, then I promise to bring Cream Puff back here with me. Will that do?"

Maisie glanced down at Cream Puff, then up at Freya. "Well, I don't know . . ."

"Come, I'm sure you don't wish to worry your parents."

"No, but—"

"If we're going to go, we'll have to go at once, before the storm gets any closer." It was still a good way off, but only a fool trifled with the weather.

Indeed, it might be wiser to take Maisie—and Cream Puff—back to the castle with her now, but Maisie's parents were sure to be frantic if the girl wasn't safe at home before the storm hit. Even now, her da was probably out searching for her, and he'd likely keep at it until he found her.

Maisie gazed up at her, biting her lip. "Do you promise you'll bring Cream Puff back here if Da says no?"

"I swear it, Maisie, and I'm not one to go back on my word." Freya got to her feet and held out her arms for the lamb. "Here, give Cream Puff to me, and I'll tuck her into my cloak."

Maisie hesitated while Freya held her breath, but at last she got to her feet. She pressed a soft kiss to Cream Puff's downy head, then laid the lamb gently in Freya's arms.

"Good lass. Come, let's go at once." Poor Cream Puff let out a pathetic little bleat as Freya tucked her into the folds of her cloak, but soon enough she settled, her sweet little lamb's head resting in the crook of Freya's elbow.

"I can't bear to see her die." Maisie raised big, tear-filled blue eyes to Freya. "You won't let it happen, will you?"

"No. I promised, didn't I?" It was a rash promise, but now that she'd made it, she'd keep it, even if it meant hiding Cream Puff in her bedchamber.

Maisie nodded, sniffling.

"Now, let's make haste, before the rain grows worse."

Freya hurried out of the stables, Cream Puff clutched to her chest and Maisie on her heels. Together, the three of them trudged toward the rise just beyond the stables.

Maisie had said she lived in one of the cottages.

It couldn't be far. She'd be back at the castle well before the storm came.

Maisie's cottage wasn't over the next rise, nor the rise after that.

Freya was growing concerned by the time they reached the third rise, but they hadn't come far down the other side of it before they saw a man with the same fair hair as Maisie emerge from a copse of trees to the south of the hillside.

"That's my da!" Maisie, who appeared to have forgotten that she'd made up her mind never to see her family again, tore down the hill, shouting to her father.

The man turned, relief flooding his face.

He said something to Maisie Freya couldn't hear, then he opened his arms, and Maisie rushed into them, burying her face in his shoulder.

Ah, a happy ending, at last.

She made her way to the bottom of the hill, Cream Puff bouncing in her arms. Even a tiny lamb became heavy after a time, and poor Cream Puff was in a bit of a temper. She'd been flailing about for the last half mile and had kicked Freya in the chin with one of her tiny hooves.

She was glad to relinquish her to Gregor Innes, Maisie's father.

"She was ever so well-behaved, Da. She's the politest lamb ever." Maisie blinked up at her father, the sheen of tears in her big blue eyes. "We can't let her die, Da."

Gregor Innes was no match for such a plea. "Aye, I suppose we can't, at that. Her mama may take to her still, and if not, you can be her mama." He smiled at the lamb he held in his arms. "She's a sweet wee thing, isn't she?"

"Yes, as sweet as anything!" Maisie clapped her hands together, gleeful. "Her name is Cream Puff."

"Cream Puff? Well, all right, then." Gregor turned to Freya. "I thank you for bringing Maisie . . . er, that is, Maisie and Cream Puff to me." He gave his daughter's braid an affectionate tug. "My little lass has a tender heart."

From what she could see, Maisie wasn't the only tenderhearted one in the Innes family. "I have a sister very much like her. You've got your work cut out for you," she added with a grin.

He threw his head back in a hearty laugh. "Aye, I know it. It might be best if you come back home with us, miss. I don't like the look of that sky."

Neither did Freya, but as it turned out, the Innes's cottage was another two miles walk to the south of where they were. Balnagown Castle was closer. It would be quicker for her to go back, and anyway, Aila would worry if she didn't turn up soon.

So, after receiving Maisie's grateful hug, she turned back toward Balnagown Castle.

The rain started falling in earnest before she'd made it

halfway, and by the time she reached the stables, the wind had risen to a frenzy and the sky had gone so dark it looked as if it were evening.

But there was no hail yet. She'd made it back just in time.

She hurried down the pathway that led to the castle, her hood pulled low over her head to protect her face from the shower of cold rain pouring down from the sky.

What a goose she was, choosing to wear Cat's old cloak instead of the warmer green one! Sentiment was all very well, but it was no match for the icy water running down the back of her neck, or the wind poking cold fingers into every tiny rip and worn seam—

Crack!

She stopped, her blood going cold.

She knew what that cracking sound meant. She'd heard it dozens of times before in Dunvegan Wood when the wind was high—

Crack, crack!

First came the series of smaller cracks, like ice breaking into pieces.

But it wasn't ice. That crack was the sound the tree limbs made right before they broke loose and tumbled to the ground.

It wasn't the smaller cracks she needed to worry about, but the much louder one that would come after them. In a wind such as this, massive limbs thicker than her leg and three times her weight could be tossed about as if they were no more than bits of kindling. Entire trees, trees that had stood for hundreds of years could be uprooted in an instant.

She froze in the middle of the pathway, her heart rushing into her throat, but she was right in the center of the copse, with a dozen or more trees surrounding her, and no way to tell from which direction the threat came.

Her only hope was to outrun it.

She caught her skirts in her fists and darted through the trees as quickly as she could, her gaze on the roof of the castle. It was just a little farther, right on the other side of the bend in the pathway up ahead—

She didn't see the limb break loose, but she heard it. There was an almighty crack, almost like the snap of a whip, then a dreadful tearing sound, then the whoosh of the heavy limb falling, falling . . .

Pain exploded on one side of her head, the ground rushed toward her, and then . . .

Nothing.

The world went dark.

Chapter 20

"You've been keeping secrets, Callum. Freya MacLeod's secrets."

Callum looked up from the letter he'd been writing. James was lounging in the doorway of his study, one shoulder propped on the doorframe. "Where the devil did you come from?"

"Here and there."

He'd closed the door for a reason, but James had never been one to let a closed door stop him from going where he pleased. "By all means, do come in."

"Good of you to ask." James sauntered into the room and dropped into one of the chairs in front of Callum's desk. "Now, about these secrets of Miss MacLeod's—"

"You're excused, Corbett." There was no putting James off when he was in a confrontational mood, but Freya's secrets were just that.

Hers. No one else at Balnagown Castle needed to know about them.

Except James, apparently.

Corbett laid his pen aside. "Of course."

Once Corbett had closed the study door behind him, Callum turned back to James. "Have you been prying into Miss MacLeod's business, James? I would have thought such a thing was beneath you."

"Not at all. There was no prying required. I merely mentioned her name to a friend who recently returned from Skye and got an earful about her and her sisters. I confess I was rather shocked, and I'm not one to shock easily, as you know."

An earful. That could mean anything. God knew there was no end to the gossip about the MacLeod sisters. Which rumors was James referring to?

"Smugglers, stolen treasure, and witchcraft?" James tutted, shaking his head. "One would never think it to look at her, but Miss Freya MacLeod is quite the hellion."

Nothing about arson, murder, or thief-takers, then. A small blessing, that.

"What of it? I don't see how it's any business of yours, James." Callum shrugged, but there was no mistaking the quiet menace in his voice, the coldness there.

James was no fool. He heard it for the warning it was, but he didn't heed it. "You've brought a suspected witch amongst the clan, and you think it's not my business, Callum?"

"A witch. What bloody nonsense. Don't attempt to persuade me you believe those rumors. I know you better than that, James."

"Of course *I* don't, but I wonder . . . do you suppose the rest of the clan would see it that way? I'm not certain they'd have your confidence in her."

Slowly, Callum got to his feet, rising to his full height and looming over his former friend. "Are you *threatening* me, James?"

There was only one acceptable answer to that question, but James didn't give it. Instead, he met Callum's gaze and said the one thing sure to snap Callum's tenuous hold on his temper. "Perhaps I'm threatening Miss MacLeod."

Did he move? Yes, he must have done, because somehow he was on the other side of the desk with James's coat clutched in his fists, the man's face only inches from his own. "Don't you *ever* threaten her, or I promise it will be the last thing you do."

Instead of blanching, as any man in his right mind would

have done, incredibly, James smiled. "Ah. I see how it is. I suspected as much, but I'm certain of it, now."

"What the devil are you talking about?" He'd never wanted to shake a man as much as he wanted to shake James right now. "Do you think this is some sort of game? Because I'm not amused. Not in the least."

"No, I daresay you're not." James reached up and carefully pried Callum's fingers off his coat. "There's nothing amusing about hopeless love is there, Callum?"

Love? What did that have to do with anything? He released James with a bit more force than was necessary, and James fell back into his chair with a hard thud. "I don't know what you mean."

"God above, but you're dim, Callum. Allow me to speak plainly. You're in love with Freya MacLeod."

In love, with Freya? No, surely not.

It was true he couldn't stop thinking of her. Or dreaming of her. He'd relived their kiss thousands of times in his head, and another thousand in his dreams. He'd lost his temper with poor Corbett merely for touching her, and last night, when they'd been alone in the garden . . .

It had taken every shred of his restraint not to kiss her again.

Even knowing what was at stake—Freya's reputation, his promise to Alistair Niven, his betrothal to Lorna, and the well-being of the clan . . .

None of it mattered, in comparison to how he felt about Freya.

But that didn't mean he loved her.

Did it? Was this what love felt like?

"You seem puzzled, Callum. Perhaps I can help. Did you or did you not nearly tear my head from my shoulders just now, when I threatened Miss MacLeod?"

"You may consider yourself fortunate all your limbs are still attached, yes."

"I thought so. A gentleman who isn't in love doesn't attempt to behead or otherwise maim his friends, Callum. You may lie to yourself all you like, but the fact is, you're in love with her."

"I think I need to sit down." He didn't so much sit as topple over into the chair.

"Now I know what I must have looked like when I realized I was in love with Lorna. It's even more pathetic than I expected." James studied him for a moment. "Or perhaps that's just you."

"Isn't love supposed to be a pleasant emotion? Because this is bloody awful."

James rolled his eyes. "This is *hopeless* love, Callum. Doomed love, if you will. I daresay the other sort of love is delightful enough, but neither of us will ever know if you won't dislodge your head from your arse."

"Me? How is this my fault?" But he knew. Of course, he knew.

But James was only too happy to explain. "You see, Callum, it's like this. I'm in love with Lorna, and you're in love with Freya, and neither of us can have our chosen ladies because of that blasted promise you made to Niven. It's like a nightmare version of Blind Man's Bluff, for God's sake."

"Alistair believed the marriage was what was best for the clan."

"But is it, Callum? Is it best for the clan for everyone to be made miserable?"

"I made Alistair a promise, James." He'd been made laird on the strength of that deathbed promise. How could he go back on his word now?

Yet how could he *not*?

"Does Freya love you, Callum?"

"Devil if I know." She felt something for him, yes, but love? How did a gentleman know if a lady was in love with him? "Does Lorna love you?"

"I haven't the vaguest idea."

They stared at each other for a moment, then James's lip quirked. "We're pathetic enough, aren't we?"

"God, yes. Perhaps we should find out before this goes any—"

"Callum!" The study door burst open behind them, and his mother rushed in, her face as pale as death. "We need you."

"What is it?" He shot to his feet, startled.

"It's Freya. It's been hours, and . . . one of the housemaids saw her in her bedchamber much earlier today, but she didn't come for luncheon, though she said she would, and no one's seen her—"

"Slow down, Mother." He rose and strode across the room to her, his chest tight. Aila Ross wasn't a lady who fell easily into a panic, but she was so distraught she was babbling. "Take a deep breath and start over again. Something about Freya?"

"She's missing, Callum." His mother clutched his arms, tears swimming in her eyes. "No one's seen her for hours, and no one can say where she went, but I've looked everywhere. She's not in the castle. I'm certain of it, and this weather . . ."

His mother's gaze shot to the window over his shoulder.

Freya had been right about last night's green sky. It had proved to be every bit the harbinger of extreme weather she'd claimed it would be.

It was as if the elements were locked in a pitched battle for supremacy, the ferocious wind competing with the deluge pouring from the sky. Balnagown Castle stood hunched against the violence, its walls shuddering in the wind, its windows rattling in the downpour.

And somewhere, amid all this destruction, Freya was lost.

"Fetch Corbett, James. I want the two of you to scour every inch of land from the south end of the grounds down to the Balnagown River. Go."

For once, James didn't argue, but shot past them, out the study door.

"Mother, fetch as many footmen as you can. Tell them

Miss MacLeod is missing and arrange them into parties of two men each. Have them search the fields, the woods, and the entire length of the front drive."

"Callum?"

He was already striding down the hallway, but he turned back at his mother's trembling voice.

"You'll find her, won't you?"

"I will. I promise it."

He would, no matter what it took. He wouldn't stop searching until he found her.

Anything less was unthinkable.

The rain lashed at Callum's face, blinding him, and with every step he took the howling gusts of wind pushed him two steps backward.

He was no stranger to wild weather. He'd been all over the Highlands, from Wick in the northeastern corner of Caithness all the way down to Fort William in the south, but never in his twenty-nine years had he seen a storm like the one now battering Kildary.

How would he ever find her?

He couldn't see. He couldn't move. He couldn't *think*. He couldn't hear anything but the roar of the wind, the distant torrent of Balnagown River pummeling its banks, and the endless recriminations echoing in his head.

That he was too late. That he should have stopped her from leaving the castle or noticed her absence and gone searching for her at once. That he should have taken better care of her. That he should have kissed her again, last night in the garden as they stood together under the strange beauty of the green-tinted sky.

Should have, should have, should have . . .

None of it mattered now. Nothing would ever matter again if he didn't find her.

He pushed on, shielding his face with one hand as best he could, the other stretched out in front of him, as if to catch the wind in his fist and hold it still until he found her. His coat flew out behind him, the wind snaking its way underneath it and searching out every defenseless inch of bare skin and twisting it in a brutal grip.

It didn't matter. Nothing mattered but Freya.

Yet she was nowhere. Not on the front drive, or on any of the garden pathways she'd visited with Gordon yesterday. He ran the entire perimeter of the castle, once and then again, turning in hopeless circles, praying for a glimpse of a worn blue cloak or a red curl whipping in the wind to guide his steps.

But there was only dark gray surrounding him on every side. He raised his head and searched the sky, but there was nothing reassuring there, just more unrelenting gray.

Anyone could get lost in this gloom, and Freya didn't know the estate grounds well. If she'd got turned around, she might stray into the open fields while thinking she was heading back toward the castle. A single misstep, and she could be wandering aimlessly for miles, getting farther from the castle with every moment.

But there was nothing for him to do but to keep going. Time slipped away as he passed the courtyard, and the walled garden and ornamental ponds beyond it. She hadn't taken refuge in the granary or the icehouse, and the wind had torn part of the roof off the old dovecote, leaving nothing but destruction behind.

A half hour passed, then an hour. After that the minutes blurred into each other until he no longer knew how long he'd been searching. Long enough that the dark day was edging into an even darker evening. The temperature dropped, then dropped again until his teeth were chattering with the cold, the rain turning to icy pellets that stung his skin, like thousands of tiny needles all sticking into him at once.

"Freya!" The wind snatched his voice and sent it flying into the vortex, but he kept calling for her until he grew so hoarse his voice was a whisper scraped from the deepest recesses of his raw throat.

How long had he been searching? Hours, days, his entire lifetime? He could no longer gauge the passing of time. His mind dulled as the cold sank into his bones, and his thoughts grew hazy, until he could no longer tell which way he'd already gone, and which way he was going.

All the while the wind became more frenzied, tearing at the tree limbs and sending detritus flying in every direction. There was no rhyme or reason to it, just chaos, and it would only grow worse once ice accumulated on the branches. Even those that might have withstood the wind would come crashing down then, bowing under the added weight of the ice.

And he was no closer to finding her than he'd been when he set out.

She wouldn't have gone to the river, would she? His heart shot into his throat, but no, Freya wouldn't be so foolish as that. She knew the storm was coming, and no one was more aware of the dangers of such a tempest than she was.

Yet once the fear had ahold of him, he couldn't shake it loose. It gnawed at him as he ran blindly through the grounds, one disastrous image after another all swarming him at once until panic threatened to steal the last few shreds of his reason.

The river would have overflowed its banks by now, and anyone who happened to be too close would be swept up in a torrent of freezing water.

Think. He had to think. Where would she have gone?

Not to the river. Freya was too smart for that. The fields beyond the stables, then? It didn't seem likely, but he'd looked everywhere else.

He'd go to the stables, and fetch Titan. He was getting nowhere on foot. The longer it took for him to find her, the more dire her condition would be.

Such a tiny, slender lady couldn't withstand this cold for long.

The pathway to the stables was flooded, the water rushing down the shallow slope, taking the gravel with it and leaving mud, leaves, and other debris in its place. He stumbled along, his boots slipping out from under him at every step until at last he reached the copse of oak trees halfway between the castle and the stables.

He stopped and stared.

A limb as thick as his thigh had torn loose from one of the taller trees, leaving a raw, gaping hole where it had once been. The wind had hurled it to the ground with enough force that a dozen branches had broken off and lay half buried in the mud, their leaves dancing in the wind.

He started to pass by, but he'd taken only a few steps before something made him turn back.

That was when he saw it. A fold of blue wool, fluttering in the breeze.

Freya's cloak.

"Freya!" He rushed forward and dropped down onto his knees beside her. "Freya, thank God."

But his thanks came too soon. She was lying on her front, her face turned toward the ground, and she wasn't moving. Long locks of her hair were tangled in the branches, and from the state of her cloak, it looked as if she'd been lying there for some time.

"It's all right, sweetheart. I've got you."

He didn't—not yet—but he would. He tore at the branches, snapping them off one by one, his hands shaking as he worked to untangle her. Cold and fear made him clumsy, and it took him a lifetime to free her.

But he managed to get her loose one branch at a time, until he was able to drag the heavy limb away from her. "Freya? Can you hear me?"

There was no answer.

He dropped to his knees again, caught her shoulders in his hands, and as gently as he could, he rolled her onto her back. "Freya? It's all right now. You're going to be—"

He broke off, the words dying on his lips.

There was a long, jagged gash on her temple. Blood was smeared across one side of her face, and her left eye was swollen shut. The limb had hit her, hard enough to knock her down, and she'd likely been lying unconscious ever since, the mud creeping closer to her open mouth with every drop of rain that fell.

"Freya." Her name fell from his lips in a whisper, his hand hovering over her face. She was so pale, so still, he was almost afraid she . . . but no, her chest was rising and falling. Her breaths were shallow, worryingly so, but they were there.

It was enough, for now. Just for now, he wouldn't ask for anything more than that.

He gathered her into his arms, taking exquisite care in case of broken bones, and staggered to his feet with her clutched against his chest. She didn't open her eyes, nor did she wake, but she stirred. Only slightly, but she . . .

He tightened his arms around her, his heart swelling in his chest.

She burrowed into him and rested her cheek against his chest.

"That's right, Freya," he whispered, pressing his lips to her cold cheek. "It's all right now. I have you, and I won't let anything happen to you. I promise it. I'm taking you back to the castle."

It was only a short distance from the oak grove to the castle's front door, but it was the longest walk he'd ever taken.

His mother must have been watching for him, because she was waiting for him at the door. Lorna was with her, her eyes wide as she peered over his mother's shoulder.

"Callum, thank God! Is she—"

"She's alive, but unconscious. The wind tore a heavy limb from one of the oaks near the stables, and it hit her. She's . . ." His voice broke. "She's so cold."

"Dear God." Lorna stared at Freya's still form, her hand over her mouth and her eyes wide with horror. "There's so much blood."

"Heads bleed." His mother was already springing into action, orders falling from her lips. "We'll have to see to the wound, of course, but the main thing now is to get her warm. Lorna, my dear, tell Mrs. Doherty what's happened, won't you? Tell her we need a hot bath as soon as possible, then gather as many spare blankets as you can find. Take Freya upstairs to her bedchamber, Callum, and then you may leave her to us."

"No. I'm not leaving her."

Lorna had hurried from the entryway, scrambling to do his mother's bidding, but she paused and turned back to stare at him. She said nothing, but an expression he'd never seen before passed over her face, there and then gone in an instant. He didn't have time to wonder at it before she turned and rushed toward the kitchen.

"You're right, Callum. She's much too cold." His mother pressed her fingertips to the pulse point behind Freya's ear. "Her pulse is weak. I'm afraid she must have been lying out there for some time. Take her upstairs. Quickly, Callum."

He took the stairs two at a time, taking care to jostle her as little as possible, his mother right on his heels. "Put her on the bed, then leave us, Callum."

"No. I told you, I won't leave her."

His mother was wrestling Freya out of her soaked cloak, but she turned for an instant, and her face softened when she saw his expression. "It's only for a short time, Callum. I need to get these wet clothes off her at once, and you need to get warm yourself before we have two patients on our hands."

"I'm not cold." It was true, somehow. Every inch of his body had gone numb.

All but his heart. It was thrashing about in his chest like a wild bird uselessly beating its wings, trapped. He eased closer to the bed and gazed down at Freya. "She's so pale and still."

"Yes, that's likely the head injury, and not the cold, but we won't know much until we examine her." His mother braced her hands on his shoulders and turned him toward the door. "You only hurt her further by staying, Callum. I will not remove this young lady's clothing with you standing here gawking at her."

It was her sternest voice. One didn't argue with his mother when she used that voice, especially not in a sickroom. "Only if you'll let me come back in."

"Yes, yes. You can come back when she's decently tucked into her bed." His mother waved a hand at the door, then turned back to Freya. "Now go."

It was the last thing he wanted to do. Fear was gnawing at him, and doubt whispering in his ear that if he took his eyes off her she'd somehow fade away, but he did as he was bid and turned toward the door.

He opened it, and nearly ran right over the top of Mrs. Doherty, who was standing on the other side, a pile of blankets in her arms. Behind her was a parade of footmen, two of them carrying the copper bathtub, and another four with steaming pitchers of water.

"This way," she said briskly, sweeping past him and gesturing to the footmen to follow her. "Make haste."

Freya was in capable hands. Until he found his way back to her, that would have to be enough.

The exhaustion caught up to him as he staggered down the staircase to the family wing, and from there into the hallway that led to his rooms. He didn't bother to order a bath. It would take too long. He stripped off his wet clothes and hurried into warm, dry ones, and then rushed back to Freya's bedchamber.

The door was closed, and a dozen or so servants were gathered outside it, whispering to each other. They fell silent when he appeared, and shuffled back, away from the door.

He gave a cursory knock but entered the bedchamber without waiting for a reply. Mrs. Doherty was standing beside the bed, her expression grave, and his mother was leaning over Freya, fussing with the coverlet and blankets.

"How bad is it?" His voice was so hoarse he hardly recognized it.

"That gash on her head is a nasty one. It will certainly leave a scar, which is a pity, but as bad as it looks, it appears to be superficial. I daresay she won't suffer any lasting effects from it, but we'll know more when she wakes up."

"She hasn't woken yet?" He crept closer to the bed.

Freya was tucked under the coverlet. The cut on her temple had been cleaned of blood and neatly bandaged, but his heart gave a wrench at the sight of her lying there, so pale and small and still.

"Not yet, no." His mother smoothed Freya's hair back from her face. "It's a bit worrying. Such prolonged exposure to the cold . . ." She shook her head and said no more.

But she'd said enough.

Freya hadn't woken. She might never wake—

No. He wouldn't even think it. She *would* wake up.

She had to. He wouldn't allow anything less.

"There's nothing you can do here, Callum. Why don't you go down—"

"No." He grabbed the chair by the dressing table, dragged it to the side of the bed, and sat down. "I'm staying with her."

His mother and Mrs. Doherty exchanged a glance, and he tensed for the moment one of them would say he couldn't stay, that it wasn't proper.

But his mother, who knew him better than anyone, took one look at his face and said only, "Very well, Callum. You may stay, if you like."

There was nothing to do then but sit and wait.

Chapter 21

Four days later

". . . need to stop fretting, Callum. I promise you sleep is the best thing for her."

The voice was soft, no louder than a whisper, and as soothing as the cool shade of the woods during the warmest summer months in Dunvegan.

But this wasn't Dunvegan. She wasn't at home in her beloved castle with its lopsided turret. She couldn't be, because she couldn't hear the waters of the loch washing against the rocky shoreline below.

Those waves were Castle Cairncross's ceaseless lullaby.

There were no waves here, and none of the comforting creaks and groans of her castle settling its old bones for the night. It must be night, mustn't it? Darkness pressed against her closed eyelids, and the voice near her was hushed, in the way that voices were always hushed at night.

Where was she? The answer was there, but it hovered just out of reach, like a butterfly fluttering over her open hand but too timid to land, its wings brushing her palm. She groped clumsily for it, but instead of answers, she found only a handful of shadows.

"She should have awakened by now."

It was a man's voice this time, low and deep and so familiar, like a warm palm stroking down her spine. His voice made her think of silvery moonlight, and deep, cool water, and . . . and . . . willow trees?

How strange.

But what would a gentleman be doing in her bedchamber? Or, no—not *her* bedchamber, but someone else's. Someone else's bed, as well, and a soft, lovely one it was, too, although it was a trifle worrying to wake and find oneself in a stranger's bed.

Something had happened, but she couldn't quite remember what. There'd been a pounding rain coming down on her, and the scent of hay and horses in her nose, and . . . a white cat? Yes, a woolly white cat—

No. Not a cat, but a lamb. A newborn lamb.

"Cream Puff." The lamb's name was Cream Puff, and she'd been nestling in someone's lap. A child, perhaps? Yes, a child with very fair hair, and . . . something, but what? It was like trying to put together a puzzle with half of the pieces missing.

If she could open her eyes, all might become clear, but her eyelids were so dreadfully heavy. Her eyeballs darted about underneath her weighted lids—left, right, then left again—but she couldn't quite manage to peel her lids off her eyes.

"She's trying to open her eyes." Someone leaned closer, their breath warm against her cheek. "Come now, Freya, you can do better than that. Let's have them all the way open, shall we?"

Someone groaned. It might have been her, but she wasn't certain. There was a pain in her head. She raised her hand to the place where it hurt, but she only grazed the edge of a bandage before gentle fingers wrapped around her wrist and eased her hand away.

"It's best if you don't touch it. We don't want it to start bleeding again."

Bleeding? Who was bleeding? Dear God, was it Sorcha? Or Cat?

She struggled once again with her heavy eyelids, and this time a sliver of candlelight found its way underneath them. Blurry shadows danced in her vision, but after a few blinks they resolved into recognizable shapes.

She was lying in a darkened bedchamber with a window opposite the bed. There was a dressing table beneath the window, and a hairbrush and hand mirror neatly lined up on top of it. There was a chair in one corner with a small table beside it. She was tucked into a bed with downy white sheets and what felt like dozens of blankets topped with a thick patchwork coverlet that had been pulled up to her chin.

At her bedside sat a lady in a wrinkled blue dress, her face lined with exhaustion.

She knew that face. She would have known it anywhere. "Aila?"

"Ah, there she is. Very good, Freya. Yes, it's me."

Aila's face came closer as she leaned over the bed. Her brow was furrowed with worry, and she looked so dreadfully pale and tired a little cry of dismay fell from Freya's lips. "Are you unwell? You look as if you haven't slept in days."

For some reason, this made Aila laugh. "Four days, give or take a few hours, but there's nothing wrong with me that a good night's rest won't cure. Indeed, I already feel much better, now that you're awake. We've all been terribly worried about you, my dear."

"Me? Why, what's happened? It's not Cream Puff, is it?"

"Cream Puff?" Aila's gaze fell on something hidden in the shadows on the other side of the room. "No, Cream Puff is fine, as far as I know. Do you remember what happened?"

Ah. Something *had* happened, then. She'd thought it must have, but the line between dream and reality was rather fuzzy just now. "I remember the rain, and there was wind, as well." It hurt her head to think, but the memories were right there. She groped clumsily for them, but they slipped from her hands before she could make sense of them.

"Yes. We had a rather bad storm. It's over now, but it's left a path of destruction in its wake." Aila hesitated, then, "You had a bit of an accident, Freya. The wind from the storm tore a heavy limb loose from one of the oak trees near the stables, and I—I'm afraid it hit you."

The stables . . . a bit more of the puzzle emerged, and painstakingly, the pieces started to fall back into place. "There was a young girl, in the stables." Margaret? No, that wasn't it. "Maisie. I came upon her in the stables, tending to a newborn lamb."

"Maisie Innes?" Aila gave a thoughtful nod. "That makes sense. That young one has a soft heart for the animals."

"Yes." Maisie had reminded her of Sorcha, who for all her mad ways tended to her animals with the gentle tenderness of a mother with a newborn child. "She ran away to the stables with the lamb, so I walked her home, but her cottage was farther than I thought, and Cream Puff kicked me in the chin. Aren't newborn lambs meant to be biddable creatures?"

Aila chuckled. "One would think so. Perhaps you got a stubborn one."

"I daresay I did." The MacLeods did tend to attract the mulish ones, of every species. "The wind was howling by the time I left Maisie with her father. I was on my way back to the castle, but I . . . well, it seems I didn't make it."

"You did make it, thanks to Callum. Not entirely in one piece, however."

"Callum . . ." He hadn't come to the stables with her, had he? But he'd come for her at some point. He must have done, because she remembered his voice, telling her . . . telling her that it was all right. That he had her, and she would be all right, because he'd take care of her.

And she'd believed him. Every word.

It all came rushing back to her then. The green sky last night, then hiding in her bedchamber this morning. Her walk, and the cowardly way she'd dodged Callum and Miss Niven, and the spiders abandoning their webs, and Titan's sleek neck under her palm. The scent of fresh hay and dust in her nose, Maisie and Cream Puff, and . . .

Callum.

Callum, his hands gentle on her face, and his voice soft and deep in her ear. He'd taken her into his arms and gathered her tightly against him, so his warmth became hers.

He'd held her hand, and she'd trusted everything would be all right, because he'd said it would be, and he . . . and she . . .

Well. He was making it difficult for her to put him out of her mind. Really, how was she meant to forget about him when he kept insisting on saving her life?

Because that's what this was. First the rampaging mob in Dunvegan, and now the wayward limb of an oak tree. For all that he was often cross and grim-faced, Callum made a rather gallant hero.

"You gave us quite a scare, my dear, but now you're awake, I daresay you'll mend quickly. I'm going to fetch you some beef broth, and perhaps a bit of toast. You'll watch over her for me for a little while, won't you, Callum?"

Callum! She turned her head on her pillow, wincing at the pain that shot through her temple. "Where—"

"I'm here, lass." A heavy footstep echoed in the quiet room, and one of the thick shadows in the corner of the bedchamber detached itself from the rest and approached the bed.

Then Callum was standing over her, his shoulders slumped, and his face so drawn and pale her fingers twitched on the coverlet, as if they would reach for him of their own accord.

"I'll be back soon with the broth." Aila rose and went to the door, but she turned back before leaving. "Callum, take my chair. You look like you're about to drop."

Then Aila was gone, leaving her alone with Callum in a dimly lit bedchamber that was now pulsing with fraught silence. Fraught, because there were dozens of things fighting to spill from Freya's lips at once, and she couldn't say any of them. Because if she did—if she dared to speak a word about her feelings for him—the rest would all come tumbling out after it like the Balnagown River bursting free of its banks.

Once the truth was out, there would be no putting it back again.

But there was one thing she could say. "Thank you, Callum, for coming for me, and . . . well, saving my life. Again." Dear God, had there ever been a more awkward thanks than that? She plucked at her bedcovers, avoiding his eyes as heat raced into her cheeks.

Callum didn't seem to notice, which was odd, indeed, as he was staring at her so intently she blushed even harder. His expression was strange, as well. She'd never seen that look on his face before, both devastated and hopeful at once, as if he were suspended between life and death.

"I'll always come for you, Freya."

They were, above everything, the words she wanted most to hear, but as lovely as they sounded on his lips, they weren't true, and wishing wouldn't make them so. She wanted to tell him that, to beg him not to promise things it was out of his power to give her—but after all he'd risked for her, she simply couldn't force such cold, ungrateful words past her lips.

"That's kind of you," she said instead. "Let us hope you'll have no further occasion to."

He said nothing in reply to this, but he took the chair his mother had abandoned, and then he was right there, his long legs stretched out in front of him, his broad shoulders and muscular bulk overflowing the confines of the small chair.

He was close enough now she could make out his features. Lines of exhaustion were etched into his brow and there were dark circles under his eyes. "There's no need for you to wait here with me until your mother returns. I'll be quite all right for a few—"

"No. I'm not leaving you alone, Freya."

The words weren't spoken in a tone that encouraged a debate, so she didn't attempt to argue, but settled back against her pillows, instinctively reaching for her throbbing head.

"Does it hurt?" Callum was on his feet in an instant, leaning over her, his gray eyes lost in the shadows. "Here, let me take a look at it."

With an exquisite gentleness completely at odds with his big, rough hands he lifted one corner of her bandage and peered underneath it. "It's a nasty cut. I won't pretend otherwise."

Despite the pain in her head, a smile twitched at her lips. No, he wouldn't, would he? He never pretended anything. "I want to see it."

He raised an eyebrow. "Are you certain of that? I don't think it will make you feel any better."

"I'm certain." She nodded toward the dressing table. "There's a hand mirror, just there."

It looked as if he was going to refuse, but then he rose to his feet, fetched the mirror, and brought it to her. "It looks as bad now as it's ever going to look."

She let out a choked laugh. "Er, yes. That's . . . very reassuring." It wasn't at all, but it was so utterly Callum she couldn't find it in herself to hold it against him.

He held out the mirror to her, and she held it up to her face.

It was worse than she'd anticipated. Her left eye was black, and the cut on her temple, was . . . well, there was no sense in indulging in squeamishness, was there?

It was a bloody, swollen mess. Her temple was a patchwork of raw, lacerated skin from the corner of her left eye to her hairline, or perhaps farther, if the caked blood in her hair was any indication.

She studied her reflection, taking care to keep her expression neutral, then handed the mirror back to Callum. "Well, that's going to leave a scar, isn't it?"

"It might, yes." He took the mirror from her and set it aside. "Hamish is going to have my head."

"And Cat's going to have mine."

She grinned at him, and amazingly, he grinned back. They sat there grinning at each other like utter bedlamites for far longer than they should have, and they might have kept it up if Aila hadn't bustled into the bedchamber just then, a tray rattling in her hands.

"Now, Callum. I insist you go bathe and have a rest while I give Freya some of this broth. Go on, now."

Callum didn't move. "I'm not tired."

"Nonsense. You're dead on your feet. You need to eat something, and it's been days since you slept."

Days? Had Callum been by her bedside all this time?

"I don't need to—"

"Callum Andrew Malcolm Ross. Not another *word*." Aila pointed her finger at the door. "Go."

Freya choked back a laugh. Callum hadn't inherited his bossiness from his father, then.

Callum glared at his mother, but he knew a lost cause when he saw one and rose to his feet. "Very well, Mother, but I'll be back before the sun rises."

"Yes, yes." Aila set the tray on the side table, then waved him toward the door. "We'll be pleased to have you back in a few hours, but not a moment sooner. Freya's bedchamber door will be closed to you until six o'clock."

Good God, his mother was a tyrant in a sickroom. All those poor newborn babies she'd ushered into the world must have been terrified of her.

But they'd been lucky to have her, and despite her high-handedness, he was, too.

He'd lied to her, just now. He *was* tired, weary down to his bones. He hadn't been near his bed in the four days since he'd found Freya lying unconscious in the mud.

There'd been no point in it. He wouldn't have slept.

But she'd woken, at last. After four torturous days, a brief but worrying fever, and endless hours of tossing, turning, and fretful muttering, those lovely green eyes had opened, and all was now right again with the world.

Now he could sleep.

"Wait, Callum." His mother emerged from Freya's bedchamber, closing the door behind her. "A word, please."

"A word, now? You just ordered me to bed, if you recall."

"Of course I recall it, Callum. It just happened. But before you go, I need a word with you, out of Freya's hearing."

This didn't bode well. He'd just as soon keep his secrets to himself for a while longer, but his mother had an uncanny knack for squeezing the truth out of him.

She regarded him in silence for a long moment, then seemed to make up her mind. "You're in love with Freya, aren't you?"

And there it was. He might have known it would come to this. His mother never missed anything, and he'd felt those searching blue eyes on him more than once over the long days they'd sat together by Freya's bedside.

Of course he was in love with Freya. Any doubt he might have had about the state of his own feelings had fled. He'd been a bloody fool not to see it sooner.

He was madly, hopelessly, and entirely besotted with her, and had been nearly from the start, since his second day at Castle Cairncross. She'd sent that tea tray sailing into the air, then scolded him about breaching her hems, and his heart had fallen right into her hands, though he'd been too dimwitted to realize it then.

But when he first declared himself, it would be to Freya, not his mother. "I never said I was in—"

"You didn't have to say it. A mother knows her son, Callum. I saw your face when you brought her back to the castle four days ago, and I've seen it every day since. You're in love with her."

What was the point in denying it? His mother had always been able to read him. "I'm in love with her, yes. But you look troubled, Mother. Do you have some objection to Freya?"

"Goodness, no! On the contrary. She's lovely, Callum. I can't conceive of another lady as perfectly suited to you as Freya is."

"No, neither can I." Freya was the calm to his storm, and the light to his darkness. She was everything he'd never realized he wanted, until he found it.

Found *her*.

"But you didn't chase me down the hallway to tell me how much you approve of Freya, did you, Mother?"

"No. I chased you down the hallway because there's something you're not telling me. Something is holding you back from confessing your feelings to Freya." Her blue eyes softened as she studied his face. "You can tell me anything. You know that, Callum."

He did know it. He'd always known it, and he'd never made a habit of keeping secrets from his mother. For a long time, she'd been all he had, and she'd never made him regret confiding in her.

But the promise he'd made to Alistair wasn't just his secret. It was Lorna's, too.

Still, he'd told James. It didn't make much sense to withhold the truth from his mother now. "I . . . there was . . . before Alistair died, he . . ."

Good Lord, it was harder than he'd thought it would be, to get the words out.

"I made Alistair a promise before he died," he managed at last. "A deathbed promise. He made me laird on the condition that I marry Lorna and make her lady of Balnagown Castle."

Just like that, his secret was out. He'd been carrying it for months, but like most secrets, it lost some of its power once it was told. He sagged against the wall as the weight of it dropped from his shoulders.

His mother caught her breath, her eyes closing. "I begged him not to ask it of you."

"What?" He stared at her. "You mean you knew about it, all this time?"

"No. I didn't know. Alistair mentioned it to me once, a few weeks before he died. I thought I'd persuaded him to give up the idea, but after seeing your reserve with Freya, I began to wonder if he'd gone ahead, after all."

"He did." He hadn't hesitated to agree to it, either. It hadn't seemed as if Alistair were asking too much of him, but at the time he hadn't understood that with a few careless words, he was giving away his future.

"It was wrong of him to ask it of you, Callum. He loved you as your own father did and would never have wanted to make you unhappy, but he grew fearful for Lorna, near the end."

"I know he didn't wish to make me unhappy." He'd never suspected otherwise. "But I'm the laird now, Mother. I made the man a deathbed promise. That's not something I take lightly."

"Of course not, Callum. If you did, you wouldn't be the man you are. I only meant to make you aware of the circumstances of Alistair exacting that promise from you."

"I'm not sure Alistair's intentions make any difference. In the end, I made the promise. Regardless of the reasons, to go back on it now feels like a betrayal of Alistair, Lorna, and the clan."

His mother was quiet for a moment, then she murmured, "What of your promises to yourself, Callum?"

Himself? What promises had he made to himself? "I don't understand."

"As laird, you do owe your loyalty to the clan. I don't dispute that. But you owe something to yourself, as well. Lorna is a wonderful young woman, and I'm very fond of her, but you don't love her. Not in the way you should love the lady you marry."

No, he didn't. He'd hoped he would fall in love with her over time. But his heart, it seemed, was as stubborn as the rest of him, and it wanted Freya.

Freya, with her wild red hair and green eyes, her sweetness and her bravery, and her way of loving those around her with her whole heart. No other lady would ever do for him, but her.

"You love Freya. Keeping your promise to Alistair means giving up Freya and giving up your own happiness. It's not fair to you, Callum, and not what Alistair would have wanted."

"I don't think it ever occurred to him I wouldn't fall in love with Lorna." Why should it have done? Everyone loved Lorna. There wasn't a single member of the clan who didn't look up to her. It only made sense he'd fall in love with her, too.

But hearts were awkward, delicate things, and love was unpredictable.

"No, I daresay it didn't. Alistair was as fond a father as I've ever known." His mother gave him a sad smile. "But I'm a fond mother, and I don't wish to see my son unhappy."

"I know." He took her hand, but what else was there to say?

It was an impossible situation. If he went back on his promise to Alistair, then he would no longer be the man he'd always believed himself to be.

But if he didn't, if he gave up Freya . . .

Then he would never become the man he was meant to be.

"I can't think on it now. My head is too muddled. Perhaps it will all become clear after I've slept." It wouldn't, but he attempted a reassuring smile.

His mother wasn't fooled, but it seemed they were both pretending now, because she forced a smile in return. "Perhaps it will."

"I'll return at six." He made his way down the stairs, his mother's gaze following him until he reached the landing and turned the corner, but halfway down the corridor that led to his bedchamber, he stopped.

There was only one other door in this corridor. It was the one that led into Lorna's bedchamber. He raised his hand without making a conscious decision to do so and his knuckles met the wood in a sharp rap.

This was a mistake. It was far too early in the morning to appear at her door. She'd be fast asleep still, hours from waking—

"Callum?" The door opened at once, as if she'd been expecting his knock, and had been hovering on the other side of it, waiting for him.

"Lorna. I beg your pardon. I shouldn't have disturbed—"

"It's all right. I wasn't asleep. Is something amiss?" Her hand went to her throat. "It's not Miss MacLeod, is it?"

"No. That is, yes, but it's good news. She's awake at last and appears likely to make a complete recovery."

Lorna sagged against the doorframe, the relief plain on her face. "Thank goodness."

"Yes. I—I don't know what I would have done if she . . ." He broke off, clearing his throat. "But that's not why I'm here."

"No? Why are you here then, Callum?"

Was he imagining that twitch of her lips, the touch of humor in her dark eyes?

He drew in a breath. This was it. Once he said the words, there would be no going back.

"I came to ask you a question."

CHAPTER 22

The following week

"My goodness." Freya stopped in the castle's entryway, staring through the window at the pony and cart waiting in the drive. "What's all this?"

Callum had appeared outside her bedchamber door this morning—she was sufficiently recovered from her injury that Aila had put a stop to his coming and going as he pleased—with an air of suppressed excitement she'd never seen in him before.

His gray eyes were shining, and the worried furrow in his forehead had vanished. Even his eyebrows weren't the stern slashes they usually were.

"This, Miss MacLeod, is your conveyance for today's outing."

"Conveyance? Where are we going?"

"You'll find out soon enough." He took her arm and led her out the door and onto the drive. "This is Clover," he added, pausing to give the pony's nose a gentle pat.

"Good morning, Clover. She's lovely."

Clover was a sturdy chestnut pony with a thick white mane and tail, and a jaunty white star between a pair of soft brown eyes. Freya offered her hand, laughing as Clover nipped gently at her fingers, her mouth as soft as velvet. "But Aila said we were going to take a walk in the garden. Surely we don't need a cart and pony for that?"

Aila had refused to permit her more than a sedate walk up and down the corridor outside her bedchamber until the gash in her head healed, and her bouts of dizziness had passed. Which was all very well, but there was only so much a lady could do while lying in her bed.

But finally, at long last, Aila had agreed to permit her to take a short walk around the garden pathways, and not a moment too soon. If she was obliged to spend another day in that bed, she was going to start climbing the walls, just for something to do.

"I have another destination in mind." Callum handed her into the cart, which was an exceedingly smart one, with a smooth, glossy wooden seat and shiny black wheels.

"It's not too far, I hope, or your mother will be furious with us both."

"As long as you can keep a secret, my mother never has to know." He joined her on the seat, his thigh resting against hers. He took up the reins and bent his head toward her, his lips twitching with a grin. "So, Freya. Can you keep a secret?"

Goodness, that smile, and the low pitch of his voice made every inch of her tingle with forbidden pleasure. "I—I'll do my best."

"Very good. Shall we go, then?"

"Indeed, although I can't imagine where you're taking me with such fanfare."

Although if the truth were told, she truly didn't care where he took her. He was so handsome in his navy-blue coat, with the breeze ruffling his dark hair and that mischievous smile on his lips, that she would have gone anywhere with him.

It was dreadfully foolish of her, of course, but she'd been trapped in that stale bedchamber for an age, and it was a lovely morning, despite the winter chill. The pale sunlight shone down on their heads, and the scent of fresh air and damp earth tickled her nose.

It was such a pretty day she could scarcely believe only days earlier a violent storm had sent the world crashing down around them.

Literally, in her case.

Even now, a week later, the remnants of the storm were everywhere she looked. Most of the fallen branches had been removed, but the heavier tree limbs the wind had tossed about were still half buried in pools of mud, and the little gray dovecote near the stables had been torn loose from its foundations.

"Here. Tuck this around you." Callum took up a thick rug from behind the seat and draped it over her legs. "If you catch a chill, I'll never hear the end of it from my mother."

"Nonsense. I've never felt better." But she did as he asked and wrapped herself in the rug, tucking it under her thighs to keep it in place.

He glanced at her, and there was that breathtaking smile again, right at the corners of his lips. The urge to press her fingertip into the fetching dimple on the right side of his mouth was so overwhelming her fingers twitched, but she kept them buried safely under the rug.

What would he do if she dared to reach out and touch him? If she traced the tempting line of his lower lip from one corner to the other, so she could feel the curve of his smile for herself?

It was a mystery, and one not likely to ever be revealed, given how missish she'd become. It wasn't cowardice, exactly, but more a bashfulness over the proper way to behave toward Callum.

Because it felt almost as if he were . . . courting her?

Not that she knew what was meant to happen during a courtship. She hadn't the vaguest idea. She'd never had a proper suitor before, but no gentleman could be more attentive than Callum had been during her convalescence.

He never failed to come and see her. He was outside her bedchamber every morning, and he spent hours on the chair beside her bed. Even when she'd slept through most of the day, she'd often awake to find him there, keeping watch over her, then when her strength returned he read to her, and brought her treats from the kitchen to tempt her struggling appetite.

He'd even brought her a new sketchbook, and with it half a dozen sharp pencils. When he'd offered them to her, it had been all she could do not to burst into tears.

But mostly, he simply sat with her. Sometimes he read to her. They'd gone through all three volumes of Smollett's *Peregrine Pickle* already and had just moved on to the first volume of *Humphry Clinker* this morning. Smollett's works were dreadfully scandalous, of course, which only made it more delicious.

But she liked it best when he talked to her. They talked for hours about everything, and about nothing at all. It seemed incredible now that she'd ever thought of him as taciturn.

When he wasn't talking, he listened.

If anyone had told her that the Callum Ross who'd first appeared on the drive at Castle Cairncross would sit by her sickbed and listen while she rambled on about her sisters and her father, and the smugglers that haunted the shores of Loch Dunvegan, she would have said they were mad.

At first, she thought he'd changed. Nearly a week passed before she realized she was wrong. He hadn't changed at all.

This was who Callum Ross had been all along.

The man who did all the different voices when he read to her. The man who leafed through her sketchbook, studying her very poor sketches of the view outside her bedchamber window as if they were great works of art. The man who cajoled the cook into making her Dundee cake, then served it to her in her bed with a generous dollop of cream, just the way she liked it.

The man who'd saved her.

He was . . . well, he was everything she'd ever wished for.

Yet at the same time, she couldn't make sense of any of this. Before her accident, he'd done his best to keep away from her, and despite his attentiveness now, he behaved like a perfect gentleman. Even on the rare occasions when Aila was called out of the bedchamber and they were left alone, Callum never tried to kiss her again.

No, not once.

Weren't suitors meant to try and steal kisses?

But it was just as well he hadn't, of course. A kiss would only encourage her to indulge in girlish fancies. He was merely doing as he'd promised Lord Ballantyne he would. He'd given his word that no harm would come to her, and he was a man of his word.

That was all.

And if she dreamed every night about the way his lips had felt on hers the one time they'd kissed, the warmth of his breath on her cheek and his arms around her, well . . . that said a good deal more about her than it did him.

It said something else, as well.

The time was drawing near when she'd have to leave Balnagown Castle and return home, but she could no longer deny that she'd be leaving her heart behind her when she did.

It was Callum's now. His to cherish, or his to break.

"The folly!" She turned to him, her green eyes shining. "You remembered."

"You sound surprised." Didn't she know he remembered her every word, her every sigh, her every glance? "I've brought us a hamper, and some blankets and rugs."

"You planned us a picnic?"

"Yes, I . . . is that acceptable?" His hand froze around the handle of the picnic basket, heat rushing into his cheeks. It was a bit ridiculous, a picnic in the middle of the winter, but—

"Acceptable? Callum, it's the loveliest thing ever!"

She clapped her hands together, delighted, and his uncertainty drained away at the sight of her smile. "Is it, really?"

"Of course. Everyone adores a picnic, don't they?"

She slid to the end of the bench, but he caught her hand before she could leap down from the cart. "No, indeed, Miss MacLeod. You stay as you are, and I'll see to everything."

"You won't let me help?"

Her lower lip poked out in the most adorable pout he'd ever seen, and he couldn't help but bring her hand to his mouth and brush his lips over her gloved knuckles. "No. You're my guest, and I won't allow you to lift a finger."

He spread their blankets out on the grass on the south side of the folly to block the breeze, then made her a snug little nest from the rugs before arranging the picnic things and returning to the cart to hand Freya down.

"My goodness! Is this all for us?" Freya gazed down at the array of dishes spread out over the blanket, her eyes wide.

"Yes. Mrs. Doherty saw to the hamper herself." He settled her amongst the rugs, then seated himself beside her. "She's outdone herself, hasn't she?"

"I'd say so, yes. There's enough here for a week of picnics. Ooh, are those fruit turnovers?"

"I believe so, yes. Will you have one?"

"Yes, please."

He offered her a plate with biscuits, cheese, and cold sliced meat, and one of the turnovers, then prepared her a cup of tea from the tea caddy.

She ate heartily, a sight that pleased him so much he himself forgot to eat and instead sat quietly and watched her, heat flaring in his lower belly at her dainty little bites.

It shouldn't have been erotic, but dear God, her white teeth nibbling at the flaky pastry and her tongue licking the errant crumbs from the corners of her lips was the most arousing sight he'd ever seen.

Slowly, one inch at a time, the space between them became narrower, until he was near enough to her he could have laid his head in her lap. What would that be like, to lie here with her warm thigh against his cheek while they listened to the sigh of the breeze through the trees together?

But he wouldn't touch her. Of course he wouldn't—

"Callum? Are you well? You're so quiet."

She reached for him with a hesitant hand, her soft fingers sifting through his hair, and that was all it took. One touch, and his restraint crumbled like sand under the weight of the incoming tide. He sat up, and the space between them disappeared as he gathered her into his arms and lowered his mouth to hers.

A lifetime had passed since he'd first kissed her.

Since then, he'd spent endless days longing for her, and endless nights dreaming of her taste, the hot, sweet glide of her tongue against his, and her soft whimper as he slid his hands into her hair to still her for his mouth. Yet for all those lonely days between now and the first time his lips had touched hers, her kiss still felt like home to him.

He'd been waiting his whole life for her. What a fool he'd been, not to realize it the first time he'd looked into her eyes, but then love made fools of them all. If Keir were here, he'd laugh himself sick. He'd say men were stupid about such things, then he'd slap Callum on the back and tell him to get on with it.

And so, he would. He could do nothing less.

Because it had been Freya, all along. For as long as he could remember, there'd been an empty space in his life. An empty space in his arms. An empty, aching loneliness in the deepest recess of his heart.

Even before he'd known her, he'd missed her.

But no longer. All those spaces were filled with her now.

It had taken him a while to find her, but she'd always been his North Star.

Freya didn't pull away from him. She remained tucked against him, in his arms, a smile playing on her kiss-swollen lips. "My, we do look serious today." She touched a teasing fingertip to one corner of his lips. "Such a glower, and on a lovely day like today, too."

He caught her hand and pressed a kiss to her fingertip. "Am I glowering?"

"Let me see." She rested her palm on his cheek and turned his face to hers, her gaze roving over him. "Perhaps glower isn't the right word, but for a gentleman who's on a picnic, you're terribly solemn. You have the sternest eyebrows I've ever seen."

"My eyebrows?" He choked out a laugh. "I have no idea what you mean, Miss MacLeod. My eyebrows are perfectly jovial. Some might even call them whimsical."

She threw her head back in a laugh. "Whimsical, are they? Very well, let me have a second look, then."

He remained as still as he could while she pretended to study them, but he couldn't stop himself from sliding his arm around her waist when she leaned forward and pressed a kiss to one, then the other. "I don't know that I'd call them whimsical, precisely, but they're exceptionally handsome eyebrows."

"Are they, indeed? I confess I've never given them much thought, but it's kind of you to say so. What of my nose, though? Are you at all fond of it?"

"Excessively fond, yes." She dropped a kiss on the tip of his nose. "It's as straight as any nose I've ever seen. Quite classical, really, in the Greek style."

"And my lips, Miss MacLeod? What do you think of them?"

"Well, Mr. Ross, now that you ask, I think them perfect. They're much softer than I'd ever imagined a man's lips could be, and quite my favorite part of your face." She traced her finger over them, her eyes darkening, and then she moved closer, and closer still . . .

Her kiss was shy, sweet.

She sighed as he opened his mouth over hers, and he stole that breath from her and took it into his own lungs so he might have that tiny piece of her inside him. It was everything, her kiss.

Everything he'd ever wanted.

"Come here, love." He wrapped both arms around her waist and eased her into his lap, holding her against his chest. A low growl rumbled in his throat as she twined her arms around his neck, his whispered name on her lips.

Callum, Callum, Callum . . .

He should release her. It was broad daylight, and he'd spread their picnic blanket right beside the folly, where anyone from the castle might stumble upon them.

Nothing was decided between them.

She wasn't his. Not yet.

But she would be, and she already felt like his with her lips against his, her breath in his mouth, her fingers in his hair, and her soft, tempting curves pressed against his hard angles. All his hopes and his dreams, everything he had and everything he was, began and ended with Freya.

His heart belonged to her now.

So, he'd let himself have this. This silk of her hair sliding through his fingers, her tongue in his mouth, tangling with his. The delicious curve of her bottom cradled between his thighs, and her sweetness, her warmth and innocence clasped tightly in his arms.

All he wanted in the world was to stay here beside the pond with her and listen to the gentle splash of the water against the banks and feel the breeze against their skin as he kissed her. To stay here with her until the sun sank beneath the horizon, and the sky filled with millions of stars.

She'd point them out to him then, the North Star and Cassiopeia, and Draco, with his long tail.

Queens and kings and serpents, and a universe of possibilities.

She let out another soft sigh and dropped a tiny kiss on the edge of his jaw before she put some space between them with a hand on his chest. "I've never kissed a gentleman before. I mean, before that night in Kyleakin." Her cheeks went pink. "I've never kissed any other gentleman but you."

Possessiveness roared through him, hot and primal, his every instinct howling at him to take her lips again, and whisper that his kiss would be both her first and her last, but there would be time enough to reveal the wild, untamed part of him.

That part of him was hers, just as every other part of him was, but she was innocent, and he wouldn't frighten her for the world. "I see. Is that something you want? To kiss another gentleman?"

"No! No, that's not what I meant. I just wondered if there's something . . . that is, am I doing it properly?"

"You're perfect, Freya." If she was any more perfect, he'd disgrace himself.

He touched his fingertip to the tempting hollow at the base of her throat. His mother had insisted upon bundling her up until every inch of Freya's skin was shrouded in thick layers of wool, but somehow she'd missed that tiny recess, and he laid claim to it now.

He stroked the soft skin, and her pulse fluttered under his fingertip. "May I kiss you here?"

"Yes, Callum." She cradled his cheeks in her soft palms, her green eyes twinkling. "Indeed, I'll be quite angry with you if you don't."

He cupped the back of her neck to hold her still for his kiss and brushed his parted lips over that fragrant oasis of skin. "So soft, Freya."

Her hands slid into his hair. "Touch me, Callum."

He groaned, tightening his fingers on her hips. He shouldn't be touching her—not here, and not yet, when there were still so many unresolved questions between them—but after a lifetime of waiting for her, Freya was the one temptation he couldn't resist.

His heart was beating in a wild tattoo against his ribs, and he couldn't refuse her any more than he could order it to cease pumping the blood through his veins.

He wanted her too much. Her mouth open under his, her sighs and whimpers in his ears, his name forever on her lips. He wanted to see the flush of passion rise in her cheeks and hold her trembling in his arms as desire rushed through her, her blood singing with it.

He wanted to bring her to release, here and now, with the pale sun shining down on them, and the breeze cooling their skin. "Come closer, sweetheart."

He steadied her with a hand on her back as she wriggled closer, her knees on either side of his thighs and her arms around his neck. "Yes, Freya. Just like that."

She was open to him, her body his to command, her green eyes so trusting as they met his, and he wanted . . . God help him, he wanted everything with her.

But no, not yet. Not until she was his.

Until then . . .

He brushed his lips over hers, then let them trail down her neck, drawn once again to the delicious hollow of her throat, her pulse quickening under his tongue.

"Callum, I need . . ."

"I know, love." He sank his hands into her curls and brought her mouth down to his. Her lips were warm, her tongue no longer shy. How easy it would be to let the world drop away! To let himself fall into her, to keep her here with him, wrapped in his arms.

He took her mouth again and again, his cock stiffening as she writhed above him, all her shyness falling away until she was meeting every eager stroke of his tongue. "Callum, I need you. Please."

"Shh. I've got you, Freya. I won't let you go."

He panted against her neck, her breathless plea setting his blood on fire. It was intoxicating, knowing she wanted him as much as he did her. He could feel her body humming with it, hear it in every ragged breath she drew.

She fumbled with her skirts, hiking them higher, and he slid his hand up her calf to her exposed thigh, stroking her there. "You're so soft here," he murmured against her throat, his palm circling her thigh in a teasing caress before his hand drifted higher, then higher still.

"May I touch you, Freya?" He brushed his fingers over the soft curls between her legs, biting back a groan when he felt the dampness there. "Right here?"

"Yes, yes. Please."

Her breath caught as he opened her with gentle fingers, parting her folds to find the center of her pleasure. Then he was stroking her with his fingertip, his breath hard and fast, another desperate groan tearing from his lips when she thrust her hips toward his hand

"Oh, I . . . *Callum*." She was lost to him, and he was drowning in her soft cries and the exquisite slide of her hot damp folds against his seeking fingers.

He stroked her slowly, circling and petting her until she was crying out for him, her back arching with pleasure. Her head fell back, exposing her long white neck, and he scraped his teeth gently over her sensitive skin as his fingers quickened against her slick flesh.

He tormented the needy bud at her center with fast strokes, bringing her close to the edge of her release, her hips moving in rhythm with his fingers.

She gazed down at him, her cheeks flushed with passion, her green eyes wild. "I . . . I can't . . . I don't know what to do."

"Nothing at all, sweetheart. Just let me touch you. God, you're so beautiful, Freya."

And she was, with her wild red curls and her eyes dark and hazy with desire. She undulated above him, incoherent pleas falling from her lips.

"Yes, that's it. Take your pleasure, Freya."

"Oh. Oh, please. Callum, please." She tensed against him, her legs stiffening, then she let out a broken cry, her hands going still in his hair as she fell apart, trembling with her release. He gathered her close, his lips pressed to her neck until at last she sagged against him.

They held each other until she calmed, long, quiet moments passing with his arms around her and their breath mingling. His cock was swollen and aching, the tip weeping with need.

But he'd never been more satisfied in his life.

"Are you . . . was that all right?" He smoothed her damp hair away from her brow. "I didn't . . . it wasn't—"

She touched her fingertips to his mouth to quiet him, her forehead meeting his. "It was perfect, Callum." A mischievous smile curled her lips. "Almost as lovely as Mrs. Doherty's apple turnovers."

"*Almost?*" He pinched her hip. "Minx."

CHAPTER 23

"You look very pretty, Miss Freya." Annie, the lady's maid who'd been assigned to assist her tonight, ran the brush through her hair in long, soothing strokes.

It was lovely, having someone else brush out her hair for her. She'd never had a lady's maid, and it must be said that neither Cat nor Sorcha had Annie's patience with the hairbrush. Cat hurried through the task, and Sorcha yanked with such force her eyes were usually watering by the end of it.

"Do you think so, Annie?" She gazed at her reflection, excitement swirling in her belly. She'd never been one to linger in front of her looking glass, but then she'd never had much occasion to, and it was such a pleasure to primp just a bit.

"Yes, Miss Freya." Annie set the brush aside and gathered the heavy locks of Freya's hair in her hands. "Such a lovely color! Shall we do a chignon for you? I daresay the other ladies will have fancier arrangements, but I think a simpler style will suit you best."

"I'm entirely in your hands, Annie. I think a chignon would be lovely, if it's not too much trouble for you."

"It's no trouble at all, Miss." Annie twisted her hair into a thick coil and held it at the back of Freya's neck, then studied the effect in the glass. "Yes, just like that, but I think we'll leave a few long locks to trail over your shoulders. It would be a pity to pin up all those pretty curls."

Freya smiled at Annie in the glass. "Since I usually just bundle it into an untidy knot, I think I'll defer to your superior knowledge, Annie."

She did wish to look her best tonight. Not because she hoped Callum would gaze at her as he'd done at the folly this afternoon, with that soft expression in his gray eyes. Her face flushed bright pink at the memory of that tender look, and she pressed her hands to her cheeks.

Very well, then. Not *only* for that reason. Goodness, a blush did give a lady away, didn't it? Such a thing as that had never occurred to her before, but then she'd never had any occasion to blush over a gentleman.

It was to be a special dinner tonight, in part to celebrate her first appearance at the table since her injury, and in part because Callum had some sort of announcement to make. He'd been quite cagey about the nature of it, saying only that it would take place at the dinner, and that several dozen members of the clan had been invited to attend.

Then he'd warned her that these dinners involved a great deal of eating and drinking, and often ran late into the night, and made her promise she'd tell him if she grew fatigued.

It was nonsense, of course. What did fatigue matter? She'd stay from the start of the dinner to the end of it, no matter how fatigued she became. She didn't want to miss a moment of it. It would give her a special memory to look back on, once she left Balnagown Castle.

But she wouldn't think of that tonight. Tomorrow would come soon enough, and reality with it, but for tonight, she let herself feel the magic of this place, so she might hold it close to her heart once she'd gone.

"Nearly finished. Just a few more pins." Annie fussed and twisted and fluffed and pinned, her expert hands a blur of motion in the glass, then stood back at last, a satisfied smile on her lips. "There we are, Miss Freya. My, the color of that gown does flatter you, does it not? It brings out your eyes, and the fairness of your skin."

Freya ran her fingers over the neckline of the dark green dinner gown Aila had brought her this afternoon. It was a simple garment, without the usual extravagant lace and ribbon trimmings, but the style suited her, and the color was divine.

"You don't think it's, ah, a touch too revealing?" The neckline was quite wide and exposed a good bit of her chest and shoulders, and the bodice fitted so tightly to her curves that if she ventured even a spoonful too much pudding tonight, she ran the risk of bursting her stays.

"Goodness, no, Miss Freya! That's the fashion now, you know, and you do it credit." Annie leaned closer, dropping her voice. "If I had your skin, I'd wear necklines down to my ankles."

At that, Freya's cheeks went positively scarlet, and Annie let out a merry laugh. "Hush, Annie, you wicked thing."

"I only wish we had some jewelry for you." Annie frowned at their reflection. "A necklace, at least. How lovely you'd look, with a string of emeralds around your neck!"

Emeralds? My, this was to be a grand affair, wasn't it? "Do you suppose a ribbon will do?" She rummaged around on the dressing table until she found the ribbons Aila had brought and held up a dark green velvet one that matched the color of the gown.

"I'd prefer to drape you in emeralds, but we can make do with a ribbon, I suppose." Annie smoothed the velvet, then tied the ribbon around Freya's neck and fastened it with a pin with a tiny pearl on the end of it. "There! I do believe you're ready."

Freya stared at her reflection in the glass, and hardly recognized herself.

She was the same Freya she'd always been, with the same MacLeod red hair and green eyes, yet not the same Freya, at once. The upraised angle of her chin, and the proud set of her shoulders was different, as if . . .

As if the lady gazing back at her was the lady she might have been, if her mother and father had lived, and there'd never been a treasure, and the smugglers had never come to Castle Cairncross, and the villagers hadn't turned their backs on them.

The Freya she might have been, if things had been different.

If she could take it all back, everything that had happened, would she? If her father hadn't died, and there'd been no treasure, and no smugglers or fire, and no enraged villagers, then . . .

Cat would never have left Dunvegan, and Sorcha would be safe now.

But there never would have been Callum, either.

She would have gone her entire life without knowing him. She wouldn't miss him then, would she? You couldn't miss a thing you never had.

Yet somehow she would have felt the loss of him, still. He would have been there, tucked into the deepest recesses of her heart. She would have carried the shadow of him in her every thought, her every word, her every step. A man she'd never known, yet still longed for with everything she had, and everything she was.

How could she wish for that?

God help her, she wouldn't change it. Not if it meant renouncing him.

Her gaze met Annie's in the looking glass. "You've transformed me, Annie."

Annie smiled, shaking her head. "Not at all, Miss Freya. You look just like yourself."

"Good evening, Miss MacLeod. You look exceptionally well tonight." Gordon Corbett, who happened to be standing near the bottom of the staircase when she came down, offered her a courtly bow. "I think we can safely say you're fully recovered."

"Thank you, Mr. Corbett. I do feel well. And you look quite gallant this evening."

"Do I, indeed? Well, I daresay I won't be, by the end of the night. If I remember correctly, I was obliged to crawl to my bed on my hands and knees the last time we had one of these dinners. Although I daresay I don't remember it correctly. To be truthful, it's all a bit of a blur."

She hesitated when he offered her his arm, but she glanced around the entryway, and didn't see a dark head towering over the rest of the company.

Callum must not have come down yet.

So, she accepted Gordon's arm, and let him lead her into the drawing room, where the rest of the party was assembled, waiting for the bell to announce dinner. "My goodness! So many people."

"Yes, I believe Mrs. Ross said we're to seat thirty-six at the table tonight. I hear the laird had two dozen bottles of wine brought up from the cellars, and that's before we even get to the whisky."

Two dozen bottles of wine, for thirty-six people? "Dear God, there'll be no one left standing upright."

"One can hope, Miss MacLeod, one can hope. You've a great deal of merrymaking awaiting you tonight." Mr. Corbett waggled his brows. "I do hope you're up to it."

"I suppose we'll find out soon enough, won't we?"

"Not soon enough for me. We were meant to sit down at seven, but I don't see . . . ah, there's the laird now, just coming down the stairs."

Freya jerked her head to the open door of the drawing room, flushing when Mr. Corbett raised a brow at her. She'd just given herself away, hadn't she? But it was difficult to regret it when she got her first look at Callum.

Her breath caught. He was . . . goodness, had there ever been a more handsome man than he? He was wearing a kilt and a matching waistcoat in Clan Ross's red and green tartan, with the traditional garter and hose and a white linen shirt and neckcloth, but in place of the usual tartan coat he wore one in fitted black wool.

She mustn't stare. Someone would be sure to notice her gaping.

With an effort she wrenched her gaze away from him, but it was no use. It was drawn back to him almost instantly. Only a few hours earlier his smiling lips had been on hers, and his hands . . . heat swept through her, and dash it, there it was, that confounded blush that gave away her every secret.

She wouldn't think of his hands just now. It wouldn't do for her to burst into flames right here in the middle of the castle's drawing room.

"Miss Niven looks very well tonight, doesn't she?"

Miss Niven? Yes, she was there too, standing next to Callum, her lips curved in a brilliant smile at something he'd said. She wasn't dressed in traditional Highland attire, but instead wore a deep red silk gown in the latest London fashion. Her sleek dark hair was gathered into a chignon set off by half a dozen sparkling ruby pins, and she wore a matching ruby necklace around her slender throat.

"She's very beautiful." For some reason, her throat caught on those words. There was no reason it should have done, but something about seeing the two of them standing there together was—

"She is, indeed. She and the laird look well together, do they not? They'll make a wonderful laird and lady."

Laird and . . . lady? "I beg your pardon?"

The way Mr. Corbett had said it, it almost sounded as if—

"The laird, and Miss Niven. They complement each other, with their dark complexions. They'll have handsome children—er, pardon the indelicacy, Miss MacLeod."

Children? Callum, and Miss Niven?

Through the open doorway of the drawing room, Callum offered Miss Niven his arm, and the lady took it with another one of those brilliant smiles. "Are they . . . is there . . . do they intend to . . ." Dear God, she couldn't get the words out. "Are they betrothed?"

"No. Not yet. Not officially, that is, but from what I understand the matter has been decided. I believe they're waiting for Lorna's mourning period to end. Her father, the late laird, passed away just eight months ago. It's a pity he didn't live to see them wed, as he was very much in favor of the match."

Freya hardly heard him. Her head was swimming, and there was a deafening buzz in her ears, as if a thousand bees had just descended on her.

Betrothed. Callum was *betrothed*, or nearly so.

And he'd never said a word about it. Not on the long, silent journey from Dunvegan to Kyleakin. Not in the four days they'd stayed alone in Brodie's cottage, not even when they'd been wagering secrets.

While she'd been telling him all about her fears and confessing to truths she hadn't even confessed to her sisters, all that while he'd known he was betrothed, and he never said a single word about it.

Not when he was kissing her. No, certainly not *then*.

Not when they'd been alone in the garden on the night before the storm, or in the countless hours he'd sat beside her during her recovery. He'd had dozens of chances to confess the truth of his circumstances to her, yet he'd remained silent.

Dear God, what a fool she was! How had she not realized it sooner?

It made sense for the new laird to marry the daughter of the previous laird, didn't it? Lorna was a beauty, with her lovely skin and that mane of thick dark hair, and much beloved by the entire clan.

Why wouldn't Callum want to marry her? Any man would.

There wasn't a lady alive who'd make a more fitting mistress for Balnagown Castle than Lorna Niven. It was as if she'd been born to it.

A fairy-tale mistress for a fairy-tale castle.

It was perfectly obvious, looking at them now. How could she not have seen it?

She hadn't *wanted* to see it, because she was in l—

"Are you unwell, Miss MacLeod? You've gone quite white." Mr. Corbett tightened his grip on her arm. "I hope you haven't pushed yourself to do too much after such a recent injury."

She pressed her hand to her stomach. All at once the gown that had been perfect only half an hour before was too tight, too confining. It was digging into her flesh, squeezing her ribs and pressing them into her lungs until she couldn't catch her breath.

"You *are* unwell." Mr. Corbett's brows drew together with concern. "Please allow me to escort you to a chair, Miss MacLeod."

"No! I mean, no thank you, Mr. Corbett. I, ah, I'm afraid I have pushed myself too hard. I believe I'll retire to my bedchamber."

"Yes, of course. I'll take you up at once."

"No, there's no need. You're very kind, but I can make my way up by myself." She'd go up the back staircase. That way she wouldn't have to pass Callum and Miss Niven, who were still lingering at the bottom of the stairs. Callum was leaning toward her, a smile on his lips, and Lorna was gazing up at him as if . . . as if she . . .

"Please, Miss MacLeod, allow me to take you—"

"No indeed, Mr. Corbett. The dinner bell has just rung, and I wouldn't dream of making you late to dinner." She didn't wait for his reply, but crossed the drawing room, her legs wobbling underneath her green silk skirts.

For an instant she almost imagined Callum's dark gaze was following her, the heat of it heavy on the back of her neck, but she kept her steps measured, her head high and her spine straight until she reached the door at the other end of the drawing room.

But once she was through it, her composure deserted her.

She flew down the corridor and up the staircase. She made it all the way to the third floor and halfway down the corridor that led to her bedchamber before the tears started falling.

When she gained her room she dropped into the chair before the looking glass.

It was a common story, really. A man who is promised to another lady trifles with an innocent and breaks her heart.

There was a word for men like that.

Scoundrel, rogue, rake, blackguard.

And yet . . . perhaps she was too credulous, too naïve, but she couldn't make herself believe Callum was any of those things.

Or perhaps she was a pathetic fool, like so many pathetic fools before her who fell so deeply in love with a wicked rogue she could no longer tell the difference between lies and the truth.

In the end, it made little difference.

She didn't move for some time, just stared at her reflection in the looking glass until, one by one, she began pulling the pins from her hair. She was still struggling with them when there was a quiet knock on her bedchamber door.

Her hands froze, her wide-eyed gaze meeting her reflection in the looking glass.

She might have known it wouldn't be that easy to escape.

But it couldn't be Callum. He'd been far too taken up with Lorna to notice—

"Freya. It's Aila."

She didn't want to see anyone, not even Aila, and for one shameful instant she considered not answering, but it wouldn't do her any good to cower in her bedchamber.

She wanted to go home. Home to her sisters, and her roof and her lopsided turret.

The time had come for her to leave Balnagown Castle.

"Freya? Are you unwell? Open the door, dear."

She brushed her tears away, rose to her feet, and went to the door, opening it to Aila. "I'm not unwell, but I . . . I need your help, Aila."

"What's happened?" Aila hurried into the bedchamber, closed

the door behind her, and seized Freya's hands. "My goodness, you're as pale as a ghost, Freya."

"I—I . . ." Oh, God, how would she ever explain herself? The last thing she wanted was to confess to Aila that she'd fallen in love with Callum only to discover that he'd betrayed her, and Lorna, as well.

Yet what choice did she have? "I've made a rather grave mistake, Aila."

"Mistake?" Aila searched her face. "I don't understand. Whatever do you mean?"

"I wasn't aware . . . that is, Callum didn't inform me that he was . . ."

Dear God, she couldn't say it.

"Yes? Callum didn't inform you that he was what? You're scaring me, Freya."

She sucked in a breath that didn't seem to reach her lungs, and choked out, "He didn't inform me he was betrothed to Lorna Niven."

Aila stared at her, as if she couldn't make sense of what she'd heard, but then she dropped onto the edge of the bed without a word, and just like that, any hope Freya had that there'd been some mistake—that Callum hadn't lied to her—died a quick death.

Every word of it was true. She could see it on Aila's face.

Yet Aila's next words contradicted it. "They are not betrothed. Not yet."

Not *yet*? Would they be betrothed soon, then? Was he . . . oh, *no*.

Was that why he'd called the clan together for tonight's grand dinner? So that he and Lorna could announce their betrothal? Could Callum be so cruel as to kiss her with such unbridled passion this afternoon, only to announce his betrothal to another lady only hours later?

Had she mistaken his character so completely?

"There is no understanding between Callum and Lorna, only an expectation."

Expectation, understanding, what did it matter? "A gentleman who expects to be soon betrothed has no more business kissing another lady than one who is already betrothed."

"You're quite right, of course, but . . . well, it's rather complicated." Aila patted the empty space beside her on the bed. "Sit down, Freya, and I'll do my best to explain it to you."

Did she even want an explanation? It would be better for her to simply wash her hands of this business, but she let out a sigh and joined Aila on the bed.

"The arrangement between Callum and Lorna is of a rather particular nature."

A particular nature? A betrothal was a betrothal, and a lie of omission was still a lie. There was nothing complicated about that.

"I see you're not persuaded." Aila sighed. "I don't defend Callum. It was wrong of him not to make his circumstances clear from the start, but what I mean for you to understand, Freya, is that the expected betrothal between them is one of necessity, and not necessarily one of inclination."

"You can't mean that Callum doesn't wish to marry Lorna?" Or was it Lorna, who didn't wish to marry Callum?

"That is precisely what I mean. He does not wish to marry her."

But why wouldn't he wish it? Lorna was everything a gentleman could want in a bride.

Freya stared down at her hands, her heart sinking. "I can't think of a single reason he could object to her."

"Can you not, Freya? I can. It may be that he simply doesn't love her."

Her ridiculous heart took up a wild rhythm at Aila's words. "Has he said so?"

Aila hesitated. "It's not for me to speak to you about the state of Callum's heart. It's up to him to do that. As for Lorna, she is a dear, lovely young lady. I'm tremendously fond of her, but she has a mind of her own, just as Callum does. I'm not at all certain that she's in favor of the match."

Nonsense. Why, there wasn't a lady in Scotland who'd decline to marry Callum Ross! It was true he wasn't charming—not like Lorna, who certainly was—but he was strong, and kind, and protective and gentle at once, and—

And she was a very great fool.

She buried her face in her hands. Dear God, what a tangle.

"Oh, dear. I'm sorry, Freya. I'm doing a dreadful job of explaining this. Let me start again. You remember I told you Alistair Niven's dying wish was to see Callum made laird of Clan Ross."

"Yes. You said he hoped it would help unite the clan."

"That's right. But Alistair was a father, as well, and Lorna his much-beloved only child." Aila took her hand. "Callum was made laird under the condition that he'd marry Lorna Niven and make her mistress of Balnagown Castle."

She stared at Aila, her chest so tight she could scarcely draw a breath.

But why should it be? None of this was at all surprising. It made sense for the only daughter of the deceased laird to wed the man who would next lead the clan.

And it wasn't as if there could be any objection to Lorna Niven. She was a lovely, accomplished young lady, and according to Mr. Corbett, a kind one.

"I—I see." Her voice was oddly hollow.

In the end, it didn't make any difference whether Callum and Lorna's betrothal was one of necessity, or inclination.

The result would be the same, either way.

If Callum had accepted the lairdship of Clan Ross on the condition that he'd marry Lorna Niven, then he would marry her, regardless of whether he loved her or not.

Callum was a man of his word. Their marriage vows were as good as spoken.

She did not approve of him keeping his potential betrothal a secret from her, and neither did she approve of him kissing her, and er . . . doing other things with her without explaining his circumstances to her.

It had been very wrong of him. Very wrong, indeed, and yet . . .

She could understand it, too. It would have been a great deal easier if she didn't, a great deal better if he were every bit the scoundrel who trifled with an innocent lady while betrothed to another.

Because her heart was still his, as much as it had ever been.

"I need to leave Balnagown Castle, Aila. It's time for me to return to my family in Dunvegan." It wasn't as if anything had changed. She'd always intended to return to Dunvegan.

If she'd hoped that Callum would . . . well, it no longer mattered what she'd hoped.

Aila's face fell. "When?"

"As soon as it can be arranged." If she could, she'd go tonight.

Aila was quiet for a long moment, then, "Friends of mine, a Mr. and Mrs. Leland, are leaving for Plockton at first light tomorrow morning. They have a daughter there who's just had a baby."

Plockton? That was only a little over fifty miles from Dunvegan. If she could get as far as Plockton, it would be a simple enough matter to make her way home from there. "Would they object to a passenger?"

"No. They'd be glad of your company, and I'd feel much better knowing you were traveling with them. They'll have two footmen and a maidservant in a second carriage. You'll be safe with them." Aila gave her a sad smile. "I've grown rather fond of you, you see, Freya."

Tears welled in Freya's eyes. Dear lovely Aila! "And I you, Aila. Indeed, I'll miss you terribly."

Aila clutched her hand. "You won't go without speaking to Callum first, will you?"

She hesitated. Could she risk seeing Callum again?

No. If she saw him, she'd never be able to leave him. All it would take was one word, one look, one kiss, and she'd end up being the reason he broke his promise to Alistair Niven, and it would only be a matter of time before Callum grew to resent her for it.

It was better, this way. "I must, Aila. I'm sorry."

Aila nodded and rose from the bed. "Very well. I'll make the arrangements with the Lelands."

So, it was decided. Tomorrow morning, before the sun crested the horizon, she'd be on her way back to Castle Cairncross, leaving Balnagown Castle and Callum Ross behind.

Her memories of them would fade, in time, just like lovely dreams did when you tried to cling to the fragments of them.

In the end, they always slipped through your fingers.

Chapter 24

Balnagown Castle was as silent as a tomb. There wasn't a whisper in the corridors, the shuffle of a tread on the staircase, or the clink of a teaspoon to be heard.

Callum sat alone in the breakfast parlor, an empty teacup and an untouched plate of toast on the table in front of him. He'd risen with the sun this morning—worry for Freya had driven him from his bed—but he was the only one eager for the day to begin.

The members of the clan who hadn't stumbled off to their cottages in the wee hours of the morning were still in their beds in the castle's guest wing and would likely remain there for the rest of the day.

There was no sign of Freya. Not in the breakfast parlor, in the library, or in the corridor outside her bedchamber. He'd spent the better part of an hour wandering from one end of it to the other, feeling like an infatuated fool, but she hadn't appeared, and there was nothing but resounding silence coming from the other side of her door.

He'd raised his hand to knock a half dozen times, then lowered it again.

It was his fault she'd been so fatigued last night that she hadn't attended the dinner. He'd kept her at the folly too long yesterday afternoon, and he wouldn't make it worse by disturbing her early this morning.

He'd just have to wait, that was all.

He poked at his toast with a finger, moving it about on his plate. He poured another cup of tea, then left it to cool in the teacup, listening to the clock on the mantelpiece mark the passing minutes.

Tick, tick, tick . . .

Was there anything more tedious than waiting?

Patience had never been one of his virtues, but nothing in the world was more tedious to a gentleman in love than the absence of the lady who'd stolen his heart. It was absurd that he couldn't think of a single thing to do with himself, and even more absurd that an entire room could throb with the absence of a lady he'd never laid eyes on three weeks ago.

But then love was absurd, wasn't it? Absurd, and wonderful, and—

The clock chimed the ten o'clock hour.

Frustrating. Had time ever moved as slowly as this? How ironic, that after three weeks of behaving with the utmost propriety toward Freya—er, for the most part, that is—and keeping his hands utterly to himself—er, *mostly* to himself—it was going to be these final few hours that would drive him to distraction.

He'd made it this far. Surely, he could survive for another hour or two.

But all he could think about was taking her into his arms. Now that he was at last at liberty to do so—to put to rest all the remaining secrets and obstacles between them—Freya had chosen to spend the morning tucked into her bed, her eyelashes brushing cheeks pink with sleep, her lovely red-gold curls spread out across the pillow, and—

He was going mad.

A footstep in the hallway made him straighten in his chair. He turned toward the door, a ridiculously lovestruck smile on his lips only for Gordon Corbett to stumble into the breakfast room, his cravat askew and his hair disheveled.

Gordon signaled to the footman for tea, then collapsed into a chair, running his hand down his face. "God above, mightn't we close the draperies? The light feels as if it's stabbing me in the eyeballs."

Callum raised an eyebrow. "Good morning to you too, Corbett."

Gordon startled, then peered at him, blinking. "Ross? Is that you? What the devil are you doing up so early?"

"Early?" For God's sake. "It's ten o'clock, Gordon."

"Is it, indeed?" Gordon squinted at the clock. "So it is. Then the better question is, what am *I* doing up so early? Or is this considered late, if I haven't yet been to bed?"

"I'll leave that to you to decide." Although Corbett's bloodshot eyes and sallow complexion argued for the latter. What had possessed the man to show up to the breakfast table in such a state was a mystery, but at least it gave Callum something else to think about other than Freya's continued absence.

"I will never drink with Jamie Graham again." Gordon pressed his fingers to his eyes with a groan. "How the devil can that man swallow so much whisky and live to tell about it? I wouldn't have believed it if I hadn't seen it with my own eyes."

Callum snorted, although it would be less amusing if Corbett cast up his accounts in the breakfast parlor, which seemed likely enough, given how green the man looked. "A touch too festive last night, were you, Corbett?"

"It seemed like a good idea at the time," Corbett mumbled miserably, but after downing his cup of tea in one swallow, he produced a wan smile. "Lovely dinner though, Ross, and a stroke of genius, making Miss Niven laird of Clan Ross." He frowned down at his empty teacup. "I don't know why we didn't all think of it sooner."

"No, neither do I." It would have saved him a great deal of trouble and heartache if Alistair had simply made Lorna the laird from the start. It was odd, really, that he'd never thought to pass the lairdship on to his daughter. He'd bestowed it on

Callum out of some misguided sense of loyalty to Callum's father, but the truth was that Lorna was far better suited to the lairdship than he was.

In the end, what mattered was the good of the clan, and Lorna was, beyond any doubt, the best choice to bring the clan together. She was calm, steady, and intelligent. Even better, there wasn't a single member of Clan Ross who didn't adore her.

As for him . . .

He'd never wanted adoration, and he never truly wanted to be laird. It had taken some time for him to realize it, but after he met Freya, the truth had come to him as easily as breathing.

Since he was a child, all he'd ever wanted was to belong. That was all. To have something that was his, that he could call his own.

He'd thought the clan was it, and they were, in many ways.

He and his mother had found a family here, and he'd be forever grateful for it, but aside from his mother, the only person he really needed, the only person who mattered to his happiness, was Freya.

She was his future, his true North Star.

"It's a pity Miss MacLeod wasn't there to see Miss Niven declared laird of Clan Ross." Corbett helped himself to more tea, cursing when it spilled over the edge of his teacup. "I think she would have appreciated it."

Yes, she would have done, and so would his mother, who'd left the drawing room before the dinner bell was rung last night and hadn't reappeared again. It was a bit odd, but she must have gone upstairs to take care of Freya.

"On our walk the day after she arrived, Miss MacLeod told me all about her father's great aunt, Margaret MacLeod." Gordon dropped three lumps of sugar into his teacup, then set his spoon aside. "It's an amusing story. Margaret was the first female laird of Clan MacLeod, and still haunts Castle Cairncross to this day. It's a pity Miss MacLeod felt too ill to remain at dinner last night."

"Wait, do you mean to say that Freya—ah, Miss MacLeod, rather—*did* come down to dinner last night?" She had emerged from her bedchamber, then, and appeared in the drawing room? How was it she'd been there, and he hadn't seen her?

"Yes, but only for a short time." Corbett frowned. "It was a bit strange, now I think of it."

"Why should it have been strange? She's still recovering from her head injury."

"Yes, I thought so too, at first, but she looked exceedingly well when she came downstairs last night. There wasn't a hint of feebleness about her. She was all smiles and appeared to be in the pink of health. Her decline was quite sudden."

"How strange." That didn't sound like fatigue. "What did she say?"

"Nothing of note." Gordon turned his teacup in the saucer, his brow furrowed. "You came downstairs with Miss Niven, and I said . . . well, I hardly remember it now, but something about you and Miss Niven looking well together."

It was an innocent comment, the sort people made all the time, but for some reason, it made Callum's chest tighten. "Is that all? You said we looked well together, and Miss MacLeod was taken suddenly ill?"

"For the most part, yes. Or, well, I confess I did say something rather indelicate, about you and Miss Niven having handsome children together—"

"Children!" Callum shot to his feet. "For God's sake, Gordon, why would you say something like that?"

Gordon was staring at him, his mouth open. "I beg your pardon. It's not gentlemanly to speculate about such things. I do hope I didn't offend Miss MacLeod, although now I think of it, it was right after that that she took ill."

Callum pinched the bridge of his nose. God above, but the man could prattle. "What else did you say to her, Gordon?"

There was no way Gordon could have told Freya about the betrothal. No one knew about it but himself, Lorna, his mother, and Alistair Niven. There wasn't even a betrothal to discuss, for God's sake! For all the endless talk of marriage between himself and Lorna, they'd never actually been betrothed.

If there had been any sort of understanding between them, he would never have kissed Freya. He wasn't a perfect man—not by far—but he wasn't some scoundrel who'd betray his betrothed, or trifle with an innocent young lady.

But the way Gordon was staring at him, his cheeks devoid of color and that horrified expression on his face . . .

He'd found it out, hadn't he? Somehow, Gordon had found out about the betrothal, and he'd told Freya. Callum knew it, even before Gordon opened his mouth.

"Oh, dear. I'm afraid I've made a dreadful mistake. I didn't realize . . ." Gordon gulped. "You and Miss MacLeod are, er . . . the two of you are. . . ?"

"Yes." Callum took care to keep his tone even. None of this was Gordon's fault—not really. This was what came of keeping secrets. They never remained secrets for long. "What did you say to Miss MacLeod, Gordon?"

"I—I can scarcely remember now, but I believe I said you and Miss Niven were likely to be soon betrothed." Gordon dragged his hands down his pale cheeks. "I'm terribly sorry. I—I didn't intend to . . . I didn't realize—"

"It's all right, Gordon. I'll explain it to Miss MacLeod." He only hoped she'd listen to him. "How did you discover there was any discussion of a betrothal between me and Miss Niven in the first place? The clan members were not made aware of it."

"Miss Niven told it to my sister Davina. They're great friends, you know. They have been, since they were girls. I believe Miss Niven felt the need to confide in someone."

Yes, that made sense. Of course she'd felt a need to tell her troubles to her friend.

Lorna wasn't in love with him, and never had been. She thought of him as a brother. The morning Freya awoke after her accident, when he'd gone to see Lorna and had asked her if she'd take the lairdship in his place, she'd confessed to having tender feelings for James Baillie.

It was as perfect an outcome as he could have hoped for, given James was madly in love with her as well, and had made himself and Callum perfectly miserable over it. But that was all forgotten now. James and Lorna had shared more than one dance last night, and by the looks of it, they were well on their way to a courtship.

Meanwhile, Freya had fled the drawing room last night. Not because she was ill, but because the news of his courtship had hurt her. She must love him as much as he did her. Or she had, before this. God only knew what she must think of him, now that she believed he'd betrayed her.

He had to see her at once and explain it all to her, before his courtship disintegrated before his eyes. He rose and strode toward the door, but paused when Gordon jumped to his feet, alarmed. "Where are you going, Ross? I advise you not to do anything rash."

"Too late." There was no use counseling restraint to a man in love.

He *was* going to do something rash. It was as good as done already.

Gordon called after him, but he ignored him and marched from the breakfast parlor to the staircase, and from there up to the guest wing on the third floor.

He stopped in front of Freya's bedchamber. All was quiet on the other side of the door.

Too bloody quiet.

"Freya?" He knocked once, loudly. "I need to speak with you at once. Open the door."

The only reply was complete silence. Not a single breath came from the other side of the bedchamber, and there wasn't a hint of approaching footsteps.

"Freya? I'm coming in."

It would have served him right if she'd barred the door against him, but no. The knob turned easily in his hand. He pushed the door open and stepped into the bedchamber, his heart hammering in his chest.

He'd make this right. Once he'd explained it all, she'd understand.

She had to.

"Freya, I . . ." He trailed off as he glanced around the bedchamber.

There was a dark green velvet ribbon and a handful of hairpins on the dressing table, but that was all. The grate was cold, and the bed was made, the coverlet pulled neatly over the top of the pillows, as if no one had slept there last night.

There was only one thing in the bedchamber that indicated Freya had ever been there.

There was a gown on the bed. It was dark green silk, a few shades darker than her eyes. She'd laid it out across the foot of the bed with exquisite care, the skirts carefully smoothed, and lined up on the floor beneath it was a pair of matching dark green slippers.

He fingered a fold of the gown, the silk slippery between his fingers, then let it go again.

Otherwise, the bedchamber was empty. The dark blue cloak she'd worn on the journey from Dunvegan to Kildary was nowhere to be seen, and her sister's half boots—the ones that were a size too large for Freya—had also disappeared.

She was gone, and every trace of her had been erased, as if she'd never been here at all.

He sat down on the edge of the bed, stunned, his chest echoing with emptiness.

"She left early this morning."

He looked up. His mother was standing in the open doorway. "Dunvegan?"

"Yes. She's gone home."

"How?" Dunvegan was a three-day journey from Kildary.

"The Lelands left for Plockton at sunrise. They agreed to take Freya in their carriage. She'll be safe with them, Callum."

He nodded.

"She found out about the betrothal between you and Lorna."

He choked on a hollow laugh. The betrothal that never existed.

His mother took a few steps into the room, and pushed the door closed behind her. "I have no idea how she—"

"Gordon Corbett told her. He didn't mean any harm."

His mother frowned. "How in the world did Gordon find out about—"

"His sister Davina. It seems Lorna needed a confidante, so she told Davina, who told Gordon."

"Ah. That makes sense. I can understand Lorna wishing to confide in someone, but she might have chosen more wisely than Davina. Davina's a dear girl, but she isn't known for her discretion."

"Freya would have learned of it sooner or later." He stared down at his hands. "I should have told her myself. I should have explained the situation from the start."

Why hadn't he done so? He'd had so many chances to tell Freya the truth, but it had taken him so long to realize he was in love with her, and then she'd had her accident, and . . .

And so, instead of telling the truth and trusting Freya to listen to him, he'd made a bloody mess of everything.

His mother sighed. "You should have told her, yes, but it was not a typical betrothal, or even a betrothal at all. I can't speak for Freya. I don't promise she'll forgive you for keeping the truth from her, but I daresay she'd listen to your explanation, at least."

"Did she say anything before she left?" He swallowed. "I just . . . I can't believe she left without a word to me."

"I think she was afraid to see you, Callum."

"Afraid? You think Freya's *afraid* of me?" The word was like a dagger buried in his chest. She'd been afraid of him, once. Had he hurt her so badly she was again?

"No. Not of you, Callum, but of herself. I think she was afraid if she saw you, she wouldn't have the will to leave you, and she didn't want to stand in the way of you doing what you felt was best for the clan."

"That sounds like her." She had every right to despise him, yet even so, she was still putting his well-being first.

"You've made mistakes, Callum. Goodness knows there isn't a thing in the world more misguided than a man in love." She took his hand. "But a few mistakes don't mean you don't deserve happiness."

They sat there on the edge of the bed for some time, neither of them speaking until at last his mother roused herself. "Well, then. What now?"

He squeezed his mother's hand and rose to his feet.

"Callum?" His mother glanced up at him. "Where are you going?"

"To Dunvegan, to fetch my lady."

CHAPTER 25

Three weeks after she'd arrived at Balnagown Castle, Freya left Kildary behind her with as little fanfare as she'd left Skye so many days ago.

She and the Lelands made it to Plockton in good time, and without incident, and from there she went on to Dunvegan in the Lelands' comfortable traveling coach, with Mrs. Leland's rather terrifying lady's maid, Mrs. Ashwell, and one of the Lelands' sturdiest footmen as escort.

The entire journey took less than three days. In no time at all, she was standing at the bottom of the drive that led to the front door of Castle Cairncross. They'd dropped Mrs. Ashwell in Portnalong to visit her daughter, and the footman was already on his way back to Plockton.

Just like that, in the blink of an eye, her mad adventure with Callum Ross had come to an end. How strange that it should be over with so little sense of occasion, as if her entire world hadn't changed in the time she'd been gone.

As if she weren't a different person than she'd been when she'd left, but the same old Freya MacLeod, with her pencils and sketchbook and her lonely roof atop her crooked turret.

As if she hadn't left her heart in Kildary, at Balnagown Castle, wrapped in Callum Ross's hands. She was alone. It had never bothered her, being alone, but she'd never been as alone as she was right now.

Her solitude would be short-lived, however. Soon enough every villager in Dunvegan would know she'd returned, and then . . . well, God only knew what would happen then, but whatever it was, she'd brave it with her head held high.

She was a MacLeod, and MacLeods didn't cower before anyone.

This was her home. She had every right to be here. The villagers weren't likely to see it that way, but she'd face that challenge when it came.

Until then . . .

She gazed up at her beloved old castle with its cockeyed turret jutting into the sky like a scolding finger, and a peace that had eluded her these past few weeks settled over her like a warm hand on her shoulder.

Life went on, didn't it?

It was all still here, the same as it ever had been. Castle Cairncross was a crumbling old pile, to be sure, with none of Balnagown Castle's fairy-tale charm, but it was home.

She pulled Cat's old blue cloak more snugly around her neck and began walking up the drive. It was late in the day. The sun had nearly vanished underneath the horizon, but the last few rays bathed the windows in a golden light, as if a candle were aglow behind each pane of glass.

The worn heels of Cat's old half boots crunched beneath her as she made her way toward the entrance. She was halfway to the door when it swung open.

She stopped, her breath held.

Catriona was standing there, her hand over her mouth, her russet hair limned in the dying sunlight. A moment later, a dark head and a pair of broad shoulders appeared over Cat's shoulder.

Freya's eyes slipped shut.

They were here. Catriona and Lord Ballantyne were home.

"Freya." Her name left Cat's mouth in a whisper, as if her sister feared saying it aloud would break some enchanted spell, and make Freya disappear forever.

"Freya." Cat's voice was louder this time, surer, and then in the next breath she was flying down the drive as if her feet had sprouted wings, her red curls streaming out behind her. Freya stopped, dropped the small valise in her hand, and opened her arms.

Cat ran straight into them, her own arms wrapping Freya up in a tight embrace, and there was nothing, not a single thing in the world that equaled being held in the arms of a beloved sister. Freya laid her head on Cat's shoulder, just as she used to do when she was a small child, and one of the jagged holes she'd been carrying in her heart since Cat had left Castle Cairncross closed.

She'd made it. She was well and truly home.

"Freya, thank God. Thank *God*." Tears were streaming down Cat's cheeks as she patted her face, her hair, her clothing, as if to make sure Freya was truly standing before her. "I've been frantic, wondering what had become of you and Sorcha. We only just returned a day ago, and when I entered the house and found you both missing, I thought—"

"I know. I know it, Cat. I'm sorry. Shh. Hush, now. It's all right. I'm all right."

Cat released her and drew back, her gaze roving over Freya's face. "What of Sorcha? Where is she? Is she . . ." She fell silent, the tremulous smile falling from her lips when Freya shook her head.

"I don't know. I don't know where she is, Cat. I—I lost her."

It all caught up to her, then. The fire, Sorcha's disappearance, and her own desperate flight from Dunvegan. Balnagown, the fairy-tale castle without a happy ending, and Aila and Gordon Corbett and Mrs. Doherty, and Lorna Niven.

And Callum.

"Freya? Dearest, what's happened?"

. . . and Callum, and Callum, and Callum . . .

The tight band around her chest snapped, and then she was sobbing in Cat's arms—great, heaving sobs torn directly from her battered heart. She couldn't hold them back any longer, and she couldn't stop, and now she'd begun she might never stop.

Cat didn't ask any more questions after that. She simply held her, murmuring soft words as Freya wept for Callum, and Sorcha, and a dream that had felt so real until it turned to dust in her hands.

"I'm going to have Callum Ross's head for this."

Lord Ballantyne was pacing from one end of the drawing room to the other, his hands clenched into fists. "Callum first, and then Keir."

"No, Lord Ballantyne. You misunderstand me. Neither Callum nor Mr. Dunn are to blame for any of this." Freya turned to Cat. "Oh, dear. I'm doing a dreadful job of explaining it."

"I don't think he means it, dearest. At least, not literally." Cat paused and glanced up at Lord Ballantyne. "You don't mean it, do you, Hamish? You don't have any plans to behead Callum Ross, do you?"

Ah, so it was Hamish now, was it? Freya hid her smile. Cat and Lord Ballantyne hadn't found her father's treasure on their travels, but they hadn't returned as empty-handed as she'd first thought.

They'd found something else, something far more precious than money.

"No, I don't mean it." Lord Ballantyne sank down into a chair with a sigh. "I realize neither of them are at fault, but dear God, what a mess they've left behind them."

"I can't argue with that. It is rather a mess, isn't it? But you do understand that it wasn't Call—er, Mr. Ross's fault, my lord?" Whatever else happened, she had to make sure he understood that. "He did nothing wrong. Indeed, Lord Ballantyne, he saved my life."

And he'd broken her heart, but she'd rather Lord Ballantyne *not* attempt to behead Callum, so she kept that part to herself. No one needed to know how foolish she'd been, and even if she wished to, she wouldn't know where to begin.

Love, as it turned out, defied every logical explanation.

"I suppose I would have done the same in Callum's place. Right, then." Lord Ballantyne rose and began once again to pace the room. "We'll go and see the magistrate tomorrow and find out the details about this fire at Stewart's."

Cat nodded. "Yes, I think that would be best. Mr. Anderson is a reasonable man. He won't see two innocent women sent to the gibbet merely because some of the villagers demand it, and we're not entirely without friends in Dunvegan."

"No indeed, and any of the villagers who attempt to wrongfully accuse or otherwise harm a MacLeod sister will be obliged to explain themselves to me first."

Freya let out a breath. She'd made up her mind not to let any of the villagers ever shame or cow her again, but goodness, it was nice to have a tall, intimidating marquess on one's side.

"As for Sorcha, we'll find her. I daresay she's in the woods, and it may be that Keir is with her. They might return to the castle on their own once they see we're back."

"Do you think so, my lord?" If only Sorcha would return tonight! Right now, even. She'd relived the moment when Sorcha had fled into the woods a thousand times and carried the weight of it on her shoulders ever since.

She wanted her younger sister back. Whole, in one piece, and as irreverent as she'd ever been.

"I hope so, Freya, but whatever happens, I promise you both, not a single stone or branch in Dunvegan Wood will be left unturned until we find her." Lord Ballantyne grinned. "It may come to that, too. No one knows those woods better than Sorcha. I daresay she's well hidden."

"Thank you, Lord Ballantyne. Neither Cat nor I can ask for anything more than that."

"On the contrary, Miss Freya, you may ask for anything you like. But I must insist you call me Hamish, rather than Lord Ballantyne." He smiled at Cat. "I'm to be your brother, after all."

"Are you, indeed?" She'd expected it, of course. Anyone with eyes in their head could see that Cat and Lord Ball—er, Hamish—were madly in love. "Why, how fortunate we are, to have gained such a brother! But are you quite sure, Hamish? You may have noticed that the MacLeods are a bit of a handful."

"I'm sure." Hamish gave Cat a smile that didn't leave a shred of doubt as to his feelings for her. "I wouldn't have it any other way."

Well, he was properly besotted, wasn't he? All was as it should be.

She turned to Cat, taking her hands and laughing at the blush staining her sister's cheeks. "How wonderful, Cat. I couldn't be more pleased for you."

Tears glimmered in Cat's eyes, and she squeezed Freya's hands. "Thank you, dearest. But you must tell me all about what happened in Kildary. My goodness, Freya, what strange adventures you've had!"

"I have indeed, and I promise I'll tell you all about it, but tomorrow, all right, dearest? Forgive me, but I'm dreadfully fatigued, and I've rather missed my bed these past three weeks."

"Of course." Cat pressed a kiss to her cheek. "Go on up to your bedchamber, and we'll talk tomorrow."

Freya mounted the stairs slowly, but she didn't go to her bedchamber. She bypassed the third floor entirely and instead made her way into the alcove and up the turret staircase to the roof.

It looked just the same as it always had. Her little corner where she sat to sketch and daydream her days away was just as she'd left it. Even the notebook she'd set aside when Callum and Mr. Dunn came up the drive was still there, waiting for her.

She crossed to the low wall and picked it up, intending to turn over a leaf or two, but the pages were stuck together from the rain that had fallen since she'd been gone, and all the sketches inside were ruined.

Not so very long ago, such a loss would have broken her heart.

Before she knew what a broken heart was.

Had it only been three weeks? It seemed impossible that so much could have happened in such a short time.

Nothing less than everything had changed.

This was her home, still. Of course it was. Castle Cairncross would always be her home, but it would never be the same again. It couldn't be, because she wasn't the same. After everything she'd seen and done, everything she'd been through, she was no longer content to while away her days on the roof.

To sit and sketch life, instead of living it.

Callum had given that to her. He'd saved her, and in so many ways. Too many to count. She'd saved him, too, but perhaps he didn't know it yet.

Perhaps he never would, but that was all right, too.

She knew, and that was what mattered.

And then, he'd broken her heart. Yet as badly as it hurt, as much as it felt like her chest was cracking in two, she couldn't begrudge him the breaking of it.

How could she when he'd given her so much in return?

She didn't regret a moment of knowing him. Not a single moment. If she had these last three weeks to do over again, she would, without hesitation.

The sky had gone dark while she'd been with Hamish and Cat. The sun had set, and the stars were making their appearance in the sky, like millions of tiny lights winking on at once.

Ursa Minor and Cepheus, Cassiopeia and Draco.

The serpent and the queen.

The North Star.

She braced her arms on the top of the wall and gazed into the sky until the stars blurred in her eyes. And if she thought of Callum, and imagined him gazing into the same sky, well . . . no one needed to know about her silly dreams but herself.

An hour might have passed, or half a dozen of them. The wind had picked up and a chill had settled over her by the time she came back to herself.

She let her dreams go, one by one, setting them loose into the night.

She'd make new dreams, in time.

But not tonight. Tonight, she'd go to bed, just as she'd told Cat she would.

She'd just turned back to the staircase when she heard it.

The clop of a horse's hooves over the graveled drive below.

Chapter 26

"Well, Ballantyne? Are you going to stand there and glare at me all night, or do you intend to let me inside?"

Hamish crossed his arms over his chest. Otherwise, he didn't move, but remained in the doorway, blocking Callum from entering the castle. "I haven't made up my mind yet."

"Well, do you think you might get on with it? I have urgent business to attend to on the other side of that door."

He'd left Balnagown Castle on horseback only six or so hours after Freya had left in the Lelands' carriage. If he hadn't had such bad luck changing horses he would have caught up to them, but as it was, he'd been trailing them for the entire journey, only just missing them in Achmore.

To say he'd reached the limit of his patience was a drastic understatement. He wanted Freya, and if Hamish didn't move out of the bloody way, he'd go over the top of him to get to her.

"It's late, Callum. Freya went to bed hours ago. Come back tomorrow. You can see her then."

Was Hamish mad? Tomorrow was a lifetime away. "Step aside, Hamish."

"For God's sake, man. I just told you she's gone up to bed. She's asleep—"

"I—I'm not asleep."

There, standing on the last step of the staircase, half obscured in the shadows, was Freya. Her clothing was rumpled, her face was pale with exhaustion, and half her hair had come loose from her braid and hung in tangled chaos over her shoulders.

He'd never seen a more beautiful sight in his life. "Freya."

She took an eager step forward, and for one breathless instant he was certain she'd rush into his arms, but then she seemed to think better of it and stopped several paces from the door. "What are you doing here, Callum?"

What was he doing here? Didn't she know he'd follow her anywhere? That he'd chase her from one end of the earth to the other if he had to? Dunvegan, Kildary, Castle Cairncross, or Balnagown Castle—wherever Freya was, that was where he'd go.

But that wasn't what he said. No, he stumbled over his words like every other besotted fool before him. "I need to . . . I have to speak to . . . I came for you."

"Well said, Ross." Hamish still hadn't moved, but he was fighting a grin. "Perhaps you'd better sleep on it, and return tomorrow morn—"

"I'm not returning in the morning. I'm not going anywhere." Callum didn't spare Hamish a glance, but kept his gaze on Freya, drinking in the sight of her. Had it only been a handful of days since he'd seen her? It felt as if he'd been chasing her his entire lifetime. "If you don't wish to see me now, I'll wait here on the doorstep until you do."

Hamish rolled his eyes. "You've always been a stubborn, willful—"

"Perhaps you'd better let Mr. Ross in, Hamish." Catriona MacLeod appeared in the doorway and laid a hand on Hamish's arm. "Freya, I advise you to speak to Mr. Ross."

"I don't know if that's such a good—" Hamish began, but Catriona interrupted him.

"Nonsense. He's come all this way to see her, after all, and . . . well, I don't fancy the idea of him sleeping on our doorstep. If we don't let him inside, we're likely to find him here tomorrow morning, frozen to a block of ice." She gave Callum a little wink.

At last, someone with some sense! "Thank you, Miss MacLeod. Hamish? If you'd be so good as to get out of my way."

"Yes, all right, but only if Freya agrees to it."

Callum's gaze found Freya's, and God, those green eyes. They'd be the making of him, or the end of him. "Please, Freya," he murmured. "May I come in?"

She'd been standing in the doorway, staring at him as if in a trance, but his words broke the spell. "Yes, I . . ." She shook her head as if to clear it. "Yes, of course, you must come in."

At last, Hamish stepped aside, but whatever brief flash of triumph Callum might have felt died a quick death. He didn't have anything to congratulate himself for, considering he'd nearly been turned away at the door.

There was nothing to celebrate.

Not yet. Perhaps not ever.

Freya might still send him back to Kildary with a broken heart. He stepped over the threshold, searching her face in the gloom, but whatever she felt, whatever she hoped and dreamed, she kept it well hidden.

She didn't speak but led him to the third floor, and from there up the staircase winding around the inside wall of the turret, and out onto the roof beyond.

He'd been here once before, on the night of the fire, when he'd found Freya hiding under her father's desk. He hadn't time to give it more than a passing glance then, but he stopped in the doorway now, his breath stilling.

Above them, the night sky was filled with stars. Millions of them, all winking at once, and from here atop the turret they appeared so close—close enough he might have reached for one, caught it in his hand, and plucked it loose from the darkness that surrounded them. "I never realized . . . it's beautiful here."

"It is." Freya wandered to the edge of the turret and braced her arms on the wall that surrounded it. "At least, I've always thought so."

She stood there gazing up at the sky, the breeze caressing the loose locks of her hair and sending her skirts dancing around her. It was as if the night welcomed her here, as if she was a part of the darkness and the wind and the stars.

"It's different in the daylight, of course. You can see for miles around Dunvegan from here." She didn't look at him, but kept her gaze fixed on the sky. "I've always preferred it at night. There's something magical about it."

Magical. Yes, that was the only word for it. There'd always been something magical about Castle Cairncross, and about the MacLeod sisters themselves.

Not witchery. There was nothing dark about them, nothing wicked.

But there was something about them that was different, something otherworldly.

Something magical.

He joined her, resting his arms on the top edge of the wall, close to her, but not quite touching. They were quiet for some time, gazing into the sky, each of them thinking their own private thoughts until at last Freya turned to him, her face still shuttered, and her expression unreadable. "Why did you come here, Callum?"

This was what he'd come for. He'd been practicing his speeches, his declarations of love since he set out from Kildary three days earlier, yet the words he'd rehearsed all deserted him.

There was only one thing to say, only one thing that mattered. "I came because I love you, Freya. I'm in love with you."

Silence.

She didn't speak, and neither did she move. She simply stood there, as still as a statue, staring into the sky. It went on for so long his heart began a deep, heavy pounding in his chest, and a bead of sweat slipped down his back.

Why didn't she speak? Did she not return his feelings, and didn't know how to tell him? Had she decided she could never forgive him, and was angry at him for following her all the way to Dunvegan, or—

Was she trembling?

She was. Her slender body was shaking like a sapling in the wind, goose bumps rising on her arms. Her jaw clenched, and her chin began to wobble, and the next he knew tears were falling from the corners of her eyes—the beautiful green eyes he loved so well, the eyes he'd dreamed about since the first time he'd seen them—and spilling down her cheeks.

"Freya, sweetheart. Don't cry." God, he couldn't bear it.

Nothing could have stopped him from turning to her then and gathering her trembling body into his arms. "I don't . . . Freya? Please don't cry. I didn't mean to . . . I shouldn't have blurted it out like that. It was badly done of me. Have I shocked you? Forgive me, Freya—"

"You're *betrothed*, Callum!" Her hands balled into fists against his chest, her words ragged, as if they'd been torn from her very soul. "You're betrothed to Lorna Niven, and—"

"No. Shhh, love. I'm not betrothed to Lorna. I was never betrothed to her."

"Then you've gone back on your word to her father, and you're not a man who goes back on your word! It will plague you, and you'll grow to resent it, and before long you'll come to resent *me*, and everything is perfectly horrid!" She buried her face in his chest and burst into a flood of tears.

He'd made a terrible mess of this. He must have done, because he'd never seen her weep as she was right now, as if her heart was shattering into a thousand pieces inside her chest.

"Freya, love, listen to me." He caught her chin in his fingers and raised her face to his. "I'm not betrothed to Lorna, and I didn't break my promise to Alistair Niven. I gave up the lairdship."

She went on weeping as if she hadn't heard him, but after a moment his words seemed to sink in, and she pulled back to stare at him. "You *gave it up*? But how can you just . . . can you do that?"

"You can, and I did. It's done, sweetheart. I asked Lorna to take the lairdship in my place, and she agreed to it."

"You gave up the lairdship to Lorna Niven," she repeated, as if she weren't sure what the words meant, and was trying to make sense of them.

"Yes." He brushed the tears from her cheeks. "She's far better suited to it than I ever could be. It should have been hers from the start."

"But . . . but don't you want to be laird?"

"I want *you*, Freya. Lorna and I were never betrothed, and there's never been anything romantic between us. The match only ever existed in her father's head, but I should have told you all this at once. I made a mistake, and I beg your pardon for it."

"You . . . you want me?"

"*Yes*, Freya. I never wished to marry Lorna. I never truly wanted to be laird, either. For a long time, I didn't know what I wanted, but I do now." He traced his fingers over her damp cheek. "All I want, all that matters to me, is you. I'm madly in love with you, Freya. I can't imagine my life without you."

"You . . . you gave up the lairdship, for *me*?"

"Don't you know? I'd do anything, give up everything else, for you. Do you think . . . could you ever come to love me, Freya?"

"Come to love you?" Her arms stole around his neck. "Ridiculous, wonderful man! I *do* love you, Callum. I love you so much I scarcely know what to do with myself."

He closed his eyes and let her words flow over him, sink into him, and wind their way around his heart before drawing her close and lowering his mouth to hers. He held her against him and kissed her with the velvety darkness enveloping them, and the stars twinkling above.

When they broke apart at last they were both panting. Freya's cheeks were flushed, her lips a dark pink and swollen from his kisses, and he'd never seen, never even imagined anyone as beautiful as she was.

His North Star.

"You'll have me, Freya?" He caught a loose lock of her hair and brought it to his lips. "You'll be mine?"

"I already am, Callum." She laid her hand on his cheek and rested her forehead against his. "I'm already yours."

His heart gave a wild leap at her words, and he drew her closer, into the warm circle of his arms, and they remained there as the night grew darker around them, a sky filled with stars above them.

He couldn't have said how long they remained there, quiet in each other's arms. Perhaps it was a moment only, or perhaps it was a lifetime, but at last she eased away from him, a soft smile on her lips.

She held out her hand. "Come with me."

He took it and let her lead him down the winding turret staircase to the second floor, and from there to a closed door at the end of the corridor. She opened it and tugged him inside, then closed the door behind them. She leaned against it, a deep flush staining her cheeks as she met his gaze. "This is my bedchamber."

He rested his forehead against hers, his grin widening. "I thought it might be."

They gazed at each other, letting the moment of anticipation draw out until he could bear it no longer. It felt as if a lifetime had passed since he'd last held her, and slowly, gently he drew her into the circle of his arms.

She pressed her slender body against his and twined her arms around his neck. "My bedchamber, and my, ah . . . my bed."

Good Lord. Had there ever been a more tempting sight than Freya MacLeod with her pink cheeks and tousled curls? He slid his hand down her back and rested it just above the delicate arch of her back. "Do you want me, Freya?"

Her flush deepened, but she met his gaze, and her answer

was there in the clear green depths of her eyes. "More than anything, Callum."

"Then touch me." He took her hand and pressed her palm over his wildly beating heart. "Please, sweetheart."

She ran her gaze over him, from the top of his dark head to the toes of his muddy boots. Whatever she saw in his face made her breath quicken, and a half smile quirked his lips at the heat in her eyes.

She was trembling a little, her slight body swaying in his arms, but there was no hesitation in her touch, no doubt in her eyes as she slid her hand down his chest to his lower belly. He sucked in a breath as the hard plane of his belly jerked under her touch. She paused for an instant, then leaned forward and pressed her parted lips to the base of his throat.

"Yes, love." He threw his head back, a groan falling from his lips. She'd hardly touched him, yet his body felt as if it were bursting into flames. "Freya." He cupped the back of her neck, encouraging her with his husky groan. "You feel so good, sweetheart."

She pressed closer, her hands sinking into his hair as she nibbled at his neck and throat, leaving a trail of fire across his skin everywhere she touched.

Dear God, she was lovely, her shy kisses the sweetest thing he'd ever felt, and she was *his*. He didn't deserve her, yet somehow, she was his.

This incredible woman who was beautiful both inside and out, wanted *him*.

"I love you, Callum," she whispered, her voice more breath than sound, the warm drift of it stirring the hair near his ear. "I don't . . ." She curled her fingers, fisting his shirt, her breath catching. "I don't know what I would have done if you hadn't come for me."

"I'll always come, Freya." He took her chin in his hand and tipped her face up to his. "I'll always come for you."

She took his hand, her green eyes soft in the dim light. "Then come with me now."

She kept his hand in hers as she led him toward the bed and perched on the edge of the mattress. "Will you . . . I thought we might . . . will you stay here with me?"

She cast a glance at him before looking away again, her cheeks scarlet and her lower lip caught between her teeth, as if she truly thought he might refuse her. Didn't she know he'd never refuse her anything it was in his power to give her?

He wanted to give her everything.

"Yes, Freya." He dragged his thumb across her cheekbone. "There's nothing I want more than to stay here with you."

She smiled. "Then come to bed, Callum."

He took her face in his hands, leaned down, and pressed a long, sweet kiss to her lips. She made a low, protesting sound when he pulled back, but it died in her throat when he slid his arms free of his coat, and let it drop to the floor. He struggled out of his boots, then stripped off his shirt so he stood before her, bared to the waist.

"Oh, that's . . . you're . . ." She stared at him open-mouthed, her cheeks on fire.

"That's a pretty flush, Freya, but if you blush any harder, you may tumble into a swoon."

She darted a glance at his face, her lips curving in a smile, but her attention quickly returned to his bare chest. Her gaze roamed over him, assessing every inch of exposed skin. "This is nice," she murmured, reaching out a hand to caress the trail of dark hair low on his belly. "It's so soft."

He bit back a groan at the innocent caress and let her explore him, his muscles tensing and releasing with every sweep of her hands and fingers over his skin. When she lowered her hand and patted the space on the bed beside her, it was all he could do not to snatch her into his arms and devour her.

But he was careful with her, so careful when he stretched out on the bed beside her and took her gently into his arms, because she was precious—the most precious thing he'd ever held—and he wouldn't hurt her for the world.

She gave him a shy glance before leaning closer, and pressing a kiss to his chest, directly over his heart. He cupped the back of her neck, his breath stuttering in his lungs as he held her against him, her mouth cool and soft against his burning flesh.

"Mmmm," she murmured, nuzzling his neck. "You smell good."

He choked on a laugh. "You must be besotted with me if you think I smell good after three days of hard riding."

"I am besotted with you. But you do smell good." She dropped a kiss on his stomach. "You smell like . . ." She paused to consider it, then shrugged. "You smell like *you*."

"Hmmm." He ran his fingers through her wild curls, slipping the pins from her hair and murmuring with approval as the long locks spilled over her shoulders and down her back. "Do I taste like me, too?"

She grinned down at him, tracing her fingers over his lips. "I suppose there's one way to find out." She leaned over him, her eyelids heavy, and pressed her mouth to his in a sweet, tender kiss that made his breath quicken and his heart leap in his chest.

But it wasn't enough. With Freya, one kiss was never enough.

He wrapped his arm around her waist and urged her closer, until she was on top of him, their legs tangled together, then he nipped gently at her lower lip until she opened for him with a gasp. He surged into her welcoming heat, his tongue sliding against hers in a sensual dance until they were panting.

He took her lips in one hot, desperate kiss after another, his hands buried in her hair, and dear God, he could never get enough of her scent, her taste, and the little sighs and gasps that fell from her lips. Had he ever wanted anyone as much as he wanted her? Had he ever imagined—

"Wait, Callum." She tore her lips from his and pressed a restraining hand on his chest. "We can't . . . this is wrong."

"Wrong?" Had he somehow misread the situation? She seemed eager, but she was an innocent young lady. Had he frightened her? He leapt off the bed and backed away from it, putting some distance between them. "I beg your pardon, Freya. I thought—"

"Wait." She clambered up onto her knees in the middle of the bed, her eyes wide. "Where are you going?"

"I, ah . . ." Damned if he knew, but somewhere away from the temptation of her. "Is there another bedchamber—"

"No! I don't want you to go, Callum." She took his hand and tugged him back to the bed. "I meant it's wrong that you're . . ." She waved a hand at his bare chest, the blush that had so charmed him earlier washing over her cheeks again. "Undressed, and I'm still wearing all my clothes."

He let out a breath, relief washing over him. "Yes, so you are."

She pushed the pillows aside and presented him with her back. "Will you unbutton me?"

His hands shook as, one by one, he slowly loosened the long row of buttons on the back of her dress, revealing one inch of soft, creamy skin after another in the most erotic unbuttoning of his life.

"There. That's better." She beckoned him forward with a crooked finger. "Come back to bed, Callum, and kiss me."

He vaulted across the floor and into the bed in one leap and pressed a kiss to her laughing lips before easing her back against the pillows and tracing the creamy swells of her breasts spilling from the top of her shift. The faint pink of her nipples was visible underneath the thin cotton, and he circled one of the rosy tips with his thumb. "So pretty."

"Oh." Her lips parted on a soft cry, her head falling back against the pillows.

"Does that feel good, sweetheart? Mmm, yes. You're sensitive here."

"Yes, I . . . oh, that's so . . ." She was squirming against the bed. "My goodness."

Her breath came in uneven pants as he stroked her nipples,

caressing the stiff peaks with gentle fingers until they turned a deep pink, and hardened for him. He held her gaze as he lowered his mouth to her breast, pausing to drop a kiss over her heart before taking one of the turgid peaks into his mouth to suckle her.

"*Callum.*" Her back arched and she sank her hands into his hair, clutching at him to hold him against her breast. "It's so . . . *oh*. I—I don't know what to do."

"Not a thing, sweetheart. Just let me pleasure you." He laved his tongue over her nipple before taking the other straining peak into his mouth. "You're so soft here." He stroked the sensitive skin of her upper thigh in a soothing caress, then he let his hand drift higher, higher . . .

"Oh, oh . . ." Freya's breath tore from her lungs in a stuttered gasp as petted her with gentle fingers, opening her to find the center of her pleasure.

"Is that good, sweetheart?"

"Yes, I . . . *please*, Callum."

He tugged at the buttons of his falls, nearly tearing them off entirely, then stripped out of his breeches and tossed them over the side of the bed. Freya's shift quickly followed, and then she was in his arms, and God, what a sight she was, with the flush of passion on her dewy skin.

He stretched out between her legs, murmuring to her as she moved restlessly against him, the tantalizing heat at the apex of her thighs coming closer to his straining cock with every twitch of her hips, but he held himself ruthlessly in check, pausing for long moments to kiss her as he cradled her face in his hands. "Do you want me, Freya?"

"Yes. Please, I—I need you."

"Open your eyes." He hovered over her, the tip of his cock poised at her entrance, gazing down into her flushed face. "Look at me, Freya."

Her eyelids fluttered open, and then she was there with him, her green gaze holding his, a gasp falling from her lips as slowly, carefully he sank into her damp heat. Once he was fully seated he went still, brushing her damp hair from her forehead as he waited for her to grow accustomed to the sensation of him inside her.

He'd had lovers before, but never—*never*—had it been like this. Her arms slid around his neck, and she tightened her legs around his hips, her warm breath on his face and her soft, fragrant skin surrounding him.

"You're mine, Freya," he growled against her lips.

"Yes. Please, Callum." She gave a tiny nudge with her hips, and then he was moving—her hot, damp flesh enveloping him, deeper with each stroke, the exquisite pleasure of being so close to her—part of her—tearing a groan from deep inside him. "You feel so good, sweetheart. I'll never have enough of you."

"All of you, Callum. I want all of you. Everything." Her hips jerked, and she let out a breathy moan that made him wild. He quickened his thrusts, his strokes careful, steady, sweat beading on his forehead as he ruthlessly held off his own release, his hips stuttering with the effort not to thrust wildly inside her, not to hurt her.

He would never hurt her, not for anything.

"Callum!" She cried out and arched against him, her slick heat pulsing around him, tight and wet and hot, the pleasure so exquisite he couldn't speak, but buried his face in her neck as his climax ripped through him.

"I . . . my goodness," she murmured when her breathing calmed. "That was . . . I had no idea."

He pulled back to look at her. Her lips were swollen and red from his kisses, her cheeks pink, and the green eyes he loved so well half hidden under her heavy lids. "Is that a compliment, Miss MacLeod? I can't tell."

She gave him a languid smile. "That is very much a compliment, Mr. Ross."

They lay there for some time, whispering to each other and listening to the waves crashing into the rocks below. Freya rested her head against his shoulder, her hair a wild tangle of red curls, and he traced her spine with his fingertips until at last her eyelids grew heavy.

He pressed a tender kiss to her lips and murmured, "Sleep, sweetheart."

She let out a contented sigh, and within moments she'd drifted into a deep sleep, the smile still lingering at the corners of her lips.

Callum didn't sleep. He held her in his arms and watched as the slice of sky visible through Freya's window lightened, and the stars disappeared into the red-gold light of early morning.

Epilogue

Castle Cairncross
Four weeks later

"I've lost Cassiopeia again." Callum squinted up at the sky, then flopped onto his back with a scowl. "I have no idea how you keep track of her. She's the slipperiest star I've ever encountered."

They were sitting on a blanket he'd spread out on the turret roof for them, the remains of their dinner picnic pushed to one corner. Cat and Hamish thought they were mad, picnicking on a roof during the cold Scottish winter, and perhaps they were, but they went to the roof at night as often as the weather permitted. They could remain there for hours, wrapped in each other's arms, studying the stars.

At least, Freya studied them. He spent more time gazing at her than he did the stars. Queens were all very well, but there was only one lady who enthralled him, and it wasn't Cassiopeia.

"Cassiopeia isn't a star, she's a constellation, and I promise you, constellations don't simply disappear. They've been in the sky for thousands of years and will remain so for thousands more."

"Hmmm." He could listen to her talk about the stars forever. Her voice took on the most adorable lecturing tone when she spoke of them, rather like the tone a stern headmistress might use, except she was an exceptionally beautiful and desirable headmistress, and he was her only pupil.

"Cassiopeia does appear to change shape depending on the time of year and the time of night, however, which I'll allow makes her tricky to find."

"Ah. She's slippery, just as I said."

"A bit, yes. There she is." Freya pointed to the sky, tracing Cassiopeia's lines from the northwestern tip down to the star anchoring the constellation's southeastern corner, then held out her hand to Callum. "Come here. I'll show you."

He eased closer to her, a low rumble of contentment rising in his chest when she slid her arm around his waist and pressed herself against him. "There she is, just where she's always been. Cepheus is northeast of Draco, and Cassiopeia is northeast of Cepheus. Now do you see her?"

"Hmmm." He took her hand and pressed a kiss to her fingertip. There was nothing he loved better than lying under the dark sky with Freya, but for all her patient lessons, he'd proved to be an indifferent pupil of astronomy.

Not because he wasn't interested in stars. He *was*. Sometimes.

But he was more interested in Freya, especially when they were nestled together under a sky filled with sparkling pinpricks of light, her warm body pressed to his and her hair tickling his neck. It was lucky she hadn't been his headmistress, or he never would have learned a thing.

She nudged him. "James and Lorna will laugh at you if you can't even find Cassiopeia by the time we return to Balnagown Castle."

He snorted. "James will laugh at me either way."

After much discussion, they'd made up their minds to remain at Castle Cairncross until Hamish and Cat's wedding, which would take place in a month's time. They'd return to Kildary afterward to attend James's and Lorna's wedding just two weeks later, in the chapel at Balnagown Castle.

When they returned to Dunvegan, they'd bring Aila with them, so she'd be there when they married next year. He'd wanted to marry Freya at once, as soon as the banns could be called, but she'd asked if they might wait until Sorcha returned home.

The only dark cloud over their happiness was Sorcha and Keir's continued absence. There were those in the village who claimed to have seen one or both wandering Dunvegan Wood. But there'd never been any shortage of rumors when it came to the MacLeod sisters, and they'd searched the woods many times and come up empty every time.

Despite their best hopes, neither Sorcha nor Keir had yet reappeared. There were those among the villagers who whispered that the devils Sorcha communed with had made off with them, snatched them up, and sent them hurtling into a fiery abyss.

More bloody nonsense, of course. He knew Keir too well to believe his friend was anywhere he didn't wish to be. For all Keir's mild temperament, he was one of the cleverest men Callum knew. He was wilier than a fox, and Sorcha no less so, and that they were both missing seemed to imply they were together still.

For now, Sorcha and Keir had chosen to remain hidden, and they likely had a good reason for it. They'd reveal themselves when the time was right. He only hoped it would be soon, for Freya's sake, as Sorcha's absence weighed on her.

As for the villagers, he and Freya hardly spared them a thought. They walked into the village regularly with Cat and Hamish and paid no attention at all to the stares and whispers they encountered as they made their way down the High Street.

The rumors about the MacLeod sisters' so-called sorcery persisted in Dunvegan, but once the magistrate, Mr. Anderson, had put a definitive end to the arson charges against them, there'd been no more talk about nooses or the gibbet, particularly after Clyde Stewart had turned back up.

He'd been spotted by one of Dunvegan's villagers at the Sheep's Heid Inn in Edinburgh several weeks after the fire. From the account they'd heard, he was very much alive, quite thirsty, and amazed to discover he was meant to be dead. It seemed he'd wandered off to Edinburgh in the early morning after the fire and had been there ever since.

"There's Perseus." Freya pointed to a collection of stars to the south of Cassiopeia. "See the tip of his sword?"

"Hmmm." He nibbled delicately at the sensitive skin behind her ear. "Lie down with me," he whispered, tugging at her earlobe with his teeth.

She laughed, even as she shivered at the caress. "You're a most disobedient student, Callum."

"Yes, but I make up for it with my exceptional skills in other areas." He brushed his lips down her neck. How could her skin be so soft?

Freya dropped her head to one side, offering the long, pale line of her throat to his seeking lips. "Come now. Don't try and tell me you're not interested in Perseus's sword. Aren't all gentlemen interested in swords and—"

She broke off with a little squeal as he tossed her onto her back on the blanket and lowered himself on top of her. "That's better." He dropped a chain of light kisses over her neck. "I'm far more interested in wee redheaded Scottish lasses with dirks than in warriors with swords."

A sly smile drifted over Freya's lips. "Is that so?"

"Indeed." He slid his hand up her leg, slowly raising her skirts and stifling a groan when the creamy skin of her bare thigh was revealed. God, he wanted to devour her.

But when he raised his heated gaze to her face and saw those green eyes on him he paused, his heart swelling with love. "You're so beautiful, Freya, all of you," he murmured, tracing the lines of her face with his fingertips.

Beautiful, and mine.

She smiled at him, her eyes hazy with desire. "I love you, Callum."

"I love you, too." He returned her smile, but it faded a little as he traced the faint scar still visible on her temple.

"So serious." She gave his lower lip a playful tug. "I'm all right now, you know."

"I know." But his gaze remained fixed on the scar, and he leaned down to press a tender kiss to it.

"I wish you wouldn't look at it. I can't bear to see that lost expression on your face."

He swallowed, meeting her eyes. "I look at it to remind me."

"Why would you want to be reminded of that? I hardly ever think of it."

He brushed her hair aside and once again pressed his lips to the small patch of raised skin where the tree limb had struck her. "I don't want to forget how close I came to losing you. I don't know what I would have done if—"

"Hush. You could never lose me." She cupped his face in her hands, and his breath caught at the stars reflected in those dark green depths. "I'll always be with you, Callum. Forever."

He smiled. "Like Cassiopeia?"

"Yes," she whispered, her hands gentle on his cheeks. "Just like that."